Crossroads

By
Wendy Saunders

Also By Wendy Saunders

The Guardians Series 1
Mercy
The Ferryman
Crossroads
Witchfinder
Infernum

The Carter Series
Tangled Web
Twisted Lies
Blood Ties

This book is the intellectual property of the author and as such cannot be reproduced in whole, or in part, in any medium, without the express written permission of the author.

Copyright © 2018 Wendy Saunders
First published in 2016
All rights reserved.

ISBN-13:978-1532704680

For My husband Paul,
Who has always been the light in my darkness,
my rock, my soul mate in this lifetime and every
other.

LINCOLNSHIRE

Library items can be renewed online 24/7, you will need your library card number and PIN.

Avoid library overdue charges by signing up to receive email preoverdue reminders at

http://www.opac.northlincs.gov.uk/

Follow us on Facebook
www.facebook.com/northlincolnshirelibraries

www.northlincs.gov.uk/libraries

CONTENTS

PART 1. THE OTHERWORLD V'S THE REAL WORLD 3
1. 5
2. 12
3. 25
4. 44
5. 57
6. 76
7. 90
8. 106
9. 123
10. 142
11. 156
12. 169
13. 184
14. 203
15. 218
16. 232
17. 250
18. 264
19. 278

PART 2. THE UNDERWORLD 291
20. 293
21. 310
22. 325
23. 341
24. 355
25. 370
26. 386

WITCHFINDER 405
1. 407

GLOSSARY OF TERMS IN GREEK MYTHOLOGY .. 415
AUTHOR BIO. 419

Part 1.
The Otherworld
v's
The Real World

1.

Louisa was bandaging three deep nasty claw marks in Tommy's shoulder, but paused and looked up as Jake stalked back into the library in Olivia's house.

'Any sign of the others?' she asked hopefully.

Jake shook his head, looking over at Veronica who was holding an icepack to the bleeding lump at the back of Mac's head. Beau jumped up at his legs, and bending down absently he scooped the pup into his arms and stroked him soothingly.

'Don't worry buddy, we'll find them for you,' he murmured to the dog who, seeming to understand the promise, leaned forward and licked Jake's face.

'Danae and Davis are still out looking, and we haven't accounted for Charles yet,' Jake told them.

Louisa's mouth settled into a thin line of worry as she turned back to her husband and taped up the end of the bandage, before helping him back into his shirt.

'I need a drink,' Tommy headed for the kitchen, reappearing moments later with a bottle of Glenfidditch and a stack of plastic cups.

'Anyone?'

'I wouldn't say no,' Mac winced as Veronica pressed a little too hard.

'Sorry Mac,' she sighed and handed him the bag of ice. 'I don't make a very good Florence Nightingale, do I?'

'No,' he smiled, 'but you make a hell of a G.I

Jane.'

She looked up at him and laughed in amusement. 'My parents would never believe you.'

'I expect most people wouldn't believe the half of what we saw last night,' he replied seriously as Tommy handed him a full cup.

'Ain't that the truth,' Tommy downed his own drink in one.

They all looked up hopefully as the front door slammed again, but a collective sigh of disappointment rippled around the room when Danae entered alone.

'Any news?' Jake asked.

She shook her head frowning. 'No, Davis is still looking. There's no sign of Theo and Olivia, and Charles is still MIA.'

Mac's face darkened at the mention of Charles' name.

'He'd better be dead,' he muttered, 'or by the time I'm finished with him, he's going to wish he was.'

'What did you say?' Danae's eyes narrowed.

'You heard,' he growled.

'Look, I don't know what happened between you two out there, but I'm sure it was necessary.'

'Necessary?' Mac laughed mirthlessly. 'I don't consider someone sneaking up on me and cracking me across the skull a necessity.'

'Charles must have had his reasons.'

'Oh, he had his reasons alright. It's because he's a selfish, stubborn son of a bitch.'

'How dare you,' Danae hissed. 'You know nothing about my brother.'

'I know plenty, and he should be thanking me for not hauling his ass back to Morley Ridge instead of trying to give me a brain hemorrhage.'

'That's enough you two,' Veronica came abruptly to her feet, glaring at them sharply. 'We're all worried, and this isn't helping.'

She turned to the window and stared out into the cold, pale morning light.

'They'll be okay,' Jake put his hand on her shoulder reassuringly, forcing her to look up into his eyes.

'But what I saw,' she whispered, as her eyes brimmed with tears.

'You could've been wrong,' he told her. 'It was dark and we were both pumped full of adrenalin…they'll be okay, I know they will.'

The front door slammed again and they all turned to the library doorway. Another disappointed sigh, as Davis stormed through, looking frustrated.

'Any luck?' Danae asked, although she knew the answer from the look on her twin's face.

He shook his head.

'There's no sign of Theo and Olivia anywhere. The truck is still parked at the foot of the private road leading up to The Boatman, the keys in the ignition. I couldn't get up to the hotel to look around, the road is blocked and the ice on the lake has completely broken up now. Which means, we'll need a boat to get to the private beach at the foot of the cliff, but even then I don't know if there's a way to reach it. I hiked through the woods, the way they would've gone, but when I reached the edge of the lake I could see that part of the cliff face had sheared away. It's crushed the Jetty, and taken out part of the steps leading up.'

'God,' Jake growled in frustration.

'I could scale the cliff face, but I don't have any climbing gear,' Davis frowned.

'How long would it take to get some?' Jake asked.

'I could probably have some here by mid-afternoon.' He pulled his phone from his pocket and began to scroll through his list of contacts.

'Could you make that two sets of ropes and harnesses?' Jake asked.

'You have experience?'

Jake nodded. 'It's been a while, but I know what I'm doing.'

'Alright then,' Davis agreed, but before he could make the call the front door slammed again.

This time they were not disappointed. They all turned to look as Charles limped through the doorway, his clothes torn and dirty. One side of his face was heavily bruised and scratched, and from the angle at which he was cradling his arm, it was fair to assume it was broken.

'Charles,' Davis breathed a sigh of relief.

'What happened?' Danae frowned.

But Charles ignored them, scanning the faces in the room, disregarding the angry glare Mac was throwing in his direction.

'Where's my daughter?'

'Mr Connell,' Louisa interrupted, glancing at the state of his various injuries. 'Maybe you should come and take a seat, and let me have a look at you.'

'Where's Olivia?' he asked again angrily.

'We haven't been able to find them yet Charles,' Davis told him quietly. 'Both Olivia and Theo are missing.'

'Charles, we're going to find them,' Danae told him 'Why don't you sit and let Louisa have a look at you and tell us what happened. We've been looking for you for hours. You were supposed to be with Mac, what the hell were you thinking?'

'He was thinking about revenge,' Mac shot back, 'that's what he was thinking about.'

'It wasn't about revenge,' Charles glared back at him, 'it was about protecting my daughter.'

'You can pretty it up all you like Charles, but going up to the hotel last night wasn't about protecting Olivia, it was about getting to Isabel.'

'You're wrong.'

'Am I?' he replied. 'Then why stop me from going with you?' 'It's because you knew I would have arrested her,' he continued mercilessly, 'and the simple fact is you want her dead…you want her dead for betraying you.'

'NO!' Charles shouted furiously, 'I want her dead because it's the only way to make sure she can't harm Olivia. You think a prison can hold Isabel? It couldn't hold me, I could have walked out at any time, but I didn't because it didn't suit my purpose. Isabel feels no such restraint, and as long as she's loose, she is a threat to my daughter. So yes, you're damn right I want that bitch dead, it's the only way to make sure Olivia is safe.'

'All right calm down,' Jake stepped in between them. 'We're all on the same side here; we all want to make sure Theo and Olivia are okay, so why don't you tell us what happened as you seem to be the last person to see them both?'

Charles sighed and shook his head, clearing his thoughts.

'When I got to the hotel Olivia and Theo had Charon. Nathaniel and Isabel were also there. Olivia shot Isabel with the tranq darts and I was holding back Nathaniel to give them time to escape. I told them to get him to the lake. I don't know what happened after that but a few moments after they were gone the whole cliff shook.'

'Part of the cliff face sheered away,' Davis explained.

'Anyway, the force of it brought down part of the ceiling in the ballroom, which is where I was. I was knocked unconscious and by the time I came round Nathaniel and Isabel were gone. I managed to free myself from under the debris, but when I got outside I saw that the lake was still and quiet. I headed for the stairs but part of them are gone and there was no way down. I had no choice but to try and climb through the fallen trees and branches blocking the road. It took me the rest of the night and part of this morning, but I made a path through. It's narrow but there is a way through. I headed back here expecting them to have been back by now. Has no one seen them?'

They all shook their heads, except for Veronica.

'Veronica?' Charles asked quietly, 'what is it?'

'I saw,' she shook her head. 'I mean, I thought I saw. It was dark and everything happened so fast, I can't be sure.'

'Why don't you just tell me what it is you think you saw.'

'They were heading into the center of the lake, at least I think it was them. I was quite far away...but.'

'But what?'

'They were still in the middle of the lake when the ice started to break up. There's no way they could have made it back to shore, not with the temperature of the water.'

'You think they went in?' Charles let out his breath slowly, closing his eyes in pain.

'I think I saw one of them go in, I couldn't tell which,' she replied miserably as her eyes filled with tears.

'No' Charles whispered, shaking his head.

'They're not dead you know,' a new calm voice spoke from the doorway.

They all turned to look in confusion.

'Mayor Burnett?' Jake frowned, 'what are you doing here?'

'I came to put your minds at rest,' she replied softly. 'Theo was pulled through the gateway to the Otherworld and Olivia went in after him. They're stranded in the Otherworld, but they are alive.'

'And how exactly would you know that?' Charles asked suspiciously.

'I know a great many things Mr Connell,' her mouth curved.

'What the hell is going on Tammy?' Mac moved closer. 'How do you know about Olivia and Theo?'

'Because' she answered slowly, 'my name isn't Tammy Burnett. It's Beckett...Temperance Beckett.'

She glanced around the room at the bewildered

faces.
    'Theo is my brother.'

2.

Olivia groaned and rolled over, gradually becoming aware that she was lying on the hard ground with her back curved at an odd angle. She sat up, blinking a few times to clear her blurry vision, and scanned her surroundings with an appraising gaze. It looked familiar, she frowned in confusion as she tried to recall the events of the previous night. Hades had promised to send her across the Veil and into the Otherworld, the Spirit realm, but as she looked around it didn't seem any different from the real world, and she wondered with a start, if it had even worked at all. Maybe she was still in Mercy.

Climbing awkwardly to her feet, she brushed the gravel and powdery residue from her jeans. She was standing at the side of an empty road, which seemed to stretch endlessly for miles, surrounded by woods. She looked up at the moody sky, watching the swirls of pale grey and white, and although the skies were overcast it wasn't cold. Glancing around, she noticed there was no snow. When she'd left Mercy everything had been covered in several feet of snow, but now it looked like the beginning of spring.

Shaking her head to clear her thoughts, she set off down the road, reasoning that sooner or later she would encounter a town, or at least a person. Readjusting her backpack so it was more comfortable, she walked at a brisk pace, anxious to find out where she was exactly. After a few miles she found she had to unzip her heavy winter coat and remove her scarf. Settling herself on the carcass of a fallen tree at the side of the road, she pulled off her backpack and opened it, reaching inside for a bottle of water.

She'd been walking for what felt like hours and she didn't seem to be getting anywhere. Taking a sip of water, she closed her eyes and listened. This close to the woods she should have at least been able to hear birdsong, or the ripple of the air through the thick green canopy of trees, but there was nothing. It was like someone had hit the mute button, either that or she was temporarily deaf.

Tucking her water bottle back into her bag, she rummaged through it, taking stock of what she had with her. Fortunately, she still had the small first aid kit she'd packed before they went after Charon. She also had Hester's Grimoire back. Breathing a sigh of relief, she pulled the book out and laid it in her lap, running her fingers over the deeply embossed leather cover. Something inside her, that she hadn't realized had been so tightly knotted, relaxed as she felt the power thrum beneath her fingertips. Opening it up, she watched as the now familiar black script curled and undulated across the page until it settled into words.

Her mother's grudging admission that she couldn't read the book had come as a surprise to Olivia. She was aware that neither Theo, nor any of her friends, had been able to read it but she had just assumed it was a charm which protected the book from anyone who wasn't of Hester's bloodline. But, if her mother couldn't read it, despite being a West, it begged the question could any of the other women in her family read it? Neither her grandmother, nor her great-aunt, had mentioned the book when she was younger. She hadn't even known of its existence until she'd retrieved it from the safety deposit box at Old Mercy Mutual. Shaking her head, she closed the book and slipped it back into the bag.

She pulled out her flashlight and flicked it on. At least that still worked and might come in useful. Sticking her hand back in the backpack, her fist closed around a chunk of cool metal. Pulling it out, her eyes narrowed as she studied it. She searched the bag until she came up with its counterpart and turned the two halves over in her hands.

It was the demon collar she'd removed from Charon's neck back at the hotel. He'd said it was used to enslave souls and neutralize supernatural abilities. He'd also said, once it was on it was impossible to remove, barring decapitation. She still wasn't sure how she'd managed to unlock it. To be fair, everything that happened in the hotel was still a little blurry thanks to the urgency and adrenalin. Still, if she could figure out how to use it…she chewed her lip thoughtfully, wondering if it would actually work on a demon, or whether it was called a demon collar because it was made by demons.

Frowning, she dropped the two pieces back into the bag. As soon as she was able, she'd have to research it further. Sooner or later, she would have to deal with Nathaniel, a powerful demon who was thousands of years old. She wasn't even sure he could be killed, let alone how to go about it. But maybe, just maybe, if she could get close enough to collar him, his power and strength would be neutralized. Then all she would have to do was to shove him headfirst back into the devil's trap at Boothe's Hollow. It wasn't ideal but it was a solution…of sorts.

Tucking her scarf into her bag, she zipped it up and removed her coat. A glint of gold flashed in the pale daylight, and Olivia lifted the compass Hades had given her, which hung around her neck on a long chain. Running her fingers over the metal, now warmed by her body heat, she studied it carefully. The front cover was etched with what looked like exquisite miniature star charts and constellations. She pressed the tiny gold button and the lid flicked open on a well-oiled hinge. Inside was a circular compass, which sat inside a larger circle, which in turn sat in another larger circle. It had several hands and dials, and once again, she was at a complete loss as to how it worked. Tapping the glass face softly with her fingernail, the hands would still not spin. Frowning in frustration she clicked the lid closed, and tucked it safely back inside her shirt.

Picking up her bag, she slung it over her shoulders, and sliding off the fallen tree trunk she picked up her coat and once again headed down the road. Another hour passed, and she was once again struck by her surroundings. She knew she should know this place, it was there tickling the back of her mind with maddening familiarity.

She continued on, and soon she began to pass even more familiar landmarks. As she approached the outskirts of the town she realized she was still in Mercy, she was just approaching it from the road on the opposite side of town to where her house was. She quickened her pace as she headed into town, cursing Hades for playing her for a fool. Well, the hell with him and his stupid cruel games, she was just going to head straight back to her house and she was going to find a way to open the doorway to the Otherworld, even if she had to go through every single scrap of paper and book in her library. If that didn't work she was going to blow up the internet for information, and if that didn't work...well, she may just damn well kidnap Charon herself. Whatever it took, she was going to get Theo back.

Her pace quickened, as she stalked angrily into the town proper and headed for Main Street. She could have blamed her stubbornness and irritation for the fact she didn't immediately notice that something was different about Mercy. She passed the town offices and turned the corner heading toward the museum. Gradually slowing her pace, her brow folding into a puzzled frown as her mind began to process something that should have been glaringly obvious the minute she stepped foot into town. She stopped abruptly across the street from the Pub, just past the Bailey's convenience store, and scanned her surroundings.

Where were all the people?

Olivia crossed into the street, slowly stopping in the middle of the usually busy road which ran the length of Main Street. There was nothing, no cars, no traffic, and most importantly, no people. She turned a slow circle, scanning the sidewalks and shops. Nothing, she was the only person there. It was like she'd woken up from a coma and found herself in the middle of a Zombie apocalypse.

'HELLO?' she called out into the silence, 'HELLO?'

So Hades had kept his word. She must be in the Otherworld, but why did it look like an exact abandoned replica of her town?

Confused, she crossed back to the Bailey's store and tried the door. It was unlocked, and swung open easily as she stepped into the cheery little store. The florescent lights glowed brightly, highlighting row upon row of fully stocked and untouched shelves. She stepped behind the counter and found the register fully loaded with cash. There was a small TV behind the counter also and although already turned on, it simply showed static. She changed the channels but each one was the same, it was as if there were no TV stations left broadcasting.

A little freaked out, Olivia stepped back out onto the street and walked a couple of blocks. Every door she tried was the same, unlocked, each room beyond pristine and undisturbed with not one single person in sight.

'Hello?' she called out again, as she wandered down the street. 'Hello, is anyone here?'

Nothing but silence.

She noticed for the first time, that the light hadn't

changed. She'd been walking for hours. In the real world the sun would have reached its midday peak and then started to descend toward the horizon and into night. But here it remained the same, covered by the strange swirls of cloud and bathing the town in a constant pale light that had a faint bluish cast to it.

Trying to think about the problem logically, she unconsciously chewed her lip. If Theo had been pulled into the Otherworld and ended up here, where the hell would he be? She tried to put herself in his place. If it'd been her pulled through the gateway, what was the first thing she'd do? she asked herself and the answer was simple. She would head to the place that was most familiar to her.

Her house…

If Theo were to head to the most familiar place, it would be her house. In fact, even if he didn't realize he'd been pulled into the Otherworld, that would be the first place he would go looking for her.

She turned the corner, intent on heading straight for the lake, when she stopped abruptly. It would take ages to walk to her house from here. Wishing she had her banged up old Camaro, which she'd affectionately named Dolly, she scanned her surroundings. Her gaze finally landed on a shiny red bicycle, which was propped against the side of a small shop.

'That'll do,' she murmured, as she grabbed the handles and swung her leg over the frame.

Stuffing her coat into the embarrassingly girly basket at the front, she set off toward the lake.

She cycled down the block, but as she turned the corner she skidded to a stop, her mouth hanging open in confusion. She turned to look behind her to the street she'd just come from, but the woods now stood at her back. Frowning, she turned back to the sight in front of her. It was her house; it should have taken her at least an hour to cycle there, yet it had taken her no more than a few moments and one turn of a corner.

Climbing down off the bike, she pushed it to the front steps of her porch. So strange, she was beginning to feel a little like she'd fallen down a rabbit hole. Nothing seemed to make sense.

She leaned the bike against the side of the house and trotted up the steps, already calling out to Theo as she opened the door and stepped into the familiar hallway.

'Theo?'

She headed for the dining room, which had become his studio. The room was silent and still. No longer holding the devastation which had occurred when Theo's dead wife had viciously materialized in her house, the room was once again neat and ordered. His art supplies were neatly stacked on the table, with pots containing brushes and tools fastidiously lined up against the wall. Many completed canvases were stacked around the room, and pencil sketches were tacked to the walls. There was not one single portrait of Mary anywhere, all of Theo's pictures were once again as he had originally painted them.

Wandering back out of the room, she headed for the library, her favorite room. After her mother had attacked her and ransacked the room in her pursuit of Hester's Grimoire, Olivia had not bothered to put it back as it originally was. Instead she had neatly stacked the books and paperwork around the room, while she sorted through hundreds of years of accumulated family history and books on magic. But, unlike the real word, here the room was once again as she remembered it from her childhood.

Deliberately turning her back on the room she checked the kitchen and then headed up the stairs, still calling out to Theo as she went. But there was nothing; the house was empty.

She moved slowly back down the stairs, her gaze snagging on Beau's leash that had been dropped on the floor by the open front door. She knew Beau wouldn't be there, she'd left him behind in the real world, but the house still felt strange without him. She only hoped someone was looking after him for her, while she was gone. Sinking down on the bottom tread of the stairs, Olivia stared out of the front door absently.

They would have realized by now that they were missing. Had they figured it out, she wondered, or did they believe that both she and Theo were dead? She sighed as her brow folded into a frown, wishing she had some way to contact her friends.

She stared out of the open front door, so lost in her thoughts that it took her a moment to fully comprehend what her eyes were seeing. She stood abruptly, and stepped closer to the open door. Directly opposite, across the grassy expanse of land which lay between the front of her house and the edge of the woods, a small wooden cottage had appeared. Nestled at the edge of the tree line, a small curl of smoke rose from the chimney, giving it a welcoming homely appeal.

That hadn't been there when she arrived, she thought curiously. She would have noticed it. She moved to step over the threshold of her house onto the porch, but paused, suddenly turning back to look behind her into the house. She felt something brush against her arm, and just for a moment she could have sworn she had heard Jake's voice.

Shaking off the strange feeling, she stepped out of the door and headed toward the strange little cottage.

Jake shivered as he crossed Olivia's doorway, feeling as if someone had just stepped over his grave. Unwrapping his scarf and removing his hat, he closed the door behind him.

'Roni?' he called out.

'In here,' a muffled voice came from the library.

'I thought I might find you in here,' he frowned as he looked around at the stacks of boxes, which she was filling with paperwork and books. 'What on earth are you doing?'

'Well, ultimately I'm going to be organizing all this for Olivia,' she looked around at the boxes she'd already filled. 'It's an absolute mess in here. Olivia and I had already discussed sorting through all of this, so she could clean and redecorate.'

'So, while she's gone you're going to clean up her mess?' his mouth curved in amusement.

'No, not exactly,' she tucked her hair behind her ear and frowned. 'Well…yes, I mean, that is a byproduct, but you're missing the point.'

'Which is?'

'There are hundreds of years of books on magic and lore in here. Some of these books I've never even heard of before. I'm willing to bet they're one of a kind. I doubt even Olivia fully understands the significance of what she's got here. These are the most comprehensive resources on the occult I have ever seen. I don't know how they managed to squeeze so much into one room.'

'So you decided to catalog it all?'

'Laugh all you like, but it's like balm to my frazzled soul,' she blew out a deep breath and turned her serious blue eyes on him. 'It makes me happy when things are categorized and in alphabetical order, it helps my stress levels.'

Jake bit back a smile, she was so cute.

'I need to feel like I'm doing something,' Veronica sighed, as she dropped down on the arm of the tatty old sofa.

'I know,' Jake replied seriously, as he stepped closer.

'I just figured that somewhere in amongst all this stuff there has to be an answer, a solution,' she shrugged helplessly. 'Some way to cross the Veil and help them, or at the very least allow us to communicate with them.'

'That's actually a very good idea,' Jake frowned

thoughtfully. Picking up a book at random he leafed through it idly. 'Have you found anything helpful?'

'Not yet,' she shook her head. 'I was just going to pack this stuff up and move it back to my apartment to sort through. I don't like being out here by myself, so close to the lake, I know the gateway's closed…but still.'

'That's understandable.'

'What are you doing here anyway?' she frowned. 'You're not still checking up on me are you?'

'No,' his mouth curved again in amusement as he dropped the book back into the pile. He knew she got really annoyed when she thought he was checking up on her. He probably didn't need to mention that she hadn't been out of his sight much since the gateway opened in the first place. 'I was just picking up the spare bag of food for Beau. I figured I'd use that up before I go and buy more.'

Her scowl softened at the mention of Olivia and Theo's cute little pup.

'How is he settling in at your place?'

'He keeps crying for them,' Jake scratched the back of his neck thoughtfully, 'but he's slowly adjusting. Problem is, he shouldn't really be left on his own and I can't really keep him with me all the time.'

'If you need to, you can drop him by my place, or the museum,' she looked up at him. 'I'll watch him when you're busy.'

'I might just do that,' he murmured, as he studied her face. 'Have you spoken with Mayor Burnett at all?'

'A few times,' Veronica nodded, 'mostly just about things concerning the museum. When it comes to Olivia and Theo, she's still not very forthcoming with information. She says she can't give us any more details, because everything that is going to happen, is supposed to happen in a particular order, or something like that. I don't really understand. I still can't believe she's Theo's sister, and that he doesn't know.'

'I know,' Jake agreed, 'it's really weird that she's

his younger sister, but that she's actually, physically older than him.'

'I'm really worried about them,' Veronica sighed. 'They've been gone weeks, surely we would've heard something by now?'

'I'm worried too,' Jake stepped closer, as Veronica stood, gazing up into his eyes.

'I feel like we should be doing something,' she frowned. 'I don't suppose you've heard anything from Charles?'

Jake shook his head.

'Charles has gone to ground, along with Davis and Danae. No one's heard from them since the day after we closed the gateway.'

'Even Danae?' She was slightly surprised that Olivia's young aunt had disappeared too, after all she was a permanent fixture in the community, although everyone knew her as deputy Helga Hanson. 'Hasn't she been into work?'

'She took some personal time,' he replied. 'Mac hasn't heard from her since then.'

'What do you think they're up to?'

'I have no idea,' he shrugged, 'probably trying to track down Olivia's mom.'

'I don't think so,' Veronica frowned. 'He seemed so genuinely concerned about Olivia, I can't believe he would just leave her trapped in the Otherworld. Perhaps he's trying to figure out a way to reach her and Theo?'

'Then why exclude us?' Jake replied irritably, 'we've all proved ourselves. If he is looking for a way to reach them then he should be including us.'

'Maybe he has his reasons.'

'Look Roni,' he stepped closer, unconsciously running his hands down her arms in a comforting and familiar gesture. 'I know Charles Connell is an extremely charming, charismatic man, but first and foremost he is a very dangerous witch, who is hell bent on finding his wife and killing her.'

'It sounds so bad when you say it like that.'

'There's no use in trying to pretty it up,' Jake's serious blue eyes bore into hers. 'He is a man capable of terrible things, you can't trust him.'

'Now you sound like Mac.'

'Well, Mac has a point, several of them actually, and he cares a great deal about Olivia.'

'I guess,' she breathed reluctantly. 'I just want them back.'

'I do too,' he muttered, as he stared down at her, his gaze dropping involuntarily to her soft full lips.

'I should go,' she murmured softly, 'it's going to get dark soon.'

'Yeah,' he replied absently, his gaze locked on hers.

Shaking her head lightly, she stepped back out of his arms.

'I should help you,' Jake cleared his throat awkwardly, 'with the boxes.'

'Thank you,' she smiled genuinely.

They worked quickly and in silence until they had several boxes loaded up into her car. The temperature had started to warm up, with spring just around the corner the snow had finally begun to melt, leaving sparse patches of it dotted across the town. Jake retrieved the large bag of dog food and locking the door up behind him, he trotted down the porch steps toward Veronica.

'I'll follow you back and help you unload them.'

'You don't have to do that.'

'Roni, you live on the fourth floor of your apartment building. It'll take you forever to get these boxes up to your apartment on your own.'

'Shouldn't you get home to Beau?' she frowned, 'he's been on his own a long time.'

'We can swing by my place first and get him, then I can help you get the boxes up to your place, and you can cook me dinner to say thank you,' he grinned.

'What if I don't want to cook?' her mouth curved into an amused smile.

'Then we can get take out,' he replied with boyish charm. 'Come on Roni, I'm starving. Have pity on a poor, overworked and dedicated public servant.'

'Fine,' she laughed, 'we can pick something up on the way back.'

Grinning one last time, Jake headed to his car and loaded up the bag of food, before climbing in and firing the engine.

They both pulled out of Olivia's drive and headed back toward town in the pale dying rays of light, unaware that at the edge of the woods, in the shadow of the trees, a tall dark figure silently watched them with dead eyes.

3.

Olivia's eyes narrowed curiously as she trotted down the front steps of her porch, her attention now fixed on the small wooden cabin at the edge of the trees. There was something comforting about it, she decided, as she moved closer, cutting through the long grass. A small tendril of smoke rose from the chimney, giving the impression of a cozy hearth and a hearty meal. Everything in her yearned toward that building she realized with a jolt. It felt like it was calling to her, welcoming her home. Strange, she frowned silently, there had never been a cottage set at the edge of the trees by her woods, yet it looked as if it belonged, as if somehow it had always been there.

Shaking her head in an attempt to clear her mind she approached the strange little house. If she had to place it in a time period, she would have said sometime around the beginning of the 18th Century, as it looked like early colonial cabins she'd seen in the historical records. It was just one level, with a low pitched timber roof and overhanging porch. As she neared the front door it opened suddenly and a woman stepped into the doorway, calmly watching Olivia with serious whiskey colored eyes.

Olivia's stomach clenched and her mouth went dry at the sight of the woman's familiar face. She stepped up onto the porch and stopped in front of her, her voice barely more than a whisper.

'Hester?'

The woman smiled in amusement.

'No Olivia,' her voice was smooth as honey and filled with affection. 'I'm not Hester.'

Understanding suddenly dawned in her mind.

'You're Bridget, aren't you?' Olivia asked softly. 'You're Hester's sister.'

'Yes I am' she studied Olivia warmly, 'and I have been waiting a long time for you.'

'Waiting for me?'

'Why don't you come in?' Bridget turned and moved back into the room, giving Olivia no choice but to follow.

Olivia stepped inside and glanced around curiously.

Although there was only one room, it radiated a warmth and coziness that Olivia instantly wanted to wrap around herself like a blanket. To one side, neatly tucked away, was a wooden cot covered with a patchwork quilt. At one end of the room was a large stone fireplace, and hanging from the ceiling above it were several bundles of herbs, which were drying out in the heat.

A pot of something delicious simmered on a large hook, suspended over the flickering flames, filling the air with a tantalizing scent. In the center of the room was a wooden table and chairs and along the edge of the room stood what could only be described as a very basic food preparation area, when compared to the modern hi tech kitchens of her time.

'Come in, don't stand in the doorway staring, you're letting in a draught.'

Olivia stepped further into the house and let the door close behind her. The wooden floor was worn and ruthlessly scrubbed to within an inch of its life. There was no glass in the windows, just wooden shutters which were open to let in the light. A small pot filled with wild flowers stood on the table. Although the cabin was crude by modern standards, it was obvious that it was well taken care of.

'Come take a seat love,' Bridget smiled, 'you must be confused and tired. Crossing over can be disorientating.'

Olivia moved obediently over to the table and pulling off her backpack she lowered herself into one of the chairs, studying Bridget's face intently.

'You look so much like her,' Olivia murmured thoughtlessly.

'Do I?' Bridget's mouth curved in amusement.

'Sorry,' Olivia shook her head, 'that was stupid. Of course you look like each other, you're twins.'

'Must be very strange for you,' she agreed.

'It is, I have a portrait of Hester painted by her daughter.'

'Miriam?' Bridget nodded, 'she was such a sweet girl. She loved to paint, always experimenting with mixing herbs and flowers and oils, trying to find a way to make them into colors to paint with. It used to drive Hess to distraction, that she would rather paint than concentrate on her lessons.'

'Lessons?'

'Aye,' Bridget smiled, 'the magic in our family has always been both a blessing and a curse, but it was our duty to pass it on to those who came after us. Miriam would have been happy spending the rest of her life painting rather than learning our craft, but eventually she followed the path, the same as all of us do in the end. It's in our blood.'

'Magic?'

'That's a part of it,' she nodded, 'but not all. It's a calling, a duty. What we were given came with great responsibility and heavy burdens.'

'Was it a burden for you?' Olivia asked softly.

Bridget stopped bustling around the small kitchen

for a moment, her eyes drowning in memories and judging from the fleeting emotion which passed over her face, they were painful ones.

'We all have our burdens to bear,' she shook her head and reached up to pull down a deep clay bowl.

'She spoke of you,' Olivia told her softly, 'in her journals. She worried about you.'

'That was Hess,' she took a long handled ladle and dished up thick scoops of stew into the bowl from the pot simmering over the fire. 'She always tried to take responsibility for everyone around her.'

'Is that a bad thing?'

'There comes a time, when we all have to take responsibility for what we've done.' She placed the bowl down on the table in front of Olivia and handed her a spoon. 'Eat.'

Her stomach growled loudly and her mouth began to water at the delicious scent wafting from the bowl. Not needing to be told twice, she dug in and almost groaned in pleasure. The meat she couldn't identify, it was something wild and gamey, not at all what she was used to. It was rich and buttery and seemed to almost melt on her tongue. The vegetables were cooked to perfection and seasoned with herbs she couldn't even begin to name, but all together it was quite possibly one of the best things she had ever tasted.

'I didn't know you could get hungry, or even eat in the Spirit world,' she mumbled through another mouthful.

'You'll find there are a lot of things possible here,' Bridget reached for a loaf of brown bread and began to cut a thick slice. 'It's simply another plane of existence.'

'Is Hester here?'

'No,' she sighed after a moment, 'I haven't seen her in such a long time.'

'Where is she Bridget?' Olivia asked curiously.

'That I can't tell you,' she handed her the generously buttered slice. 'I don't know where she is.'

'But?'

'No buts,' she sat down opposite Olivia, 'that was the agreement we made. That she would disappear so that no one could compel her soul to reveal the location of Infernum and I...,' she paused as her clear gaze met Olivia's, 'I would wait here for you.'

'For me?' jolted by Bridget's words, the spoon tumbled from her suddenly nerveless fingers, 'but how...why?'

'My sister saw a lot of things Olivia, she was an incredibly gifted seer, but she was so much more than that. She could see people's threads.'

'Threads?'

'Every living thing has threads attached to them, joining them to others. I'm told it's like looking at the world through a spider web of different colored yarns. Every line has a different color, every color has a different meaning, love, loyalty, friendship, betrayal, pain, all of them binding souls to each other. It isn't common, but there are some gifted witches who can see the threads of life. Hester could not only see the threads binding everyone together, but she could follow individual threads down through generation after generation. I don't really know how she was able to do it, there has never been another witch like her, not before, not since.'

'So she could see the future; not just any future, but the future of specific individuals and their descendants?'

'Something like that,' Bridget smiled.

'Wow,' Olivia breathed heavily as she picked up her spoon once again. 'I bet that was a hell of a headache.'

'Perhaps,' Bridget shrugged, 'if it did cause her distress she never showed it. To her, her magic was a gift, a celebration and she found so much joy in it.'

'And you?'

'It was a nail in the coffins of all the people I loved.'

'I'm sorry,' Olivia murmured.

'I made my choices,' she shrugged, 'but there is something you need to understand.'

'And that is?'

'That there is no such thing as white magic nor black, it is the witch who takes the power to a light or dark place. There is no good and evil, only personal responsibility. You are an extremely powerful witch, more so than you even realize. I know what has happened to you Olivia, and I know everything that has brought you to this point. I know why you are here.'

Olivia's defenses were immediately up.

'You know nothing about my life,' she said coolly

'Yes I do,' she breathed tiredly, 'and I understand more than you think.'

'Where are you going with this Bridget?'

'A warning,' she shrugged, 'and also I'm here to help you. Everything you are holding inside, bolted down so tightly, is eventually going to tear its way loose. All that pain and rage and betrayal will take your magic to a dark place and you along with it.' Her voice dropped low, 'you must have felt the beginnings of it already.'

Olivia gripped the spoon so tightly, her knuckles turned white. The delicious food she'd wolfed down only moments earlier now sat like lead in her stomach and ash in her mouth.

Bridget was right, she had felt it. That moment she'd called down the Hell fire and felt it flood her body, vast, dark and seductive. Even now she could feel it coiled deep inside her, restless and all-consuming, waiting to unfurl like a dragon of raw flame and power. She'd felt its dark call the first time she'd killed one of the Hell Hounds, an intimate kill even in her injured, weakened state. As she'd closed her hands around its throat and made it burn, she'd felt its panic, tasted its fear and pain. She'd reveled in it. To her shame, instead of feeling pity, she'd made the fire burn hotter, because she could, because she'd liked it.

Shame colored her cheeks, as her memory flashed back to the moment she had stood out in the snow wearing nothing but Theo's shirt, blood dripping from the wound at her thigh staining the crisp, white snow, scarlet beneath her naked feet. She'd reached up into the sky and pulled down lightning bolts of pure silver flame.

Like Zeus, standing high above on the pinnacle of Mount Olympus, as he rained down fire and lightning and retribution upon the Titans.

She'd rode the whip of power and gloried in it. In that moment, she knew she could have burned everything surrounding her, but she hadn't. She hadn't... she reminded herself.

She closed her eyes and drew in a shaky breath, her body trembling in remembrance, almost reliving the moment her body flooded with such an arousing ancient magic. Her hand involuntarily slipped beneath the table and squeezed the thigh which still bore the partially healed cut she had sustained that night. She winced at the slight pain and squeezed harder, as if the pain could somehow keep her grounded.

'There has never been anyone like you Olivia.' Bridget whispered, 'Daughter of fire. No one but a God has ever been able to control such a vast elemental power as the five ancient fires.'

'What do you mean?'

'There are five types of fire, the oldest and most unstable magic; Earth fire, Spirit fire, Hell fire, Witch fire and Demon fire, and you can wield three of those already. That kind of power in the wrong hands... if you don't reconcile your own demons Olivia, the power will overwhelm you. It will take you down a road there is no coming back from. I know...' her voice trembled as she fixed her penetrating gaze on Olivia, her eyes deeply troubled. 'Don't walk the path I did.'

'You're trapped here, aren't you?'

'In a way,' she sighed. 'I have my part to play in

this, we all do. Our family Olivia,' she shook her head, 'our history, it's, well…it's very complicated; stained with blood, and pride, and betrayal. We have so much to atone for, each generation has added to this mess.'

'I don't understand?' she frowned.

'Did you ever stop to wonder how we came to be in possession of Infernum, the most powerful book in history, or how Nathaniel came to walk the earth free and unfettered, while his brother remained imprisoned by Hades? How he knew about our connection to the book?'

'What are you saying?' Olivia asked slowly, her stomach tying in knots.

'Each generation has passed our history down daughter to daughter, colored by our own perceptions and our desperate desire to paint ourselves as the heroines, the warriors, who were chosen to protect the most powerful and sought after artifact ever known.'

'That's not true, is it?'

'No,' her mouth hardened. 'The truth is, our family is vastly flawed, unstable and susceptible to the darkness we find so seductive and irresistible. Do you really think your mother was the first West to covet the book and its powers? Our hands are stained with generations of betrayal, going all the way back to the first of our bloodline. Her name was Carrigan and it was her fault Nathaniel escaped from the Underworld.'

'What happened?'

Bridget shook her head.

'That's a story for another time.'

'But…'

'What you need to understand is that with every retelling of our story, it has become warped and changed. Ashamed of our past, each generation has tried to rewrite our history,' she let out a mocking laugh. 'Our glorious history, how we came to be the powerful protectors of the book, such a sacred duty, a sacred trust, such an honor, but the simple ugly truth is, that it was bestowed upon us as a punishment, that our children and our children's children have been enduring for nearly two thousand years. That book has been a plague on our bloodline, a disease we have never been able to rid ourselves of.'

'God,' Olivia whispered painfully.

'God had nothing to do with it, even the Goddess herself stood by and watched us suffer. Generation after generation of her daughters, living out a never-ending punishment, simply because of the blood that flows in our veins.'

'She's not like that,' Olivia frowned.

'Not with you,' Bridget murmured, 'that's how we knew you were different. Hess looked into our future and she saw you were the answer to the one question we'd never dared ask.'

'What question?' the color drained from her face.

'It's you Olivia, it's always been you. We have been waiting such a long time for you to be born. That's why you are different, that's why you can wield Hell fire. You're the one…the only one who can break this never ending cycle of blood and betrayal. You can set us all free.'

'No,' she shook her head in denial, 'you're wrong.'

'We're not wrong,' Bridget replied calmly. 'We have been trapped on this spinning wheel for so long; round and round we go. That book has spilled more blood than all the wars there have ever been, put together. The darkness won, time and time again, because we have never been strong enough to end it, but not this time, this time we have you.'

'No, you don't have me,' Olivia replied coldly. 'I don't want this. I didn't sign up for this, and it's sure as hell, not why I crossed over to the Otherworld. I'm here for one reason, and one reason only…to find Theo. I don't care about anything else.'

'Yes you do,' Bridget replied calmly. 'You're scared, I know you are, but it's time you faced up to your responsibilities.'

'What, like you did?' she stood abruptly, the chair legs scraping loudly against the wooden floor. 'Because from where I'm standing you and your sister didn't do such a great job yourselves, and you have the nerve to sit there and lecture me about my responsibilities? How dare you. I'm not here to clean up your mess, I'm here to find Theo, that's it.'

'You're right Olivia,' she sighed tiredly, 'my sister and I made a lot of mistakes and it isn't right to ask you to shoulder such a burden. It isn't right, and it isn't fair, but there is no one else. It has to be you, because it can be no other. I wish I could spare you the dark days ahead. I wish I could go back and undo all the mistakes our family has made, but I can't, because it's not up to me. I am here to instruct you and to help you, but I can't change the way things are, no matter how much I might want to.'

'I don't need any instruction and unless you are able to tell me where Theo is, I don't want a damn thing from you.'

'I don't know where Theo is; the Otherworld is different for each of us. I only knew where you'd be, because Hess saw it. He's here somewhere, I can sense that much, but it will be up to you to find him.'

'Fine,' Olivia snapped, as she snatched up her backpack. 'Thanks for the meal.'

'Olivia,' Bridget rose from her chair, 'you can't ignore this, or ignore me. I'm not going away, you need guidance. Your power is raw and undisciplined, as is your knowledge of our craft. It's not your fault, you didn't have those who came before you to guide you and nurture you through this, but you cannot just walk away.'

'Just watch me.'

She headed for the door.

'Olivia,' Bridget spoke quietly, causing her to pause and look back. 'I'll be here, when you change your mind.'

'I won't.'

'We'll just see about that,' Bridget murmured as she watched the door close behind Olivia.

Mac looked up at the tap on his door.
'Jake,' he nodded.
'Have you got a moment?'
'Sure,' he closed the file that had been giving him a headache for the past 45 minutes and beckoned him in. 'What's on your mind.'
'It's about Olivia and Theo.'
'Have you heard anything? Are they back?'
'No,' he shook his head, 'but a couple of nights ago, I helped Roni haul a load of Olivia's books over to her apartment to sort through. She says it's the most comprehensive collection of obscure occult and magic books she's ever seen. She thought by going through them, she might find something helpful on how to contact them on the other side. Or even better, find a way to bring them back, and seeing as Charles and the others have done a disappearing act, I figured what harm could it do?'
'So,' Mac leaned back in his chair, 'has she found anything?'
'I don't know yet,' he frowned, 'she called earlier and left me a message. She sounded quite excited about something, but she didn't want to talk about it on the phone. I'm going to swing by her place after I'm done here. I just thought you'd want to be kept in the loop.'
'Thanks Jake, I appreciate it,' he blew his breath out slowly. 'I have to admit, I'm getting worried. It's been weeks and nothing, no sign of them or Charles, and when that man goes radio silent it makes me itch. He's up to something, and I can guarantee it's something we wouldn't approve of, or he would have involved us.'
'Are you so sure of that?' Jake asked. 'You seemed pretty steamed at him the night after the gateway was closed.'
'That's because he tried to cave my skull in with

the butt of his gun,' he frowned. 'However that being said, looking back and knowing what I do of him, I can't quite bring myself to believe he would abandon his daughter. He had her watched over and protected for years while he was incarcerated, but then again, who really knows the man? I say we rely on ourselves this time around. Tell Roni, whatever she needs we've got her back. Let's bring Olivia and Theo home.'

'You can't do that,' a soft voice spoke from the doorway.

Mac looked up and his expression instantly hardened.

'Mayor Burnett,' Jake nodded.

She glanced over at Mac's chilly expression and sighed. It seemed he was still pretty mad about finding out her true identity, but unfortunately that couldn't be helped.

'I don't mean to intrude, but what is happening now with Olivia and Theo is important. It has to happen, which means that no matter how much you want to help them, you can't interfere.'

'You keep saying that, but you're not really giving us much to work with here,' Jake frowned.

'I know it's hard for you to understand, but I can't give away too much information. We have to let events unfold in their own time.'

'And how long will that take? Months? Years? They've already been gone three weeks,' Jake replied, 'people are starting to notice.'

'I know how long it's been for us, but it's not the same for them.'

'I don't understand,' Jake frowned.

'In the Otherworld time passes differently, in fact time doesn't actually pass at all.'

'You're really not making any sense.'

'Here three weeks have gone by, but in the Spirit world time has no meaning, so to them they've only just arrived. It will feel like hours not weeks.'

'That's messed up.'

'I don't make the rules,' her mouth curved into an amused smile, 'I just try to work around them.'

'You're asking us to take a lot on faith here Mayor,' Jake sighed.

'I know,' she replied sympathetically, 'I know you want them back. I do too, but there is a lot at stake here. I need you to trust me.'

'That's asking a lot,' Mac finally spoke up, his voice low and cool, 'from someone who has lied about her identity for the last forty years.'

'Okay fine, I deserved that, but you don't understand what will happen if you interfere.'

'What will happen?' Jake asked.

'I will die,' she answered quietly

'What?' Mac's expression lost a little of the cool hostility, as his brow creased into a frown.

Tammy sucked in a breath and tried to organize her thoughts.

'I was nine years old when I was brought to Mercy,' she began softly, 'and I was dying from what I would later discover was Scarlett Fever, a condition easily treatable in the present day, but from my time it was a death sentence. I was a premature baby, my mother died giving birth to me, and throughout my early childhood I was sickly and prone to illness. I would never have survived if I had been left in Salem. Even once I was brought to Mercy, it was still touch and go for a while as to whether or not I would survive. My past is your present. What is happening now, directly leads up to the events which brought me to Mercy. If you interfere now, those events will never take place and I will die in Salem, just another faceless statistic of childhood mortality in the 17th century colonies.'

'Jesus Christ,' Jake raked his hands through his hair. 'I thought it was bad enough trying to get my head wrapped around Theo being dragged through time, but seriously, time travel is giving me a brain aneurysm right now.'

'I know it's a lot to take in, and a lot to ask, but please don't try to interfere.'

'Alright,' Jake blew out a breath, 'I'll talk to Roni. We won't try to pull them back across the Veil, but that doesn't mean we're not going to try and contact them.'

'Fair enough,' she nodded as her gaze locked on Mac, who was silently studying her. 'Can you give us a minute Jake?'

'Sure,' he noticed the look that passed between them, and felt the atmosphere grow heavy. 'I'll just head over to Roni's now.'

Neither of them answered, in fact they barely noticed when he clicked the door closed quietly behind him, leaving just the two of them shut in the small office.

'You're still mad at me?'

'Is that a question or a statement?' he replied coolly.

'Layton,' she sighed, 'I'm sorry I never told you, but it's really not that big a deal.'

'Excuse me?' his expression darkened, 'not that big a deal? You lied to me about who you are.'

'I didn't, not really,' she replied. 'Look, after I was taken to the hospital and treated, I was adopted by the Burnetts. They gave me their name legally and they shortened my name to Tammy, and it just kind of stuck. I never lied to you about who I was, I'm still me. I just didn't tell you where and when I was born.'

'A lie by omission, is still a lie.'

'For God's sake Layton,' she snapped angrily, 'stop being so obtuse.'

'Obtuse?' he stood abruptly, facing her over his desk. 'You should have told me.'

'Really?' she asked incredulously, 'tell you what? That I was born in Salem in 1676, and magically pulled through time? Tell me Layton, exactly how am I supposed to start a conversation like that? You wouldn't have believed a damn word out of my mouth. You'd have thought I was crazy, and with good reason. Admit it, if I had told you back then, before all of this happened, before the things you've seen since you came back to Mercy, there is no way you could've believed me.'

'Maybe not the first time around, but I have been back in Mercy for months,' he snapped, 'months Tammy, and at any point you could've come to me and told me the truth, but you didn't.'

'I couldn't.'

'You mean wouldn't,' he replied bitterly. 'You're not the woman I thought you were. I don't know you at all.'

'That's not fair,' she whispered, 'you were the only one who did know the real me.'

'How can I believe that now?'

She could feel the tears burning the back of her eyes and the hot hard knot forming in her throat. Not wanting to let him see how much his words had stung, she turned and headed toward the door. But she paused with her hand on the handle; she couldn't leave him like this, after everything. She'd hurt him, she knew it and he deserved as much of an answer, as she was able to give him.

'I never had the chance to know my mother,' she began so softly he almost missed it.

Mac watched her carefully, ignoring the heaviness in his chest as she spoke.

'My father was an abusive alcoholic, my eldest brother became a cold blooded killer and my sister in law was violent and unstable, because she was probably suffering from paranoid schizophrenia. Theo was all I had. He pretty much raised me from the moment I was born, it was me and him against the world.

You can't begin to imagine how painful it was, being separated from him, and not only that, but to be placed in a world I didn't understand, with people I didn't know, and I couldn't tell anyone, not another living soul, where I came from.

I've waited forty years to see my brother again. Do you think I didn't want to tell the truth? The minute he landed up in Mercy, do you think I wasn't desperate to go to him and tell him who I was? Of all the time I have spent with Olivia, do you not wonder why I was so careful to never be in the same room as Theo? To make sure our paths didn't cross?

Because I couldn't take the risk of him recognizing me, or figuring out who I was before now. Things are about to get bad Layton, really bad. Nathaniel is even more dangerous now, and Isabel West is not only losing her grip on her sanity, but on her control over him. I never wanted you to get caught up in the middle of all of this. It's my fault, I should never have asked you to come back to Mercy,' she shook her head, her voice low and filled with pain.

'I am truly sorry, for the hurt I have caused you Layton.'

Her eyes were burning but she couldn't bring herself to look at him. She turned to the door and fumbled with the handle, trying to swallow past the misery lodged in her throat. She was so focused on trying to get out of the room, she didn't notice him round the desk and close the distance between them in two quick strides. All she knew was she was suddenly caged against the door by his arms. She felt the heat and hardness of his body pressed against her back and his breath whisper across her cheekbone. As he bent low his voice washed over her, familiar and gravelly; she'd always loved the sound of his voice.

'Tell me just one thing.'

She turned and looked up into his piercing blue eyes.

'Is this the reason you wouldn't marry me?'

If her silence hadn't given him the answer he needed, he would have read it in the guilt swimming in her glassy eyes.

'Damn it Tammy,' he growled low.

Before she could open her mouth to respond, his crashed down on her. A gasp escaped, as he took her under, his fingers tangled in her sleek bob length hair, holding her close as his mouth tasted her like he was a man starving. She couldn't think, couldn't breathe.

It all crashed in on her with painful acuity, the familiarity, the heat, all those feeling of longing, of need, and she embraced them all and gave like she had never given before. For the first time ever there were no barriers between them, no secrets, it was just the two of them.

Her fingers grazed his jaw and slid up to his cheeks tracing the indentations of what had been cute dimples in his youth, but had now deepened into sexy creases. His stubble scraped at her sensitive skin, but she didn't care. His hard body pressed her soft curves, as he held her trapped against the door.

When the insistent need for oxygen finally drove them apart they stood, breathing heavily, his forehead pressed to hers, his hands still tangled in her hair and her fingers still gently cupping his ridiculously handsome face.

'Tammy,' he breathed against her mouth, 'I don't need you to protect me, I just need you. I always have.'

'Don't,' the word came out as a choked sob, 'I can't lose you Layton, not like this. I won't have your blood on my hands.'

Something about the way she said it set alarm bells going off in his head. He grasped her chin gently, and brought her face up, so she had no choice but to look into his eyes.

'There's something else,' he frowned, 'something you're not telling me.'

'Layton please,' she tried to shake her head but he held her firmly with gentle hands.

'Tell me Tammy, I know the truth about who you are now. There will be no more secrets between us.'

'I can't.'

'Are you in danger?'

She stared at him silently.

'Tammy,' he warned.

'When Nathaniel finds out who I am...and he will,' she whispered, 'he will come after me, for no other reason than to hurt Theo.'

'I'm not going to let that happen,' he stroked her jaw softly.

'This is exactly why I didn't want to tell you. Nathaniel will kill whoever stands between me and him, and then he will kill me in the worst way possible. I told you before Layton, I won't have your blood on my hands.'

'You think I'm just going to stand by and watch you get hurt?' he asked angrily.

'Do you think I'm going to use you as a human shield?' she fired back.

'It's not your choice Tammy.'

'Yes, it is,' she pulled his hands from her face and pushed him away.

She couldn't think when he was crowding her space, she could only feel and it was that stupidity which had made her confess everything to him in the first place.

'Stay away from me Layton, I mean it.'

She turned and yanked the door open and disappeared.

He let her go, he knew she wouldn't run far and they both needed the space to process all that had happened.

His heart was still thundering in his chest and he could still taste her on his lips. He pressed his forehead against the cool wood of the door, and took a deep breath. So this was how she wanted to play it, was it? Pushing him away so he wouldn't get hurt? Well fuck that, this time there was no way he was giving her up without a fight. He was going to damn well protect the woman he loved, even if it meant going up against a demon.

4.

Jonathan Bailey slowly rose from his kneeling position on the cold hard floor. He leaned heavily on the shelving he had just been restocking and straightened his aching back, wincing as he felt his knees click. He gazed through the window at the rapidly melting snow and breathed a sigh of relief; his bones were definitely looking forward to the warmer weather.

Glancing around the quiet store his eyes flicked to the clock, which hung above the cash register. Good, he'd be closing up soon. There was no use denying it, especially in quiet contemplative moments like this, but he was getting too old to manage the store by himself.

He knew his wife loved the store and helped immensely. Despite her rather frightening reputation for being a busy body, and the town gossip, she had a good heart, one she didn't let the rest of the town see. She would perch on her throne behind the cash register and freely dispense her mind, and opinion, to the good people of Mercy, often with brutal practicality and razor sharp honesty.

It wasn't always appreciated or even warranted, but the residents had come to accept her the way she was. He was the only person who knew the real Eustacia Bailey.

They'd never been blessed with children. They'd

never spoken of it, even after the first ten years of their marriage and their joint failure to produce a child.

She'd begun to change after that. As more of their friends and acquaintances subsequently married and produced large families with ease, the harder it had been on her. Sure, he'd wanted kids, he'd dreamed of passing the store on to his son, or daughter, just as the store had been passed to him by his father and grandfather before him. But he'd accepted along the way that some things were just not meant to be.

It always sat there between them, the unspoken heartbreak and regret, but as the years rolled by the sharper her tongue became and the harder it was to dredge up the past. They had made a comfortable life for themselves, there had been good times and laughter, but he often wondered, if by keeping them tied to the store, to the legacy left by his family, he had held them back. Perhaps, when it became clear to them there would be no children, they should have created a new dream together.

He looked around at the general store which had been in his family for three generations, realizing how much he loved it. It held so many memories of his own family, of his childhood, and his parents, and of his life with Eustacia, but perhaps...perhaps it was time to let it go.

Lately, he had been thinking more and more, about selling the store and retiring. They could take one of those fancy cruises, somewhere warm and exotic, where his bones wouldn't creak and complain like a rusty hinge. He'd never had the chance to take her on a honeymoon as his father had suffered a stroke just before their wedding, and he'd had to take over the store. Yet she'd never complained.

Well, he thought with a silent chuckle, she'd never complained about him, though she damn well complained about nearly everything else.

A small smile played on his lips as he scooped the

empty cardboard cartons off the floor beside the newly stocked shelves, his mind still caught up in a lifetime of memories. Eustacia Bailey may have henpecked him to within an inch of his life, liberally and often with great gusto, but the truth was, she had been the sun and the moon to him for the last fifty years.

'Jonathan!' her familiar tone snapped, 'what are you doing standing around with that silly grin on your face. It's nearly five past and you've not locked the doors yet.'

'Yes dear,' he smiled softly at her, with infinite patience, 'I was just about to.'

'Well get on with it,' she stood with one hand fisted on her hip and the other tucking the cash drawer under her arm. 'I'd like to get home some time tonight.'

He shuffled over to her, dropping the empty boxes by her feet. He leaned toward her, as she watched him with wary eyes and dropped a sweet kiss on her cheek.

'I love you Eunie,' he smiled, 'I don't think I've said that to you often enough.'

'Have you been drinking?' her eyes narrowed suspiciously.

'No,' he replied in amusement.

'Then what are you after, trying to soften me up?'

'Nothing,' he chuckled.

'Well,' her lips pursed speculatively, 'you'd better get on with it then.'

He watched her as she turned abruptly and headed toward the back, where the office was located. Suddenly she stopped, hesitated, and slowly turned back toward him.

'I love you too,' she added, a faint blush staining her cheeks under layers of pressed powder.

He smiled, as she disappeared into the back room. Maybe it was time to start thinking about selling up after all. The soft tinkle of the bell shook him from his thoughts, and still smiling he turned towards the door.

'I'm sorry we're closing…'

His voice trailed off and the smile fell from his

face, as he watched the tall figure of a man enter.

He was uncommonly tall, must've been nearly seven feet in height. He was immaculately dressed in a crisp white shirt, black waistcoat and trousers. His heavy black overcoat was so long it hung to his lower calves, and his silver hair was almost completely concealed by a large wide-brimmed black hat.

His skin was papery and heavily lined with age, his cheeks hollow and his mouth a thin tight line, but it was his eyes which caused Jonathan Bailey's own to widen in shock. The stranger's eyes were completely black, with no whites at all. But, it wasn't just that they were black, Jonathan found himself staring, inexplicably drawn into those shiny orbs, unable to move or even gasp in fear. The blackness seemed to go on endlessly, vast and all encompassing, a soulless void of nothingness.

He couldn't move. Caught, like an insect in a web, his mouth fell open and yet no sound emerged. His eyes widened in fear, but he could not close them to shut out the vast, inevitable pit he was being sucked down into.

He vaguely registered the stranger's palm pressing against his chest, the abnormally long, elegant fingers sinking into his skin, as if he were no more than a shadow. There was no blood, no wound, but he suddenly felt a shocking tear, as if something precious had been ripped from him.

The color drained from his eyes, taking them from a merry twinkling brown, to the pale, colorless white of a serpent. His lips, still open in a silent scream of stunned agony, held a faint blue stain, as his skin turned grey.

Then he felt nothing but a shocking emptiness, and crushing cold, his body falling backward in slow motion. He could see it somehow, as if he were suddenly watching from a different vantage point, and when it hit the ground, he felt nothing.

The stranger withdrew his clenched fist from the discarded body, his long tapered fingers wrapped around a small ball of pure white light, which pulsed brightly in his palm.

His other hand dipped into the folds of his heavy overcoat and withdrew a small clear glass bottle. He tipped the light into the bottle and pressed a stopper into the neck, as if to prevent the strange ball of light from escaping. He shook the bottle a couple of times, seemingly satisfied when it shone even brighter. Tucking the bottle into his breast pocket he turned back to the door, disappearing into the dark street in a tiny tinkle of bells.

Olivia crossed Main St. lost in thought. She settled the weight of her backpack more comfortably on her back, but paused suddenly and frowned.

For a second she could've sworn she'd seen a large black shadow emerge from the doorway of the Bailey's convenience store. A sudden blast of icy air crashed against her, and she took an involuntary step back, drawing in a shaky breath.

Curious, she headed toward the Bailey's store and stepped over the threshold. She'd been in that store so many times, and this was an exact replica, right down to the chipped wooden door frame and the faded, open sign, but it felt different this time.

The store was one of the first places she'd been to when she arrived in the Otherworld and although it was abandoned, it had still retained the warmth and smell of home. Not this time though, the air was freezing. She could almost feel the hairs rising on the back of her neck, and a strange smell lingered on the air. If she had to guess, she would have sworn it was the pungent scent of lilies.

It just felt all wrong; she couldn't describe the what or how, but she could feel it. Stepping further into the store a wave of nausea washed over her.

Forcing herself forward she searched the store thoroughly, but she couldn't find anything. Opening the door at the back of the store she stepped into a small windowless room, which held a small desk and chair, an ancient computer and a tall metal filing cabinet.

Once again she found nothing amiss, just the inexplicable sense of wrongness. She turned back to the door and paused, tilting her head to listen carefully. In the little room, she could hear several low pitched sounds. She had to concentrate, straining to separate them. One sounded like the frantic clatter of nails on a computer keyboard, another made her think of the clink of coins being counted and finally, she thought she could hear the low murmur of a familiar voice. In fact, it sounded like Mrs Bailey.

Just when Olivia thought it couldn't get any stranger, she saw a flicker at the edge of her vision and when she turned, just for a split second, she saw Mrs Bailey kneeling down to place a stack of money into the small safe tucked underneath the desk. But, as quickly as she had appeared, she was gone again.

Olivia shook her head, she must be losing her mind. She was probably hallucinating, after all technically she hadn't slept since the night before they closed the gateway and even then with the revelation of Theo's wife, she hadn't slept particularly well that night either. With the sudden thought of Theo, the pressure in her chest once again flared. Forcing down a wave of guilt, pain, and loneliness, all wrapped up in a helpless messy bow of love, she turned and withdrew from the tight, unpleasant confines of the room.

Stepping back out into the store, she headed to the door. She probably needed to find somewhere comfortable and safe to get her head down for a few hours and sleep.

'JONATHAN!' The scream of panic ripped through the air, unmistakably loud and clear.

She spun around, and saw Mrs Bailey emerge from the office, her wide, shocked eyes focused on something behind Olivia. Before she could react, Mrs Bailey rushed forward, passing straight through her and disappeared once again.

Olivia sucked in a deep sharp breath and shivered. It felt as if she had just been doused with a bucket of ice cold water. Her gaze once again scanned the room, but Mrs Bailey was nowhere to be seen. Shaking her head lightly, a tired, almost hysterical laugh catching in her throat, Olivia once again headed for the door, determined to get out of the store which now felt entirely too small and confining. It was almost as if Mrs Bailey had been a ghost, appearing and disappearing like that. What with the whispering voices and the strange feelings, if she'd been back in the real world, Olivia thought as she stepped back out into the street, it would have felt like a haunting. Except, she realized with a jolt, they weren't the ghosts, she was.

She sank down onto a nearby bench and leaned back against a huge Realtor advertisement. She stared up at the grey sky and released a deep sigh.

What was she doing? Everything felt as if it were going wrong and she was being swept along, caught in a riptide, unable to catch her breath. Unable to find anything to anchor herself to or, she thought grimly, no one to anchor herself to, and with that realization came the brutal truth, she needed Theo. Nothing made sense without him, she didn't know when or how it had happened, but he had become as necessary to her as the air she breathed. He was her rock, her anchor. Through everything that had happened since she had returned to Mercy, he had been the one holding her together, even when she hadn't realized it.

God she missed him. She closed her eyes, squeezing them shut against the sudden onslaught of images. She missed the way he looked at her, like he couldn't quite believe she was real, and the way he smiled at her, content to just sit and listen to her waffle on about history, as if it was the most riveting subject in the world.

The way he touched her, how it felt to have his fingers trailing down her skin, burning even as it soothed. The way he tasted, and the feel and shape of his lips against hers. The way he would fold her into his arms and hold on, and when he made love to her, it felt as if the whole world had faded away and they were the only two people in existence.

She let out her breath and leaned forward, propping her elbows on her knees and cradling her head in her hands. She could feel the tide of grief and loss rising up in her throat, howling to get loose. She hadn't even told him she loved him. He had been pulled to God knows where, thinking that she didn't care, that she was angry with him. She'd been selfish and ungrateful; she'd yelled at him and told him she couldn't trust him. He must hate her, she thought miserably.

'He's not angry with you, you know,' a soft, comforting and painfully familiar voice spoke quietly next to her.

Olivia jolted in shock and sat up, her hands dropping limply to her thighs and her mouth falling open in stunned silence.

'Aunt Evie?' she whispered, after what felt like an eternity.

'Hello Olivia,' Evelyn West smiled, crossing her legs and resting her arm along the back of the bench comfortably.

'Why are you here? How are you here? What…?'

'I'm just visiting…from,' she pointed upward to the cloudy sky, 'up there.'

Olivia was lost for words. She sat staring numbly at the aunt she had spent most of her late childhood and teens thinking didn't want her.

'You looked like you needed a little support,' she smiled sympathetically. 'Feeling a little lost right now, aren't you?'

Olivia nodded, her eyes filling with tears and when Evie held out her arms Olivia hesitated for a second and then leaned forward into the familiar embrace. She was immediately transported back to her childhood, to the aunt she had loved, with whom she had shared a tight bond and an affinity for the woods.

'There, there, sweetheart,' Evie rocked her gently against the hot flood of tears, 'it's really not as bad as you think. You're tired, and your heart is sore, but soon things will start looking up.'

Olivia couldn't speak. It was as if a dam had broken, and everything came flooding out, even things she didn't know she had stored deep inside her. She cried for them all, her Nana, her mother, her father, her destiny, Theo, it was like a purge that came crashing out in a flood of tears and anguish.

Evie held her shaking and exhausted body, until her harsh sobs finally slowed. She soothed her hair and crooned to her softly, until her tears were no more than a few hiccups and a shaky intake of breath.

'I guess I needed that,' Olivia croaked.

'I'd say,' Evie tucked her hair behind her ear, just as she had when Olivia was a child. 'I've never seen anyone so in need of a crying jag as you. You hold too much in Olivia, there's something therapeutic about a good cry every once in a while.'

'If you say,' Olivia sniffed. 'I bet my face is a splotchy mess right now and it feels like my eyes are full of grit.'

'It will pass,' Evie chuckled, 'but you needed to get that out of the way so we could talk properly.'

'I suppose,' she sighed, 'I've been behaving like a bit of a brat lately, haven't I?'

Evie watched her quietly, a small smile twitching at the corner of her mouth.

'I'll take your silence as a firm yes,' Olivia raked her hair back from her face. 'I guess I've been on my own for so long, so used to going my own way that…'

'That as soon as someone comes along and tells

you that you have a destiny, you fight it for all its worth,' Evie finished for her.

'Yeah,' she admitted quietly. 'I never have liked being told what to do.'

'You were like that even as a child, even before your mother betrayed us all.'

'It's too much,' Olivia whispered, 'I can't…I can't do it. I can't have everyone relying on me. I mean, killing a demon, finding and protecting one of the most, if not THE most powerful object in history. I'm not ready, I'm not enough.'

'You're more than you think you are Olivia,' Evie shook her head. 'I'm sorry this has fallen to you, but we rarely get to choose when destiny comes knocking. Your mother won't stop until she has the book, and Nathaniel won't stop until he takes the book from her. If a demon lord, as old, and dangerous as Nathaniel, gets his hands on the Book of Hell, it will mean the end of days, Armageddon, the Apocalypse, whatever you want to call it. He will unleash Hell on earth, and he will use Mercy as the gateway. Everyone you love will burn in fire, and ash, and flame. So destiny came knocking on your door instead of someone else's. She's just asked you to save the world, are you really going to tell her no?'

'I guess not,' Olivia blew out a breath. 'I have so many questions.'

'I imagine you do and I'll answer as much as I can, but I'm kind of on a Cinderella deal here. I had to pull some serious strings to get in here, and I only have so long before my carriage turns into a pumpkin, and I have to return.'

'Okay.'

'But there is one thing we need to clear up before anything else,' Evie told her seriously, 'and that is to tell you I'm sorry. I'm so sorry Olivia; I was wrong.'

'About what?'

'I thought, by keeping you away from Mercy, by

refusing custody of you, I was keeping you safe. I can see now that I made a huge mistake. What you needed was your family, or what was left of it. I should have taken you and loved you, for as long as my broken body was able to. I should have taught you everything I knew about our history, and our magic, to prepare you for what is to come. But I was selfish. I wanted you safe, and happy, I wanted you to have a normal life, not bear the curse of our family. I thought I was doing what was best for you, but instead I only made things harder.'

'It's alright Aunt Evie,' Olivia whispered after a moment, and she found, much to her surprise it really was. The hard ball of resentment she had always carried deep in her gut was gone. Evie had loved her, and that was what made it alright. 'You made the best decision you could at the time, and what's done is done, it can't be changed.'

'I know, but unfortunately you are coming into the middle of this mess, with no proper training in magic and no real understanding of our history. You need to listen to Bridget. She really is here to help you, and if you give her the chance, you may find she understands what you are going through, better than anyone.'

'I suppose I owe her an apology, I was pretty rude to her earlier.'

'Yes you were, and although it was understandable, there's really no excuse for bad manners.'

'Alright, I'll go and find her later. I just want to find Theo. I can't focus on anything else right now. I have to find him.'

'Olivia,' Evie sighed, 'you'll find him when he wants to be found.'

'What do you mean?'

'Theo has his own issues he's working through right now.'

'So what are you saying? That I shouldn't look for him?'

'No, I'm saying it may be harder than you think to

find him, and while you are looking make the most of the advantages that come your way.'

'I don't understand.'

'Olivia, you must've noticed by now that the sun hasn't set.'

'I did actually,' she frowned.

'Time has no meaning here,' she tried to explain. 'Time is passing at a different rate in the real world, just as it passes differently in every realm and dimension. While you are here, time has slowed to an almost infinitesimal rate. When you return to the real world things are going to happen very fast. You need to be ready, so while you're here take the time to learn what you can.'

After a moment she nodded and Evie relaxed.

'I have to go now,' she told her, 'but there is one more thing.'

'What's that?'

Evie pointed over the road to Jackson's pub, The Salted Bone.

'There's someone over there who needs you.'

'Theo?' Olivia breathed hopefully.

'No, someone else you will recognize, but he might not be exactly the man you know,' she replied cryptically.

'What?'

'Just go and take a look,' she nudged her off the bench.

'Will I see you again?' Olivia asked quietly.

'Oh, I expect we'll run into each other, sooner or later. What is it my friend Fiona is so fond of saying? The dead never stay dead.'

Olivia smiled and turned toward the pub.

'Oh and by the way,' Evie called out causing Olivia to turn back, 'cut Mags some slack. She was only doing what I asked her to, and it hurts me when she hurts.'

Olivia nodded and headed to the pub. Her thoughts drifting back to Mags. She'd been pretty hard on her too. It hadn't helped that she had found out the truth about her friend's relationship with her late Aunt and that she had kept her silence for years, allowing her to believe that her Aunt hadn't loved her, or wanted her. A fresh wave of guilt left a sour taste in her mouth, as she pushed the door to the pub open and stepped into the darkened room. Maybe she should make peace with Mags when she got back, if she got back.

She made her way through to the bar area, easily navigating the tables and chairs in the dim light. She could see a figure with dark hair sitting at the bar with his back to her, an open bottle of Johnnie Walker Blue on the counter next to him as he raised a glass to his lips. She stepped closer and caught his reflection in the mirror behind the bar.

'Sam?' she gasped loud enough for his back to stiffen, and for him to turn slowly on his stool to face her.

'Sam?' she breathed in relief, as she moved closer to him. 'I'm so glad to see you, how the hell did you find me?'

It took her a moment to realize something was wrong. Sam didn't look as if he was pleased to see her. In fact, he was looking at her very strangely and as she stepped closer to stand directly in front of him, she got a bit of a jolt. He didn't look right, in fact he looked younger, much younger. The man she knew, was about the same age as her, if not slightly older, but this Sam looked barely more than seventeen.

'Sam?' she asked uncertainly.

'How do you know my name?' he asked accusingly, 'and who the hell are you?'

Olivia's heart plummeted. Great, she thought, that's just great. The one person in the world who could've helped her find Theo, and find a way back to the real world, and he didn't have a clue who she was.

5.

'Who the hell are you?' Sam asked angrily. 'Did my father send you?'

'I have no idea who your father is,' she replied carefully.

'How do you know who I am then?'

Suddenly his eyes lost some of the anger and he focused on her more closely, as if he were seeing something for the first time. 'You don't belong here.'

'No kidding,' she murmured.

'No, I mean you're not dead. You're not a spirit,' his brow furrowed in confusion. 'You still have a mortal body. How did you get here?'

'Hades,' she answered honestly. Even if he didn't exactly remember who she was, he was still the closest thing she had to a friend on the other side, and if she was going to find Theo, and get the hell outta Dodge, she was going to need all the help she could get.

'Hades?' his eyes widened. 'THE Hades?'

'Yeah, that's the one.'

'How do you know who I am? What do you want with me?' he asked suspiciously.

'Look, I know this is going to sound strange. I don't know why you don't remember me, or why you look about fifteen years younger than the last time we met, unless of course you have a hell of a plastic surgeon, but we have met. We're friends, sort of.'

'Friends?' he replied skeptically, 'but you're human.'

'Yeah and you're not, I get that.'

'You know what I am?' his eyes widened in surprise.

'Well no, not exactly. I know you aren't human and I know you can kind of,' she did a strange little flapping gesture with her hand, 'you know, appear and disappear, and travel from one place to another instantaneously.'

'Translocate,' he replied curiously.

'Oh, okay then, translocate yourself from one place to another, and that you can…' she stopped and frowned. 'What do you call it when you jump through time?'

'Through time? Are you mad? No one can translocate through time. Distance yes, over different dimensions yes, but not through time.'

'You can,' she shrugged. 'I've seen you do it.'

'Impossible,' Sam scoffed.

Sam lifted the glass back to his lips, his eyes narrowing as he scrutinized her thoroughly, perhaps trying to figure out why she would make up such an outrageous lie.

Olivia watched him observing her, and a sudden thought occurred to her. Every time she had met up with Sam, or rather the older version of Sam, he had been adamant he knew her, that they had met before, but she knew she had never met him. What if the tables had finally turned? If the Sam she had known, had travelled back to her time. What if she had finally caught up with an earlier version of him, and from his point of view they were just meeting for the first time.

'God,' she breathed with the sudden realization, 'time travel is enough to give you a brain hemorrhage.'

She took the glass from his hand and downed the contents in one go.

'Hey that's mine.'

'Oh please' she sighed, 'are you even old enough to drink?'

'That's a stupid human rule,' he frowned.

'Okay, here's the thing,' she took a deep breath, 'you can believe me, or not, but it's the truth. At some point, in your future presumably, you are going to discover you are capable of skipping back and forth through time. That's how we meet, well how I met you. You apparently are just meeting me for the first time now.'

'Huh?'

'Try and keep up Sam, we don't have all day. The older version of you,' she continued, 'the one I know, travelled back to the year 1695 to a town called Salem, in Massachusetts. You saved a man named Theodore Beckett, from burning to death in a barn. You pulled him out minutes before the barn collapsed in. The people in his time assume he has died in the fire, but you pull him forward over three hundred years into his future, and drop him in my lap, or rather in front of my car, in my hometown of Mercy.'

'Let's just say you're right,' he replied skeptically, 'and that you are telling the truth about the whole travelling through time, and I'm not saying I believe you, but why would I do that?'

'I have no idea,' she shook her head and slid tiredly onto the barstool next to him, pulling out another glass and refilling it.

'He's important to you, isn't he? This Theodore?'

'Yes he is,' she stared into her glass for a moment before taking a sip. 'I know you don't know me right now, and you have no reason to trust me, but I need you Sam. I need your help to find Theo, and get back to the real world.'

'I can't help you,' he frowned.

'But…'

'Look lady…what's your name?'

'Olivia,' she replied, 'Olivia West.'

'Well Olivia, Olivia West,' he mimicked, 'I couldn't help you even if I wanted to. The truth is, I'm stuck here too.'

'What do you mean?'

'My father trapped me down here as a punishment, and I can't guarantee when he'll decide to let me out.'

'What did you do?' Olivia asked curiously.

'Nothing,' he answered a little too quickly.

Olivia found herself studying him closely, his eyes were guarded and his spine stiff, but there was something else in his expression. A sneaking suspicion had her mouth curving into a small smile.

'Who was she?'

'I don't know what you're talking about.'

'Yes you do, nobody puts an expression like that on a guy's face but a girl, so what's her name?'

'Look,' he snapped irritably, 'I'm sorry but I can't help you.'

She blinked and suddenly found herself sitting alone at the bar.

'Well, that went well,' she murmured, her gaze catching on the mirror behind the bar, as she raised her glass and toasted her reflection.

Roni winced as she stubbed her toe painfully on the coffee table. Easing around it, she hobbled toward the door and tripped over the pile of books she'd forgotten she'd stacked on the other side of the table. She hit the floor in an unladylike tangle of limbs, and with a loud thud. Her elbow cracked sharply against the hard surface and she found herself seeing stars, as she let loose an unintentional cry of pain.

'Roni?' Jake's muffled voice came from the other

side of the door. 'Are you okay?'

Groaning, she took a deep breath, hauled herself off the floor and limped slowly to the door. He always seemed to have an unfortunate knack for being around when she was at her most ungraceful. As she swung the door open Jake stood watching her carefully. He had Olivia's rather appealing puppy tucked under one arm, his blue leash dangling down to the floor. As soon as Beau saw her he scrambled against Jake, trying to get to her, his tail wagging madly.

Jake's gaze tracked slowly down her body, from her tank top and pajama pants to her bare feet, and back up until he met her eyes. She flushed under his intense appraisal. She thought she saw a flash of something in his eyes, heat perhaps, but dismissed it.

He didn't see her like that, he only saw her as a kind of cute, klutzy sister type. She really needed to stop obsessing about him she thought, as she took in his gorgeous face and blonde hair. It was starting to fall forward into his eyes a bit, he obviously needed a haircut and she found her fingers twitching slightly. Fighting the urge to reach out and push his hair back, she swallowed and cleared her throat.

It shouldn't be awkward between them. Over the past month or so they had settled into an easy friendship, and she was finding that lately she enjoyed his company more and more. She didn't want anything to change that, after all it wasn't his fault she had a pathetic crush on him. She watched as his jaw clenched and his eyes involuntarily dipped to her chest again. It was only then she realized in horror that she wasn't wearing a bra, dammit. Her face flushed pink and she automatically folded her arms over her chest.

'I wasn't expecting you,' she muttered in mortification.

'You called and left a message earlier,' Jake explained after a moment.

'Yes, but it was getting late, so I assumed you'd just call me back tomorrow.'

'Yeah,' he replied ruefully, 'sorry about that, I would have called you earlier. I got called out on an emergency, but...' he held up a bag of takeout, 'I brought dinner. If I know you, you've been so caught up in Olivia's books you probably forgot to eat anything.'

She looked down to the bag and her mouth watered at the scent wafting toward her. He was right, she had forgotten all about eating.

'Oh alright,' she sighed, moving back so he could step into her small apartment.

She closed the door as he placed Beau down on the floor and unhooked his leash. The minute the puppy was free he scrambled across the floor and began to sniff everything in sight, acquainting himself with his new surroundings. Jake watched him in amusement for a moment, as he bumped into another pile of books and rolled over on the floor.

'He's as clumsy as you are,' he smiled fondly.

Veronica's heart sank. That was probably how he looked at her, with that same indulgent smile. He'd never see her as a sexy confident woman, who the hell was she kidding? He was way out of her league.

'I'll get some plates,' she sighed softly in resignation.

'Hey, what's wrong?' he frowned at her tone.

'Nothing, I'm fine,' she turned to the kitchen.

''Did you hurt yourself?' he noticed her limping slightly, and as she cradled her elbow, his frown deepened.

'It's nothing,' she replied.

There was no way she was embarrassing herself further by telling him that, she'd not only tripped over her own feet, but also the coffee table and the books, in the short distance between her couch and the door.

'It doesn't look like nothing.' He dropped the bag of food down by the door and effortlessly scooped her up into his arms.

'Jake,' she flushed again, 'it's really not that bad. Put me down.'

'Be quiet, he murmured as he headed over to the couch, easily dodging the small land mines of books scattered across the floor.

He was so agile and full of quiet understated strength as he moved fluidly, settling her on the deep cushions of the couch.

'Stay there,' he ordered quietly as he scooped up the bag of food and disappeared into her small kitchen.

She heard him rustling around, the clank of plates being lifted out of the cupboard, and the tinkle of glasses clinking together.

Taking a moment to draw in a shaky breath, she willed her heart to settle into a normal rhythm. It was mortifying having this reaction around him. All he'd done was carry her to the couch because she was being a klutz again, but the smell of him as he'd pressed her against his chest and his arms tightened around her, set her pulse racing She shook her head and blew out the breath she was holding, she was beginning to annoy herself. She needed to get rid of this fluttery schoolgirl feeling whenever she was around him, and settle into the friend zone, where he was already firmly planted.

He stepped back into the room, a wine bottle and two wineglasses in one hand, both fully loaded plates balanced on his other hand and forearm, and what appeared to be an icepack tucked under the arm which held the wine. He moved with thoughtless precision, and that same graceful economy of motion, completely unaware of how appealing he was.

Damn it, she wished she could be like that; he made it all look so easy. If that had been her, the dinner would already be splattered up the walls, the plates in pieces on the floor and she'd probably have cut open a major artery with the glasses, while quite possibly knocking herself unconscious with the wine bottle.

'Where's Beau?' she asked as he set the plates, glasses and wine on the table and pulled two packs of chopsticks out of his back pocket, dumping them on the table too.

'He's in the kitchen with his own food,' he dropped down on the sofa next to her with a grin. 'I learned the hard way, if I actually want to eat all the food on my plate I have to distract him.'

'Smart.'

'I like to think so,' he picked up the icepack. 'Okay, where does it hurt?'

'My elbow.'

'Not the ankle?'

'Stubbed toe, its fine.'

'Okay, elbow it is then.' He took her injured arm carefully and examined it thoroughly, before pressing the cold pack to her skin. 'You're going to have a hell of a bruise.'

'Wouldn't be the first time.'

'I don't get it,' he shook his head in amusement.

'Get what exactly?' she pulled the plate into her lap, and with one hand awkwardly scooped up some noodles .

'You can't seem to stay upright most of the time, yet I've seen you stand there cool as a winter's breeze, and take down monsters with a shotgun,' he shook his head and chuckled. 'It's like you're two completely different people; you're Clark Kent and Superman.'

'That's not actually very flattering,' she frowned. 'Can't I be Diana Prince slash Wonder Woman?'

He pursed his lips thoughtfully and his gaze once again dropped to rake across her body, which heated unconsciously under his perusal.

'Actually, you'd look good in the star spangled hot pants.'

'Shut up,' she murmured, as her cheeks flushed

pink once again. 'Although,' she continued, 'if we're talking superheroes, my choice would be Elektra. Okay, she's Marvel instead of DC, and she was created to be the love interest of Daredevil, but she is awesome, plus she fights with a pair of Sai, the daggers that look like tridents. Seriously cool weapons.'

Jake sat there, his own dinner forgotten as he watched her in fascination.

'That's it, I'm in love,' he grinned, 'if for nothing else but your knowledge of comic books and ancient Chinese weaponry.'

'Actually the Sai was also used in Japan, Thailand, Vietnam, Malaysia and Indonesia, and there is some speculation that it originated in India.'

'You're like a walking text book,' he shook his head incredulously.

She laughed lightly, as she scooped up another mouthful of noodles.

'Of course Elektra's not just from the comic books. In Greek mythology Electra, spelled this time with a C not a K, was the daughter of King Agamemnon and Queen Clytemnestra and therefore she was a princess of Argos. Both she and her brother Orestes plotted revenge against their mother Clytemnestra and stepfather Aegisthus for the murder of their father.'

'You're so cute,' he chuckled, attacking his own plate of food.

And there it was she thought with a quiet sigh. In the space of two minutes they had gone from star spangled hot pants to cute. When was she going to learn to keep her mouth shut? Maybe her mother was right after all, no guy was ever going to be interested in a woman who constantly had her nose in a history book.

Slightly embarrassed, she casually changed the subject.

'So you got called out on an emergency earlier? I hope it wasn't anything too bad.'

'Actually,' he frowned, 'we got called out to the Bailey's store. Jonathan Bailey was found collapsed on the floor by the cash register.'

'Oh my God,' Roni gasped, 'was he attacked? Is he okay?'

'We're not really sure what happened at this point, there seems to be some confusion,' he replied. 'He was alive, barely; he's been rushed to the hospital. Louisa's on tonight, she's going to keep me updated as to his condition. Nothing seems to have been taken, so we can rule out robbery, but there seems to be some confusion as to what actually happened. I've got a witness that says he wasn't alone when he collapsed. We're still trying to make sense of it all.'

'I really hope he's okay, he seems like such a sweet man.'

'Yeah,' Jake blew out a deep breath, as he placed his empty plate on the table and picked up the wine.

'You not driving tonight?'

Jake shook his head.

'Snow's mostly gone now, so I figured I'd walk Beau over as it's only around the corner from my place.'

She accepted the glass he handed to her and settled back against the couch.

'So,' Jake picked up his own glass and leaned back too, 'why don't you tell me what you found in Olivia's books.'

Her face lit with excitement, as she remembered the reason she'd called him in the first place. She leaned over to the nearest pile of books and lifted an old book. It was small and covered with a dark red, cloth binding, which had split at the spine with age and now almost hung off. She flipped through the dry pages, ignoring the stale dusty smell.

'I found this,' she handed the book to him. 'It's not exactly what I was looking for, but it's close enough.'

'A summoning spell?'

She nodded enthusiastically, smiling as she unconsciously edged closer, so she could look down at the page too.

'It's a spirit summoning. Theoretically we should be able to summon Olivia's spirit and speak with her.'

'That sounds a little too easy,' he frowned suspiciously.

'Well it's not,' Roni murmured, as she gazed down at the open page in his hands. 'Some of these items we'll need for the spell are pretty hard to come by.'

'Pretty hard to come by?' he repeated scanning down the list. 'A pentagram, bound at the corners with white silk ribbon, and made from the wood of a Willow tree, harvested in the light of the full moon?'

'That's actually one of the easy ones,' she picked up her notepad and scanned down the notes she'd made. 'I've already ordered the ribbon online, that should arrive in a couple of days. As for the wood, there is a hiking trail through the woods, south-west of the lake. According to Glenn Gordon, the guy who runs hiking groups for tourists down that way, there are some willows just west of the trail. It shouldn't take more than a few hours to hike up there from the visitors center.'

'In the dark?' Jake asked her pointedly. 'You said it needed to be harvested in the light of the full moon. You can't hike unfamiliar ground to look for a willow tree in the middle of the night.'

'It's not ideal' she agreed, 'but unfortunately it's necessary. As luck would have it, the full moon is only a week away, so we can cross that one off the list.'

He shook his head and sighed, resigning himself to hiking through the woods in the middle of the night, as there was no way he was letting her go alone. His eyes dropped down to the list and scanned past the more mundane items of candles and salt, to the more exotic herbs.

'What the hell is Kuzu?'

'Japanese arrowroot,' Roni told him.

'Why would we need Japanese arrowroot?'

'I don't really know,' she wrinkled her nose in thought. 'It was used for drawing poison out of wounds. Maybe it has some other magical property, I'm not really sure. I'm just kind of approaching this spell from a recipe standpoint.'

'What, just follow the instructions and hope it turns out looking like the picture?' Jake cocked an eyebrow in amusement.

'Something like that,' she smiled. 'I think we're just going to have to take a lot of this on faith, and hope that the person who wrote the spell knew what they were doing.'

'Fair enough,' Jake continued to scan the list. 'Uh, what is Silene undulata?'

'That's a small white flower used by shamans, it's more commonly known as African dream root. I think it's supposed to induce vivid hallucinations or something.'

'What?'

'Relax, we're not going to be ingesting it, probably just inhaling some of the fumes.'

'Huh?'

'Never mind,' she shook her head.

'Roni, where are we supposed to get all these herbs and flowers from?'

'The internet,' she replied. 'Don't worry, I've already ordered most of them.'

'Er, Roni?' he frowned, 'I don't think you're going to be able to get this last item from the internet.'

'What's that?'

'The blood of a necromancer?'

'Ah yes, that one,' she pouted thoughtfully. 'I'll admit that one was a bit of a challenge.'

'A challenge? This isn't World of Warcraft Roni, there is no such thing as necromancers.'

'Of course there is,' she shrugged, as if the answer

should be painfully obvious. I'll admit it's a bit of an archaic word to use, but then again I don't know how long ago the spell was created.'

'What are you talking about?' he shook his head. 'Necromancers are dark wizards who raise corpses.'

'You're thinking in terms of modern popular culture, TV, films and games which deal in the fantasy and science fiction genres. But although they are wildly exaggerated for dramatic emphasis there is a grain of truth, a seed from which the myth grew. If you go right back into antiquity, necromancy evolved from shamanism, the practice of calling upon the spirits of ancestors. Necromancy was widely accepted as a way to communicate with the spirits of the dead, or shades as the Greeks and Romans called them. It wasn't until the middle ages, when the medieval Christians believed that only their God could resurrect, the Catholic church condemned it as demonism, and the work of the devil.'

'How the hell do you know all of this?' his mouth fell open in surprise. 'You're like a female rain man.'

'My point is,' she sighed, 'you just have to take it out of its historical context and move it into the modern day. In the Middle Ages, alchemy was considered heresy, yet today we call it science. Back then necromancy was the domain of demons, witches, and practitioners of dark magic, but today we call it spiritualism, and it is practiced by mediums.'

'Mediums?' he replied slowly, suddenly understanding. 'Fiona?'

'Yes,' she nodded sympathetically. 'Fiona.'

'We need to talk Fiona into giving us some of her blood?'

'Not just that, as she is an extremely talented medium we could really use her help.'

He groaned again.

'What have you got against Fiona?

'Nothing exactly,' he shook his head, 'it's just the

woman is whole bucketful's of crazy.'

'I'll admit she's got a few quirks.'

'A few?'

'Alright a lot,' she conceded, as she took a sip of her wine, 'but at least there's no guessing with her. You know exactly what you're getting.'

'That's true I suppose,' he grimaced, 'I just don't want to deal with her legion of cats, and that's after navigating the minefield of garden gnomes just to get to her front door.'

'You don't like gnomes?'

'Not when they number more than the entire population of the state of Texas.'

She laughed warmly and lifting her feet she curled them comfortably under her, turning to face him more fully. Casually propping her uninjured elbow on the back of the couch, she rested her head against her hand, and took another sip of wine.

Jake leaned back and tilted his head, watching her quietly. She looked so comfortable and relaxed in his company, her intense blue eyes watching him, her cheeks flushed from the warmth of the room, and the wine. One of the straps of her tank top had begun to slide slowly off the curve of her shoulder, and his fingers curled involuntarily with the urge to reach out and stroke her skin, to see if it felt as soft as it looked. His jaw tightened and he fought the urge for his gaze to dip once again. It was pure torture, knowing she wasn't wearing underwear, and he had to keep reminding himself, that they were just friends, but damn he wanted his hands on her desperately. For a nerd, she was pretty damn sexy, and the crazy thing was, she didn't seem to know. He watched mesmerized, as her tongue slid slowly across her lower lip to catch a drop of wine.

'It's getting late,' she murmured.

'Late,' he repeated absently, his gaze fixed on her lips.

A small series of yips from across the room drew his attention and broke his gaze as they both looked across to where Beau was laid out on his back across a cushion, his paws in the air twitching madly.

'He's probably chasing rabbits again,' Jake shook his head.

'You can leave him here tonight if you want.'

He turned back to look at her.

'I can take him to work with me in the morning, you're probably going to be busy with the Baileys.'

'Are you sure?'

'It's not a problem, really. He's such a sweetheart,' she gazed across to the cute little twitching ball of golden colored fur. 'I always wanted a dog,' she murmured absently.

'You didn't have one growing up?'

'Mother didn't like dogs,' she replied blandly as she drained the last of her wine.

It was telling he thought, the way she referred to her mother. He'd noticed on several occasions, she never called her mom, it was always mother, and he got the distinct impression her childhood had been a lonely one, filled with impossible expectations. It was no wonder she couldn't see how great she was.

'You could get a dog of your own now.'

'Maybe,' she slid the empty glass onto the table. 'Maybe if I get a bigger place, a house, perhaps with a yard,' she mused thoughtfully. 'I'd like my own little house in Mercy, somewhere I could put down roots, that is of course if I end up staying.'

Jake jolted slightly in surprise.

'What do you mean, if you end up staying?'

'I'm still on probation remember. If they decide to hire someone with more experience to run the museum, I'll have to move to wherever my next job is.'

'I'm sure Mayor Burnett has no intention of hiring someone else, it's probably just a formality.'

'No, I'm pretty sure I'm going to have to work my ass off to impress her.'

She smiled at him as she unfolded her legs and stood, slowly stretching out the kinks as she went. Jake's mouth went dry, as his gaze slid to the smooth skin of her flat stomach, when suddenly his eyes narrowed and he tilted his head.

'Is that a tattoo?'

'What?' she looked down at him and saw his gaze firmly fixed on the small splash of color peeking above her pajama pants, which were now riding her hip bone. 'Oh um…'

She yanked her tank top down to cover it, but merely succeeded in revealing even more of her cleavage.

'Damn it,' she muttered, her cheeks flaming red in embarrassment.

'Ah, come on Roni,' he looked up and grinned. 'You can't flash me and then leave me in suspense. What is it?'

'My pathetic attempt at teenage rebellion.'

'Let me see.'

'No,' she laughed.

'Please.'

Sighing in defeat, she rolled her eyes and hooked her finger in the waistband, lowering it just enough to reveal the small tattoo riding high on her hip.

'It's a…a…a bat?' his eyes widened and a laugh bubbled out. 'Why on earth do you have the Batman symbol on your hip.'

'I was in college, there was a party…' she shrugged. 'The one and only time I ever got really drunk, and I ended up waking up with the bat signal permanently etched into my skin.'

She rolled her eyes and fisted her hands on her hips, as Jake continued to laugh.

'You know it's really not that funny,' she shook her head, 'and it taught me a valuable lesson on the merits of sobriety.'

He continued laughing as he stood up.

'You're a wild woman Roni,' he smiled. 'Still waters run deep, don't they?'

'Don't,' she shook her head in amusement, 'can you imagine what my mother would say. She still thinks I'm going to marry a stuffy accountant or a lawyer.'

'For what it's worth I love it, and compared to some of the drunken tats people get, it's really not that bad.'

'Really?'

'I've got one too you know.'

'What? A Batman tattoo?'

'No,' he laughed again, 'a drunken tat, you want to see it?'

He moved his hands to his belt, clearly intending to drop his pants.

'No!' Roni laughed, 'I do not want to see it, and I'm kicking you out now so I can go to bed.'

He slowly walked backward, still laughing, as she pushed him toward the door.

'Okay, okay I'm going, spoilsport.'

He turned to retrieve his jacket and her eyes automatically dropped to his rather fine ass. She let out an involuntary sigh, and allowed her mind to drift for a moment. God, she was willing to bet money he'd look real good without his clothes on, it was obvious he was fit, and well-toned. He had the physique of an athlete, in fact she'd also be willing to bet he'd been quarterback in high school.

'That's a sucker bet,' he laughed as he turned around to face her, 'of course I was the quarterback in high school. I was a God.'

'What?' the color drained out of her face.

'You said, you bet I was a quarter...'

'I didn't say that,' she shook her head, 'I thought it.'

'No, you definitely said it. I heard you quite

clearly.'

Her brow folded into a frown. No, she'd thought it, she could've sworn she hadn't said a word. How much wine had she had? Maybe she was drunk…funny she didn't feel drunk in the slightest.

'It's also true, that I have a very fine ass,' he smirked.

Her face blazed red.

'That's not…I didn't say…'

She looked so cute floundering like that. He couldn't say if it was her mortified expression, or the amount of wine he'd also had, that had him leaning in, but as his lips settled on hers she stilled.

He'd only intended it to be a light teasing peck on the lips, but one touch of her soft, warm mouth, had him pausing and leaning in further. The scent of her wrapped around him, crawling under his skin luring him in. Her lips opened in a surprised gasp and he deepened the kiss, helpless to do anything else, one taste of her and he was lost.

The jacket dropped to the floor from his nerveless fingers, and he found himself wrapping his arms around her impossibly tiny waist, and pulling her in closer. His fingers toyed with the hem of her tank top, teasingly gliding underneath, as the pads of his fingers traced the incredibly soft skin of her lower back.

She rose up on tiptoes, and wound her arms around his neck, her fingers tangling in his hair at the nape of his neck. She tilted her head and kissed him back, and every thought drained from his head, every thought but her.

They broke apart suddenly, breathing heavily, both staring at each other in something akin to shock.

'I…uh…need my jacket,' Jake frowned, as his eyes dropped to the heap on the floor at his feet.

They both reached for it at the same time and managed to bang their heads.

'Are you okay?'

Roni pressed her hand to the top of her head, her blue eyes wide. Not trusting herself to speak, she nodded slowly.

'Good…that's ah…good, I'm just going to go then, get you to bed,' he shook his head. 'Let you get to bed…to sleep.'

She watched him in silence, as he turned to the door and opened it abruptly, catching it on the toe of his boot, and managing to smack himself in the forehead.

'Shit,' he swore as he stepped out into the hallway and shut the door behind him.

'Shit,' she heard from the other side, and as she glanced down, she noticed half of his jacket wedged in the door.

The door once again opened, and Jake pulled his jacket loose.

'Um, I'll see you tomorrow, I mean I'll get the dog tomorrow.'

He shut the door behind him.

Roni stood for a couple of minutes staring at the closed door, before she finally leaned forward and double locked it. Turning around, she leaned back against the cool wood of the door, and let out a deep breath. Slowly sliding down until she was sitting on the floor, she touched her fingertips absently to her swollen lips.

'What the hell just happened?' she thought in confusion.

6.

Olivia glanced up at the large forbidding building in front of her. Funny, she thought to herself, she'd never thought of it that way before. Then again, it was usually a hive of activity, brightly lit, noisy and full of drama. Now it was silent as the grave, its white walls washed in the strange blue grey light of the Otherworld.

She pushed the double doors open, and stepped inside. It really was creepy she decided, as she took in the empty gurneys and trolleys lined up against the wall. She moved further into the emergency room, past the unmanned desk. All the charts were blank and stacked neatly on the edge of the desk, and the computer was nothing but an empty screen.

Walking slowly past the curtained cubicles, the beds and bays were all vacant, with neatly stacked, fully stocked supply trolleys, and silent monitors. Ignoring them she headed for the room Theo had first been taken to when he'd collapsed in front of her car. She walked slowly down the corridor to the private rooms, the only sound the dull click of her boots and her shallow, nervous breaths. It was ridiculous, there was no one else there but her, and yet she still felt a chill run down her spine, and her palms grow clammy.

She stopped and turned back to the still dullness

of the corridor behind her, and stared. There was nothing there, but her unease continued, causing her to swallow hard. Turning back around she resumed her slow search, despite feeling the primal 'fight or flight' impulse clawing in her chest. It felt like she was being followed. Her eyes cut across to a picture frame on the wall beside her and just for a second, in the glass, she could've sworn she'd seen a large dark shadow.

She spun around, but the corridor was still deserted. The cloying scent of lilies suddenly filled her nose and throat. She felt a whoosh of air next to her, so close it brushed the skin of her cheek, icy and unfamiliar. She spun again to face the other direction, her heart pounding in her chest, knowing she was no longer alone. The hairs on her arms stood up, as the air began to crackle with static electricity. Not waiting for whatever it was to catch up with her, she bolted down the corridor toward the private rooms, hoping desperately that Theo was there.

She rounded the corner and suddenly hit a solid warm chest. She felt herself tip backward, but a pair of arms wrapped around her to stop her from falling. She looked up and found herself staring into familiar blue eyes.

'Sam,' she breathed in relief, as she straightened, disentangling herself from his hold. She looked back down the corridor from which she'd come, but the feeling was gone. She turned back to Sam, her eyes narrowing suspiciously. 'Were you following me?'

'No,' he frowned, 'why, what's wrong?'

'I just thought...' she turned back to glance uneasily down the corridor once more. 'Nothing, it's nothing, I guess I'm just a little spooked.'

She drew in a deep shaky breath and she stepped back, looking up into his curious blue eyes.

'What are you doing here Sam?'

'I told you, my father...'

'No, I mean what are you doing in the hospital?'

'Looking for you,' he shrugged.

'Why?'

'Because you interest me.'

'Why do people keep saying that,' she muttered sourly. 'I'm really not that interesting.'

'I want to ask you some questions, about what you said before.'

'Well,' she resumed walking, glancing up as he fell into step beside her, 'I'm not sure exactly how much I should be telling you. I don't really know how the whole time traveler thing works.'

'You're serious about that, aren't you?' his eyes narrowed thoughtfully. 'You really do believe I can translocate through time?'

'Sam, I know for a fact you can,' she sighed, stopping abruptly, turning to face him once again. 'The truth is, I don't know much more than what I've already told you, and I'm sorry, but I really don't have time to chat. I need to find Theo, and apparently after that I have to stop a demon from getting his hands on the most powerful book in history.'

'What?'

'Sam,' she retorted irritably.

'I tell you what, how about a deal? I'll help you find your friend.'

'And in return?'

'You tell me what you know about me, this demon and the book.'

She pursed her lips thoughtfully. She wasn't entirely sure telling him everything was the right thing to do, but…she decided, what the hell? She needed all the help she could get at this point, and even though he wasn't the same Sam she knew, she still felt as if she could trust him.

'Fine,' she agreed, 'deal.'

They wandered the deserted corridors of the hospital and she told him everything, starting from her childhood, her parents, arriving back in Mercy, the murders, Chief Walcott, and Theo being dumped in front of her car. She spoke of Charlotte, Charon, the gateway and the spirits overrunning Mercy. Nathaniel, Infernum, her mother, everything just came pouring out, right up to the moment Hades dropped her in the middle of the Otherworld. When she finally finished they stopped walking, and Sam stared at her thoughtfully.

Although he looked a little disturbed she felt so much better, it was almost like a purge, being able to talk through everything from start to finish. He'd only interrupted a few times to clarify, or to ask a question, but for the most part he'd just listened patiently and it had been very cathartic.

'So, let me get this straight?' he frowned. 'Your mother raised a demon?'

She nodded, as he continued. 'And she is using him to find the Hell book?'

He frowned again.

'What?'

'We were taught the books were just a myth.'

'Books?' she repeated slowly, 'books as in plural?'

He nodded thoughtfully.

'Five of them in total, no one seems to know for certain where they came from. In fact, no one has even seen one in nearly two thousand years, and slowly all knowledge of them passed into myth. Most people have never even heard of them.'

'But you have?'

'I have a…friend who has some knowledge of them.'

She didn't question him too closely, but a fleeting look had crossed his features when he mentioned his friend, and for a moment Olivia wondered if his banishment to the Otherworld had something to do with it.

'Okay,' Olivia spoke slowly, prompting him to keep talking, 'so…'

'Well, like I said, there are five books, Infernum, Caelorum, Purgatorio, Alterum and Terra.'

'Latin?' Olivia replied, recognizing some of the names. 'Hell, Heaven, Purgatory, Otherworld…?'

Sam nodded.

'It's an older version of Latin with some slight variations, but that's essentially what it translates to.'

'And Terra is Earth?'

'That's right, each book contains within it, all the secrets and magic of each of the five domains.'

'And you don't know where they came from?'

Sam shook his head.

'No, but they're old, I mean seriously old, like from before the Gods.'

'Before the Gods?' her eyes widened.

'The story goes that the five books were created by an ancient race, who understood the most primal and elemental powers. They harnessed them and locked their secrets inside the books. Each book had its own guardian, the only one who could understand its secrets.'

'So what happened to them?' Olivia leaned closer in fascination.

'War, sickness, or maybe they just died out? We just don't know, but I do know, that Infernum was supposed to be the most powerful of all of them. Terra was hidden on Earth, but it was destroyed during the holy wars; the humans claimed it was heresy when they couldn't read it and unlock its secrets. As for Caelorum, Purgatorio and Alterum, I don't know if they've even survived, they've been lost for so long, and now you're telling me that Infernum has been hidden by your family for generations?'

'That's what I've been told.'

'That's incredible,' he shook his head. 'What I don't understand is, where Theo fits in? I mean, why would I pull him through time?'

'I don't know,' Olivia shook her head, 'maybe

because he kept dreaming about me, and about Infernum.'

'What?'

'Oh,' she frowned, 'didn't I mention that? Theo has visions, dreams mostly.'

'And he had a vision of Infernum?'

'Not exactly. From what he's told me, it's more like he's dreamed about me, and in those dreams we've been talking about the book, but he hasn't actually seen it. Although, he did save my ancestor Hester, who was apparently the last person to have seen the book.'

'So, he is connected to it somehow,' Sam mused.

Olivia stopped in front of the door of a private room. Beyond it, lay the room in which she had first seen Theo. It was the night he had realized she was real, and not a figment of his imagination. So, logically this room should hold some meaning for him.

Reaching out with trembling hands, her fingers closed around the handle. She pulled in a deep breath and allowed the door to swing silently open. Her heart sank as she beheld the empty room, the bed was neatly made and nothing was amiss.

'I'm sorry Olivia,' Sam murmured quietly behind her.

'I don't know where else to look,' she replied hopelessly. 'I've tried the house, the pub, Jake's apartment, the hospital, I don't know where he is.'

'To be honest, he could be anywhere,' Sam drew her away from the room. 'If he was pulled through as abruptly as you say, he might not even realize he's not in the real world anymore, and just to complicate things, he might be in a different time frame from us.'

'What do you mean?' Olivia stopped abruptly and turned to stare at him.

'Time doesn't run the same way here as in your world.'

'My aunt said something like that to me,' she cast her mind back, trying to recall exactly what she'd said.

'Something about time has no meaning here.'

'That's not entirely correct,' he replied thoughtfully, 'it's more like, time is fluid.'

'I don't understand,' she frowned.

They slowly started walking again as Sam tried to put his thoughts into an explanation she would understand.

'In your world, time is like a river, it only flows in one direction. You divide it, into minutes, hours, days, months, years, but essentially it all flows at the same rate and only ever in one direction. It is inevitable, you are born, you grow old, you die. It's linear, it's flesh and blood. In the spirit world, you cast off your mortal body and with it, your mortal lifespan and all its restrictions. The soul is infinite, it exists as pure energy. If time on Earth is a river, which flows in only one direction, time in the spirit world is like a giant ocean moving in all directions.'

Sam stopped suddenly, his eyes distant and lost in thought.

'Time is an ocean,' he murmured to himself.

'What is it?'

'Time is an ocean,' he murmured again, like he was trying to figure something out. 'What if time is like an ocean? The energy produced from the motion of the currents and tides changes when it encounters land mass, it slows, dissipates or is diverted. What if time is the same, only instead of land masses, there are fixed points in time, events of such importance they are embedded deep within the fabric of existence?'

Olivia stared at him blankly.

'When the wave hits the land, or in this case the fixed point in time, it fractures and is deflected outward in different directions, creating alternate time lines. What if you can ride those time lines like a wave?'

'Er Sam?' Olivia interrupted his random trail of thought, 'could you dumb it down for me a bit? I'm not really up on temporal mechanics.'

'Sorry,' he shook his head, 'the point I was trying to make was that time in the Otherworld can exist at any point in time. It is the soul that chooses where it wants to be, where it wants to return to. It's not even a conscious decision.'

'Not a conscious decision? So I can't just choose to jump to whatever time I want to?'

'No,' Sam shook his head, 'I mean there are some souls who are able to. Souls, who are very old and gifted, but for most of you, you just end up where you end up.'

'Great,' Olivia sighed, as they reached the emergency department and headed for the main entrance. 'So, Theo could be stuck in another time period, and I'm stuck here?'

'Theoretically.'

'Well that's just fucking great,' she blew out a frustrated breath.

'I'm sure that's not the case though,' he replied sympathetically, 'after all this is specifically where Hades sent you. That must mean Theo is here somewhere.'

'I don't know,' she sighed. 'I can't rule out Hades sending me on a wild goose chase just to amuse himself.'

They stepped through the main entrance and back out into the daylight, heading back toward town.

'It'll be alright Olivia, we'll find him.'

'I hope so,' she let out a deep disappointed breath.

A shiver suddenly danced down her spine making her pause. The hairs on the back of her neck stood on end and her skin began to crawl. Turning back to the hospital she caught a glimpse of the same strange black shadow she'd seen twice now. It hovered by the entrance of the hospital. Her breath caught in her throat, and for a brief second it almost seemed to stare right back at her, as if it were challenging her somehow, and then it melted into the shadow of the building.

'Did you see that?' Olivia whispered.

'See what?' Sam turned back to the hospital.

'There was…' she shook her head frowning, 'never mind.'

'Come on,' Sam drew her attention, 'there's a few more places we can try.'

Louisa took one last deep drag on her cigarette, and dropped it to the floor, crushing it under her boot. Blowing out a breath, she buried her hands deep into the pockets of her jacket, and stared up into the dark, starlit sky. Even though spring was now fast approaching there was still enough bite in the air to cause her to shiver.

'Dr Linden?'

She looked across at one of her interns, standing out in the cold without a jacket, clutching a chart, and shook her head. So much for her break.

'What is it Adams?' she snapped irritably.

'I'm sorry to disturb you Dr Linden, but it's Mr Bailey, his stats have dropped again.'

She pushed herself off the wall, and plucked the chart out of the young woman's shivering hands.

'You really shouldn't be out here without a jacket,' she frowned, as she gazed down at the chart. 'This isn't the West Coast. You're not in Santa Barbara anymore.'

'Santa Cruz,' she corrected.

'Just get inside before you end up sick,' Louisa sighed, as she headed through the hospital entrance.

The young intern scurried after her, trying to keep up.

'Are the test results back in.'

'No, not yet.'

'Go and chase them up then,' Louisa replied, stopping so abruptly the intern nearly crashed into her.

The young woman stared at her.

'Now Adams.'

'Oh right, test results, sorry.'

Louisa watched in exasperation as she scurried off.

'Still traumatizing interns,' a warm familiar voice

chuckled.

She turned and found herself staring into a pair of amused brown eyes. Dr Achari was the newest addition to the staff. Although the young Indian doctor had only been with them a few months, he'd arrived just as they'd been slammed with massive intakes of patients suffering with all types of different diseases, common and otherwise.

She found out later that it was because of a supernatural creature who'd escaped through the gateway into Mercy and liked to infect humans with sickness. Unfortunately for them, not only had half the town been affected but most of the staff as well. They'd had to borrow staff from nearby Salem, and Georgetown.

Dr Achari, and herself were the only two most senior staff unaffected, and after several weeks of total chaos, they'd emerged with a kind of war buddies' friendship that came from surviving such an intense situation.

'Sachiv,' she smiled, as he handed her a cup of coffee, 'I thought you were off an hour ago?'

'I was, but I was just waiting on a patient transfer,' he took a sip of his own coffee. 'Why do you look like you're about to tear someone's head off?'

'I'm just tired,' she shook her head, 'and frustrated. I've been here for sixteen hours straight, I haven't seen my husband in two days and I still can't figure out what's wrong with Mr Bailey.'

'You run his bloods again?'

'Yeah,' she nodded, 'but they still keep coming back normal, I just don't get it. Meanwhile, his stats keep dipping, we can't seem to keep him stable. It doesn't help that I have his wife who refuses to leave his side.'

'Well come on, you can understand that, he's her husband. She is bound to want to stay close, it's a natural reaction.'

'I understand that, and I don't have a problem with it, what I have a problem with, is tripping over her every time I turn around, and her demanding that I explain and justify every single decision I make with regards to his treatment.'

'We've had worse Louisa,' he chuckled. 'Do I need to remind you of Mr Trevino?'

'God no, I still have nightmares about him,' she chuckled, taking a sip of her coffee. 'I just want to be left alone to get on with my job, maybe then I can figure out what the problem is.'

'Unfortunately overbearing relations are part of the job description.'

'I know,' she sighed, staring into her cup absently, 'but half the time they're worse than the patients.'

'Do you want me to take a look at Mr Bailey's chart? Might help to have a fresh pair of eyes?'

'Well it certainly couldn't hurt,' she handed him the clipboard.

Dr Adams hurried back down the corridor, and collided with a tall dark haired man wearing a white coat. Unfortunately, there had also been a large cup of coffee added to the mix, which had exploded on impact, drenching the front of her scrubs, her white coat and covering the blood test results in her hand.

'Hayley, where's the damn fire at?'

She glanced up at Lucas Garcia, her fellow intern and roommate. She lifted up the soggy piece of paper, which now dripped coffee and stared at it, her eyes filling with tears.

'Hey, Hayley I was only kidding, what's wrong?'

'Nothing,' she swallowed hard, 'I'm just tired. I was up all night, and I've just pulled a double, and Dr Linden has been riding me all day.'

'Really?' he frowned, 'she's not usually that bad.'

'I know,' she blew out a breath.

'You need a break,' he told her pointedly.

'I can't,' she shook her head miserably. 'I need to

get these test results back to Dr Linden before she kicks me off her rotation.'

'She won't do that, and you know it,' he took the mangled and almost illegible paper from her hand. 'I'll go get a fresh copy and drop it down to her, I'm heading down that way. You go grab a sandwich and take ten.'

'Are you sure?' she smiled gratefully.

'Get out of here,' he grinned, and remember you owe me when it comes around to my turn to clean the bathroom.'

'You're still not getting out of it,' she told him, 'but I will make you breakfast tomorrow.'

'Blueberry pancakes?'

She nodded.

'Sold.'

She laughed and headed down the corridor feeling lighter. She quickly stopped by the cafeteria, and grabbed a ham on rye and a bottle of water. Taking the elevator down to the lowest floor, she stepped out into the stillness of the deserted corridor.

She was well beneath ground level, and not far from the boiler room. To some it would have seemed creepy, but to her it was a place of solace, no one else seemed to go down there, and it was so peaceful. She climbed up on an empty gurney parked up against the wall, and folded her legs under her.

Unwrapping her sandwich, she took a bite and sighed in pleasure. She hadn't realized she was so hungry, after all she hadn't stopped in hours. Taking a deep gulp of water, she leaned her head back against the hard concrete wall and closed her eyes. God, what she wouldn't give to just curl up on the gurney, and go to sleep. It felt like she hadn't stopped in forever, and she was alarmingly close to selling her soul for a solid eight straight.

Her family had thought she was crazy when she told them she was going to medical school. With her blonde hair, blue eyes, and west coast roots, she looked every inch the surfer chick rather than potential doctor. From the moment she'd hit med school, she'd had to fight twice as hard to be taken seriously. But she was good at her job, she knew she was, and even though Dr Linden had been hard on her, Hayley knew she was capable of proving them all wrong.

She was going to be a Cardiologist, in fact she was determined to be the best Cardiologist in the whole damn country, then perhaps it would finally silence the California Barbie jokes once and for all. Although, she sighed, she doubted it, as there was always going to be some asshole who mistook her for a beauty queen instead of a medical professional.

She picked up her sandwich and took another bite, chewing thoughtfully. Maybe she should dye her hair. She shivered suddenly and frowned. It was cool down in the lower levels, but not usually this cold. She dropped her sandwich onto the gurney next to her, and unfolded her legs. The sudden and strange scent of flowers filled her nostrils. It smelled like…lilies, she decided. She remembered the scent well from her grandmother's funeral, the whole place had reeked of them.

She looked up, and glanced down the corridor, she could have sworn she'd heard something. Screwing the lid back onto her water bottle, she placed it down next to her half eaten sandwich. She dropped her legs down to the ground and stood up, moving slowly and cautiously in the direction where she'd heard the faint sound.

'Hello?' she called into the stillness, 'is anyone there?'

She was met with silence, a cold clammy shiver crawled slowly down her spine and she swallowed in unease. Suddenly this place didn't seem so peaceful, maybe she should just go back up she decided. She turned around and her heart slammed into her mouth. An extremely tall man stood silently in front of her. He was dressed in a long dark heavy overcoat and wore a strangely dated, wide brimmed hat.

'Um,' she cleared her throat trying to ignore her heart hammering in her chest. Forcing herself to appear more confident than she felt, she confronted him. 'Sir, are you lost? These lower levels are off limits to visitors, you need to be four floors up.'

He didn't answer, instead he raised his chin and slowly his face was revealed from under the brim of his hat. Her mouth fell open in a silent scream at his pale papery skin and pitch black eyes. She felt a sudden pressure and as she looked down in horror, she could see his hand plunged into her chest. Slowly he withdrew his hand and for a second she saw a bright pulsing white sphere of light, before her eyes rolled back, and her body collapsed to the cold hard floor.

The stranger watched the light pulsing and throbbing in his palm like a heartbeat. His abnormally long, tapered fingers squeezed slightly and it burned brighter. He brought the strange ball of light to his face and inhaled deeply, his black eyes burning with a dreadful kind of hunger.

His mouth suddenly split into a grin, revealing brown rotting teeth, a sharp contrast to his skin, which was so white it was almost transparent. His other hand dipped into the folds of his long coat and pulled free a small glass bottle. Removing the stopper with his teeth he tipped the glowing ball of light into the bottle and sealed it. Cradling the bottle gently he turned and disappeared through the solid concrete wall, leaving Hayley laying grey skinned and lifeless, alone in her sanctuary of solace.

7.

Jake stared at the screen with a confused frown. He flicked back to the beginning of the security footage he'd retrieved from the Bailey's store and watched it through again.

'What the hell?'

He turned it back and watched it again.

'Shit,' he swore silently under his breath.

Pulling the flash drive, he headed out of the room and toward Mac's office.

'Don't you ever knock anymore?' Mac looked up from the file he'd been reading.

Jake checked to make sure no one else was listening and then closed the door to Mac's office and rounded his desk.

'There's something you need to see,' he told him, handing him the flash drive.

He reached out and took it, raising an eyebrow at Jake's cryptic mood as he plugged it into his laptop.

'What is this?'

'The security footage from the Bailey's store.'

Mac turned back to the screen and watched intently.

'What the hell?'

He flicked it back and watched it again.

'Shit,' he swore.

'I know,' Jake shook his head, as Mac flicked the footage back and watched it once again.

His gaze narrowed, and he unconsciously leaned closer to the screen, studying the tall dark figure wearing a strange dark hat, standing in front of Jonathan Bailey.

Some kind of visual disturbance ran across the screen obscuring the stranger's face but they both saw, clear as day, as he reached into Jonathan Bailey's chest and pulled out what looked to be a ball of light about the size of a tennis ball.

'What the hell is it?'

'I haven't a clue,' Jake shook his head.

'Has anyone else seen this?'

'Just you and me,' he replied.

'Jesus,' he scrubbed his hand over his face in frustration. 'I thought all the creatures got pulled back in when we closed the gateway?'

'Maybe they did; maybe this is something different.'

Mac sighed deeply.

'Do you remember the days when all we had to worry about was a serial killer on the loose.'

'Simpler times,' Jake nodded.

'I have to admit, I don't even know where to start with this,' Mac stood and paced his office. 'Without Olivia and Theo, or even, although I hate to admit it, Charles, I wouldn't know how to even begin to figure out what that thing is.'

'Is there no way to contact Charles at all?' Jake asked.

'No,' Mac scowled, 'we're not exactly best friends.'

'How about Danae?'

'We could try leaving a message on her cell, because I'm willing to bet money that she's with Charles and Davis.' He pulled open his desk drawer, and retrieved his weapon, holstering it at his side as he picked up his jacket and shrugged it on. 'Let's go and see your sister, and find out if Mr Bailey has regained consciousness yet.'

Jake nodded and followed him from the room.

Louisa looked up tiredly from the chart she was furiously scribbling in. Her brother strode confidently through the department, with Mac following behind him looking equally as serious.

'Hey,' she greeted them both.

'Louisa,' Mac nodded, 'we're here for an update on Mr Bailey. Is he awake yet?'

'No,' she sighed. 'I don't even know if he is going to wake up.'

'Have you found out what's wrong with him yet?' Jake asked.

Louisa shook her head.

'I hate to admit it, but I just don't have a clue. His test results keep coming back clean. We've done bloods, scans and CT's, in fact nearly every test we can think of, but we just can't find a cause for the coma.'

'Damn it,' Mac muttered, 'I was hoping we'd be able to speak with him. Is there nothing you can give him to bring him around?'

'Sorry Mac, right now we don't even understand why he's unconscious.'

Her eyes narrowed suspiciously, as she saw the look that passed between her brother and the Captain.

'You know something, don't you?'

'Is there somewhere private we can talk?' Mac asked quietly.

'Sure,' she nodded, leading them into a small private lounge nearby.

'Okay, what's going on?' Louisa asked the minute the door was closed.

'I retrieved the security footage from the Bailey's store earlier today,' Jake told her. 'When we watched it back, it seems Mr Bailey wasn't alone when he collapsed.'

'Okay,' she replied in confusion, 'so what's that got to do with him being ill? Because I'm telling you now, he has no evidence of injuries at all, especially ones that would cause a coma.'

'I wouldn't be so sure about that,' Jake shook his head. 'The footage showed a very tall figure dressed in black. There was some sort of interference on the recording, which obscured his face, so we couldn't get an ID, but the tape very clearly shows him reaching into Mr Bailey's chest and when he withdrew his hand he was holding some kind of ball of light.'

'I'm sorry, what?' she frowned, rubbing her temples tiredly. 'Some guy shows up at the Bailey's store, and reaches into Mr Bailey's chest? I told you he doesn't have any kind of injury, not so much as a bruise.'

'I know,' Jake told her pointedly.

'Well Jesus,' she blew out a breath, 'you think it's some sort of supernatural creature?'

'It seems to be a distinct possibility,' Mac interrupted.

'God,' she muttered, 'I'm too tired for this. I wish Olivia was here, this is her deal.'

'Believe me we wish she was here too, but she isn't, and neither is Charles,' Jake replied. 'So until that changes we're on our own.'

'You think whatever it is, was left behind when we closed the gate?' she asked.

'It seems to be the most logical explanation,' Mac answered.

'The problem is,' Jake threw a look at his boss, 'we need to figure out what it is, before anyone else gets hurt.'

'I think it's already too late for that,' Louisa sighed.

'What do you mean?'

'One of my interns collapsed yesterday evening. She hasn't regained consciousness, and is showing the same symptoms as Mr Bailey. We're trying to stabilize her, but like Mr Bailey her vitals are all over the place. It's like her body is just trying to give up. We've got them both on life support at the moment.'

'Damn it,' Mac swore.

'There's something else you should see,' she told them cryptically, as she moved to the door.

They followed her through the hospital corridors in silence until they reached a private room. They stepped through and saw a young, attractive woman with pale blonde hair lying still and lifeless on the bed, attached to various tubes and beeping monitors.

'This is Hayley Adams, she's one of my interns,' Louisa told them, as she rounded the bed and beckoned them closer. Satisfied she had their attention, she leaned over her patient and very carefully peeled back one of the girl's eyelids to reveal her pale colorless eyes.

'I take it that's not her usual eye color?' Mac frowned.

'No, she usually has really blue eyes, like Forget-me-nots.'

'Is there any medical condition that could cause this?'

'We see something similar in older patients, and it's usually caused by cataracts, a condition very easily corrected by minor surgery, but these aren't cataracts. I've had a colleague who specializes in optometry check thoroughly, and her eyes are still fully intact, it's like they just drained of color.'

'And Mr Bailey is showing the same symptom?'

Louisa nodded.

'Hayley has been an intern of yours for how long?'

'She's been here for several months now. She's very bright, driven and hardworking.'

'Does she live alone?'

'No, she shares an apartment with Lucas Garcia, one of the other interns.'

'Was she found at her apartment?'

Louisa shook her head again. 'She was found here

in the hospital.'

'Nobody saw anything?'

'No, she was taking a break down on one of the lower levels and before you ask, that particular corridor didn't have any surveillance, but you can check the rest of the cameras.'

Mac nodded. 'We'll do that. How about this Lucas Garcia? Is he in today?'

'He's on rotation in the ER at the moment; you should be able to find him down there.'

'Okay, I'll take the intern,' Mac turned to Jake, 'you head down to the security office and check out the footage. See if this stranger shows up anywhere else.'

Jake nodded and watched silently as Mac slipped out of the room, before turning to his sister.

'I want you to be careful.'

'Jake come on, I'm perfectly safe.'

'I expect that's what Hayley Adams thought too.'

'Alright, fair point,' she conceded grudgingly.

'Look, until we figure out who this guy is or even what he is, you need to be careful. We don't know how he's picking his victims, or what he's doing to them. So just make sure you're not on your own if you can help it.'

'I'll try,' she sighed, 'but I still have a job to do.'

He wrapped his arms around her, and dropped an affectionate kiss on her head.

'I'll stop by and see you and Tommy later.'

Louisa nodded, watching as he also stepped from the room.

Jake was deep in thought as he approached the security office. Knocking lightly on the door and entering he found the security guard, who would normally be seated in front of the screens, standing off to the side of the small enclosed room, his arms folded in front of him and a scowl on his face. In front of him, a technician was kneeling on the ground with a hard drive in several pieces.

'Hey Todd,' he nodded to the security guard, someone he'd known since high school.

'Jake,' he replied.

'What's going on?'

'Something's wrong with the equipment, we keep getting a line of interference over several of the cameras.'

Jake glanced over at the screens on the wall, some still showed feeds from the cameras and a couple were showing snowy static.

'Is it constant?' Jake asked, 'the interference? Is there a pattern to it?'

'Nope, doesn't happen all the time. We caught it on some of the cameras last night. They've been checked and they seem to be working just fine, but Kurt here can't seem to find the root of it.'

The skinny tech looked up and scowled back at Todd.

'I know how to do my job, but I'm telling you it isn't a hardware problem.'

'And I know I wasn't imagining it, I've got the tapes to prove it.'

'You have recordings?' Jake repeated.

'Yeah, because some of us know how to do our jobs properly.'

'Now just a minute,' Kurt threw down the screwdriver clutched in his fist.

'Whoa, time out you two,' Jake stepped in between them and turned to Todd. 'Can I see the recordings.'

'Sure,' he replied, still shooting daggers at Kurt, as if somehow it were all his fault.

He hit a few buttons, and turned back to the screens.

'Take a look at three, four, eight and twelve.'

Jake flicked back and forth between the four different screens.

'These were taken last night?' he queried.

'Yeah.'

Jake turned back to the screens and watched. Although each feed was taken from a different camera, in different parts of the hospital, they all showed the same thing. A tall, thin, dark clothed man, wearing a wide brimmed hat, and a line of interference running across the screen obscuring the features of his face.

'This man,' Jake leaned forward and tapped the screen, 'have you seen him in the hospital before?'

Todd squinted, leaning closer to the screen as if noticing for the first time.

'No,' he shook his head frowning lightly. 'I'd remember someone like that, he's pretty distinctive. He looks like he's at least seven feet tall.'

'You're sure?'

'Positive.'

'Can I get a copy of these?'

'No problem,' Todd replied. 'I'll get them sent over to the station for you.'

'Appreciate it,' Jake nodded.

As Jake stepped out of the small airless room, the sound of raised voices began once again. Ignoring them, he clicked the door closed behind him and headed down to the main entrance, where Mac was waiting for him.

'Any luck?' he asked as he approached.

Mac shook his head.

'Roommate didn't know anything. What about you?'

'Same thing on the security cameras that we saw in the Bailey's store, tall, dark figure, face obscured by interference. Todd's going to send the footage over to the station.'

'Damn, so it looks as if it's the same guy then.'

'Looks like.'

'According to the roommate Hayley had been fine in the days leading up to the incident. She wasn't acting strange, and she hadn't mentioned being followed. Both she and Mr Bailey have nothing in common, no connection that I can see.'

'Could be he's picking his victims at random then,' Jake mused. 'Opportunity?'

'Maybe,' Mac agreed. 'I think you should go talk to Veronica.'

'What?' his eyes widened in panic, 'why?'

'Is there a problem?'

'No,' he shook his head, 'why would there be a problem?'

'You're just acting weird,' he shrugged. 'Anyway, she's the best person we've got when it comes to research, and you said yourself, she has access to all of Olivia's books. Show Veronica the security footage from the Bailey's store, and see if she can figure out what that thing is, and what that ball of light was.'

'Maybe you should go and see her instead?'

'Jake,' Mac frowned, 'what's wrong with you? I thought you two were friends.'

'We were,' he shook his head, 'I mean, we are.'

Mac looked down at his watch.

'I'm due back at the station, I don't have time for this,' he shook his head. 'Look whatever the issue is between you and Veronica I suggest you deal with it. We need to find out what's going on around here before anyone else gets hurt, and in Olivia and Charles' absence she's our best chance at figuring it out. So suck it up, and go see her.'

'Fine,' Jake frowned, 'but I need to go back to the station and collect the security footage for the Bailey's store.'

'No need,' Mac smiled, 'got it right here.'

'Great,' Jake replied sourly as Mac pulled the flash drive from his jacket pocket and handed it over.

'Let me know what she says,' Mac nodded and headed out.

Jake turned and reluctantly headed in the direction of the museum, figuring he might as well walk. It would at least give him time to figure out what the hell he was going to say to Roni. He'd been a coward, he knew it. He'd been avoiding her since the 'kiss', he hadn't even been able to face going back and picking up Beau yet. Instead he'd messaged her and asked her to keep hold of him for an extra few days.

It was pathetic, he sighed, and shook his head. What the hell had possessed him to kiss her like that? He shouldn't have done it, she just looked so damn cute, all flushed and embarrassed. He'd only meant to give her a teasing little peck on the lips, but the second his mouth landed on hers he stopped thinking completely. God, now he was thinking about her mouth again. It wasn't fair, he just wanted to go back to the comfortable friend zone they'd been in, but now he'd made it awkward between them.

It didn't help that he couldn't sleep, couldn't stop thinking about her, about how she'd tasted, how she'd sighed into his mouth, how smooth and soft her skin had been under his fingers. How she'd snaked her arms around his neck, and wrapped herself around him until he couldn't breathe without inhaling her. Damn it, he almost growled, he should've just kept his mouth to himself.

It wasn't like he wasn't attracted to her, he was. In fact he would've liked nothing better than her naked and beneath him, but that wasn't going to happen. It was too complicated, and he didn't do complicated. Roni wasn't the kind of girl a guy had a fling with, she was the kind of girl a guy married.

He entered the museum, pausing only briefly to ask the girl at the desk where Roni was, before heading up to her office, still muttering to himself. It was just one kiss he reasoned, he was probably making a big deal about nothing. She hadn't called him, she hadn't messaged him back, other than to say okay, when he'd asked her to keep hold of Beau. He was totally over-reacting, she hadn't mentioned it. In fact, she'd probably already forgotten all about it. It was probably fine. He knocked lightly and opened the door.

It wasn't fine.

Roni looked up from her desk at the intrusion, and the second she caught sight of Jake her eyes darkened, and her jaw clenched. She looked furious. Damn it, Jake thought absently, she looked sexy as hell when she was pissed.

'Is there something I can do for you Deputy?' her eyes may have blazed hotly, but her tone was chillier than an ice floe heading for Greenland.

Yep, definitely pissed.

Veronica looked at Jake, leaning casually against her door, and her temper spiked again. She ruthlessly shoved it back down, and turned back to her work. She didn't want to talk to him now, or possibly ever.

She was mortified beyond words, not only because he'd heard her innermost private thoughts, although she still maintained she hadn't spoken the words aloud, but what other explanation was there? But she was also pissed at herself as much as him, the whole situation was embarrassing and just plain uncomfortable.

He'd meant to give her a light teasing peck, she knew it, she'd read it in his expression, but the minute his lips had touched hers she'd latched on. He was obviously embarrassed she'd taken things too far, and had run as far and fast as he could. He hadn't even come back to pick up Beau. God, she wished she could just hit the rewind button, but she couldn't she thought with a sigh. She'd probably ruined their friendship, all because she couldn't keep her pathetic crush on him under control.

'Roni?' he stepped into her office and clicked the door closed behind him.

'Jake, I'm really rather busy. If you've come to pick up Beau, he's not here. Mitchell took him out for a walk for me.'

'No, I haven't come to…wait who the hell is

Mitchell?' he frowned.

The door suddenly opened behind him and an enthusiastic ball of fur bounded through and tried to scramble up his legs, barking happily in recognition.

'Hey Boy,' Jake kneeled down and stroked Beau who collapsed to the floor ecstatically, and rolled over to expose his belly. 'You've no shame,' he chuckled.

Jake glanced up as a shadow fell over him, his frown deepening as he caught sight of a tall, good looking, guy with short dark hair.

'Thanks Mitch,' Roni smiled at him, as he strode over to her desk and handed her Beau's leash.

'It's no problem, anything for you Roni you know that,' he grinned.

Jake stood abruptly, glaring at the guy standing comfortably close to her.

'Mitchell, this is Jake,' she introduced them. 'Jake, Mitchell Nash.'

'Hey,' Mitch inclined his head and held out his hand.

'Hey,' Jake replied, grasping his hand a little more firmly than he'd intended as he stared at him intently.

'Mitch?' Roni interrupted, as she glanced back and forth between them in confusion.

'Yeah?'

'There was a delivery from the Peabody while you were out, could you make sure the items on loan are unpacked carefully and cataloged.'

'No problem,' he smiled, as he released Jake's hand and stepped back, closing the door behind him on his way out.

'He works here?' Jake asked as he turned sharply back to Roni.

'Yes he does, not that it's any of your business. He's my assistant, and I'd appreciate you not shooting him daggers. He's actually very good at what he does.'

'I'll bet,' he muttered sourly.

'Jake,' she sighed in exasperation, 'why are you here? I really am quite busy, so if you just came to collect Beau I'd appreciate it if you just take him and leave me to get on with my work.'

'That's not why I'm here', he closed the distance between them, and skirted around her desk. 'I have something I need to show you.'

'What?' she asked suspiciously.

'This,' he pulled the flash drive free and handed it to her. 'It's the footage from the Bailey's store, the night Jonathan Bailey collapsed. It seems the eye witness was correct, he wasn't alone when it happened.'

She took it from him and loading it up onto her laptop, she hit play.

Jake watched in concern as her eyes widened and her skin paled.

Roni clenched her fists to stop them from trembling, her stomach was doing somersaults and her heart hammered in her chest. She shook her head unconsciously, almost as if in denial, as she looked up into Jake's concerned face.

'Roni what is it?'

She stood abruptly, her mind racing as she slammed the laptop shut and disconnected the power cable. Pulling her jacket off the hook and yanking it on roughly, she snatched her keys off the desk. She scooped up the laptop and tucked it under her arm.

'Come on,' she headed for the door, 'we have to go now.'

'Where? Why? I thought you had to work?'

'It will have to wait, everything will have to wait.'

'Roni,' he caught her by the arm to still her frantic movements, 'tell me what's going on?'

'Not yet, there's something I need to check. Are you coming or not?' she pulled away from him impatiently.

He studied her face carefully. Her eyes were wide and fearful, her skin pale and her breath coming in shallow nervous waves. Something was very wrong here; he'd never known her to look so freaked out, even when she'd dealt with ghosts and monsters.

Nodding in agreement, he let go of her arm and bent down to scoop Beau into his arms as he followed her out of the office. He decided it was probably best not to push her right now. She obviously knew, or thought she knew, something important about the man in the footage. It seemed Mac was right, she was their best chance at figuring out what the hell was going on, and he had the uncomfortable feeling he wasn't going to like what she was about to tell them.

He followed her down to her car and before he knew it they were pulling up to the garishly colored house on Fairfield Avenue guarded by a whole platoon of freakishly happy garden gnomes.

Veronica snatched up her laptop and was out of the car and striding up the path toward the front porch before Jake had even managed to get his seatbelt off. He scooped Beau up, and hurried down the path after her. He debated on whether or not to put Beau down, but knowing the legion of cats Fiona had, he was willing to bet that would be an incredibly bad idea.

Veronica frantically pounded on the door, dancing on the spot impatiently as she waited for the crazy old British woman to answer, and when she did, she certainly didn't disappoint.

The door was abruptly jerked open, and Fiona stood there scowling. She'd obviously tried to tame her wild grey wiry hair into some semblance of order, but it still stuck up in all directions, except for a small patch at the front, which was pinned ruthlessly by a small barrette with a ladybug on it.

She wore a bright yellow sweater, red leggings with giant daisies on them, and her trademark red Birkenstocks. Her eyes appeared hugely magnified behind her cat's eye glasses, and her mouth was covered in white foam, with a toothbrush handle protruding from her lips.

'Why are you brushing your teeth now? It's like three in the afternoon,' Jake asked in confusion.

She pulled the brush from her mouth and pursed her lips.

'Got something stuck in my teeth, was annoying me, not unlike you. What do you want?'

Veronica pushed past her impatiently and moved into the hallway.

'Well by all means come on in,' she added sarcastically. 'Please make yourselves at home.'

'I have something I need to show you Fiona, and I'm sorry it couldn't wait.' Veronica breathed heavily.

Fiona's eyes narrowed as she took in her pale face and trembling hands.

'Better go on through then,' she nodded in the direction of the lounge.

Beau barked suddenly as he caught sight of one of the cats, and scrambled madly in Jake's arms. Roni headed into the room with Jake right behind her. Once satisfied there were no cats in the room, Jake shut the door and dropped Beau to the ground. The puppy rushed over to the nearest sofa and started sniffing madly, following a trail all over the room with his tail wagging.

Fiona slipped into the room and shut the door firmly behind her, wiping her mouth with a cloth, her toothbrush still clutched in the other hand.

'So what is it that's so important you had to come barging into my house?'

Veronica dropped the lap top onto the nearest table and opened it up.

Fiona stood silently watching the footage on the screen as it played through.

'Well,' she folded her arms across her ample chest and fixed Veronica with a steely eyed stare, 'you already know what it is, don't you?'

Roni breathed heavily, and numbly dropped into a

deeply cushioned chair.

'I was hoping I was wrong, that you'd tell me I'm wrong.'

'Sorry girl,' she replied, her voice gentling slightly, 'but you're not wrong.'

'What?' Jake interrupted, 'what is it?'

'The figure in the footage,' Roni answered, her voice no more than a whisper, 'he's the Soul Collector.'

Her eyes bore into his, a deep worried blue.

'And he's stealing human souls.'

8.

'I'm sorry, what?' Jake replied as if he couldn't quite believe the words coming out of her mouth.

'You heard the girl,' Fiona bustled over to a drinks cabinet at the side of the room and retrieved a bottle and filled three glasses.

'I'm on duty,' Jake shook his head as she offered him a glass.

'Trust me boy, you're going to need it.' She thrust the glass into his hand and passed the other to Veronica. Picking up her own glass she lifted it in a mocking salute. 'To the utter shit hole we are currently up to our necks in.'

Veronica threw back the fiery liquid, but even as it burned a trail down her throat, her body still felt cold.

'Roni,' he placed his untouched glass down on the low coffee table, and kneeled down in front of her, taking her icy cold hands in his. 'Explain to me what's going on.'

'You'd better take a seat and get comfortable,' Fiona dropped down into a nearby chair, her knees cracking loudly as she went.

Jake took a seat next to Roni, staring at her patiently.

'His name is Charun, I came across his name when I was helping Olivia research Charon. Quite often the two of them are confused for the same person, but they're not. Charon as you know is Greek, the Ferryman of the Underworld and servant of the God Hades. Charun is Etruscan, it is thought that his name is derived from the Greek Charon, as he is also known as Charu. He is a Psychopompoi of the Underworld.'

Jake looked at her blankly.

'Psychopompoi comes from the Greek word Psychopomps, which literally means, 'guide of the souls'. These creatures, depending on the religion, can be spirits, angels or even deities, and it is their responsibility to escort the newly deceased souls from Earth to whichever afterlife they are destined for. It is not their place to judge the souls, only to provide safe passage.

In Greek mythology Charon is considered a Psychopompoi as is Hermes, Hecate, Mercury and Anubis, because they all share a common role, even if they are from different civilizations. A more recent example of a Psychopompoi, is the English version of the Grim Reaper, which originated from the 15th Century, but has since been adopted by many cultures.'

'So this Charun is some kind of Angel of Death?'

'Not exactly. Like I said, Charu is Etruscan. Both he and his counterpart, the female known as Vanth, were demons of the Underworld. It was their job, not to punish the dead, but like Charon to escort them to their final destination in the Underworld. Vanth was always portrayed as quite benevolent, despite her origins as a demon. Charu was her opposite, he was often portrayed as menacing and dark.'

'So,' Jake frowned, 'this Charu is taking these souls and sending them to the Underworld?'

'That's just it, he's not doing what he's supposed to. These people aren't dying, it's not their time to cross over. He isn't escorting their souls, he's harvesting them.'

'What for?'

'I have no idea, but if you look carefully on the video footage, you see him trap the soul in a glass bottle.

What he is doing with them after that, I couldn't say.'

'That ball of light? That's a human soul?'

Veronica nodded.

'These people aren't ready, it's not their time to cross over, which means there is only one way to harvest the souls from their mortal bodies, and that's by force. That's what he's doing, he's ripping these souls from their bodies. That's why Mr Bailey is in a coma and on life support, his soul is gone. His body is just an empty vessel now. The body cannot survive without the soul. Sooner or later it will shut down permanently, and no amount of medical intervention will be able to save him.'

'Where is his soul now? Is there any way to return it to his body?'

Veronica shrugged helplessly. 'I just don't know.'

Jake turned his gaze on Fiona.

'I don't know either,' she poured herself a drink, 'but what I do know is that he won't be satisfied with just one soul.'

'You're right about that,' Jake murmured.

'He's taken someone else, hasn't he?' Roni breathed heavily her eyes filled with worry. 'It's not just Mr Bailey?'

Jake shook his head. 'He took one of Louisa's interns, her name is Hayley Adams.'

'God,' Roni held out her glass to Fiona and watched her fill it almost to the brim, before she tossed her head back and downed it in one.

'Roni,' Jake frowned, 'I think you'd better slow down there.'

'You don't understand,' she turned her troubled gaze on him, 'there is no way to stop him.'

'What are you talking about? There must be something, some way to…'

'No,' she cut him off. 'He can't be killed, he can't be reasoned with, he can't be stopped. He is going to go through this town like a plague, harvesting every soul, until he is wading through the corpses of everyone you have ever known, or loved. Mercy will become nothing more than a desolate wasteland of ash and bone.'

'I don't accept that,' Jake replied stubbornly, 'I'm not giving up. If we can't stop him or kill him, then we find a way to send him back to wherever he came from.'

'He must have come through the gateway with the others,' Fiona mused as she swirled the amber liquid around thoughtfully in her glass. 'Question is, why wasn't he pulled back through?' she looked up at them both and took another sip. 'Makes you wonder doesn't it?'

'Wonder what?' Roni asked.

'How many others weren't pulled back through, how many were left trapped in Mercy.'

'Jesus,' Roni dropped her head into her hands.

'One problem at a time,' Jake murmured absently, as he rubbed soothing circles on Roni's back. 'Just breathe sweetheart, it's going to be okay.'

'How is this possibly going to be okay?' she looked up at him. 'None of us have the skill, or the power to send him back.'

'No, we have something better.'

'What?'

'Someone on the inside,' he smiled. 'If we can't open the gateway from this side, maybe Olivia can from the Other side.'

Fiona cackled in delight. 'I guess you're not just a pretty face after all boy.'

'We need to contact Olivia,' Roni replied.

'We need to contact Olivia,' Jake agreed.

Olivia sat perched on the edge of the roof, staring at the town laid out before her like a miniature replica. She took another swig from the bottle of Johnnie Walker she'd swiped from the pub, and stared down at the sidewalk far below her, wondering idly how far a drop it was. If she fell would she actually die she pondered, after all she was already in the Spirit world. Did that mean she was now invulnerable to injury, or even death?

'Not a good area for experimentation,' Sam appeared suddenly next to her.

'For God's sake Sam,' her hand jumped involuntarily to her rapidly beating heart. 'Give me a heart attack, why don't you?'

'Sorry.'

'You'd think I'd be used to that by now, wouldn't you?'

He grinned at her boyishly.

'I swear you do that on purpose.'

'Do what?' his eyes widened innocently, 'and in answer to your earlier question, I don't think you'd actually die, but I can't be sure. You're not a true spirit, you're technically still wearing your mortal body, which means if you damage it in here you probably won't survive out there.'

'Fair enough,' she took another swig from the bottle, 'and just for the record, I wasn't planning on actually doing it. I'm frustrated, not suicidal.'

'If you say so,' he took the bottle from her, and drank deeply himself.'

'It makes me really uncomfortable when you do that,' she frowned, 'you don't look old enough to drink.'

'Don't let the face fool you,' he laughed comfortably, 'I'm older than I look.'

'How much older?' she asked curiously.

He shook his head in amusement. 'I wouldn't want to make you more uncomfortable.'

Smiling she turned back to the view. Letting out a deep breath, she gazed up at the sky.

'It's a little disconcerting you know.'

'What is?'

'Not knowing how long I've been here for.'

'It's not really relevant you know.'

'I know, I know, time has no meaning here, blah, blah, blah,' she rolled her eyes and took the bottle back. 'I just…' she shrugged and sighed a little, 'I miss the sunset.'

'You really don't have a clue how it works here, do you?'

'What?'

Sam turned to face her more fully.

'Tell me what you love about the sunset,' he asked softly.

'The feel of it,' she replied quietly, 'that quiet moment when you feel the air change. When the world slows, and the sky softens into swirls of vivid pink and purple. For that one moment everything shifts, and the whole world is still, holding its breath, waiting for the stars.'

She looked into Sam's eyes and saw him smile.

'Olivia.'

'Yes.'

'Look up.'

She did and a delighted laugh fell from her lips as she drew in a breath of wonder.

'Oh my God,' the strange blue tinted daylight was gone, and the sky was now ablaze with magnificent swirls of sleepy pink and purple. 'How did you do that?'

'I didn't,' he whispered smiling softly, 'you did.'

'Oh my God,' she breathed, looking up to the sky, 'that's so cool.'

'In this place, anything is possible. If you can imagine it, you can make it happen.'

She looked back at him as he held out his hand to her. She took it gently and he smiled.

'Now think of any place you want to.'

She did as he asked, and even as the thought began to take shape in her mind, her surroundings began to shift and blur, like a painting left out in the rain. When she looked around they were no longer perched on the edge of the roof top, but were now standing inside the museum in front of Hester's portrait.

'Wow,' she breathed, 'is this what it's like for you

when you translocate?'

'Close,' Sam smiled letting go of her hand. Turning to face the portrait he studied it closely, 'she looks like you.'

'So I'm told.'

'Why here?' he asked curiously.

She shrugged. 'It just sort of popped into my head, this was one of my favorite places when I was a kid. I thought it was so cool my family had their own exhibit. I don't know, I guess it made me feel important.'

He nodded in understanding, as they slowly started walking, looking at the exhibits as they went.

'So what about you Sam?'

'What about me?'

'I've told you pretty much my life story, how about telling me yours?'

His brow folded into a sudden frown and he sighed. 'I can't, I'm sorry Olivia but there are rules I have to abide by.'

'Whose rules?'

'Nice try,' his mouth curved slightly in amusement.

'Well, can you at least tell me how you ended up here?'

He blew out a deep thoughtful breath as they continued to walk past the glass fronted display cases.

'My father wanted me to do something that I didn't agree with. I refused and he cast me down here and locked me in, to give me some time to think.'

'How long have you been here?' she frowned.

'Time is irre…'

'Yeah, yeah, I know irrelevant, forget I asked,' she shook her head. 'What did he want you to do?'

Sam hesitated for a moment, as if he were unsure how much to reveal.

'He wanted me to betray someone I cared about,' he replied finally.

'Who was she?'

'So sure it's a she, aren't you?' he smiled.

She simply raised her brows and waited.

'Fine,' he answered after a moment, 'she was…is a friend, sort of.'

'How can someone be sort of a friend? If you care about her enough to be exiled because of her, either she's important to you or not.'

'She is,' his voice was soft and tinged with an emotion she couldn't quite name, sadness perhaps? Or maybe remorse. 'You remind me of her actually,' he looked up at Olivia. 'She is beautiful and clever, but she can be incredibly stubborn, and she's sweet and kind. She has a deep love of lore and history.'

'She sounds like my long lost twin, except for the sweet and kind part,' Olivia chuckled lightly, 'so what's the problem? She sounds pretty perfect.'

'She's the daughter of a traitor.'

Olivia stopped suddenly, and stared darkly at Sam. 'And you hold that against her?'

'No,' he realized she'd got the wrong idea, 'I would never hold what her mother did, against her. It was not her fault, she had nothing to do with it, and yet she is paying the price for it. Even her own people,' he shook his head in disgust. 'You should see how they treat her, it's like they look at her and see her mother. They can't see who she truly is. Even my people treat her with distrust and suspicion.'

'I see, so it's like a forbidden love kind of thing?'

'No,' he shook his head, 'it's not like that.'

'Isn't it?'

'We're not even the same race.'

'So! There's nothing wrong with mixed race marriages.'

'For humans perhaps, but not for us. Our races have hated each other for thousands of years, they barely tolerate each other. Any inter-race interaction is kept to a strict minimum. There's no mixed race friendships, let alone marriages. I don't even know if…' he shook his head in denial. 'It's impossible, especially after what I've done.'

'What did you do?'

He turned away and started walking again, almost as if it were easier to confess when he wasn't looking directly at her.

'I used to be like them, the rest of my people. I was raised to view the others as my enemy, not to be trusted. My father chose me, said he had something very important for me to do. He wanted me to seek her out and befriend her, secretly of course. He was convinced she was just as much a traitor as her mother. Tainted blood he called it. He was obsessed with the idea she was going to continue where her mother had failed.'

'What did you do?' she asked softly.

'I refused at first, but my father convinced me it was important, and with my ears ringing with words like duty, honor, and loyalty, I did as he asked. At first I was so resentful, I'm surprised she even bothered to speak to me.' His eyes grew distant, tangled up in memories, 'I think she was so surprised I was even speaking to her. She was so used to being shunned, by both her own people and mine.'

'Sounds like a lonely life.'

'It was,' his voice dropped low, 'I didn't understand that at first. She once told me when she first met me, it was like being allowed to take a breath for the very first time.'

Olivia watched him silently, watching the silent play of emotion across his face until he began to speak again.

'She's never going to forgive me when she finds out.'

'I think she will,' Olivia told him gently, 'if she's the person you think she is. She may be hurt, but she knows you love her, so she'll forgive you.'

He looked up at her and stared.

'She doesn't know how you feel about her, does she?'

He shook his head slowly.

'Sam,' she breathed.

'You don't understand Olivia,' he frowned, 'this isn't just about overcoming prejudice. If they found out about us we would both be executed.'

'Are you serious?'

'I was protecting her.'

'Sam,' she spoke after a moment, 'I'm not trying to interfere, and I certainly don't want to tell you what to do, but I do know one thing, love is a gift that should be treasured, not denied. Sometimes it's worth the risk. You just need to decide, is she worth it?'

'Is Theo?' he asked in return.

'Yes,' she whispered, 'and I would rather live minutes with him then spend my whole life without him.'

He wrapped his arms around her impulsively and pulled her into an affectionate hug.

'You're like the sister I never wanted.'

Olivia laughed, squeezing him gently before pulling back and looking up into his eyes.

'Then take some sisterly advice and tell her how you feel Sam. Trust me when I tell you, that you may never get another chance. You have to make the most of every moment.'

'Carpé diem?'

'Something like that,' she smiled in amusement.

Suddenly the ground trembled beneath their feet causing them to break apart.

'Did you feel that?' Sam frowned in confusion.

'What was that? An earthquake?'

'That's impossible, this isn't like earth. It's not a physical plane, it's not subject to seismic shifts.'

The ground trembled again, this time harder, making them stumble slightly.

'If it's not an earthquake, what the hell is causing

that?' Olivia breathed in alarm.

'I have no idea,' Sam's eyes widened.

Suddenly there was a great tearing sound, and the ground beneath them shook so violently they were thrown to the floor. The glass display cases shattered, sending glass showering over them. The floor heaved and groaned beneath them. Olivia curled into a ball and covered her head with her arms, trying to protect herself from falling debris. Priceless pieces of history tumbled to the floor and smashed, causing her a momentary jolt, until she reminded herself they were just replicas and not real. The frantic shaking seemed to go on forever until it suddenly stopped as abruptly as it started. Olivia looked up, coughing lightly in the dust filled air, her gaze searching the devastation for Sam.

'Sam?' she coughed again. 'Sam, are you hurt?'

'He's not here,' a cool voice broke the silence.

Olivia looked up and her eyes landed on a familiar figure. Still impeccably dressed in an elegant suit he sat on the edge of a toppled over cabinet, his glossy black cane propped between his legs, his hands wrapped neatly over the deep blue jeweled handle.

'Hades,' she breathed, 'where's Sam? What have you done with him?'

'Nothing,' he shrugged dismissively. 'I simply wished to speak with you without the time traveler overhearing.'

Olivia climbed cautiously to her feet, careful not to cut her hands on the crushed glass which littered the floor.

'Did you do this?' she asked accusingly.

'No.'

'If it wasn't you, then what happened?'

Hades was silent for a moment, seeming to draw in a breath, as if to rein in a wave of temper.

'Something we did not anticipate,' he answered finally.

She took a minute to study him closely, his hair was no longer a deep shiny well-groomed blue black as it had been in the human world. Now it burned with the ebony and sapphire flames of Hell fire, banked low but still snapping and crackling as he turned his head. His expression had also lost the curious amusement it had borne the last time they met. Despite being in the overwhelming presence of a God she'd sensed a kind of playful curiosity then. That too was gone and in its place was a barely concealed anger.

'Hades, what's going on?' she asked carefully, 'why are you here? Last time we met you said you'd be watching me, that this was some kind of an amusement for you.'

'It is no longer a game Olivia,' his dark eyes burned into hers.

'Tell me what's going on then.'

Hades tapped his long tapered fingers against the handle of his cane impatiently, his jaw clenching tightly.

'Nathaniel has destroyed one of the Crossroads.'

'What?' Olivia gasped, 'why would he do that?'

Hades stood abruptly, causing her to flinch nervously, as he paced the debris strewn floor, restless and sleek like a caged panther. He turned back to her suddenly.

'It seems we underestimated Nathaniel. I assumed he wanted the book to raise his brother from the Underworld, to use Infernum's power to breach the prison I created for Seth and set him free, so they could both move unhindered through the human world, causing whatever carnage and chaos they pleased.'

Olivia kept silent as Hades paced the floor angrily.

'It seems they have both set their sights higher, or rather lower, I should say.'

'Ohhh,' Olivia breathed out slowly, 'they want to gain control of the Underworld.'

'In order to do that, they must first deal with me,' he stopped pacing and turned to face her. 'By destroying one of the oldest and most powerful places in the

Underworld, he has not only upset the balance, but sent a message to all those who are opposed to me. What he has done is start an insurrection. He had to have had help destroying the Crossroad, he doesn't have the access or the means to do it alone, even with your mother and her limited abilities.'

'But why destroy the Crossroad?' Olivia frowned. 'I thought he wanted my mother to make a deal with the Keeper?'

'He does, I suspect he will attempt to destroy all but one of the Crossroads, to shift the balance of power and to prevent anyone from stopping or following him and Isabel. We have run out of time Olivia, you must reach the Crossroad before he does.'

'Can't you stop him?' she breathed heavily. 'You're a God, surely you can do something.'

'We are tearing the Underworld apart, but we don't know how many of the souls in the Underworld have sided with Seth and Nathaniel, and how many are still loyal to me. We are on the verge of war. The stakes are beyond high now, there is no turning back.

This isn't about a second rate witch getting her hands on the book, it's about two very old Demon Lords gaining control over all the Hell dimensions, and if they do they will rise up and destroy the Earth. The mortal world will burn, and they will climb over the corpses of your people to attack the very gates of Heaven itself.'

'Oh my God,' Olivia gasped, her hand covering her mouth.

'God?' he scoffed, 'don't expect him to do anything, He can't even keep his own house in order.'

'What do we do?'

'I cannot find Nathaniel, he is being too well hidden by his allies. You will have to find him.'

'How the Hell am I supposed to do that?' she frowned.

'Your mother,' he replied, 'you are bound to her

by blood, the oldest magic there is. Find her and you find the demon.'

'And then what?' she snapped angrily, 'just how am I going to stop a demon?'

'You won't have to,' he replied. His eyes burned black, his voice cold and menacing. 'I will deal with him, but you have to find him before he reaches the final Crossroad. Forget Theo, there isn't time to deal with him. Once Nathaniel leaves the boundaries of the Underworld, I cannot stop him. I have no authority in the human world, my brother Zeus saw to that when he cast me down into the pit.'

'Are you fucking kidding me?' Olivia ground out from between clenched teeth. Somewhere in the back of her mind, a small voice was screeching at her not to provoke a God, but that voice was rudely elbowed aside as her temper erupted into a blinding fury.

'Watch your mouth mortal,' Hades hissed. His hair flared up as if someone had just turned up the gas, before bursting into a bright halo of blue fire.

'Or you'll what?' she spat angrily, as she stepped closer to him, 'you'll do what exactly Hades? From where I'm standing, you need me far more than I need you. I am sick to death of everyone expecting me to clean up their mess the minute they snap their fingers. Like I don't have anything better to do, like I don't have the right to choose my own destiny. I am not a tool to be picked up and used whenever you feel like it. Find the murderer Cinderella, find the book Cinderella, stop a demon Cinderella, oh and yeah while you're at it save the world.

I don't think so, I am going to find Theo and when I do, then I will find my mother and even stop the damn demons, both of them if I have to. Not because you've told me to, or because it's my destiny, or some other bullshit like that, but because it's the right thing to do, because I care more about the human world than any of you, because the mortals you so happily dismiss as inferior, or just there for your amusement are the people I care about. So you can go straight back to Hell Hades, because I am not leaving here without Theo.'

Hades watched her contemplatively, his gaze sliding from her blazing eyes down her arms to her hands. Sometime during her rage-filled rant at the God of the Underworld her hands had burst into flame. Her fingers clenched onto burning spheres of churning, writhing, sapphire and jet flames, like tiny, fearsome, primordial worlds, burning in the palms of her hands. The flames licked up the skin of her arms, burning the same electric blue as Hades' hair.

His fingertips ran softly down her arm, skimming her skin as if the flames weren't even there; they certainly didn't seem to burn him. When he reached her hands he cupped the back of her hand turning her palm face up to reveal the spitting and hissing ball of raw Hell fire. He raised her hand up between them, so the fire was reflected in his dark eyes, before turning his serious gaze back on her.

'This is why it has to be you Olivia,' he spoke quietly, 'why it has always had to be you.'

'I will do what needs to be done Hades,' she replied resolutely, 'but we do it my way. No man rules my destiny, not even you. I choose… that's not negotiable.'

'I almost feel sorry for Theo,' his mouth curved suddenly at the corner. 'You remind me very much of Persephone, and if you are anything like her, you will make his life hell.'

'Then we have an agreement?'

'Very well,' he conceded, 'find Theo, but do it quickly. There isn't much time. The more damage Nathaniel does to the Underworld, the quicker it will spread through all the adjacent worlds, this one included.'

'What will happen to this world?'

'I couldn't say for sure, but it will sustain heavy damage as the walls between worlds begin to break down.

We have to contain this rebellion and quickly.'

'You know, it would go a lot faster if you would just tell me where Theo is?'

Hades sighed heavily, rolling his eyes in exasperation.

'Olivia, you already know where he is, you just need to figure it out.'

'Riddles Hades?'

'Listen, once you have found Theo you need to get to the Crossroad. There is a doorway hidden in this world, which will allow you to pass through into the Underworld, you need to find it and use it. Once you are there…' he hooked a slim elegant finger through the exposed golden chain at her throat and pulled, allowing the compass he had given her, to slither from the open collar of her shirt, 'use this.'

'I still don't understand how it works, if you could just tell me?'

'I can't tell you until you know, and if you know, I don't have to tell you.'

'More riddles? Seriously? That'll really make this so much easier.'

'I don't know why I like that smart mouth of yours so much Olivia,' he shook his head. 'It's a compass, so ask yourself, what does a compass do?'

'This is just crazy,' she sighed as she turned the compass over in her hands. 'Sometimes, I wonder if I am actually insane and just hallucinating this whole thing.'

She looked up and caught Hades' amused smile.

'Then maybe you should take a look at the place where all the crazy people go.'

She blinked and suddenly Hades had disappeared.

'Olivia?' Sam gasped in relief, 'I've been looking everywhere for you. Where the hell did you go?'

'Where all the crazy people go,' Olivia murmured as Hades' voice echoed in her ears. 'My God…'

'What is it?' Sam asked anxiously as she turned her

wide eyes on him.
>'I know where Theo is.'

9.

Olivia looked up at the building in front of her. Riverside psychiatric facility looked much as it had the last time she'd seen it, a tidy rectangular building with whitewashed walls, surrounded by uniformly manicured lawns.

She swallowed nervously and her heartbeat increased as she wiped her palms on her jeans. Taking a deep breath she started to move, passing by the neatly trimmed shrubbery and heading for the main entrance. Once inside she turned and headed past the main reception. The building wasn't as neat and tidy inside, the small earthquake caused by the destruction of one of the Crossroads had obviously affected many of the buildings.

A vase had toppled from the nearby reception desk, shattering across the floor in a rainbow of blue pottery and colorful flowers. Several magazines had slid from a small coffee table in the waiting area and were now heaped on the floor. She passed by overturned, cheerful, colored plastic chairs, and headed for the day room.

It seemed like such a long time ago now, but this was the place where she'd found Theo after Sam had brought him forward into the 21st century and rather inconveniently dropped him in front of her car. After he'd been treated at the hospital for his injuries they'd transferred him to Riverside, believing that he was suffering from amnesia. He'd been sitting in the day room that day, painting at the table by the window with his small palette of watercolors, amused by the place where they supposedly sent all the crazy people.

She reached the entrance to the room and could see more debris scattered across the floor from the earthquake. Counters and plastic pieces of board games were scattered across the floor, mixed in with scrabble tiles and dominoes. The walls were still the same bright, happy, sunshine yellow, and the paintings hung on the wall had not moved, not really a surprise as they had been screwed to the wall in the first place. She headed further into the room and stopped abruptly as her heart leapt into her throat and thudded there dully.

Theo sat to the side of the room on a green plastic chair, with an artist's easel in front of him. He was surrounded by scattered pieces of paper, some crumpled up, others covered with pencil and charcoal sketches. His shirt sleeves were pushed up to his elbows revealing the winding blue, black and silver lines of the supernatural tattoo etched deeply into the skin of his arm. His dark hair fell forward partly obscuring his face, but as he moved, frantically swiping the brush over the canvas, she caught a glimpse of his dark eyes fixed on the painting he was working on in fierce concentration.

'Theo,' she whispered.

He couldn't hear her from the doorway. She stepped further into the room, moving toward him slowly, almost afraid of moving too quickly in case he disappeared, and she found herself once again alone. As she neared him she paused, frowning when she caught sight of one of his sketches which had been swept across the floor. She bent down and picked it up with shaky fingers. It was a pencil sketch of something she'd seen him draw before. He'd tried to keep her from seeing it, but it was obviously something that bothered him greatly.

She took a step closer and picked up another drawing and then another. Soon she had a small pile in her trembling hand as she sucked in a shaky breath. They were all the same, a huge gnarled tree beneath a storm laden sky. From the lowest, thick twisted branch swung several nooses and from one of them hung a limp female body, dangling as if it were caught in the sway of an unseen wind.

Her fist clenched involuntarily, crushing the pictures in her hand. Dropping them to the ground where she'd found them she straightened and looked back toward Theo. Her heart broke for him, he'd carried the pain and guilt for so long he didn't know how to let it go.

'Theo,' she spoke a little louder this time.

He didn't acknowledge her, but kept painting, the muscles of his forearm corded tightly as he swiped angrily at the canvas, as if he were trying to exorcise some sort of personal demon. She kept walking slowly, approaching him as if she were afraid of startling him.

'Theo?' she called to him loudly this time, but still he didn't answer.

She crossed the distance and stopped next to him, but he didn't even so much as look up. Olivia's face creased into a scowl of confusion; what was wrong with him? It was like he wasn't even aware of her presence.

'Theo?'

She dropped down next to the chair he was sitting in, crouching beside him so she was almost his eye level. She reached out tentatively and laid her hand gently on his forearm in an attempt to still his frantic movements, but he didn't even acknowledge her.

'Theo?'

'He can't hear you, you know,' a cool female voice spoke from across the room.

Olivia's head snapped up and her eyes widened when she saw the person who had spoken. She shot to her feet, her hands bursting into silver Spirit fire before she'd even consciously summoned it. Placing herself protectively in front of Theo her eyes blazed angrily.

'Mary,' Olivia hissed.

Mary Alcott-Beckett sat on one of the tables by the window overlooking the gardens, her hands folded neatly in her lap and her feet resting on one of the plastic chairs. She watched Olivia with calm detachment, her gaze wandering slowly down to the silver fire burning in Olivia's hands.

'Go ahead,' she replied tiredly. 'Trust me, it would be a kindness.'

Olivia's forehead creased in confusion. She slowly relaxed her hands, letting the tension in her body ease a fraction. She took in Mary's appearance, noticing that she no longer resembled the angry spirit who had attacked herself and Theo back at her house.

Gone were the red eyes lost to madness, the rotting teeth, the matted wild hair and the dirty 17th century smock and apron she'd worn. Instead Olivia now saw a young woman with serious blue eyes, and hair the color of a corn field. Her smooth flawless skin had lost the sickly chalky pallor and was once again a pale fine porcelain. Her feet were bare, but clean, and she wore a pale blue summery dress, which stopped just above her knees. If Olivia had been meeting her for the first time now, she would never have guessed she was from the 17th century, but more from her own time.

Curious, but still suspicious, her fire banked and she looked to Mary cautiously.

'What are you doing here Mary?'

'I can't leave,' she sighed softly, as she gazed back at Theo.

Olivia followed her eye line back to Theo, who was still painting obliviously.

'What did you mean when you said he can't hear me?'

'He's trapped,' Mary replied quietly, her attention turning back to Olivia. 'His guilt is keeping him imprisoned within his own mind. He's stuck. He can't move past it and he can't let it go. It is slowly consuming him, eventually he will be lost to the madness, just as I was.'

'No,' Olivia whispered.

'I can't reach him, believe me I've tried.'

'Why are you still here Mary? Why can't you leave?'

'Because he won't let me,' she whispered, her gaze tracking across to the man she'd once called husband.

'I don't understand?'

'He blames himself for what happened to me,' she replied. 'His guilt is keeping me bound to him.'

Her eyes dropped down, she raised her ankle and as Olivia's eyes followed hers, she saw for the first time a thin silver chain, delicate and intricate, shimmering in the dim light. It wound around Mary's ankle and then dropped down to the ground, running along the tiled floor to Theo where, Olivia realized with a start, it was attached to Theo's wrist.

'He doesn't even realize he is doing it,' she breathed in frustration, 'but he has been dragging me through time with him like an anchor. Until he lets me go, until he forgives himself and moves on, I am trapped here with him, watching him slowly going mad.'

Her eyes filled with tears and suddenly Mary seemed so much younger.

'I want to go home,' her voice broke with grief. 'Maybe this is my punishment; as he bore witness to my madness, maybe I must now suffer through his. We are damned, both of us.'

'Not if I can help it,' Olivia replied quietly.

Silent tears slid down Mary's face. Unable to speak anymore, she turned back to the window and gazed out into the garden longingly.

Olivia watched, unsure what to do. She had been so consumed, with only one thought in her mind since the first moment she'd set foot in the Otherworld. Find Theo, that was her only purpose, but she had never expected to find him like this. Her heart sank as the joyful reunion she had envisaged evaporated before her eyes. How the hell was she supposed to reach him? He was incapable of even acknowledging her presence.

'Mary?'

The young woman turned back with watery eyes.

'Have you tried to talk to him?'

'For longer than you can imagine,' she sighed brokenly, 'he just doesn't want to hear me.'

'Have you forgiven him?'

'There's nothing to forgive,' she frowned. 'What happened to me in Salem was not his doing.'

'But he thinks it was, maybe he needs your forgiveness.'

Mary regarded Olivia thoughtfully.

'Maybe,' she murmured.

She slipped from the table and padded slowly over to Theo on bare feet.

'Theo?' Mary spoke softly next to him.

He growled and tossed the paint splattered canvas aside, retrieving another one before once again slashing jagged swipes of paint angrily across the surface.

'Theo,' she tried again, kneeling down next to him much as Olivia had. 'I don't know if you can hear me, or that you just don't want to hear me, but this has to stop. Hurting yourself won't change what happened. You think you know what happened, but you are remembering it wrong.' She touched his forehead lightly, laying her fingertips across his skin and closed her eyes. 'Think back to that moment Theo. Think back to Salem and see the truth.'

Theo was drowning, surrounded by darkness. He could feel the icy slash of rain against his burning skin, like thousands of tiny needles piercing his tender flesh as the fever ravaged his weak body.

He could smell the stormy scent of ozone and the stink of horse sweat beneath him. He clung desperately to his mount, his fingers tangled in its drenched mane. Jagged spears of lightning split the heavy storm laden sky, causing the dark grey clouds to swirl and boil like witch's brew.

Darkness shrouded his path, yet he urged his horse on, through the trees and across fields. He was lucky it was his own horse, Kane, whom he'd trained from foal. Kane could read his master's slightest movement and intent. He'd also made the journey from Salem Village to Salem Town so often he barely had to direct the horse at all.

It was fortunate, for even now he could feel the fever burning through his veins, his mind felt as if it were bundled with hay. He fought to focus through the haze. He had failed Temperance, she was gone. His heart clenched painfully and he bit his lip to keep the animal like howl of agony contained deep inside of him. There would be time enough for grieving later.

He should never have left her, he should never have left Mary. He could not fail her, not like he had failed Temperance.

They'd taken Mary in the night. They'd come to his home and dragged her screaming from the house, while his body was racked by painful chills and consumed with fever, too weak to stop them. Even now, she was chained in Salem Jail. She would not survive it, he had to reach her, before they killed her.

He swayed in the saddle as another wave of dizziness swamped him. Grasping onto Kane he sucked in a deep shaky breath and fought down a wave of nausea. He could not stop now, he was so close. He urged Kane on, through the deep darkness and into the storm.

Mary curled onto her side on the filthy straw of the cold, damp smelling floor. Her eyes were glazed, and her hair matted and stuck to the side of her face, which lay against the foul straw. Her arms rested numbly in front of her, bound together brutally, the cord biting mercilessly into the torn skin of her wrists as she absently traced circles against the ground with dirty cracked nails.

'Little child, little child sing unto God,

*praise his name when you wake,
little child little child glory unto God,
lest the devil your soul to take.'*

She murmured the child's rhyme over and over, her voice barely more than a cracked whisper.

She could feel the little demons surrounding her, breathing over her skin with their hot breath and picking at her flesh with tiny needle pointed fingers. Digging, digging, digging, with eyes like fire and tiny goat's horns jutting from their temples. She hissed loudly as one danced across her eye line, baring its razor sharp teeth in a malicious grin.

'You're next,' it whispered gleefully as it nipped at her skin.

She let loose a scream, which burned as it tore painfully from her dry throat. Scrambling across the dirty floor, she clawed and clawed at her skin, drawing blood.

The door crashed open and two men entered. She looked up at them imploringly, then she screamed again. In her delirium, all she could see were masks of disfigured red flesh, their mouths hanging open, drooping as if the flesh were melting from their jaws, their eyes were missing, displaying nothing more than fleshy hollow caverns.

'Demons!' she screamed, scurrying across the floor, trying to get away from them. 'Demons!'

Logan looked down at her, the pitiful creature squirming in the filth of human excrement and rotting hay, and yet he felt no pity, only blind hatred and disgust.

'Take her,' he spoke quietly to the man next to him.

'Are you sure?' Stephen turned back to him. 'They say her father is on his way, and she is still a preacher's daughter, he can make life very difficult for us if he chooses.'

'Look at her.' Logan's dark eyes fell on her, clawing at the ground, her eyes wild, and almost feral, 'she has condemned herself. She is in league with the Devil.'

'He will require proof,' Stephen replied.

'And he shall have it,' Logan answered coldly. 'Pick her up.'

Stephen hauled her off the floor, pinning her in his arms as she fought him wildly. With her back pinned to his chest she faced Logan as he slowly approached. His fingers moved to her bodice and began to unlace it deftly, exposing her soft white breasts. She growled and struggled against them, but Stephen's arms tightened around her, his eyes widening in arousal.

Logan reached out with cold hands and pinched the soft flesh of her breast, his fingers digging in so viciously the blood vessels beneath her skin burst and bruised. She howled in pain, but Stephen kept her immobile in his vice-like grip, the evidence of his excitement digging into her buttocks through her dress.

When Logan finally let go, and withdrew his hand an ugly red welt marred the snowy flesh of her breast. He quickly and efficiently re-laced her bodice.

The sound of horses outside split the tension filled air.

'I'll be back,' he growled, 'watch her.'

Logan disappeared and closed the door behind him. Stephen licked his lips, grinding his hips against her and leering.

'You know,' he whispered into her ear, his breath hot and foul, 'under all that filth you're a pretty girl. Lucky for you, I don't mind the dirt.'

Mary struggled as his hand fumbled roughly beneath her skirt and between her thighs, pinching her savagely. She screamed again, and tried to pull away from the torment of his fingers. She threw her head back, and felt a sickening crunch, as the back of her head collided with his nose.

He howled in pain and threw her to the hard ground, but with her hands bound she couldn't break her fall. She crashed to the ground and hit the side of her face painfully, causing her lip to split.

'You bitch,' Stephen hissed, bright blood spilling from between his fingers as he cupped his nose. Growling dangerously, he dived down on top of her, punching her hard and rolling her over onto her stomach. Dazed and unable to defend herself, he ripped up her skirt and fumbled with his belt.

'What the hell are you doing!' Logan roared as he pulled Stephen off her and threw him across the tiny room.

'She's a whore!' he hissed, the blood bubbling from between his lips.

Logan reached out and struck Stephen hard across the face, causing him to howl in pain at the pressure on his obviously broken nose.

'That may be true, but she is a devil's whore!' Logan ground out from between clenched teeth. 'No man of God should be touching her.'

Logan hauled her to her feet in disgust and dragged her from the room.

'What is going on!' the enraged voice of George Alcott thundered down the narrow passageway. 'Where are you taking my daughter?'

Logan nodded coolly in greeting as he approached the preacher, his hand wrapped in a death like grip around Mary's upper arm.

'She is guilty of witchcraft and is in league with the Devil himself. She will hang for her sins.'

'No!' his face reddened and his lips thinned, 'she will be examined by the authorities fully.'

'She has been examined,' Logan told him coldly, 'the evidence against her is sound.'

'I have seen no such proof,' he hissed.

'Then look for yourself,' Logan tore open her bodice revealing the ugly welt marring her naked breast.

George tried to avert his gaze from his daughter's bared chest but it was too late, he had seen the mark and sucked in a sharp breath.

'Behold the teat with which the Devil suckles,' Logan hissed. 'We have all witnessed her speaking with her familiars, demons we cannot see.'

Mary looked down, and saw one of the small spindly creatures clawing at her skirt, trying to climb up her body.

She screamed and began to struggle against Logan's grip.

'Get it off it me, it will bite me,' she cried, tearing at her skin once again, not caring that her body was exposed to the small crowd of people appearing around them.

Stephen had reappeared behind Logan, scowling murderously at the back of Mary's head. Behind George stood Cotton

Mather, having just taken over as Minister for Boston's North Church from his father Increase Mather. He had been visiting George and Margaret Alcott when word of their daughter's arrest had reached them.

'Witchcraft you say?' Cotton's eyes lit with curiosity as he stepped closer staring at the mark on Mary's breast. 'What other evidence is there?'

'She murdered my sister,' Logan replied flatly, his eyes dark with hatred. 'and she burned her body upon the instruction of her devil master.'

'Is this true girl?' Cotton asked.

'Burning, burning, burning bright, or devil catch you by morning's light,' she began to laugh hysterically. 'She is free, he freed her.'

'Who did?'

'The man with dark hair,' she cackled, 'he disappeared…he made her disappear.'

'Well it seems quite clear the girl has been driven mad by the devil she chose to serve,' Cotton replied piously.

'Forgive me for interrupting,' a smooth cool voice spoke up from behind Cotton.

Cotton stepped to the side and a tall man with burning dark eyes and dark hair stepped forward, his collar crisp and white against the stark black of his coat, as he clutched a thick book to his chest.

'Ah Nathaniel,' Cotton nodded, 'I wondered where you were. Well speak up, you know I value your council.'

'Like I said, forgive me if I speak out of turn,' he inclined his head and when he spoke his voice was soft and humble, but as his head rose and his black eyes locked with Logan's, they seemed to sparkle with suppressed mirth. His gaze dipped to Mary's mark, lingering for a moment before flickering back to Logan. A ghost of a smile whispered across his lips before it disappeared, almost as if he knew what Logan had done. 'It seems to me that the girl is indeed in league with demons, this kind of madness could be catching. I would suggest you deal with her quickly before others succumb to the same affliction.'

'Witchcraft here?' Cotton Mather stroked his chin thoughtfully. *'You're right of course Nathaniel, we must guard against such evil. Very well Beckett, deal with her quickly. We will accompany you and make sure that it is done.'*

Logan nodded and pulled Mary roughly past George Alcott.

'Father,' she reached out to him as she passed, *'father please help me…'*

George swallowed hard and turned his face away from his only child.

'FATHER!' she screamed as she was pulled out into the cold night air. She tripped and fell forward into the wet mud, the rain beating down on her, stinging her raw skin.

'Bring her,' Logan commanded, watching callously while she was roughly pulled from the ground and tossed carelessly into the back of a wagon.

Stephen climbed into the back and held her down roughly so she couldn't escape, watching Logan climb up onto the bench and take the reins. Cotton and Nathaniel stepped out into the downpour and the sky cracked with lightning. Adjusting his tall dark hat Cotton climbed up onto the seat next to Logan, while Nathaniel moved to the rear and climbed up into the wagon bed beside the still screaming girl.

Logan shook the reins and headed away from the jail. The journey did not take long, though Mary felt every bump and rut in the uneven surface of the road, that the wagons wheels travelled over. Her face was pinned to the damp, pungent smelling wood, which splintered and pricked her rapidly numbing flesh. By the time they had reached the huge tree on the hill, her screams had quieted and her body was wracked with violent tremors. She barely murmured, as she was lifted from the wagon, just stared lifelessly up into the sky watching the icy splinters of rain spearing down toward her face.

A small wooden stool was produced from the wagon and placed beneath the lowest, thickest, branch. A noose was placed around her neck and tightened, before the rope was slung over the branch and secured. Stephen lifted her up and stood her on the stool and the rope was tightened once again, not enough to cut off her air supply yet, but enough to pull her to her toes.

Cotton Mather and Stephen stood before her as witnesses, while Logan opened his bible and began to read. Nathaniel moved to stand beside him, watching his every move, his flat eyes flaring every now and then with a spark of interest. The night roared again with an ominous growl of thunder and lightning blazed angrily across the sky.

Logan looked up as he heard hoof beats above the howl of the wind and rain. His eyes narrowed as he tried to identify the rider approaching in the darkness.

Theo breathed heavily as he reined in Kane. He'd arrived at the jail only after they'd left and made haste to the hanging tree, praying he wasn't too late. He slid down from the saddle, his legs collapsing weakly beneath him. He drew in a breath and pushed himself painfully to his feet.

'STOP!' he roared angrily.

Logan's eyes narrowed and he continued to speak from memory, his gaze fixed on the sight of his brother struggling through the mud and rain, as he tried to reach the tree and his sentenced wife.

'Let her go!' Theo stumbled forward. He hadn't even worn his coat, his thin shirt was now plastered to his skin causing his fever wracked body to shake violently.

Cotton stepped into his path.

'It is done,' he told him firmly, 'her soul is damned. She must pay for her crimes.'

'Logan please,' Theo struggled weakly against Cotton as Stephen stood by, smirking at his feeble attempts to break free.

Logan ignored the heart wrenching pleas of his brother and continued to read, his voice almost lost in the violent turmoil of the storm.

'May God have mercy on your soul,' he whispered as Nathaniel kicked the stool out from under Mary's feet.

'NO!' Theo screamed, 'NO!'

He clawed weakly at Cotton his vision narrowing, and graying at the edges, as he saw Mary kicking and twitching at the end of a rope. When her body was finally still, swaying slightly and buffeted by the wind and rain, Theo sank to the ground exhausted and numb.

'He has been bewitched,' Cotton touched Theo's forehead. 'He burns with fever, we can only hope that now the witch is dead, he can fight whatever enchantment she inflicted him with.'

Cotton looked up into Logan's eyes.

'It is in the hands of God now,' he stared at Logan speculatively. 'You have proved yourself today Logan Beckett, you are truly a faithful servant of God. You placed what was right and just above the needs of your own brother, that takes a strong heart and an even stronger loyalty to God. I will not forget that.'

Logan held Cotton's gaze unaware of the amused smile on Nathaniel's lips, and as he watched an idea began to form in his mind.

Theo was drowning, unable to separate memory from dream. His body was wracked with a fever long since healed, as his mind tried to break the surface.

It felt like someone was trying to call him, why did that voice seem so familiar? Why did he yearn toward it with everything inside him? He blinked as the cool rain bathed his face and suddenly realized he was alone.

He sat up in confusion, his body didn't feel as weak as it had a moment before. He looked around. Cotton, Logan, Stephen and Nathaniel were all gone. Even his horse and the wagon were gone. He pulled himself to his feet noticing that he was able to move quite easily. His body felt normal, strong even. The rain slowed to a drizzle and the skies quieted. He looked up at the tree where Mary's lifeless body twisted and swung in the breeze.

His heart thumped painfully in his chest and his eyes filled with tears as he neared her. Her head hung forward limply, but as she twisted in the wind to face him her eyes opened slowly.

'Theo,' she whispered.

His heart jolted as his dead wife fixed her broken eyes on him.

'Theo,' she whispered again, 'this was not your doing. You tried to save me but it was not meant to be. I was supposed to die like this, nothing you could have done could have changed that.'

'I wanted so badly to save you,' his voice was a choked

whisper.

'I know but you can save me now, you have to let me go Theo.'

'How?'

'I'll forgive you, if that's what you need, but you need to forgive yourself.'

Theo sank to his knees in the damp sod. The pain in his chest was suffocating, the guilt and remorse eating him alive as he leaned forward and wept bitterly.

'There's nothing more I can do,' Mary shook her head as she turned to look at Olivia.

'There must be something,' Olivia replied as she watched Theo in concern. Although he'd stopped painting he sat, catatonic, staring at the canvas.

Mary shook her head. 'I was wrong.'

'What do you mean?' Olivia frowned.

'He doesn't need forgiveness, I think deep down he knows it wasn't his fault.'

'I don't understand,' she shook her head.

'What he needs is hope.'

Mary stepped back. 'He needs something to fight for,' she told Olivia softly, 'he needs you.'

'But he can't hear me.'

'Oh, I think he can, you just need to show him the way back. Don't give up on him Olivia, this is what you came here for, not to find him…to save him.'

Mary turned and moved back toward the window giving Olivia some space. She looked down at Theo staring vacantly at the paint splattered canvas. Her eyes caught on the half-finished painting and she looked, really looked and what she saw made her gasp in sudden realization.

He'd painted the hanging tree beneath a storm laden sky, but if she took a step back and looked beneath the surface there was a painting within the painting. The jagged slashes of lightning looked like long, wild, windswept hair, the voids in the clouds looked like eyes and the swirls of cloud themselves looked like the dips and planes of a face. It was her face, he'd painted her into his nightmare. Mary was right, he was reaching out to her, if she could just make him hear her.

'Theo,' she kneeled down next to him taking his paint stained hand.

She pulled in a deep breath. It was time to be honest with him and hoped that he heard her.

'Theo,' she spoke again, her voice a little stronger. 'I'm sorry for the things I said to you back in Mercy. I didn't mean it. I was angry, I was scared that if I gave in, if I loved you and let you in, that you would hurt me. That if I gave you that much power over me, you would break me. I'm still scared, only for a different reason now.'

She sucked in another breath, ruthlessly blinking back the tears threatening to fall.

'I'm scared of losing you. Theo, there is no me without you. None of this means anything to me if we're not together. So if you're trapped here for the rest of days, then I'm not moving either. I'm not leaving you Theo.'

Theo looked up at the sky, the rain had stopped completely and grey clouds swirled across the starlit sky, for a moment it almost looked like a woman's face.

Shaking his head in confusion he looked back to the tree. Mary was gone, as was the rope and the stool. He was completely alone, except he didn't feel alone. He raised his hand to his face, studying it in the pale moonlight, flexing his fingers. They tingled as if someone was grasping his hand.

A soft voice fluttered against the edge of his mind, a voice that seemed so familiar that his heart clenched in his chest. The voice came again. It was a woman and she was telling him she was sorry, that she was afraid.

He cast his gaze around looking for her, as some strange emotion grasped him by the throat, a sense of urgency and desperate kind of need. He had to find her, she was afraid and he would have given anything to take away her fear, to keep her safe.

'I'm not leaving you Theo…'

He had to find her, he had to tell her…

Something, what was it he had to tell her? He couldn't quite remember. He glanced down at his hand once again, he could almost feel her smaller hand in his, gripping tightly.

He turned his hand over noticing the strange blue, black and silver markings, which ran up from his hand all the way up his forearm to disappear under his shirt.

Suddenly he was assaulted by a reel of images flashing through his mind with such force, the intensity of it drove him to his knees. When he finally looked up, gasping for breath, only one word fell from his lips.

'Olivia…'

'A war is coming Theo,' Olivia sighed, 'everything we know is about to change. The people we love are going to get hurt. Everyone is looking to me to be some kind of hero, but I can't do it, I can't do it without you.'

She looked down at their joined hands, as the first tears began to fall, smearing the paint as it hit the skin of his hand.

'I crossed worlds for you Theo, I defied a God for you, and all because I love you.' Her heart burned hopelessly with grief and love, the sight of their joined hands blurred as her eyes filled with tears. 'I love you Theo, and I will continue to love you until the end of days, and probably beyond that.'

A choked sob escaped.

'Please,' she whispered brokenly, 'stay with me…'

'Always,' she felt a hand slide along her jaw and softly cup her cheek. She drew in a sharp breath and looked up into Theo's warm brown eyes.

'Livy,' he whispered.

His mouth crashed down on hers, swallowing her gasp of shock and relief. He stood abruptly, dragging her to her feet, the plastic chair he had been sitting on scraping loudly across the floor. Wrapping his arms around her, he pulled her in tightly to his body, drinking her in. The feel of her against him, the scent of her skin, the feel of her long dark silky hair in his hands, her mouth, her taste. He drank her in as if they'd been apart for years.

They broke apart breathing heavily, his forehead pressed to hers.

'I thought I'd lost you,' she breathed painfully.

'Never,' he brushed away her tears with the pad of his thumb leaving a small streak of paint across her cheek. 'We'll always find each other Livy, no matter what.'

'Theo,' another voice spoke softly.

He turned his head and his eyes widened.

'Mary?'

For a moment time seemed to stand still. The air was silent, filled with an strange kind of recognition. A quiet understanding passed between them.

'It's time to let her go Theo,' Olivia told him quietly.

She took his hand and raised it between them. Catching hold of the thin silver chain she showed it to him. His gaze followed it as it dropped down to the ground and trailed across the floor, where it wrapped firmly around Mary's ankle.

'You've been dragging her through time with you,' Olivia told him gently. 'Your guilt has kept her bound to you.'

Theo squeezed his eyes shut momentarily and shook his head.

'I didn't know,' he turned to look at her, 'I'm sorry.'

'It's time to let her go Theo.'

Theo grasped the delicate chain at his wrist and tugged causing the links to break. He held it out to Mary who watched as it began to disintegrate in a shower of tiny sparks until there was nothing remaining.

Her face broke into a smile, and she sighed deeply in relief. She began to glow brightly, her form blurring until they could no longer see her. The room was flooded with a pure, brilliant light. As it reached flash point they were forced to cover their eyes from the sheer blinding intensity. When it finally subsided and they looked up, Mary was gone and they were alone.

'Do you think she's at peace now?' Theo asked.

'I hope so,' Olivia smiled, 'what about you? Are you at peace now?'

Theo looked down at the woman in his arms and his embrace tightened.

'I am now,' he kissed her gently murmuring against her lips, 'because without you there's no me either.'

10.

Theo stared out across the lake as the sun dipped low on the horizon, his arms tightening around Olivia, almost as if he were afraid she'd disappear if he let go. They stood on a beach, backed by a small precipice overlooking the lake. From where they stood they could see Olivia's house on the opposite bank, nestled amidst the tree line. They could almost see the ruins of the cliff, which led up to The Boatman, the old abandoned art deco hotel where they had rescued the Ferryman.

'Where are we exactly?'

'On the north-west side of the lake. I used to come up here on my bike when I wanted to be alone…well mostly when I wanted to sulk.'

He looked behind them to the blankets spread out on the sand, and the small bonfire they'd laid out.

'So, this is the Otherworld?'

'Yeah, bit of a letdown isn't it?' she smiled.

'I don't know what I expected,' he pressed a kiss against her hair.

She turned in his arms so she was facing him, tracing his jaw lightly with her fingertips as a sigh escaped her lips.

'What is it?' he frowned.

'A lot has happened since…' she shook her head,

'since that night. We really should talk.'

'I don't really remember much,' he stroked her back gently, as if he couldn't help but maintain the contact between them. 'I remember everything up to the moment we were on the ice and that's where it gets a bit distorted.'

'Charon opened the gateway and it created a kind of vortex. All the spirits and creatures caught in Mercy were sucked back through, but you got caught at the tail edge of it and were pulled through with Mary.'

'What happened to you? Did you come through after me?'

Olivia shook her head. 'The ice started to break up and I couldn't hold my grip. I fell through.' She shuddered at the memory of the black, icy cold water engulfing her, and dragging her down into the crushing darkness below.

'God Livy,' Theo's grip on her tightened involuntarily, 'you could have drowned.'

'I very nearly did. I cracked my head on the ice as I went in. I was practically unconscious before I even hit the water.'

Theo's heart pounded heavily in his chest at the thought of her nearly dying alone in the icy water, because he wasn't there to protect her.

'Don't do that,' she smoothed the wrinkles between his brow. 'You couldn't have done anything even if you had been there.'

'How did you survive?'

'Charlotte,' she whispered, 'she saved me. She dragged me to the shore. So, there I was, half dazed, probably suffering from hypothermia, you were gone and I didn't know if you were dead, or…' her voice cracked slightly and she cleared her throat and tried again. 'I didn't know if I'd ever see you again. I was in pretty bad shape, I have to admit I gave some serious thought to just lying down and dying.'

'Jesus Liv,' he swore angrily.

'I didn't though,' she stroked his face soothingly. 'I

was lying there on the sand when Hades appeared.'

'Hades?' Theo repeated in confusion. 'What, THE Hades?'

'Why does everyone keep saying that,' she murmured, 'but yes THE Hades, as in the God of the Underworld and Charon's boss.'

'What did he want?'

'Front row seats to the Olivia and Theo show apparently.'

'Huh?'

'Hades knew that I was able to conjure Hell fire and he was curious about me. He offered to send me to the Otherworld to find you.'

'In exchange for?'

'Help in stopping my mother and Nathaniel from getting their hands on Infernum, but at the time, I think he mostly just wanted to see what I would do. It was kind of like an experiment. He said that there was a way out, a way back to our world, but I had to figure it out. I think he wanted to see how I would handle it.'

'So it was like a test?'

'Exactly.'

'And how did you do?'

'I threw a bit of a tantrum.'

Theo's brow rose questioningly.

'Okay, I haven't got to that bit yet,' she replied. 'Anyway, Hades sends me over to the Otherworld, and at first I'm a bit pissed because I figure, you know, that I'm still in Mercy and that he's having a good laugh at my expense. Then I finally get wise, and figure he really did send me to the Otherworld, but before he did, he gave me this.'

She pulled the small golden compass from the neck of her shirt. Theo took it gently as it was still slung around her neck on a delicate chain, and flicked open the face of it.

'It's a compass?' he tilted his head as he studied

the exquisite craftsmanship. 'It doesn't work?'

'Well apparently it does, I just haven't figured out how to use it yet.' She took it back and closed it before tucking it back into her clothes.

He stood and listened patiently as she filled him in on her meeting with Bridget and her aunt, and on finding Sam.

'Sam's here?' Theo repeated.

'Well, yes and no,' she replied. 'He is here, but he's not exactly the Sam we know. This is a younger version of himself. Not only does he not know us, but he hasn't figured out how to use all his powers yet.'

'I see,' he mused thoughtfully.

'There's something else,' she began. 'Just before I found you Hades came to me.'

'Why? I thought you said he was just watching you?'

'Well it certainly started out that way, but things have changed.'

'Why? What happened?'

'When Nathaniel and my mother escaped from The Boatman, apparently Nathaniel smuggled my mother into the Underworld so that they could find one of the Lost Crossroads. There are five of them scattered through the Underworld, and if any human finds one they can ask a boon of the Crossroad keeper.'

'A boon? You mean like a wish?'

She nodded.

'They're supposed to be very powerful. Nathaniel couldn't make a deal with one of them himself, because he's not human.'

'I take it that's what he is using your mother for?'

She nodded again. 'He seems to think that the keeper can either tell them the location of the book, or send them to it. I'm not entirely sure what he is planning. But I was supposed to go after them once I found you.'

'Supposed to?'

'That was part of my deal with Hades,' she blew out a breath. 'He would send me to the Otherworld to find you and once I had, I had to get to the Crossroad before them and prevent them from making a deal with the keeper.'

'So what's changed?'

'Nothing,' she shook her head. 'I still have to stop them from using the Crossroad to find the book. The problem is, for whatever reason, Nathaniel is destroying all the other Crossroads so that no one can use them.'

'Why would he do that?'

'I'm not sure, but what I do know is that by destroying something as old and powerful as the Crossroads, it has sent ripples out across all the worlds. It has upset the balance and it is being felt even in this world. I felt it when he destroyed the first Crossroad and the shock wave felt like an extremely powerful earthquake. Hades seems to think that the more Crossroads he destroys, the more it will tear away at the fabric between worlds, until every wall begins to break down.'

'And when that happens?'

'The Underworld will fall. Hell will spill out onto Earth and once those creatures get loose, what we saw in Mercy will pale in comparison to what will be unleashed.'

'God,' Theo raked his hand through his hair.

'I know, it's a hell of a head fuck,' she sighed, 'but…I gave my word. I can't go home, I have to stop Nathaniel and my mother.'

'How are you supposed to do that?' he frowned. 'If there are still another four Crossroads how are you supposed to figure out where they are, let alone which one Nathaniel will go for next?'

'Hades says there is a gateway hidden here, which will take me directly into the Underworld. Once I'm there I just need to figure out how to use the compass. It's the key to finding them, I know it is. I'm tied to my mother by blood, the oldest and most powerful magic there is. If I find her, I find Nathaniel.'

'Olivia,' he shook his head.

'I know it's a lot to take in. I'm not asking you to go with me. I can find a way to get you back to the real world. If there's a hidden gateway to the Underworld there must be a way back home.'

'You really think I'd leave you now,' his grip on her tightened angrily, 'after everything we've been through? Where you go, I go.'

'I don't want you to get hurt,' she whispered closing her eyes against the pain. 'I thought I'd lost you once before, and I can't go through that again. It felt like my insides had been ripped out, and there was this big dark pit inside me, which just got bigger and deeper.'

'Livy,' he whispered.

'I want you safe.'

'And you think I don't want the same thing for you? You think it wouldn't kill me to lose you?' He brushed his thumb across her lower lip, his voice low and intense. 'You crossed worlds to find me Livy, do you really think I wouldn't do the same for you. Neither of us wants the other one to get hurt. Well I can't give you any guarantees, but I can make you a promise that no matter what happens we will always find each other. No matter what,' he repeated. 'It's you and me Olivia, nothing will ever change that. Not even death will keep us from each other.'

She closed her eyes and pressed her forehead to his.

'Do you promise?'

'I swear,' his lips brushed hers.

Her arms snaked slowly around his neck and pulled him in closer as she sank into his kiss.

'Tell me again Livy,' he breathed against her mouth. 'Tell me the words.'

She didn't need to ask what he meant. It was the one thing he'd wanted to hear her say to him for months and when she'd finally told him, he had been too lost within the prison of his own mind to hear her.

'I love you Theo,' she breathed. 'I will love you until time no longer exists.'

He took her mouth again, walking her back slowly until he could lower her to the blanket. He stripped away her shirt so he could find her soft bare skin, which warmed under his touch. Her fingers tangled in his hair and she gazed up into his dark eyes.

'Say it again.'

She smiled against his mouth. 'I love you,' she whispered.

'God Livy,' he shuddered in her arms, 'you have no idea what you do to me.'

She dragged her fingers up his torso taking his shirt with them as she went, allowing him to pull away long enough to draw it over his head and discard it.

'Theo,' she breathed heavily, the words choking in her throat.

She wound her arms tightly around him, pulling him in impossibly close, so they were pressed warm skin to warm skin. He took her mouth once again, sinking down into that place where time slowed and nothing else existed but the two of them.

Everything felt different, so much sharper and more intense. His lips left hers and trailed down her throat to her collar bone, causing her to shiver and the fine hairs on her arms to raise. When he reached her breast and drew the tip into his hot mouth, she arched helplessly, unable to do anything but feel.

It was dizzying to know that he held this much power over her, that he was able to give so much pleasure. He switched to the other breast and her hands trailed down his chest to his stomach, scraping the skin lightly, causing him to bite down on her softly. She undid his jeans and pushed both them and his boxers over his lean hips before reaching down to wrap her hand around him. He released her breast on a gasp of pleasure, pressing his flushed forehead to her skin and unable to do anything but rock slowly into her firm grip.

Reluctantly he pulled away from her, far enough to strip the rest of the clothes from them and when they were both finally naked he crawled back up the length of her trembling body, nestling himself between her thighs.

'Say it again.'

'I love you,' she whispered as he plunged inside her deeply.

He stilled inside her, holding himself at the deepest point, breathing heavily and trembling at the intensity of her body squeezing him so tightly. His lips brushed against her lightly once and then twice. He rolled his hips slowly, causing her to gasp once again at the wave of pleasure. His tongue swept in and he tasted her, savoring the moment as if it would last forever. She wrapped her legs tightly around his hips, pulling him in closer as her arms tangled around his neck keeping him anchored to her. He slid his arms underneath her and pulled her in just as closely until they were one tangle of long limbs and flushed skin, unable to tell where one ended and the other began.

There was an uncertainty between them, an undercurrent of desperation that hadn't been present before. The unspoken fear between them of what was yet to come and whether or not they would both survive it, but surrounding it all was the overwhelming love between them, which they had both finally embraced. It was empowering, the feeling they could do anything as long as it was the two of them together. Her fingers dug into his skin as her core tightened viciously and the pleasure ripped through her like a tornado, leaving utter devastation in its wake.

'I love you,' he breathed against her ear, 'always…' He felt her clamp down and could do nothing but follow her down into oblivion, spilling himself deep inside her.

At some point the sky had changed from a violent swirl of purple and pink to a clear star lit canvas. Olivia settled comfortably, sitting between Theo's legs with her back to his chest, as he wrapped a blanket around them both and folded her sweetly into his arms. The fire they had laid out earlier now danced and snapped merrily, bathing them both with warmth and flickering light.

'What are you thinking about?' Theo's voice rumbled quietly against her ear as she absently traced the tattoo along his forearm.

She sighed loudly. 'I was just wishing we could stay here forever, in this moment, just you and me.'

He smiled against her hair. 'Forever is a long time love, you'd be bored after the first decade.'

'That's true' she chuckled. 'Fine, I'll amend that statement to, I wish we could disappear somewhere where no one could find us.'

'This is about Hades, isn't it?'

'Not just about him,' she frowned, entwining her fingers with his and studying their joined hands absently. 'I gave my word, which means I have to face Nathaniel and...'

'Your mother?' he guessed.

He felt her nod silently.

'You don't have to do this alone Livy,' he untangled his hand from hers and grasped her chin, tilting her head so she could see him. 'It's going to be alright.'

'Is it?'

'We are going to deal with Nathaniel and Isabel.'

'And then?'

'And then we're going to live happily ever after.'

She laughed lightly. 'There's no such thing as happily ever after.'

'Alright then,' he smiled, 'would you settle for growing old together?'

She turned more fully in his arms so she could

look into his eyes.

'Yes,' she murmured, reaching out to stroke his face. 'I'd settle for that.'

He brushed her lips gently with a soft kiss filled with promise. Before, such a sweet gesture would have sent her running, but now she held onto it like a lifeline.

'So,' Theo smoothed her rumpled hair back from her face, 'now we need to decide what our next move is.'

'We need to find the gateway to the Underworld, but more importantly we need to figure out how to find Nathaniel and my mother when we get there.'

'Not only that,' Theo frowned, 'we need to figure out a way to stop them, if we manage to reach them in time. When we went up against them at The Boatman, your Hell fire had no effect on Nathaniel and neither did my knife.'

She rubbed her face tiredly. 'God, if we ever manage to pull this off it will be a damn miracle.'

'Is there any way we can summon Diana?' he asked, 'she's helped you a few times now. She seems to have taken a certain interest in your wellbeing. Perhaps she would be inclined to help us?'

'Even if she was, I don't know how to call her. Every time she appeared it was to further her own agenda, not at my instigation.'

'Perhaps we should speak with Bridget then?' he suggested.

'That's probably the best option at the moment,' she agreed.

A sudden rumble beneath them had them pulling apart abruptly.

'What was that?' Theo frowned.

The ground trembled again.

'Damn it,' Olivia hissed. 'Last time this happened Nathaniel destroyed a Crossroad.'

'You think he has destroyed another one?' Theo grabbed his jeans and jerked them back on, standing up as he pulled his shirt over his head.

Olivia shook her head. 'The tremors aren't strong enough, trust me you'll know it when he destroys another one.' She grabbed her own jeans, lifting her hips off the blanket to slide them on, before grabbing her bra and shirt. 'It could mean that he's getting close to one. Either way we need to move soon. There are only four more Crossroads, and with the destruction of each one, the more damage the Veil between worlds will sustain.'

Theo leaned down and yanked his boots on.

'We should probably head to Bridget's house then and see what she knows.'

Olivia nodded, pulling on her own boots. She reached up and grasped Theo's hands as he leaned down to help her up. She swayed dizzily on her feet as soon as she was standing, stumbling against him.

'Are you alright?' he asked, holding onto her tightly.

Olivia drew in a shaky breath as the spinning feeling began to subside.

'I'm fine,' she breathed against his chest, 'just a little dizzy.'

He pulled back and tilted her head so he could look into her eyes, concern etched on his face.

'Are you sure?'

'I'm okay.'

'When was the last time you slept?'

'I have no idea,' she sighed. 'I don't even know how long we've been here. Honestly Theo, I'm fine. I'm sure it's just the stress of everything catching up with me.'

Frowning, he bent down to scoop up the blankets and Olivia's backpack, before wrapping his arms around her tightly.

'Hold on,' he told her softly.

'What?'

He closed his eyes the way Olivia had shown him and thought about the place he wanted to be. Their surroundings blurred, and shifted, and suddenly they found themselves back in their bedroom at Olivia's house.

'What?' she looked around in confusion, 'why have you brought me here?'

'Because,' he dropped the blankets and backpack down on the chair by the fireplace and scooped her up into his arms. Pulling down the bedding, he laid her down and pulled off her boots. Kicking off his own he climbed up onto the bed next to her and wrapped her up in his arms.

'Theo,' she struggled to sit up, 'we don't have time for this. We have to find Bridget.'

'We can do that tomorrow.'

'We might not have tomorrow.'

'I doubt Nathaniel will manage to find and destroy four Crossroads in the space of a few hours. You're exhausted, physically, emotionally and mentally,' he pulled her back down and wrapped his arms around her once again. 'You can save the world tomorrow, but for now you need some sleep.'

'You're so bossy,' she yawned against him.

He smiled as he felt her slowly relaxing into his arms.

'Yes I am,' he murmured. 'Sleep now love, tomorrow will come soon enough.'

He could tell by her lax body and rhythmic breathing that she had already drifted into sleep. However, sleep would not come so easily for him. He'd spent God knows how long trapped in a dreamlike state, while she had searched for him and worried for him. She'd faced down a God, and learned that she had a terrifying destiny in the same breath. A destiny that could cost her, not only her own life, but those of the ones she loved most dearly, and yet here she was, exhausted and drained but still ready to fight, to do what was right.

He looked down at her, stroking the soft dark satin of her hair, and tracing the soft curve of her lip. He marveled at her, not quite believing she was really his. She was fierce, a warrior, even if she didn't know it. She may have thought she was chosen because of her ability to control Hell fire, but the truth was, it was her strength, and love, and loyalty, which made her so special, even if she couldn't see it.

Satisfied she was deeply asleep, he slipped from the bed and padded over to the window, staring out at the lake glistening in the moonlight. The ground trembled softly again under his feet, and the pictures on the wall rattled quietly.

He was worried about what she had told him and he knew they had barely glanced the surface yet. None of them knew for sure what Nathaniel's end game was. They had been so certain it was Isabel using the demon, but it was now becoming obvious that it was the other way around.

Nathaniel was allowing Isabel to believe she held the upper hand, but he was manipulating her. The more unstable she became, the more danger she was to her daughter.

He turned back and looked at Olivia's sleeping form. The darkness was coming. He could feel the oppressive weight of it in the air. Whatever Nathaniel's plan was, he was going to do whatever was necessary to achieve it, even if it meant destroying this world, and theirs, and everyone in between. Drawing in a shaky breath, he turned back to the window, leaning heavily against the frame with one arm, his face bathed in pale moonlight.

Nathaniel was going to come after Olivia sooner or later. He had to, she was the only one standing between him and the book. He knew it and so did Nathaniel.

Hell, even Hades and Diana knew it. They'd all put her in the line of fire, not caring that it might cost her life. His fist involuntarily tightened in frustration, this time it was going to be different. He was going to learn everything he could about the demon Nathaniel and the next time they faced him he would make damn sure he killed the bastard, because one thing was for sure, if Nathaniel wanted Olivia, he was going to have to go through him first.

11.

Olivia stepped down from her front porch and looked up at the sky. It was back to the strange bruised daylight, but there was something else, something different about it. She glanced across the sky, and a dark ominous shadow caught her attention. She squinted slightly, shading her eyes with her hand as she tried to make out what it was. It was too dark to be a cloud; it was almost pitch black and stretched out, far back over the choppy waters of the lake.

She heard Theo close the door and jog down the steps after her. He picked up her backpack from the ground by her feet and slung it over one shoulder.

'There's no food in the house, but I did refill your water bottle. You should drink something.'

'I'm fine,' she murmured absently. 'Look at that, what do you think that is?'

Theo looked up to where she was pointing.

'It's a…' he frowned, his eyes narrowing as he looked closer. 'I don't know…what is that?'

It seemed to be rippling, like a wave lapping at the shore. A sudden gust of wind pulled and tugged at Olivia's hair, brushing it forward into her face.

That was also strange. Ever since she'd arrived in the Otherworld, there had been no deviation in the weather at all. The temperature had stayed the same; there was no bright sunshine, no rain, not so much as an errant breeze. Now all of a sudden a current of air swept in from nowhere and tugged at her clothes, buffeting her body slightly.

Olivia glanced across at the small cabin nestled amongst the tree line and saw the door open.

'We should go,' she tugged lightly at Theo's sleeve. 'Looks like Bridget is expecting us.'

Theo turned and looked across the small expanse of grass to the small wooden cabin. It gave him a start to see such a familiar looking place. The Salem of his childhood had been filled with such dwellings. He saw a familiar looking woman step into the doorway, wearing a long dark dress and drying her hands on an apron, before leaning casually against the door frame waiting for them.

He felt Olivia's small warm hand slip into his and give a little tug to get his feet moving. They walked slowly across the grass, hands linked comfortably, as the wind tugged and pulled at them. As they neared the doorway the sight of Bridget gave him a jolt. She was almost the spitting image of Olivia. It seemed the West line bred true, with a strong familial likeness passed to each generation.

'I see you found him then?' Bridget spoke softly as they stepped onto the covered porch.

'Bridget,' Olivia greeted her quietly, 'I owe you an apology. Last time I saw you I was pretty rude. I was frustrated, and I took it out on you. It wasn't fair and for that I apologize.'

Bridget nodded slowly after a moment.

'Unfortunately that temper and stubbornness runs true in our family,' she looked past Olivia to Theo and smiled. 'Hello Theo, it's been a long time.'

'Yes it has,' he murmured, studying her closely. The last time he had seen her was the night he had saved Bridget and her sister Hester, when they had been just children.

'Well come in, come in you two.'

She stepped back to allow them to enter, but as her gaze once again fell on Olivia she paused. Her eyes ran down the length of Olivia and then back up again. Her gazed narrowed, before once again meeting Olivia's eyes.

'What?' Olivia frowned.

'Nothing,' Bridget murmured, but as she stepped back a small smile curved the corner of her mouth.

Theo pulled Olivia into the small welcoming cabin out of the wind, which had now reached a howling pitch. Bridget turned to close the door, casting an ominous glance up at the blackness in the sky before joining them. A fire burned merrily in the hearth and a small pot bubbled on a large hook suspended over the flames.

'Sit down,' she pointed them toward the freshly scrubbed table and reached up for two bowls.

Doing as they were told, they watched as she retrieved the pot from the fire and ladled out two deep bowlfuls of porridge, to which she added a generous dollop of honey and a pinch of cinnamon.

Olivia's stomach rumbled in appreciation as she picked up her spoon, even though she'd never particularly liked porridge. The stuff her Aunt Evie used to make when she was a kid had resembled a thick grey glue, but the glorious scent wafting from the bowl made her stomach clench and her mouth water.

'So good,' she sighed after spooning some into her mouth.

Bridget took a seat at the table next to them and smiled as they ate.

'Where did you learn to cook like this?'

'My mother,' Bridget smiled. 'As the older sister it was always my job to care for Hester and even if I was older by only a few minutes I always felt like she was my responsibility, especially after mother was killed.'

'What was she like?' Olivia asked, 'Hester, I mean.'

'She was sweet hearted and kind, but so serious.

Maybe that came from being able to see what was yet to come. She understood the great burden on our family.'

'You said the book was a curse on our family.'

'Aye, that it is. Are you finally ready to listen?'

Olivia glanced across at Theo who squeezed her hand under the table gently. She turned back to Bridget and nodded slowly.

'Tell me everything.'

She leaned in and folded her hands neatly on the table.

'Our history is a long one,' she began quietly, 'and to fully understand everything that came after, you must first understand the 'why'. For that we must go back to the very beginning, to Ancient Greece in the year 128 AD, and to a woman named Althethea. She was married to a Roman by the name of Gaius, who had been appointed by the Senate as Governor of Eboracum, and so they journeyed to their new home in Albion.'

'Albion?' Theo frowned.

'It was what England was called before the Romans arrived and Eboracum, unless I'm mistaken, would be York,' Olivia replied quietly.

Bridget nodded and continued.

'Unhappy in her arranged marriage and homesick for her native Greece, she befriended one of the slaves in her husband's house, a young Celt of Irish descent by the name of Áedán. Well, to cut a long story short, they fell in love and when Áedán's brother Èibhir came searching for him and helped him escape, he took Althethea with him. In the dead of night they stole away, like thieves, across the wall to the wilds of Scotland, and within a year their daughter Carrigan was born.'

'Carrigan?' Olivia interrupted, 'you mentioned her before. You said all this was her fault somehow.'

'I'm just coming to that part,' she answered patiently. 'Althethea's husband Gaius tracked them down and killed both her and Áedán. Carrigan survived because her uncle Èibhir hid her. She was raised by him in a small isolated Scottish clan. Once she was grown Carrigan had a brief affair with a Irish traveler named Eòin, and bore him a daughter of her own, whom she named Bronagh.

It is here our story begins. The murder of Carrigan's parents hurt her very deeply, even more knowing that Gaius not only survived, but went unpunished. As the years passed she became bitter and hateful. Driven by the desperate need for vengeance she sought out an old witch who lived deep in the Highlands and begged her to teach her the secrets of magic.'

'I assume she did?'

Bridget nodded sadly.

'But, as I tried to tell you before Olivia, it is not the magic itself that is light or dark, but the witch. The more that hate and bitterness took root in Carrigan's heart, the darker her magic became. Consumed by the need for revenge, she used an ancient and forbidden summoning magic, and raised a demon lord named Nathaniel, who tells her there is a way she could have power beyond her wildest dreams.'

'The book,' Olivia whispered.

'Yes, Nathaniel told her of Infernum's location. It was hidden deep in the mountains and protected by a spell he couldn't break. Only a child of pure heart and spirit could cross the protective line and retrieve the book. The problem was, Carrigan knew her heart was no longer pure, if it ever had been.'

'She used her own child, didn't she?' Theo asked quietly.

Bridget sighed. 'She took Bronagh to the mountains, tiny little thing that she was, barely more than six years old. They found the primitive and crude temple, where the book had lain undisturbed for countless centuries. Bronagh did as her mother bade and crossed the line, retrieving the book. But Nathaniel betrayed her and tried to take the book for himself.'

'Big surprise there,' Olivia muttered.

'So what happened?' Theo frowned.

'Bronagh. She took the book. Carrigan told her to run to the temple as it was the only place Nathaniel couldn't enter. He killed Carrigan, but he couldn't get to the child.'

'God,' Theo frowned. 'How did she escape?'

'Diana,' she answered simply.

'The Goddess?'

'Diana appeared to the girl and alongside her was the God Herne, in the form of a great white stag. They waited until nightfall and under the cover of darkness Diana cast an illusion to fool Nathaniel. She made him think the girl was trying to escape to the East, and when he took off in pursuit they spirited the child away to the West, all the way down to the coast. Once they arrived at the shore, Diana summoned a Silkie.'

'What's a Silkie?' Theo asked.

'They are from Irish folklore,' Olivia told him, 'magical creatures who resemble seals. It's said that when they shed their pelts they can take the form of a human.'

Bridget nodded in approval.

'Aye, Fintain was his name and he was but a boy himself. He stole Bronagh away across the cold, icy waters to Ireland, the land of her father, grandfather and great uncle, under the watchful eye of Diana and Herne. The years passed by and Fintain stayed with Bronagh for he had come to love her deeply, and from them came the next child of our line.'

'Wait a minute,' Olivia held up her hand. 'Are you seriously telling me, we're descended from a witch and a Silkie?'

'Yes I am,' Bridget smiled.

'That is so cool,' Olivia laughed in delight. 'No wonder I like swimming so much.'

'So, Bronagh kept the book?' Theo frowned in confusion, 'or did she leave it in the temple?'

'She couldn't leave it in the temple, for it had been disturbed. The book was awake and it was calling for its Guardian.'

'Guardian?'

'I don't know the exact origins of the book, but I do know that it had a Guardian once, long ago. The Guardian is the only one who could read it and understand its secrets. Diana knew it could not be left in the temple where anyone could find it, so she gave it to the girl and told her that as she was the one who had awoken it, it was her responsibility and that of all who came after her. She was told to keep the book safe, but never to use it. She understood that she was its keeper only, until the day came that its rightful owner lay claim to it.'

'So what happened to Nathaniel?'

'He knew from that point on our family were tied to the fate of the book. In order to find the book, he had to find the descendants of Bronagh's bloodline. So he stalked the earth looking for any trace, but we always managed to be one step ahead of him. Whenever he got too close the family would move again. When they eventually left Ireland they headed to England, where they stayed until the great migration across the water to the Americas. There they joined the colonists and settled in the Massachusetts Bay Colony, which is how they eventually ended up in Salem.'

'So Nathaniel has been walking the earth for the best part of a thousand years?' Theo asked.

'That I know of,' Bridget replied, 'but he has been searching for the book for much longer. There's more though. How much do you know of his brother Seth?'

'Not much admittedly,' Olivia replied, 'only that he's Nathaniel's brother and that Hades has him trapped in a prison in the Underworld.'

'They are more than just brothers, they are two halves of a whole. One cannot be fully complete without the other and together they will be unstoppable. If

Nathaniel ever gets his hands on the book the first thing he will do is free his brother and if that happens, not even the Gods themselves will be able to stop them.'

'God,' Theo breathed.

'Then we will just have to make sure he never gets his hands on the book,' Olivia replied.

'We should...' Theo began speaking, but broke off suddenly as the ground beneath them began to shake violently.

Something behind them toppled from its shelf and smashed on the ground. The simple homely furniture began to rattle and shake. A terrible grinding sound began and the house itself began to toss and shake so violently they were almost thrown from the chairs they sat in. Suddenly, there was a loud splintering sound above them and as the main support beam began to give way a large crack appeared in the roof.

'Get down,' Theo yelled above the grinding of bowing wood. Both Bridget and Olivia crawled under the stout wooden table followed by Theo. There they held on tightly, while the house began to tear itself apart.

Nathaniel sucked in a deep, pleasure filled breath as he felt the blade slide into the warm, soft body with a soft hiss of metal, feeling the point of the blade clink and spark slightly when it passed straight through and embedded itself in the moss covered stone.

The man looked up at him, his wide green eyes filled with shock and pain. His mouth hung open in a silent scream as blood bubbled from the side of his suddenly lax lips. Although it was unnecessary, Nathaniel twisted the blade viciously, causing the body to twitch and arch under his slick, blood soaked hands. A final sigh of breath escaped the man's mouth and it was done.

He yanked the knife out, making the corpse jerk once again. Nathaniel laid his hand over the wound in the dead man's chest and felt warmth flood his hand. The tattered flaking skin of the flesh prison Isabel had forced him into glowed like the embers of a fire. He absorbed the rush of energy and felt the high, as the power rushed through his body, weakening his prison and strengthening his own body trapped beneath.

When he was done he looked down at the keeper of the second Crossroad. No longer a powerful being of ancient power, he lay at the center of the Crossroad he was bound to, callously discarded and pitiful. Now nothing more than an empty decomposing carcass for the filthy parasitic creatures of the Underworld to feed upon.

He stepped back and flexed his hands, reveling in the euphoric feeling of power spiking through his body. Isabel's feeble power pulsed once through the dead flesh she had stitched to his true form and settled into a dull itch. He reached down at the flap of skin on his forearm and grasped it with his fingers, tearing a long strip off and revealing a raw wound underneath. His eyes, one dead and colorless and one a cloudy blue glanced down to the gaping wound in his chest where Olivia had pierced his body with Hell fire, and he grinned.

The little bitch had done him a favor without even realizing it. By breaching the fleshy prison, she had hastened its decomposition, weakening the binding magic Isabel had used. He turned back to the small puddle of water which had pooled in a crack at the edge of the crossroad and caught his reflection. The wound at his throat, which Theo had inflicted with the strange blade, caused him more pain than he would like to admit. It had seared through his skin and although it hadn't killed him it slowly ate away at his flesh, like one of the filthy human diseases. The wound had blackened and spread down his neck and up to his jaw where the flesh had rotted away and partially dissolved the bone of his jaw, leaving an unpleasant cavern like void in his face.

Still, it wouldn't be long until he freed himself from the disgusting, rotting, pig flesh and emerged in his true form. The power he stole from the corpses of the Crossroad keepers were not only sustaining him, but feeding him, making him stronger.

He'd lied to Isabel, he'd convinced her that it was prudent to destroy all the other Crossroads so no one else could use the advantage against them. It hadn't been hard to convince her, she was obsessed by her desire for the book. It consumed her every waking thought, making her easier and easier to manipulate as she descended into madness. At this point it would be very easy to dispose of her. The binding magic she had used to keep him under control and unable to harm her, had long since crumbled, but he wouldn't kill her, not yet. She may still be of use to him.

They all underestimated him. He smiled in cold amusement through the ruin of his jaw. They all scrambled, like tiny little pieces on a chess board, unaware that every move they made was predestined because of the events he had set in motion thousands of years ago. If there was one thing he knew it was infinite patience. The pieces were finally moving into place, he was so close. Gaining possession of Infernum was just the beginning. Even Hades, who at this moment hastened to consolidate his armies against him, had no clue as to his true intent.

Turning back to Isabel who watched calmly from the edge of the stone walkways, he moved slowly toward her. Her gaze flicked to the corpse lying sprawled at the center of the Crossroad and then back to Nathaniel.

'Enjoying yourself?' she asked acidly.

'More than you could possibly imagine Isabel,' he smiled coolly.

'I still don't understand why we have to destroy all the Crossroads? Why can't we just make a deal with a keeper and go after the book?'

'Patience Isabel,' he replied smoothly, 'you are in Hades domain now. Do you really want him coming after you, trying to stop you from getting your hands on

Infernum. After all you've suffered, all you've sacrificed, do you want to risk Hades' interference?'

She watched him with dark unfathomable eyes.

'If we destroy all the Crossroads first, we not only minimize the risk of anyone following us, but we destabilize the Underworld and keep them busy. It's a win-win situation.'

'So you say.'

His mouth curved as he watched Isabel turn to the Crossroad, studying it thoughtfully.

A circular cover stone sat at its center, with its former keeper grotesquely sprawled across it. Four roads struck out from the center in the direction of the four compass points. Each road was made up of heavy stone slabs, each etched with strange spidery symbols, and deeply embedded with moss and lichen.

Each road ended in a huge, dark stone archway and each of the four archways were connected by a tall circular stone wall, which encompassed the whole Crossroad. Blackened thorny vines crisscrossed the tall boundary walls in a vicious cruel looking lattice.

It looked like the briar patch which guarded Sleeping Beauty's slumbering castle, Isabel thought absently, only this wasn't Disney and there sure as hell wouldn't be a happy ending. Well…she amended her thoughts, there wouldn't be a happy ending for anyone else. But for her, once she got her hands on the book, she would have everything she had ever wanted, everything that was ever meant to be hers.

Nathaniel knew he had her the moment her mouth curved into a smile and she turned back to him.

'Destroy it,' she whispered.

'Your wish is my command,' he bowed mockingly.

He pooled his power carefully. He couldn't risk letting her know how weakened the body she had created for him was; it wasn't time yet.

He could have easily destroyed it himself now.

After absorbing the life force of two Crossroad keepers he could feel the strength and power roaring through his veins, but it would make Isabel too suspicious. So instead he raised his hands and used his power to unlock the four huge stone gateways.

The great doorways burst open as huge plumes of black shadow rushed in like thick, inky looking tentacles. When the shadow finally dissipated the Crossroad was filled with men and women of all ages and descriptions, each dressed in black, with eyes the color of rubies.

'Nathaniel,' a young man who looked no older than twenty human years stepped forward. 'You summoned us?'

He tried to keep the disgust from his face as he took in the decaying rotten flesh of the body Nathaniel had been forced to wear. His gaze raked across to Isabel and his lips peeled back as if he were about to give a feral snarl.

'That's enough Zachary,' Nathaniel replied calmly. He'd known Zachary for countless centuries and he was one of his most trusted lieutenants. In fact, Zachary had joined him on earth at Constantinople, and Nathaniel had been forced to concede that, when it came to finding the most inventively excruciating ways to cause pain to humans, Zachary far outstripped himself. Watching the young looking demon working had been absolutely breath taking. He could tell, even now, the outrage he held in by iron hard control only. The slight tension in his body, the subtle flare of his nostrils and the glare in his eyes said that he would love nothing more than to strap the human witch to a table and go to work on her. It was an interesting idea, Nathaniel mused absently. He'd always intended to deal with Isabel West himself when she had outlived her usefulness, but the thought of handing her over to Zachary and watching the little Maestro working his magic was…slightly arousing.

'What do you require?' Zachary asked quietly.

'Break every last stone, not one single symbol

must remain.'

'As you wish,' he turned to the others and nodded.

They fanned out across the Crossroad, each choosing a stone inscribed with an ancient symbol and began to smash them all one by one. Bright blue light flooded the space with each stone broken; the ground trembled and shook, filling the air with a loud grinding sound. It was as if the ground itself were protesting the desecration and destruction of such an ancient place of power. Once the last stone had been smashed the demons disappeared, coalescing once again into shadow and vanishing through the doorways, leaving Isabel and Nathaniel standing in the ruins of the Crossroad, with Zachary watching them closely.

The muted blue glow beneath the cracked stones seemed to throb once, then twice, faltering like a dying heartbeat, before finally fading into darkness leaving the Crossroad as cold and dead as its keeper.

'What are your orders?' Zachary asked.

'They remain the same as before,' he answered quietly. He threw a quick glance in Isabel's direction but she wasn't paying attention. Her gaze was once again fixed on the, now silent, ruins. 'You know what to do.'

Zachary nodded and he too disappeared.

'Isabel?' Nathaniel called.

She stared silently, giving no indication she'd even heard him.

'Isabel?' he repeated.

She turned to him slowly, preoccupied, as if her mind was somewhere else entirely.

'Are you ready?'

'For what?'

His deformed mouth curved into a terrifyingly clown-like smile.

'To find the next Crossroad.'

12.

'Roni wait up,' Jake frowned, as he cast his flashlight in front of him. 'Damn it, where are you?'

'I'm right here,' she sighed in exasperation. 'I don't need you to hold my hand you know. I told you I was perfectly capable of doing this on my own.'

'Yeah, I'm going to let you go hiking through the woods in the middle of the night with a soul stealing demon on the loose,' he replied sarcastically.

'He probably isn't out here you know, the pickings are too slim. If its souls he's after, he's going to stick close to town, where it's like shooting fish in a barrel.'

'You don't know that,' he frowned, his face concealed by the darkness. 'He has to be hiding out somewhere. For all you know he could have a secret lair around here.'

'A secret lair?' she replied in amusement as she pointed her flashlight down at the compass she held in her palm.

'Well, you know what I mean.'

'So you what?' the amusement flipped to irritation as she adjusted her direction, 'came out here to protect me?'

'Of course I did,' he sighed. 'In case you hadn't

noticed I'm a cop. That's what cops do, protect people.'

She wasn't sure why that statement annoyed her even more. No, to tell the truth she knew exactly why it bugged the crap out of her, because it was painfully obvious he didn't feel the same way about her as she felt about him.

It was embarrassing and just plain depressing. After kissing her boneless he'd just shrugged it off and pretended it didn't happen. In fact, she was beginning to wonder if it had happened at all, or whether she'd just imagined it in the first place.

'So, you're just out here protecting me as your civic duty,' she replied in disgust.

'Not just,' he jogged to catch up with her, grabbing her arm and turning her to face him. 'Christ Roni, would you just listen?'

She stopped and turned to face him, pointing her flashlight at an angle, so it lit up both their faces. It was hard to talk to someone when you couldn't see their expressions.

'Look,' he frowned, 'yes I would protect you as I would anyone else, because it's my job, but also because that's who I am. I can't help wanting to keep you safe. I'm sorry if that pisses you off, but I'm not going to change. It's not because I think you're not capable, it's because I can't stand the thought of you getting hurt.'

He blew out a frustrated breath and tipped his head back so he could see the stars peeking through the canopy of trees.

'Stop saying such sweet things before I end up liking you more than I already do…'

He turned his gaze back on her, a smile playing on his lips.

'I like you too.'

'What?' Roni whispered, the color draining from her face.

'I said I like you too,' he clarified, seeing her

puzzled expression. 'You told me to stop saying sweet things to you because its making you like me.'

'I didn't say that,' her eyes widened in shock.

'Yes you did, I heard you,' he frowned in confusion.

'No,' she repeated firmly. 'I thought it, I didn't say it.'

'That's not...'

His voice trailed off.

'Wonder if it's part of his gift he unlocked the night he cast the circle. Perhaps it was a dormant gift, which has been awoken...'

'What?' Veronica asked, 'why are you looking at me like that?'

'You were just wondering if it was a dormant gift, which was woken up when I cast the circle.'

Her mouth fell open.

'Holy shit!' Jake breathed, his eyes widening. 'Do you know what this means?'

'What?' Roni whispered.

'I'm Charles Xavier.'

Her expression hardened and she shook her head. 'I don't think you're taking this seriously.'

'I'm very serious.'

'Patrick Stewart or James McAvoy?' she asked after a moment.

'Now who's not taking it seriously?' he raised a brow in amusement.

'I can't believe we're having this conversation,' she sighed.

'And McAvoy obviously,' Jake replied. 'I'm too young to lose all my hair.'

He raked his hand through his hair, shaking his head dramatically and pouting as if he were part of a shampoo commercial.

She couldn't help the laugh that bubbled out.

'So, are we good?' he asked.

She rolled her eyes, a small smile still hovering

over her lips as she sighed in defeat.

'Yeah we're good,' she turned back toward the trail. 'Just stay out of my head.'

'Sorry, can't make any promises,' he fell into step next to her. 'I haven't a clue how to control it although it does answer a few questions.'

'How so?' they walked along companionably.

'I've been hearing some very strange conversations around town lately.'

'Like what?' she asked curiously.

'Like Mr Wilson wondering if he should order some red stilettos online.'

'That's not so strange.'

'In his size?'

'Oh,' she chuckled.

'And Marisa Thompson wondering if Laurel Martin stuffs her training bra with tissue. Lewis Clark thinking his wife would look good with butt implants. Josh Anderson wondering what dog food tastes like. Lonnie Wright wondering if her husband gets a vasectomy whether or not he'll still be able to get an erection and trust me you do not want to know what the sweet little eighty-year-old Ms Betty Nelson wants to do to Todd Roberts, who is forty-five years her junior.'

Roni let loose another laugh.

'Seriously I'm traumatized, I may require counseling.'

She smiled at him even though he couldn't see her in the darkness.

'I'd say maybe it was just a fluke, but now I'm guessing you're stuck with it.'

'At first I thought I was going crazy.'

'I'd say given everything that's happened recently, you reading peoples' minds ranks pretty low on the Mercy crazy scale.'

'Maybe,' he mused, 'but I feel like Mel Gibson in the film 'What women want'. I can see it becoming a real pain in the ass.'

'Well maybe there's some way to switch it back off,' Roni replied thoughtfully, 'or at least teach you to control it, so you're not picking up every random thought.'

'I hope so.'

'Although I have to say I may never look at Ms Nelson again in the same light.'

'Roni please,' he replied in a pained voice, causing her to laugh again.

She stopped abruptly as her flashlight landed on a Willow tree. 'Here we go,' she looked the tree up and down. 'This one should do.'

'Do we have to get naked and chant or something?' Jake asked.

'Very funny,' she rolled her eyes, handing him her flashlight.

She tucked her compass into her bag and removed a knife with a slightly curved blade and white handle.

'What's that?'

'A boline,' she answered absently, as she selected the branches that she wanted. 'It's for harvesting herbs and wood for spells.'

'Oh,' he replied. 'You know you could have just used the magic knife Olivia gave me.'

She shook her head, as she cut several small lengths of wood and tucked them into her bag.

'No, that's an athame, which you've also used for killing. Different knives, different purposes.'

She stepped back and retrieved her flashlight from him. The beam suddenly highlighted his face and she paused just taking him in. He was smiling at her again, she wished he wouldn't do that, it just made her want to sink her teeth into him. She'd never known anyone like him, never had someone that could make her laugh the way he did. Looking at him now watching her, she just wanted to latch onto him again. She wanted her mouth on his, she wanted to taste him, God, it just plain sucked that he didn't want her that way.

'Roni,' his eyes widened in surprise.

Oh no.

'Please tell me you didn't just hear that.'

He didn't need to tell her, his face said it all.

'Stay out of my head,' she snapped angrily, turning away from him in absolute mortification.

Great, now she was going to have to move to another state.

'Roni, wait…'

Possibly another country.

'Roni damn it,' he grasped onto her arm and pulled her up against him. 'Will you just wait a minute.'

'Forget it Jake,' she shook her head.

'Roni…'

'No, seriously just pretend you didn't hear that.'

'Roni will you just…'

'Look, I think I've embarrassed myself enough for one lifetime, possibly even two, so will you just let me go.'

'Roni if you would just…'

'Jesus, stop saying my name,' she hissed, 'I'm dying here Jake.'

Before she could say another word his mouth crashed down on hers. Unlike the sweet slow exploration of last time, his tongue swept in hot and needy, tasting her like he just couldn't help himself.

He yanked her body up against his and took, and took, until she was dizzy, and when she thought she couldn't give anymore he pushed her into a spiral of desperate need, until she was practically clawing to get him closer. It was like being burned alive with painful pleasure and she was as lost to it as he was. The insistent need for oxygen finally drove them apart, so that they were leaning against each other, breathing heavily, their foreheads pressed together and hearts pounding.

'Do you really think I don't want you?' he breathed against her mouth.

'I...'

She was about to answer him when she suddenly broke off frowning. She fumbled for her flashlight.

'What is it?' he asked sensing the tension in her body.

'Do you smell that?'

He did, it was a sudden strong scent of lilies. He'd never particularly cared for those flowers; they always reminded him of funerals.

'Lilies?' he replied, 'what's so strange about that? We're in the middle of the woods.'

'Yes,' she replied quietly, 'but...' she swept the ground around them, 'there are no lilies here.'

They both shuddered violently at the sudden icy cold feeling. It felt like being plunged into freezing cold water as the sensation trickled down their backs, settling uncomfortably between their shoulder blades.

She jolted slightly as she felt a tall shadow rush past the edge of her vision.

'Did you see that?' Veronica whispered urgently.

'Roni,' Jake grabbed her hand tightly and turned to look at her, 'RUN!'

He yanked on her arm causing her to stumble slightly, but she managed to remain on her feet as they both took off in a flat run. Even though it was a full moon, barely any light penetrated the thick canopy of trees. She had no idea which direction they were heading in and could do nothing but cling on to Jake, trying not to trip and fall on the uneven ground. Her lungs were burning in protest, and her legs ached. It felt like they had been running forever, when they finally slowed and stopped in the shadow of a huge old tree.

'Are you okay?' Jake whispered.

She nodded, a small unconscious habit, even knowing that he couldn't see her. She sucked in a deep labored breath. 'Yes,' she wheezed, 'just a bit out of shape.'

He shut off his flashlight and shoved it into his

pocket, drawing his weapon, listening for any sound other than their harsh panting.

'Do you know where we are?'

'I think we're coming up on the beach to the West of the lake.'

'We're heading in the wrong direction,' Roni breathed heavily.

'I know,' Jake frowned, 'but it can't be helped. If we can get out of the woods and back to the main road, I can call Tommy to come and pick us up. We'll come back for the car in the daylight.'

'Do you think that was him? The Soul Collector?'

'I think it pays to be cautious,' he took her hand again. 'Ready?'

'Yes.'

'Keep your flashlight pointed dead ahead otherwise I can't see where we're going.'

'Okay.'

The sudden pungent smell of lilies washed over them and a gust of cold air rushed past them.

'Shit,' Jake swore, 'GO!'

They set off again but each time they tried to veer west toward the main road, whatever it was herded them back into the deep shadow of the wood, until they were being pushed north. Veronica's legs felt like jelly, and she was panting hard when her luck finally ran out and her foot tangled in an exposed tree root. She went down hard, dropping her flashlight, which rolled away into the undergrowth.

'Jake,' she whispered urgently, trying to push herself upright, 'Jake!'

She felt a warm hand grab her and pull her to her feet. When the scent of Jake wrapped around her she almost wept in relief.

'I've got you Roni,' he held onto her as he fumbled in his pocket for his flashlight.

The beam sputtered once, twice.

'No, no, not now,' Jake muttered. 'Damn it, I knew I should've changed the batteries.'

He hit it a couple of times in frustration before it finally flicked on. The beam of light slowly scanned the surroundings, then suddenly highlighted a pale, white, heavily lined face with black eyes.

Roni let loose a scream. Jake spun her around, placing her protectively behind him. With his weapon raised and propped atop the flashlight, he scanned his surroundings again, turning in circles, trying to train his gun on the shadow that flitted across the edges of his vision.

'Damn it's fast,' he muttered trying to get a shot.

He could feel Roni's hands wrapped around his waist as she pressed against his back. He turned again sharply and she turned with him, but he couldn't see it. He spun once again.

He jolted as the beam of light fell upon another face, only just managing to pull back in time before he let loose a shot. The barrel of another gun was pointed at them and a flashlight shone in their eyes.

'Jake?' a surprised voice spoke in the darkness.

'Mac?' Jake tried to shield his eyes.

Mac lowered his flashlight.

'Veronica?' Mac recognized the young woman standing pale faced behind Jake. 'What the hell are you two doing out here in the middle of the night?'

'We could ask you the same thing?'

'We've got a missing hiker, I'm helping to organize search and rescue, just north of here.'

'Are you alone?' Jake asked.

Mac nodded.

'What is it?'

'It's here,' Jake told him as he glanced around uneasily.

'What is?'

'The Soul Collector,' Roni told him. 'We've seen it,

it was chasing us.'

'Damn it,' Mac hissed, recalling Jake's explanation of the shadowy man on the security footage. 'I've got people all over this section of the woods.'

He holstered his weapon and unclipped a radio from his belt.

'This is Chief Macallister, everyone return to base immediately. I repeat, return to base.'

The sudden static of the radio split the air.

'Come on,' Mac clipped the radio back to his belt and once again drew his weapon. 'We need to get back to the others.'

They headed quickly through the woods, the strong sense of unease prickling at their backs. Every now and then they would get a waft of lilies on an icy cold breeze. It was obvious it was tracking them but strangely enough it didn't attack, it almost seemed to be toying with them as it stalked them patiently.

'What's that?' Veronica asked suddenly.

'What?' Mac replied.

'Over there to the left,' she reached out and grabbed his arm, aiming the flashlight toward whatever it was that had caught her attention.

'Damn it,' he muttered, as they headed over quickly, 'it's the hiker.'

He handed the flashlight to Roni and grabbed his radio.

'This is Macallister, we need paramedics.'

Roni dropped down to the damp ground next to the guy, as Mac relayed their coordinates. He was coiled on the ground on his side, his bright red jacket peeking out from beneath his backpack, which was what had alerted her. Mac dropped down next to her as Jake continued to scan their surroundings warily.

'Is he alive?' he called over his shoulder.

Mac turned him over and sucked in a sharp breath. The hiker's face was chalky white and his lips tinged a deep unpleasant blue. Mac leaned forward and pressed his fingers to the guy's ice cold throat.

'No pulse,' he grabbed the radio. 'Forget the paramedics, we're going to need the coroner.'

'We should go,' Jake grabbed Roni and pulled her to her feet, his hawk-like gaze still trained on the trees surrounding them. 'We'll have to come back for him in the daylight, but for now we need to get out of here.'

Nodding in agreement he joined them and together they disappeared into the woods.

By the time the sun had risen Roni was standing in the makeshift base, wrapped in a blanket and clutching a disposable cup of coffee. It was barely palatable, too bitter and much too strong, but it was warm at least.

She watched nervously as a couple of the volunteers disappeared back into the woods with Mac, Jake and the coroner to document the scene and retrieve the body. She couldn't sit, she was too worried and so she paced in front of the small canvas canopy, which had been erected on a wide patch of grass at the edge of the woods. Inside the canopy was a foldable table covered with a large map, which had been divided into search areas. A smaller table was set up at the side with flasks of coffee and a stack of paper cups.

'Miss Mason?' a voice spoke up behind her and she turned, recognizing deputy Carl.

'Yes?'

'Chief radioed in, they're going to be a while documenting the scene. He asked that someone drive you home.'

'I don't think...' she shook her head.

'Chief's orders I'm afraid,' he apologized. 'It's a crime scene now, you can't be here.'

'I suppose,' she frowned.

'If it helps, Jake said he'd meet you back at your place once he was done,' Carl replied, seeming to realize the cause of her distress.

She nodded and followed quietly as he led her toward one of the squad cars.

Jake scanned the tree line warily, ignoring the hive of activity taking place behind him. Even running on no sleep and five cups of really bad coffee, he was still not tired, in fact he was almost painfully alert. It was probably the adrenalin, which even now coursed through his veins.

Unfortunately, he knew when he eventually did crash, he was going to crash hard. But not yet, he frowned. Even with everything brightly lit with the pale rays of morning there was still a sense of foreboding, like they were being silently stalked. He paced the edge of the crime scene, impatient and filled with restless energy, like a caged animal.

The unease didn't shift and he rolled his shoulders uncomfortably. At least by now Carl should have had Roni back at her apartment, where she would be safe. He knew she probably wouldn't have been happy about that, but when Mac realized the Soul Collector was still loose in the woods, he'd given Carl strict instructions to get her back to her apartment, even if he had to cuff her to do it. They'd relieved as many of the volunteers as they could, but there were still too many people out in the woods for comfort.

'Jake!' a voice had him turning back to the crime scene, 'you'd better come and have a look at this.'

He turned around and headed over. Dr Achari and Mac were leaning over the corpse, now partially concealed inside a body bag which was zipped up to the chest leaving the hiker's face exposed. He looked to be in his mid-fifties, and given his build, and his well-used boots and equipment, it was fair to assume the guy was not only in good shape, but an experienced hiker.

'Do we know who he was?'

'Businessman from Salem,' Mac replied. 'Brent Myers, on a hiking trip with two of his buddies. They got separated on the trail, but Brent here was an experienced hiker, so they figured they'd just meet him back at their hotel. When he was a no show they called it in.'

'Any idea how he died?'

Sachiv shook his head.

'There are no obvious signs, I won't know anything until I perform the autopsy.'

'There is something else though,' Mac told him. He turned to Sachiv and nodded.

Sachiv leaned down and peeled back one of the guy's eyelids. His pupils were cloudy and drained of color.

'Damn it,' Jake swore, 'just like Mr Bailey and Hayley Adams?'

'Unfortunately,' Sachiv nodded. 'I have to admit I've never seen anything like it, but that's three victims now. If this continues we may have to consider some sort of disease as the cause.'

He shook his head frowning.

'I need to get him back and run some tests. If it is the same thing that is affecting Mr Bailey and Hayley perhaps we might discover something which could help them.'

'I seriously doubt it,' Jake muttered under his breath.

'What was that?' Sachiv frowned.

'Nothing,' Jake shook his head. 'How long until the autopsy's finished?'

'A few hours,' Sachiv stood. 'I'll head back now. I'll bump him up to the top of the list as a priority just in case we are looking at some sort of virus. We need to find out what is affecting these people before anyone else succumbs.'

Jake nodded and stood back, allowing Sachiv to zip the bag closed. Both he and one of the volunteers lifted the corpse onto a stretcher and headed out. Jake blew out a breath in frustration. He didn't want to be in the woods, he wanted to go and check on Roni and make sure she was okay.

He knew Sachiv wasn't going to find anything helpful from the autopsy, just as he knew the cops documenting the scene wouldn't find anything. It was frustrating, as he and Mac were the only ones who knew the truth, but they still had to keep up appearances which meant running procedures and collecting evidence. It was a huge waste of time as well as being potentially dangerous, after all the Collector was still somewhere out there in the woods.

The Collector watched through the tree line, with shiny black eyes which seemed to descend down into endless nothingness. His mouth opened a fraction, giving a glimpse of rotting brown teeth, at odds with the stark whiteness of his deeply lined skin.

His hawk like gaze followed the human with pale hair with interest. He raised his face slightly, almost as if he was tasting his scent upon the air. That one interested him.

When he had held the female in the darkness he'd shone. His soul had pulsed a bright, blinding white in the darkness of the woods and it was that which had attracted him to them.

He wanted it. His long tapered spindly fingers flexed involuntarily as he recalled the tantalizing lure of the human's soul, so pure and blinding. He licked his thin lips and swallowed, his obsidian eyes filled with a dreadful kind of hunger, the kind of hunger that could devour worlds and yet never be satisfied.

He had to have it. Perhaps he would take the female too. She had shone as well; slightly less than the male, but still enough to interest him.

His gaze once again locked onto Jake, and his mouth widened into a sickening smile. He could take it now but, he glanced around the small clearing, there were too many others.

He didn't want them, they didn't interest him.

There was nothing special about them at all, but that one… a low hiss rumbled deep in his throat.

He could wait. He melted back into the shadow of the woods. He would be back, after all he had the human's scent now.

13.

Jake leaned up against the concrete wall outside the morgue and yawned. Taking another sip of coffee, he rubbed his eyes tiredly. He didn't know why he was waiting around for the autopsy report on the hiker. Christ, he couldn't even remember the guy's name. He was willing to bet the autopsy wouldn't show anything. After all, he was pretty sure there was no medical test that would show if someone's soul had been yanked out of their body or not.

But, he thought with a tired sigh, Mac wanted him to double check just in case anything did show up. He took another deep gulp of coffee, draining the cup and looking up at the sound of footsteps approaching along the stark sterile corridor.

His expression softened as he saw his sister heading toward him.

'Hey,' he greeted her softly.

'Hey,' she wrapped her arms around him and hugged him hard. 'Mac told me what happened; are you okay?'

'I'm fine.'

'What about Veronica?'

'She was okay when we made it out of the woods, I haven't seen her since.'

'You're definitely sure this thing has been stealing souls?'

'Yeah,' he muttered sourly as he stared into his cup.

'Damn it,' she swore softly.

'I know. Looks like we've got another vic, only this time he didn't make it,' he frowned thoughtfully. 'I wonder what made this one different? Why did he die when the other two didn't?'

'Four.'

'Sorry?'

'Other four,' she shook her head in worry, 'that's one of the reasons I came to find you. We've had another two admitted with the same symptoms.'

'Well shit,' he scowled.

'Jake,' she whispered quietly, 'it's the Baxter twins.'

'No,' he shook his head crushing the now empty cup in his hand. He knew the Baxter twins, girls, no more than eight years old. 'Are they stable?'

'For now,' she replied worriedly, 'but the truth is, I don't know how long they'll stay that way.'

They both looked up as the door opened and Sachiv stuck his head around the corner.

'Oh good you're here,' he nodded to Jake. 'Hey Louisa.'

She smiled at him as he stepped out into the corridor.

'You coming in then?'

Jake pushed himself off the wall and tossed the screwed up paper cup in the trash, before he headed into the cool sterile room, followed by his sister.

'So,' Sachiv scooped up a brown folder and flipped it open. He stopped next to the body, which was laid out on a stainless steel slab and covered to the waist with a white sheet. 'We have here Mr Brent Myers, age 56, of Loring Avenue, Salem.'

'And?'

'And I've got nothing,' Sachiv closed the folder with a snap and looked at Jake seriously. 'I've never seen anything like it. There is absolutely nothing wrong with him.'

'Apart from being dead,' Jake replied mildly.

'That's just it, I can find no reason for it. His heart is in beautiful condition for a man his age, there's no damage to the muscle. He didn't have a heart attack, no stroke, no brain aneurysm, no clots, tumors, fever, injury…nothing. His body appeared to be fit and healthy. It's literally like he went from being alive to being dead.'

'Tox screen?' Louisa asked.

'Preliminary findings didn't flag anything up. I'm still waiting on some other test results, but I have to say if it comes back clean, the cause of death will have to go down as SADS.'

'SADS?' Jake asked in confusion.

'Sudden adult death syndrome, it's similar to SIDS which is sudden infant death syndrome, or cot death as it's also known.'

'That's it?'

'Sorry I couldn't be more specific,' he handed him the folder, 'but apart from the strange eye discoloration, I can't find anything.'

'Well thanks anyway Sachiv,' Jake shook his hand. 'I'll make sure Mac gets the report. Let me know if anything shows up in the test results.'

Sachiv nodded.

Louisa waited until they were both alone in the corridor before she spoke again.

'I think I might know why he died and the others haven't yet,' she mused thoughtfully, as they started walking back to the elevators.

'Yeah?'

'Well, if you think about it, all the other victims were discovered very quickly and given medical attention, or rather should I say medical intervention.'

'They were all put on life support?' He punched the call button and as the doors opened they both stepped inside.

'Exactly, and within maybe an hour of the attack. When I spoke to Mac earlier, he said Mr Myers went missing at approximately 3pm yesterday afternoon but he wasn't reported missing until after 6pm. The search didn't begin until 8pm, and his body wasn't discovered until what? 1am?'

'I see where you're going with this,' he scratched his chin.

'Without life support all of them would die. It's a commonly held belief that the body can't survive without the soul. So I'm thinking that if we don't get to them within an hour or so of being attacked, they won't stand a chance.'

'Shit,' Jake blew out a breath. 'We need to do something, and fast.'

'Are you making any progress with that?'

'Roni seems to think we have just about everything we need to try and contact Olivia.'

'Still no word from Mr Connell or the others?'

'No,' he shook his head as they both stepped out onto Louisa's floor and headed toward the exit. 'Charles is off the grid, he's not responding to the contact protocol he set up, and Helga, I mean Danae, isn't answering any of her messages. Her phone is permanently switched off and we don't know how to contact Davis.'

'I can't believe they'd just disappear on us after everything that's happened recently. What do you think they're up to?'

'Haven't a clue,' Jake replied, 'and right now they're the least of my worries.'

There was a sudden commotion down the corridor as an alarm went off and several nurses rushed toward one of the private rooms.

'Dr Linden, Mr Bailey's coding!' a voice called out

urgently.

'NO, NO, NO!' Louisa took off at a run, followed closely by Jake.

'Do something!' Mrs Bailey shouted with angry tears burning her eyes.

'Somebody get her out of here.' Louisa rounded the bed, dropping the head of the bed down and yanked the pillow away to lay him flat.

Jake took the sobbing Mrs Bailey in his arms and pulled her out of the way into the corner of the room to allow the nurses to move more freely. He watched as Louisa began chest compressions.

'Epinephrine and Atropine?'

'Got them,'

'Okay push the Epi,' Louisa watched the monitor as she pumped the old man's chest firmly.

He held onto Mrs Bailey, smoothing her back and rocking her gently, the tears streaming down her make-up free face. Come to think of it, he didn't think he'd ever seen Eustacia Bailey looking anything less than perfect, but there she was, her hair flat, her heavily lined skin pale, and her clothes wrinkled. Her only thought was for the man lying on the bed, the man she had devoted her whole life to.

'Damn it,' Louisa swore, 'charge the paddles.'

She listened for the whine of the machine charging as the nurse rubbed the paddles together.

'Clear.'

She yanked her hands clear, watching as Mr Bailey's body jerked violently.

Her eyes flicked to the monitor.

'Again.'

'Clear.'

Another spasm racked his poor body.

Louisa resumed compressions. 'Charge to two hundred.'

Jake watched in amazement as they worked

tirelessly to bring him back. When the seconds ticked into long minutes, into ten, into twenty, Louisa was still there, giving chest compressions even as the nurses looked to each other knowing there was no use.

'Dr Linden.'

Louisa shook her head, 'no, keep going.'

'Dr Linden,' the nurse placed her hand over Louisa's to still her movements. 'He's gone, it's time to call it.'

Louisa let her hands fall helplessly to her sides breathing in painfully, her eyes filling with tears as she looked up at the clock.

'Time of death 10.42am.'

She turned to Mrs Bailey, watching in deep sorrow as the old woman's legs went from under her. Eustacia Bailey crumpled to the floor in Jake's arms and when her mouth fell open, the sound which tore from her lips was the most piercing, heart wrenching, animal like howl of despair Louisa had ever heard in her life.

Veronica paced her living room in agitation. Beau was curled up on the new, bright blue bed she'd bought him and in the kitchen sat new, bright plastic food and water bowls. She'd figured it was probably just easier to have spares at her apartment, as she and Jake seemed to have joint custody of Olivia and Theo's cute little dog, at least until they returned. If they returned.

She chewed her nail, absently glancing at the clock again. She couldn't settle, she'd tried. She'd showered and changed into her pajama pants and tank top, and crawled into bed, but despite her exhaustion sleep just wouldn't come.

She jumped at the sudden banging at her door. Sprinting to the door, she yanked it open. Her gaze landed on Jake's face and her heart almost broke at the expression deeply etched into his features.

'What is it?' she asked worriedly, stepping back to

allow him into the apartment. 'What's happened?'

She clicked the door closed and turned to face him.

'Jake,' she studied him closely, 'what's wrong?'

He didn't say anything, he simply leaned in and wrapped his arms around her, pulling her in tightly and burying his face in her neck.

Her arms came up slowly and she rubbed soothing circles on his back. He didn't know why he'd reached for her, or why he was content to just stand there holding her tightly, breathing in the scent of her.

He'd intended to check on her, make sure she was okay and then he was going to head back to his apartment and get some sleep. But she'd opened the door and with one look at her, something inside him had crumbled. He'd reached out to her like a lost little boy, allowing himself to take the comfort, he didn't know he needed so badly.

He could've just stayed there all day, clinging on to her like a lifeline, but she needed answers and he could feel Beau scrambling at his legs trying to get his attention. He took one final breath and pulled away to look into Roni's questioning eyes.

'Mr Bailey died a few hours ago.'

'Oh no,' she breathed, shaking her head sadly. 'I'm so sorry, he seemed like such a sweet man.'

He bent down and scooped Beau up into his arms, stroking his soft coat as much to soothe himself as the pup. Dropping down to the couch with a sigh, he looked up at Roni.

'I've known him my whole life. Lou, Olivia and I would race down to his store after school, to buy candy and make a nuisance of ourselves. Mrs Bailey would be yelling at us and shooing us out of the store, but Mr Bailey would just laugh and sneak us an extra tootsie roll each. Once, when I was 11 years old, I fell out of the tree Tommy had dared me to climb. I not only broke my arm, but gave myself a concussion. I was laid up in bed, stiff, sore and covered in bruises, when Mr Bailey dropped by to bring me a whole box full of comic books and sweets.'

Roni dropped down onto the arm of the sofa next to him and rubbed her hand across his tense shoulders soothingly.

'It sounds like you have some really great memories of him.'

'I just can't imagine Mercy without him; he seemed as permanent as the town itself.'

'I know,' she murmured.

'I was there when he died Roni,' he admitted quietly. 'Louisa and her team were trying to save him. They tried for over half an hour, even knowing that it was useless.'

'I expect your sister probably felt the same way about him as you did.'

'I held Mrs Bailey in my arms as she watched them working on her husband. She always seemed to tower over me, even when I got to be taller than her. She was such a formidable woman and a little intimidating, but she felt so tiny, so broken.' He released his hold on Beau and leaned forward, cradling his head in his hands, his elbows propped on his knees. 'The sound she made when they pronounced him, Roni. I think it will haunt me for the rest of my life, I've never seen anyone in so much pain.'

She scooted Beau off the sofa and sat down. The puppy turned to look at her indignantly, before curling up at Jake's feet and letting out a sigh.

'It will be okay,' she murmured, running her fingers through his hair.

'Will it?' he raised his face to hers, 'because I don't even have the comfort of knowing he's in a better place. All I know is, while his soul is trapped God knows where, he can't find peace or even move on. He was a good man and he doesn't deserve for it to end like this.'

She reached out and grasped his hand firmly and when he looked into her eyes he found a deep, genuine sympathy.

'We will figure this out, I promise. We will find out what he is doing with the souls and if we can, we will find a way to set them free.'

'God I hope so,' he blew out a breath as she stood up and moved toward the kitchen.

'Do you want a coffee? Something stronger?'

He shook his head. 'I've already had too much coffee. I'm so wired it feels like my hair is standing on end.'

'Tell me what you need Jake,' her eyes softened as she looked at him.

'I just don't know,' he frowned, he slowly stood and moved closer to her. 'Roni, about what happened earlier…between us.'

'Jake, don't…' she stopped him, shaking her head. 'We don't need to do this now.'

'Yes we do, we've danced around it for too long as it is,' he paused trying to find the right words. 'I had no idea you felt that way about me.'

'Jake please,' she whispered, 'don't.'

'You think I don't want you?' he stepped closer. 'I think I've wanted you from the first moment you tripped and fell in a heap at my feet.'

Her mouth curved into a small amused smile.

'I bet I'm not the first girl to fall at your feet.'

'You'd be surprised,' he replied with a sigh. 'Look I wanted you, and I kissed you…twice. Maybe I shouldn't have, it's only made things more complicated.'

'What exactly are you trying to say here Jake?'

'I can't do this with you Roni and it's not because I don't want you, please don't think that.'

'Don't worry I get it,' she forced a smile, but it didn't quite meet her eyes. 'Its fine…I'm fine.'

She turned away.

'Roni don't be like this. If I could just explain.'

'You don't need to, I said its fine.' She shook her

head, swallowing back the hard ball of misery that ached at the back of her throat, not daring to turn around and look into his deep blue eyes, seeing the pity there. 'I didn't expect anything really, I always knew you were way out of my league.'

'It's not like that,' he frowned. Did she honestly not know how great she was, how beautiful and sexy? Did she really not understand how hard it was for him to keep his hands off her?

'Look I said its fine,' she turned back toward him keeping her pain tucked away tightly. 'We shared a few kisses, no big deal. No harm done. Anyway you should probably get home and rest. You haven't slept yet and I'm pretty tired so...'

She headed back toward the door.

'Roni, damn it would you just listen,' he swore and headed toward her, grabbing her arm to spin her around and as she did his mouth descended on hers again. He pressed her up against the door and feasted on her mouth. His fingers tangled in her glossy hair, dragging her head back, changing the angle so his tongue could sweep in and taste her.

He tore his mouth away, pressing his forehead to hers and breathing heavily as he closed his eyes, trying desperately to find his control.

'Do you have any idea how much I fucking want you Roni?' he breathed against her mouth. 'I don't want to hurt you.'

'Then don't,' she whispered as she looked up at him, her blue eyes wide and her heart pounding in her chest.

'It's not that simple. I don't do serious relationships, I never have. I don't know how, I'm too selfish. But you,' his bruising grip gentled as he toyed with the ends of her hair, 'you've got serious written all over you Roni. You deserve someone who can give you serious, someone who can give you marriage and children.'

'And you can't?'

'I thought I could for a while. I thought I could be that guy,' he shook his head, 'but after seeing what Mrs Bailey went through, I never want to feel pain like that.'

'Well,' Roni's expression hardened, 'then you're not only a coward, but you're an idiot too.'

'What?'

'With everything that is going on, do you really think I'm sitting around writing your name in little hearts on my notebook? You think I'm sitting around dreaming of a white picket fence, two point four children and the faithful family dog?'

'I didn't think that…'

'That's just it Jake,' she pushed him back so he wasn't crowding her space. 'You didn't think at all. You can spout all the crap you want about me deserving better, and about you not being able to give me what I want, but it's all bullshit. Pretty it up all you like, it's just an excuse to protect yourself from taking a risk, from getting hurt.'

'That's not fair,' his eyes darkened, 'I care about you.'

'If you did, you would have stopped and asked me what I actually wanted, instead of just assuming for me.'

'Fine, what do you want?'

'I don't know!' she blew out a frustrated breath. 'Do I want a husband and kids one day? Yeah probably, but I can't even think about that right now. Because right now, the world's a pretty fucking scary place and I'm afraid. I don't know what's coming, but I do know that we could all be dead tomorrow, or worse having our souls ripped out and taken God knows where. So what do I want? I want someone who'll stand beside me, I want someone to hold on to, to give me courage and be there when I'm hurting. I want someone who SEES me the way my parents and my family never have.'

'Roni…'

'I want to feel…real,' she breathed painfully.

'Jesus Roni,' he pulled her closer to him, gently grazing her jaw with his fingertips, 'you are real. You're the most real thing in my life right now.'

She looked up into his eyes.

'Do you want me Jake?'

'More than I want my next breath,' he murmured.

'Then take me to bed,' she watched him carefully. 'Stop worrying about tomorrow, we'll deal with it another time.'

He shouldn't, he knew he shouldn't, but he just couldn't stop himself. She deserved better than him but it was true, he was selfish, and right now all he wanted, all he could think about was her, and to hell with the consequences.

He wrapped his arms around her as his mouth found hers, once again soft and slow. Her arms snaked around his neck and as his hands slid down to her hips he lifted her against him, so she could wrap her legs around his waist.

He turned and headed toward the bedroom, kicking the door shut behind him, after all Beau was too young to see what they were about to do. He dropped her down beside the bed and stepped back.

Removing his gun, he ejected the magazine and checked the safety, before laying it on the top of her dresser. He kicked his boots off and slid out of his jacket, laying it over the chair she had propped in the corner of her room. Moving back toward her, slowly pulling his shirt from the waistband of his pants, he watched her watching him.

'Are you sure this is what you want?' he asked as he moved to stop in front of her.

'What do you think?' she whispered, her fingers already beginning to unbutton his shirt, peeling it slowly from his shoulders and revealing more of his body. She sighed softly in appreciation, as her smooth inquisitive fingers stroked his skin, tracing all the dips and curves of his hard muscled body. When she reached his waistband she unhooked his belt and rolled his zipper down. Hooking her fingers in she pushed them slowly over his hips, taking his boxers with them and letting them drop to the floor.

She gasped as her mouth fell open.

'Jesus Christ.'

The man was just beautiful everywhere.

'Thank you,' his mouth curved into a cocky grin.

He kicked out of the rest of his clothes until he was totally and unapologetically naked.

'My turn,' he smiled, lifting her easily and depositing her on the bed, so that she was kneeling up against him.

His fingers raked tantalizingly down her ribcage and grasped the bottom of her tank top, pulling it up and over her head in one swift movement. His eyes flashed appreciatively at the sight of her naked skin.

'You are perfect Roni,' he murmured, taking her mouth again, filling his hands with her beautiful plump breasts.

She moaned into his mouth when one of his hands skimmed down her torso and under the waistband of her pajama pants, finding her naked beneath. His fingers stroked her lightly in a teasing glide.

'Jake please,' she gasped against his lips.

'Tell me what you want,' he whispered.

She placed her hand over his and pressed him more firmly against her. He circled teasingly as her body trembled against him and just when she was about to cry out in frustration he slid one finger inside her, followed by another and then curled them slowly. Her eyes almost rolled back in her head and she could do nothing but rock against his hand, as her body instinctively sought the slow build and blinding release that was so close.

'Christ Roni,' Jake broke their kiss, breathing heavily and pressing his face against the soft heavenly scented skin of her shoulder. Nipping the skin lightly he felt her tense around his fingers and growled, pressing his hips against her firmly. 'If you don't stop making noises like that it's going to be over before it starts.'

'I'm sorry,' she gasped, 'I just…'

She threw her head back as he hit a spot deep inside that made her go blind, and without realizing it she let loose a loud moan of intense pleasure.

Jake's control snapped with an almost audible ping. He pulled his hands free and tossed her back on the bed ripping her pajama pants down her legs and tossing them aside, before crawling between her thighs and taking her with his mouth.

Roni arched off the bed and her hand reached down and tangled in Jake's hair as he ruthlessly drove her body up to the highest peak and held her there. Her body hummed like a finely tuned instrument as he nipped and feasted on her. When he finally drew that tight little bundle of nerves into his mouth and sucked hard her orgasm ripped through her, white hot and blinding, and she let loose a scream.

Roni lay staring up at the ceiling as Jake slowly slid up her body resting comfortably between her thighs, a cocky grin curving his lips.

'I've been thinking about doing that to you for weeks,' he slid his arms under her back pressing her breasts against his chest. 'Didn't peg you for a screamer though.'

'I'm not usually,' she mumbled her face flaming red.

'What's that?' he smiled against her lips, kissing her softly.

'God, the neighbors probably heard that,' she breathed in mortification.

'I wouldn't worry about that sweetheart,' he chuckled, as he nibbled her jaw lightly, 'because we're not done yet.'

He took her lips again, kissing her deeply as she

felt him press against her. Lifting her hips slightly he slid into her slowly, inch by deliriously delicious inch and just when she thought he couldn't get any deeper he tensed up and pressed further.

'Jake,' she breathed against his mouth.

'I've got you sweetheart,' he rolled his hips against her setting a slow deliberate pace, 'just relax.'

Her arms tangled around him, pulling him in as close as possible. She wasn't by any means a virgin but the few disastrous relationships she'd had, hadn't even come close to making her feel the way Jake did.

She wasn't kidding when she said she didn't usually make any noise, she'd never really felt the need to. She simply let them satisfy themselves and roll over to sleep. She had wondered at one point if she was just defective. Maybe she wasn't capable of feeling that level of passion.

Jake however, made her feel like her skin was wired into the mains electricity. She could do nothing but feel every raw nerve and jagged edge of pleasure. He owned her body in a way she hadn't even known was possible. All she knew was she wanted more, she wanted deeper, faster. Now she'd experienced it she was greedy for it.

She drew her legs up his thighs, past his hips until she was wrapped around him like a pretzel. He growled and set the pace faster, and grasping her leg he hooked it up over his shoulder. She was so close, she could feel it just dancing out of her reach. Her body arched and yearned toward it as his hips ground against her.

It built viciously in her core and when she couldn't hold on anymore she let go and clamped down hard. Jake gasped in pained pleasure and fell against her, his hips slowing as he drew out the last of the pleasure, until they collapsed in a sweaty pile of limbs and gasping bodies.

'Jesus Christ,' Jake panted, 'you're bendy.'

'Yoga,' she managed to gasp out.

He laughed against her skin, burying his face into her neck and breathing her in deeply as she chuckled against him.

The insistent ringing startled Jake out of sleep and he fumbled on the nightstand for his phone.

'Jake here,' he mumbled as he pressed his face back into the pillow.

'Jake?' Mac replied, 'you still asleep? I figured you'd be up by now'

Jake lifted his head and stared at the blinking numbers on the clock by the bed. It read 9pm.

'Jesus,' he rolled over and scrubbed his hand over his face. He'd slept most of the day away.

'Listen,' Mac continued, 'I need to speak to you about something important. Can you come by the station?'

'You still there?' Jake frowned.

'Yeah,' Mac replied tiredly. 'Oh and I want to speak with Veronica, so find her and bring her with you if you don't mind.'

'No problem.'

He hit the disconnect button. Dropping his phone back down on the nightstand he rolled over, at least he didn't have to look far to find Roni. He smiled as he wrapped his arms around her warm naked body and pulled her in closer, nipping her shoulder gently with his teeth.

She sighed and rolled into him, snuggling sleepily against him.

'Who was that?' she yawned.

'Mac.'

'Umhum…' she drifted back off to sleep.

'Roni,' he smiled, shaking her slightly.

'What?' she murmured.

'It's nine o clock.'

'Hhmm.'

Suddenly her eyes flew open and she sat up abruptly, the covers pooling around her waist.

'Nine? What, in the evening?'

'Uh huh,' he replied enjoying the sight of her naked body.

'Damn it,' she hopped out of bed and pulled her robe on.

'What's wrong?'

'Beau will be starving by now, which means he's probably chewed through everything in sight.'

He watched in amusement as she yanked the door open and disappeared into the other room. He let loose a small chuckle when he heard her voice.

'Bad dog! Bad!'

Rolling out of bed with a yawn, he reached for his pants and pulled them on. His stomach growled loudly and he realized with a frown he hadn't actually eaten in over twenty-four hours and he was ravenous.

Perhaps it was just as well Mac had woken them up. This way they could grab something to eat, see what Mac wanted to speak to them about that was so important, and with any luck he could seduce Roni back into bed by eleven, eleven-thirty at the latest. Smiling to himself he pulled on the rest of his clothes.

Mac looked up as Jake opened the door and strode in, with Roni following behind him, yawning slightly.

'Still don't know how to knock then?' he asked dryly.

'Hey, you invited me,' Jake shrugged.

'Take a seat both of you,' he said seriously.

'What's going on Mac?' Jake frowned at the Chief's expression.

Once they were settled in the chairs in front of his desk he rose and began to pace slowly. 'It seems we have a bigger problem than we originally thought, the five victims of this Charun or Soul Collector or whatever you want to call him.'

'Five?' Roni interrupted in a startled voice.

'I didn't get the chance to tell you earlier, but there have been another two victims admitted to the hospital with the same symptoms as the others,' Jake told her seriously.

'Who are they?'

'The Baxter twins.'

'Ted and Jan Baxter's girls?'

'You know them?'

She nodded. 'Jan volunteers at the museum. Jesus the girls can't be more than eight years old.'

'I know,' Jake replied soberly.

'God. He's taking children now?'

'They're not the first,' Mac replied quietly.

'What do you mean?'

Mac turned and picked up a tall stack of files and dropped them on his desk. Picking up the first one he read, 'Juliet Smith, age 62, Georgetown, deceased.' He picked up the next one, 'Loretta Johnson, age 16, Georgetown, coma of unidentified causes'. He dropped it and picked up the next one. 'Aaron Williams, age 43, Georgetown, coma, Della Jones, age 38, Georgetown, deceased, Derek Brown, age 47, Lawrence, deceased, Adrian Taylor, age 19, Lawrence, coma, Joley Wilson, age 4, Andover, deceased, Lewis Anderson, age 87, Boston, deceased, Lilly Martinez, age 15, Boston, coma.'

He continued picking up file after file and dropping them on the desk.

'Lawrence, Andover, Ipswich, Cambridge, Boston, North Reading, Quincy, Weymouth, Plymouth...the list goes on. Unexplained deaths with no known cause, comas of unidentified causes, leaving the patients on permanent life support. Over one hundred and thirty-four victims so far and that's just the ones we know about. Forty-seven fatalities, and all the others still in comas. This son of a bitch has been hunting the whole of Eastern Massachusetts.'

'What?' Jake frowned, as he began to pick up random files and leaf through.

'The first one we can trace it back to, was February. This bastard has been stealing souls for months.'

'February?' Roni frowned, 'that would put the time line at roughly around when the gateway was left open. He must've been one of the first to come through.'

'Exactly, and he was either powerful enough, or clever enough, not to get dragged back through when it was closed.'

'There could be a lot more victims than this,' Jake frowned as he continued to look through the pile.

'I know,' Mac replied, 'which is why we have to do something and soon. Where are we at with contacting Olivia and Theo?'

'We harvested the willow during the full moon last night,' Veronica told him, 'that was the last thing we needed. We're pretty much ready to go.'

'Good,' Mac nodded. 'Contact Fiona and set it up for tomorrow. I'll be there too and then we'll see if there's a way to kill this son of a bitch.'

14.

The shaking gradually subsided and Theo crawled out from under the table, followed by Olivia and Bridget.

'That was worse than the last one,' Olivia frowned, as she looked around at the devastation.

Furniture was broken or overturned and pots, bowls and plates had crashed to the floor and lay in pieces. But the worst of the damage was the main beam, which had started to split and bowed alarmingly. Bridget surveyed the damage with a calm detachment, her gaze drew up to the ceiling and her eyes narrowed on the broken beam. Olivia and Theo both watched in wonder as the beam heaved itself back into place with a resounding crack and smoothed out as if it had never been damaged.

'How did you..?' Theo began.

'It's this place Theo,' she told him. 'If you can imagine it you can make it real.'

She bent down and picked up an overturned chair and retrieving her broom she began to sweep up the fragments of pottery.

'If you can make anything you want happen, can't you just…I don't know…wish it all clean? I mean why clean up at all?' Theo asked curiously.

'Why do anything?' she shrugged. 'Why cook if I

don't have to? Why clean? The answer's simple Theo, because I want to. Because I enjoy it.'

'Why would anyone enjoy that?' an amused voice spoke from behind them.

Olivia turned around and caught sight of Sam who was sitting comfortably in one of Bridget's chairs, a cocky smile on his face.

Bridget's eyes narrowed in annoyance. 'You,' she made a small sweeping gesture with one hand, 'out!'

Sam suddenly disappeared and after a moment there was a loud banging on the door.

'Hey! How did you do that?' Sam's muffled voice came from the other side. 'I can't get back in.'

Bridget walked casually over to the door and opened it.

'Yes?' she asked coolly. 'Can I help you?'

'Why did you throw me out, and how?'

'Didn't your mother ever teach you not to enter a witch's house without permission?' she glared at him. 'This is my home, and you will not enter it without first asking permission. It's not only arrogant, it's just plain rude.'

He blinked as he took in the sight of the irritated woman before him. A small smile played at the edge of his lips.

'You're right,' he replied, 'it was rude of me. I apologize. I'm Sam, a friend of Olivia's and you are?'

'Bridget,' her lips pursed as she studied him.

'Bridget,' he held out his hand and as she took it reluctantly he smiled at her, his dimples winking to life. 'There, now we're friends.'

'Is he always like this?' she turned to Olivia.

'Pretty much.'

'I suppose you'd better come in then,' she sighed in resignation and stepped back, allowing him to pass, but as she was about to close the door behind him, something caught her eye. She stepped slowly out onto the porch and looked out at the lake.

The strange dark patch of sky Olivia and Theo had witnessed earlier, had grown. It stretched down to the lake, half of which was now missing. It looked like it had been cut in half and the furthest section of the lake, and all the trees surrounding it, were just gone. The water lapped and tipped over the edge into nothingness, like the old Norse concept of the edge of the world.

Bridget heard a gasp and a sharp intake of breath behind her and turned to find Olivia staring wide eyed, with Theo and Sam flanking her.

'What is it?' she asked quietly.

'The Void,' Bridget cast her gaze back to the terrifying emptiness. 'It is the space between worlds.'

'What is inside it though?'

'A vast well of nothingness,' she shrugged, 'infinity? Who knows? Why do you think we use the gateways between worlds? They are like bridges across the Void, you cannot simply punch a hole in the fabric of the world and cross into the next.'

'What would happen if you did?'

'You would fall,' Bridget turned back to Olivia. 'All I know is, anyone who has ever fallen into the Void has never returned.'

'But why is it here?' Theo asked.

'I suspect the destruction of the Crossroads has caused much damage. All of our worlds exist as a delicate system of sets and balances. If something happens in one, all are affected. It's like an underwater earthquake in your world would cause Tsunamis, which would affect several different continents and cause great devastation. That is what is happening here. The destruction of the Crossroads has torn a hole in the skin of this world, exposing it to the Void.'

'Is there any way to stop it?' Olivia asked, her brow creasing in worry.

'No,' Bridget shook her head, 'the damage is done and it's permanent. It's contained for now, but if any more

Crossroads fall the tear will expand, consuming everything in its path until this whole world is gone.'

'We have work to do then.' Olivia straightened her back, her eyes filled with firm resolve as she turned and headed back into the cabin, followed by the others.

'First we need to locate the gateway to the Underworld,' Theo answered as he wandered into the cabin behind her.

'I might be able to help there,' Sam replied, jumping up and sitting on the edge of the table.

'Does that look like a seat to you,' Bridget asked coolly.

'Sorry,' he muttered contritely as he slid down and sat in one of the chairs.

'What do you mean you can help with that?' Olivia asked. 'Do you know where the gateway is?'

'No,' he shook his head, 'but that's what I've been doing since the first earthquake. I've been searching for it.'

'I wondered where you'd got to,' she murmured.

'I'd have stopped by but you were,' he glanced at Theo and grinned, 'busy…'

Olivia blushed and cleared her throat.

'So what did you find?'

'I think I've narrowed down its location,' he turned his gaze back on Olivia. 'A concealed gateway has a different feel than everything else, almost like a different resonance. If you know what you are looking for you can detect it.'

'And you know what to look for?' Theo asked.

'That's right,' he nodded.

'Okay, so the next question is, when we get to the Underworld how do we find the Crossroad? And more importantly how do we find the one where Nathaniel and Isabel are?'

'Hades said, once I got to the other side of the gateway I had to use the compass,' Olivia replied.

'Compass?' Bridget repeated.

Olivia slipped her fingers through the chain and slid it from her shirt. Pressing the little golden button, the lid flipped open to reveal several complicated circles within circles. Bridget stepped closer and leaned in to study the strange dials and symbols.

'And Hades gave you this himself?' she looked up at Olivia who nodded in answer.

'I don't suppose you know how to use it do you?'

Bridget shook her head contemplatively. 'I've never seen anything like it before, but it hums with power.' Her fingers hovered over it but did not touch the warm golden metal, almost as if she were afraid to.

Olivia frowned as she looked down at it.

'I haven't a clue either.'

'There are some spells we could try on it that may reveal its secrets.'

'Yeah,' Olivia mumbled thoughtfully as she stared at it, 'but maybe it doesn't work here.'

'What do you mean?' Theo asked.

'Well Hades said, when I get to the Underworld I should use the compass. Maybe it needs to be in the Underworld for it to work.'

'What do you think Bridget?' Theo asked.

'It's possible,' she mused.

'We'll try the spells first,' Olivia decided. 'If we still can't get it to work, we're going to have to take a chance and hope I can figure it out once we get to the Underworld.'

'So I guess that leaves one more problem,' Theo frowned. 'How do we stop Nathaniel and Isabel if we reach them in time?'

'I'll deal with my mother,' Olivia replied darkly.

'And Nathaniel? We don't have any weapon that would work on him. I don't even know if he can be killed.'

'That's Hades' problem.'

'What?'

'Hades told me to find them,' she told Theo. 'He

said once I did he would deal with Nathaniel as long as they haven't left the confines of the Underworld.'

'What if they have?' Sam asked.

'We'll just have to make sure that doesn't happen,' Olivia shook her head and blew out a frustrated breath. 'God, all this over a book.'

'I don't suppose you know where the book is, do you Bridget?' Theo asked.

She shook her head. 'No I don't.'

'But Hester definitely had the book? I mean, are you sure it was passed to her?'

'It wasn't supposed to,' her penetrating gaze fixed on Theo.

'What do you mean?'

'As the oldest it was supposed to pass to me.'

'Why didn't it then?' Olivia asked in confusion.

'Because I made a choice, she turned her eyes on Olivia, her voice low. 'I felt it… the darkness. I heard it's call.'

Olivia didn't have to ask her what she meant, she understood exactly. She had felt it herself. When the whip of power had held her in its grasp she had felt the dark edge to it, gloried in it, welcomed it even. She'd ridden it right to the edge and stared into the abyss. It would have been so easy to embrace the darkness and the vast power it offered. But she hadn't, she reminded herself, her hand once more unconsciously gripping the slowly healing wound at her thigh.

'You gave it to Hester, didn't you?' Olivia whispered.

'I wanted it,' Bridget spoke quietly as if she and Olivia were the only two people in the room and in a way they were, because Olivia's aunt Evie had been right. Bridget was the only one who could understand what it was like for Olivia, because she too had felt the darkness, been tempted by it. She alone knew the seduction of its call. 'I wanted it, not to keep it safe, but to use its power. I couldn't trust myself, so I gave it up and laid the burden upon my sister, with the promise that she would never tell me its location.'

Olivia nodded in understanding.

'And you have no idea where she might've hidden it?' Sam asked.

Bridget shook her head.

'It's okay,' Olivia replied, 'it was always going to be a long shot. If we can get to my mother and Nathaniel before they use the Crossroad, and stop them, we won't need to find it. It can stay hidden for the rest of time for all I care.'

'Unfortunately it's not that simple Olivia,' Bridget told her.

'Why?'

'Because even if you do stop them from gaining possession of the book, there will always be someone else looking for it. You have to find it and protect it.'

'I can't,' she whispered as her eyes locked with Bridget's. 'You know I can't.'

The plain truth was she didn't trust herself with the book any more than Bridget had. Her problem was, she didn't have a sister to step in and take it off her hands.

'I'm sorry Olivia, more than you can possibly imagine, but you have to find the book. I think Hester hid it for you, she wanted you to find it.'

'You can't know that for sure.'

'I do know, which is why I've waited here for you for three centuries.'

Olivia blew out a deep resigned breath. 'I guess I should...' she broke off suddenly and frowned.

'What's wrong?' Theo asked in concern.

'I don't know,' she looked up, 'something doesn't feel right, it's like...'

She cried out as she leaned over and stumbled, wrapping her arms around her middle. It felt like someone had lassoed her and was jerking her backward. She looked up and her eyes met Theo's for a brief second before she was jerked back roughly and then she disappeared.

'OLIVIA!' he reached for her, but his fingers grasped onto thin air.

'Theo!' Bridget grasped onto his arm, 'calm down. I need you to focus.'

'Where is she!'

'She hasn't left the Otherworld, she's still here somewhere,' she shook him firmly. 'You can find her.'

'How?'

'The same way you jump from one place to another. Close your eyes and instead of thinking about the place you want to be, focus on her.'

Pushing down the wave of panic he tried to focus his mind, and as he closed his eyes and thought of Olivia everything around him blurred and shifted.

Olivia sucked in a deep shaky breath and pushed herself up onto her hands and knees. Whatever had pulled her out of Bridget's cabin hadn't hurt her, but had dropped her unceremoniously down in a heap on some sort of garishly patterned carpet. Her forehead wrinkled and she realized she recognized the ugly bright print. She looked up and gazed around her, taking in the brightly colored, mismatched furniture and artwork hung haphazardly on the walls. All the room was missing was a legion of cats.

She pushed herself to her feet and dusted her hands off on her jeans. The room was much the same as she had last seen it, except for the large circular table in the center of the room, surrounded by four chairs.

She was definitely in Fiona's house, but why? How had she ended up there? She blinked, and for a second she thought she saw people sat around the table. She blinked and the scene flashed in front of her once more, then disappeared. She thought she'd caught a glimpse of Jake.

Moving forward, she slowly circled the table as the scene flashed again, almost like there were two images laid one over the other. She took a deep breath and focused and suddenly the scene in front of her stopped flickering. She found herself staring at Fiona, Roni, Jake and Mac all sat around the table holding hands and at the center was a large silver bowl filled with what looked like a jumble of herbs, and was that blood? She frowned as she leaned closer and caught the pungent smell of burning herbs. It was then she realized the bowl was smoldering with tiny tendrils of smoke, rising up and filling the room with a sweet sickly smell. What the hell were they doing?'

She could see Fiona's mouth moving, but she couldn't quite catch the words. They were fragmented like a TV channel with a bad signal, she could only pick out a few words here and there.

'Olivia?' She heard Fiona's voice, 'Are...there?'

A séance? Seriously? Olivia resisted the urge to roll her eyes, but instead moved closer, straining to hear whatever it was they were obviously trying to say to her.

'Olivia?' Theo breathed in relief as the room shifted around him and he found her leaning over a table. 'Olivia?'

'Theo wait.'

Bridget caught his arm and held him back as she watched Olivia carefully. 'I don't think she can hear you.'

'What? Why?'

'She's looking through a window.'

'What?'

'Look at her, she's witnessing something we can't see. Don't interfere, let it play out and see what happens.'

Bridget sniffed at the air. 'Willow bark and African dream-root.'

'What's that supposed to mean?' Theo scowled in frustration.

'I can smell it on the air,' she replied thoughtfully. 'Someone's trying a summoning spell, a very old and potent one. Whose house is this in your world?'

Theo looked up and scanned his surroundings. It certainly looked familiar, but it wasn't until his gaze landed on the garish mustard yellow couch that he grimaced in recognition.

'This is Fiona's house.'

'Who is Fiona?'

'She's a medium, she speaks with spirits.'

'I see,' Bridget replied, as she watched Olivia who was engrossed in something only she could see. 'She must be trying to relay a message specifically to Olivia.'

Olivia strained to hear what was being said, but it was like trying to watch a film with no volume, and no damn subtitles. It was at that point she realized, that frustratingly, she had absolutely no aptitude for lip reading either.

'Arghhh,' she hit the table and yelled in annoyance, 'I can't hear you.'

The volume suddenly roared in, too unexpected, too loud, and as she clamped her hands over her ears she managed to pick out one word before the volume disappeared again.

'Soul Collector?' Olivia frowned, what the hell was a Soul Collector?

Suddenly the scene in front of her flickered and disappeared. She glanced around the room and found both Theo and Bridget staring at her intently.

'What the hell's going on?'

'You were pulled here by a summoning spell,' Bridget told her. 'What did you see?'

'I saw Fiona,' she turned back to the now empty table.

'Was she alone?'

Olivia shook her head. 'She was with Jake, Roni and Mac,' Olivia looked up at Theo. 'They looked like they were trying to hold some sort of séance, but I couldn't understand what they were trying to say. It was like I could see them, but I couldn't really hear much. I only managed to pick out one word.'

'What was the word?' Bridget asked.

'What's a Soul Collector?' Olivia asked suddenly.

'The Soul Collector?' Bridget repeated slowly as her face drained of color. 'Goddess have mercy.'

Fiona slumped forward on the table sweating slightly, her hands trembling.

'Fiona,' Roni jumped up and rushed to her side, 'are you alright?'

'Phew, that was jolly hard work' she breathed heavily. 'Bit shaky.'

'Jake get her some water.'

'Best make it a brandy,' Fiona amended as he rose from the table, 'and don't be stingy.'

Shaking his head and smiling he moved to her drinks cabinet and poured her a large glassful.

'Thank you,' she took it from him with trembling fingers and downed it in one go, coughing slightly. 'That'll hit the spot.'

'So what now? We try again?' Jake asked.

'Why would we do that?' Fiona replied.

'Because it didn't work?'

'Who says it didn't work?' she replied indignantly.

'But I thought?'

'Best leave the thinking to the grown-ups, boy,' she handed him back the glass, nudging him in the direction of the drinks cabinet again.

Rolling his eyes, he rose and refilled her glass.

'Are you sure it worked Fiona?' Mac asked. 'I mean, Jake's right, nothing happened. I thought she might appear or something… I don't know.'

'Oh she was here alright, I could feel her although it was very faint,' she frowned. 'This was never going to be a two-way conversation you know, it's not a phone call and it's not an exact science. It was always about getting a message to her.'

'Do you think it worked?' Roni asked 'Do you think she understood?'

'I guess we'll see?' she took the refilled glass from Jake and this time sipped slowly.

'So now what?' he frowned.

'Now…we wait.'

'That's it?' he replied incredulously, 'we just wait?'

'That's all we can do,' Fiona replied. 'We're not equipped to deal with the Soul Collector, not without help. We can only hope Olivia received the message and can come up with some way of helping.'

'And in the meantime the son of a bitch keeps taking souls?'

'Unfortunately,' Fiona murmured thoughtfully swirling the liquid in her glass, 'but maybe there is something else we can do.'

'What?'

'Perhaps we can figure out what he is doing with the souls?' she mused. 'If he's keeping them, maybe we can find a way to set them free. Theoretically, those souls whose physical remains are on life support should be able to return to their bodies. Those whose bodies are deceased should be able to move on to whichever afterlife they are destined for.'

'That's a good idea actually,' Roni's eyes lit up. 'I'll go back to Olivia's books and see if I can dig anything else up on Charun, or the harvesting of souls.'

'There is one thing that is bothering me though,' Fiona looked up at Jake.

'What's that?'

'Why did he let you go? You said he was following you in the woods?'

'That's right,' Jake nodded.

'I wonder what attracted him to you in the first place? I mean, you would have thought he would stay closer to town, where it's easier pickings.'

'That's what I said,' Roni spoke up.

'So what was he doing in the woods? And why go after you? What were you doing at the time?' She turned to Roni, 'I mean, I know you went out to harvest the willow branches, but what were you doing at the exact moment you first realized he was there?'

'I umm...' Roni flushed bright pink, 'well we were...um...'

'Oh for God's sake,' Jake sighed, 'I was kissing her.'

Mac's brow rose as his mouth curved in amusement.

'I see,' Fiona answered absently, 'a strong emotion, perhaps that's the lure?'

'What?'

'I don't know,' she shook her head, once again brisk and businesslike. 'I need some time to think this over, so all of you out of my house and I'll call you if anything changes.'

Being summarily dismissed they stood and retrieved their jackets, filing out of the house in silence and leaving the strange old woman, surrounded by an army of cats, muttering thoughtfully to herself.

Slamming the door open, Olivia stormed out of the house and stalked angrily down the path, past legions of overly cheerful gnomes.

'HADES!' She yelled as she flung open the garden gate and headed out into the street. 'HADES!'

'Olivia,' Theo rushed out after her with Bridget close behind him, 'calm down.'

She stomped out into the middle of the road and raised her face to the sky.

'HADES! I KNOW YOU CAN HEAR ME!' she turned in circles staring up at the sky, as it began to churn with dark grey clouds. 'HADES!'

'Why don't you shout a little louder Olivia,' a calm voice spoke up behind her. 'I don't think they quite heard you in Tartarus.'

She spun around and saw Hades standing behind her. No longer wearing his immaculately tailored suit he was now clad in ancient armor, which was splattered with blood and other fluids she didn't even want to try and identify.

'IS IT TRUE?' she stalked towards him angrily.

'Is what true?'

'Is the Soul Collector loose in Mercy?'

Hades drew in a deep breath as if he were searching for some patience.

'Yes, Charun is loose in the mortal world.'

'Why didn't you tell me?'

'Because there is nothing you can do about it.'

'But he is stealing human souls.'

'You mortals are so excitable,' he sighed in annoyance.

'People are dying,' Olivia's voice dropped to a deathly whisper.

'Mortals die all the time, I told you there is nothing you can do about it.'

'But you can,' Olivia demanded. 'You can pull him back to the Otherworld.'

'No I cannot,' he explained patiently. 'I can walk the Earth but I have no authority there. If you have a problem with that I suggest you take it up with my brother Zeus, although I can guarantee you won't find him nearly as accommodating as I am.'

'Then what use are you?' she whispered angrily.

'Be very careful Olivia,' his voice was low and dangerous, 'I have tolerated a lot from you. I have killed mortals and stripped the flesh from their bones for a lot less. There is a line…be very careful you do not cross it.'

She watched him with hot angry eyes, but wisely kept her mouth shut.

'Now, if you've quite finished with this little tantrum, go and find the Crossroad before it's too late.'

He disappeared and Olivia found herself standing in the middle of the road clenching her fists, as she tried to rein her temper in.

15.

Charles paused and looked up at the darkening sky, breathing in deeply. New Orleans was always at her best at dusk. Like a sultry temptress, she flaunted herself with the teasing promise of pleasures sated and deep secrets revealed, and both the natives and visitors alike loved her for it.

The air itself seemed to sizzle with a vibrant energy, so vibrant it could almost be seen flowing through the streets like rainbow colored ribbons. The city was alive, pulsing and throbbing like a heartbeat. After all, there was nowhere else in the world that exuded Southern decadence quite like New Orleans.

He turned onto Bourbon Street, heading through the bustle of people. The air hummed, music pumped from doorways in dozens of varieties, from Jazz and blues to Creole and back again, which all coalesced to form the unique sound that was pure New Orleans. The air was scented with the mouth-watering scents wafting from nearby restaurants and cafes.

The buildings were elegant and gracious. Spanish colonial railings edged romantic balconies, each different in design. Some were strung with ropes of fairy lights, which laced around brightly colored flowers in full bloom. Some hung great swaths of bunting in riotous colors, which looped across the street connecting the buildings.

Charles crossed the street and paused in front of a large corner building with peach colored walls. The first floor boasted a beautiful balcony with deep green shuttered windows overlooking Bourbon St. The ground floor was warm and welcoming, with Cafe Lafitte in Exile scrawled above the open doorway, and music pumping out into the warm evening air. Dating back to 1933 and the end of prohibition Cafe Lafitte was the oldest operating gay bar in the whole of the United States. An incredibly unique landmark of the quarter, it had been frequented by the likes of Truman Capote and Tennessee Williams. But famous or simply infamous, local or visitor they all came and all were welcome.

He stepped across the threshold and glanced around, grateful it wasn't yet too crowded. The main floor was dominated by a large angular bar with seats set up around it. He didn't have to look far to see two familiar faces.

'Charles,' Danae waved him over to where she sat comfortably next to her brother at the bar, sipping from a tall glass.

'What's wrong with you?' Charles frowned as he looked down at Davis, who was scowling at his sister.

'Don't pay any attention to him,' she laughed. 'He's just annoyed because he's been hit on three times since we walked in.'

'Shut up Danae.'

'Awww, it's not your fault you're so pretty,' she tapped his cheek insultingly.

'You're enjoying this, aren't you?'

'Yes,' she took another sip, 'it's payback for saddling me with the name Helga.'

'That's enough you two,' Charles sighed. 'Davis are you sure this is the place.'

'Yes I am,' he nodded.

Suddenly Danae's phone vibrated in her pocket. She slipped it out and scrolled through her messages.

'Damn it,' she frowned.

'What is it?'

'It's Jake again,' she looked up at her brothers. 'Jonathan Bailey has died and now it looks as if it's attacked two kids in Mercy, and that's just the tail end. Apparently it's been hunting along Eastern Massachusetts since the Gateway was first opened. Charles, we need to do something.'

Charles frowned as he regarded her thoughtfully.

'Charles?' she repeated, 'it's getting out of control.'

'We can't,' Charles replied quietly, 'we're so close.'

'I know you want Olivia back, I do too, but at what price? Because from what little I know of her, she wouldn't trade her life at the cost of a hundred and forty others.'

Charles' jaw clenched tightly.

'You know I'm right.'

'I can't,' Charles whispered, shaking his head. 'I can't leave her there Danae, she's my daughter.'

'I know,' she stood up, fishing in the pocket of her jeans. She pulled a couple of bills and dropped them on the bar before grabbing her jacket.

'Where are you going? Davis frowned.

'Back to Mercy,' she replied. 'You two can do this without me. You don't need my help, but they do.'

'Danae...'

'No,' she shook her head firmly, 'you don't get it. These people are my friends. I have lived among them and worked alongside them for nearly two years now. I can't just abandon them.'

Charles nodded and stood aside to let her pass.

'Danae wait!'

She turned back and looked at her brother.

'Just be careful, okay?'

'You know me,' she grinned suddenly.

'That's what worries me,' he muttered sourly.

They both watched her disappear through the main entrance before Charles finally turned back to the bar and signaled the bartender.

A young blonde guy in a black t-shirt with the bar's logo on the pocket, sauntered over casually. 'What can I get you honey?' he smiled warmly.

Charles leaned over the counter and replied quietly, 'I'm here to see Julien.'

The guy pulled back, his eyes narrowing as his gaze swept over Charles from head to toe, his mouth pursing in contemplation before finally nodding to the left of the bar, where a set of stairs led up to the first floor.

Charles nodded in thanks as he turned and headed up, closely followed by Davis. The first floor was set up in a similar way to the lower, with another large angular bar sat at the center of the room surrounded by bar stools.

'Julien?' Charles leaned over the bar and asked another bartender.

He pointed to the left, to an archway that led into a smaller, cozier room with a pool table in the center and uniformed sofas stretching around the edges of the room. They both headed into the dimly lit room, which seemed somehow more muted, intimate even. Several people congregated around the edges on the sofas, in pairs or small groups, talking in hushed tones. Two slightly older men played pool while a third stood and watched.

'Excuse me,' Charles interrupted the man standing and watching. 'Julien?'

He nodded toward the corner sofa where a young man in his thirties was sipping a tall cocktail. He had a slim elegant build and silky ash blonde hair which fell to his shoulders in smooth waves. He wore black tailored slacks with a smoky grey shirt, open slightly at the collar. He watched them as they approached slowly, his pale watery blue eyes unreadable.

'Julien?' Charles stopped in front of him.

'Who's asking?' he replied, his voice smooth and cultured.

'My name is Charles Connell and this is my brother Davis,' he held out his hand.

For a moment Julien simply stared at him curiously, before finally leaning forward and grasping Charles's hand with his own slender one. He gripped his hand firmly and pulled him closer, leaning in and inhaling deeply.

'A witch?' Julien's eyes sparkled with interest, 'and a powerful one at that,' he murmured. He inclined his head toward the sofa, indicating that they should take a seat.

Charles settled on the sofa next to him turning to face him more fully, while Davis chose to remain standing, hovering protectively over him.

'Now Mr Connell,' Julien's mouth curved in amusement as he took a slow sip of his drink, 'why don't you tell me what it is you think I can do for you?'

'I understand that you are able to procure certain things from other worlds, for a price.'

'Is that what you heard?' he smiled, 'and just what is it you want me to procure for you Mon Cher?'

'I want two souls pulled back from the Otherworld.'

'Souls from the Otherworld?' his perfectly sculpted brow rose questioningly. 'I'll just bet there is a fascinating story to go with that.'

'Can you do it or not?'

'Sorry honey, that's above my pay grade. Only a Psychopompoi or a God has enough juice to pull a soul back from the Otherworld. Once a body is deceased it cannot be returned to the mortal world. Unless you want to arrange a rebirth into a new body? Now if you're talking reincarnation, a deal can be made, for a price.'

'Not a rebirth and they are not deceased. They're both still in mortal bodies, just trapped on the other side.'

'Now I'm even more curious about the back

story,' he leaned forward in interest. 'Are the bodies intact? If they've sustained any damage they cannot be returned.'

'They're intact,' he replied, 'as far as I know, but I'm willing to take the risk.'

'Hmm,' Julien studied him carefully. 'It can be done, but it's going to cost you.'

'Name your price.'

Julien nodded to a slightly stocky man with brown hair, who stood over his shoulder. He reached into his pocket and pulled out a folded piece of paper and handed it to Charles.

'A standard fee, not negotiable and non-refundable.'

Charles looked up at Julien and nodded.

'Excellent Mon Cher,' he smiled as the stocky brunette lifted a laptop and opened it on the low table in front of them.

It only took a few moments for him to complete the wire transfer. They waited tensely for a few moments before the guy nodded at Julien in confirmation.

'Well then,' Julien sipped his drink, 'what you need is Cora.'

'Who's Cora?' Davis spoke up behind Charles.

'An associate of mine,' he replied smoothly. 'If anyone can bring your friends back from the Otherworld, it's her.'

'So you can't actually do it yourself?' Davis frowned.

'I like to outsource whenever possible,' he turned to the guy standing next to him. 'Shane, be so good as to have the car brought around, would you?'

He nodded and disappeared as Julien stood and lifted his suit jacket from the back of the sofa. Slipping it on he straightened his sleeves, revealing delicate golden cuff links, each in the shape of a tiny doorway. 'Shall we gentlemen?'

'Where are we going?' Davis asked.

'To see Cora of course,' he replied in amusement, 'although I should warn you, she has a price of her own… and she doesn't deal in money.'

'We have to pay her too?' Davis replied indignantly, 'after what we've just paid you?'

'Oh Mon Cher,' Julien laughed in delight, 'that was just for the introduction. Trust me, pulling two souls from the Otherworld won't come cheap.'

'It's fine Davis,' Charles silenced him, seeing another heated retort hovering on his lips.

He clamped his mouth shut, but his eyes still blazed hotly as they turned to follow the enigmatic Julien back into the main bar and down to the lower level. By the time they stepped out onto the street, a dark shiny sedan had pulled up to the curb and the driver stood, holding the door open.

'Thank you Omar,' Julien breezed past him and climbed in.

They rode in silence as they headed through the busy French Quarter and out toward the edge of the city. Before long, the bustle and noise of the city had given way to the relative tranquility of a balmy Louisiana night. The further into the Bayou they travelled, the more the close night air was filled with the cacophony of bush crickets and grasshoppers, interspersed every now and then by the loud croak of a bull frog. The air hung heavily with the scent of vegetation and algae covered waters.

Davis' temperament began to deteriorate as the sweat began to roll ponderously down his collar and somewhere at the back of his neck a mosquito began to nip at him savagely. But Charles sat calmly, unruffled and cool as always, his expression unreadable. He watched out of the window as they passed by Cypress trees. After a while they left the main road, turning toward the undergrowth and deep into the heart of the Bayou.

Finally, the car rolled to a stop and the driver stepped out to hold Julien's door open for him. They climbed out and followed him down to the water's edge, where a small wooden boat sat. In it was a tall thin man with dark skin.

'Are we going in that?' Davis replied in disgust, as he pulled a handkerchief from his pocket and mopped his brow. His pale almost white hair was now saturated with sweat, clinging to his head and giving him the appearance of a drowned person.

'We are,' Julien smiled in amusement as he climbed into the boat and sat down, his voice low and smooth. 'That is of course unless you'd like to stay here and keep the raccoons company Mon Cher.'

Davis glared at him in annoyance, before climbing into the small boat behind Charles. The boatman pushed away from the edge and began to pole through the slow, sluggish, greenish brown water.

He slapped his skin again as he felt a sharp nip at his jaw and tried to draw in a breath, but the air was so close it was like trying to breathe underwater. He heard a small splash in the water next to him and turned to look. Just for a second he saw a long thin shape undulating through the murky depths.

'I'd keep your hands to yourself Mon Cher,' Julien told him, 'the snakes aren't too friendly.'

Davis threw him another glare, which was lost in the darkness of the swamp. He swatted at the back of his neck with a resounding crack as something bit viciously at him again. With a deep frustrated sigh of resignation he settled down into his seat for the most uncomfortable boat ride of his life, with the dubious bonus of Julien's amused laughter ringing in his ears.

The small boat weaved through the Bayou, meandering slowly between tall stark trees, which speared up out of the water to tower over them like spindly giants. The slow sluggish water lapped against the side of the boat, which was bumped every now and then by something large and submerged, something Davis didn't want to examine too closely. The night air, while hot and thick, was filled with the sounds of life, of Katydids and the skittering Whirligig beetles, and the occasional lone cry of the night heron.

Finally, they bumped alongside a long thin jetty and stepped out of the cramped boat. Either side of the slim wooden walkway the surface bobbed with lily pads. A small alligator sat, still and watchful on the path in front of them. Julien didn't even break his stride. It looked up at their approach, regarding them with lazy eyes, before letting out a hiss and sliding back into the water.

The walkway ended in a ramshackle building, which seemed to be comprised of a mishmash of different styles, as if the builder couldn't decide on the building he was going for and kept changing his mind. It seemed to be at least two levels, but thin and slightly overhanging the water on long spindly legs that couldn't possibly sustain the building's weight. Yet it sat there sturdy as a rock, defying all the laws of nature.

Julien reached the door. Knocking politely, he waited until the door swung open slowly, before stepping through. Davis also followed Charles through the doorway and stopped abruptly.

The inside of the building in no way matched the outside. He'd expected a rough wooden cabin but instead he was greeted with a thick deep, blushing pink, shag pile carpet, which seemed to him to be absolutely insane. Surely it would add to the heat of the already unbearable Bayou, and it was just another place for insects to nest in, but funnily enough, nothing seemed to make sense inside the cabin. It was actually cooler than it was outside, and as he looked around he noted frilly pink curtains at the windows, framing sparkling clean glass. The walls were decorated with pale cream wallpaper and covered in tiny little pink rosebuds.

Over the top of the wallpaper were dozens of delicate china plates mounted on the walls. Each were hand painted with pictures of what looked like the English countryside, one was even scattered with a flock of sheep being chased by a sheepdog. A small pink sofa was pushed against one wall and strewn with frilly cushions. Next to it stood a display cabinet, which housed dozens of little china figurines, ladies with long swishing skirts and bonnets, kittens and dogs, even a cow being milked. To the other side of the room was a small neat table with matching chairs and each chair was tied with a pink ribbon.

Davis blinked a couple of times, wondering if he'd inadvertently caught a fever from the mosquito bites and was hallucinating the whole thing, when a small tidy little woman appeared. She looked to be in her sixties with neat white curled hair and a flowery dress with a white cardigan over it, buttoned demurely up to the neck.

'Is she English?' Davis turned to Julien.

'She's whatever she wants to be Mon Cher, this is just the flavor of the month,' he shrugged. 'When it no longer amuses her, she'll be something else. Last time I was here she was a four foot Tibetan monk and before that a six foot Lithuanian.'

'Cora,' he greeted her with open arms, 'Chére, you look positively darling.'

'Julien, you handsome devil, I was wondering when you'd come back to visit. I was beginning to think you'd forgotten me.'

'Never my love, but this is not a social call. I have brought you some new friends, I know how much you love having visitors.'

She clapped her hands together in delight. 'Splendid, why don't you introduce me and then we can have a spot of tea.'

'Cora, this is Charles Connell and his brother Davis.'

'A witch no less,' she pursed her lips as she studied him thoughtfully. 'Why have you brought him here?'

'He wants two souls brought back from the Otherworld.'

'And you told him I could do that Julien?' she tutted, shaking her head in admonishment. 'Bad man, teasing him so. You know that isn't possible.'

'Chére,' he interrupted, his eyes glittering with mirth. 'They aren't dead, they are still wearing their mortal bodies.'

'Really?' she turned back to Charles studying him with renewed interest. 'How fascinating… I'll bet there's an awfully good story to go with that.'

'That's what I said,' Julien replied.

'Well come along and sit down then, I have cucumber sandwiches and a Victoria sponge.'

'I would love to stay Cora darling, but I'm afraid I have business elsewhere, so I'll leave you to come to terms with them.'

'Oh if you must,' she sighed in a resigned girlish voice, 'but you make sure you come back and make it up to me.'

'It would be my very great pleasure Chére,' he grinned and kissed her hand softly.

'You really are a terrible man,' she told him primly. 'Run along then.'

Julien turned back to Charles and Davis.

'I'll leave you in Cora's capable hands; the boat will be waiting for you when you are ready to return.'

'What about you?' Davis frowned in confusion. 'How are you going to get back.'

'Oh sweet, sweet Cher,' he smiled, 'I never reveal my secrets.' He stepped closer and traced a long slender finger against his jaw. 'You be sure to stop by and see me again, I do so like a challenge.'

Davis scowled as Julien blew him a kiss and with a saucy wink slipped out of the door, leaving them alone with the strange little woman.

'Sit, sit,' she ushered them toward the table, which

curiously now held three place settings of fine china teacups and side plates. In the center of the table sat an elegant long spouted teapot, with matching milk jug and sugar bowl. Next to it was a four tiered china cake stand, which held several different varieties of delicate sponge cakes and pastries, and beside that a large plate of tiny little sandwiches cut into dainty triangles.

'Now,' she took a seat and began to pour three cups of tea, 'who exactly is it you wish to be pulled back from the Otherworld?'

'Her name is Olivia,' Charles told her as he accepted the tiny little cup of tea she offered him.

'Milk?' she picked up the small jug and tipped some into his cup. 'She's important to you?'

'She's my daughter,' he replied.

'One lump or two?' she picked up the sugar bowl. 'You said two souls?'

'One please,' he watched her drop a sugar cube into his cup, 'the other is a man named Theo. He's her...' he cast about trying to find the right word... 'companion.'

'I take it by companion, you mean lover,' she smiled in amusement as she handed Davis a cup.

Charles' jaw tightened as he picked up the small silver spoon and as he began to stir his tea, Cora let loose a silvery peal of laughter.

'We don't like to think of our children as grown up do we?' she smiled in amusement. 'Why don't you tell me how they came to be trapped on the other side?'

'There was a gateway between worlds which had been left open. We were trying to close it, when they were inadvertently pulled through.'

'That's not the whole story is it?' she picked up the sandwich plate and offered it to each of them in turn.

'No, it's not.'

'Well,' she set the plate down and lifted her own teacup and sipped daintily, 'it is of course possible to bring them back.'

'But?'

'But it won't come cheap.'

'Your price?' he asked bluntly.

'Nothing so trite as money.'

'Then what do you want?'

She sat for a moment sipping her tea and regarding Charles thoughtfully.

'I'm willing to waive my usual fee, after all you're not my usual clientele.'

Charles raised a brow questioningly.

'You're different,' she mused tapping her pale pink nails against her china cup, 'a powerful witch no less.'

'So what exactly is it you want from me Cora?' he asked.

'A favor.'

'What's the favor?' he asked suspiciously.

'Oh no,' she smiled softly, 'it's not that easy. There's nothing I want from you…right now.'

'So you want a future favor from me.'

'That's right,' she replied, 'to be redeemed at my pleasure.'

'Alright.'

'Alright?' her brows raised slightly, 'that's it? No Caveat's? No restrictions? No, thou shalt not kill or steal?'

Charles placed his cup down slowly and deliberately, his penetrating gaze boring into hers as he leaned forward.

'I don't think you understand Cora,' his voice was low and dangerous, 'I want my daughter back. I don't care what it costs.'

'Well, we have a deal then,' her eyes glittered hungrily.

'Yes we do,' he replied sitting back in his seat once again.

'I'll need it in writing you understand,' she added, 'you know, just in case.'

'Just show me where to sign.'

Her eyes glanced down to the table in front of him, where a document lay rolled out before him alongside an old fashioned ink well and sharpened feather. The parchment the agreement was written on was old and brown with age. The writing itself was strangely archaic with elegant loops and swirls. He scanned through the document checking it was in order, before dipping the nib in the well and signing his name at the bottom.

She learned forward trapping his hands with hers before he could roll it up and hand it back. Her gaze hardened.

'Sealed with blood.'

His gaze held hers as he reached into his pocket and pulled out a small penknife. Flicking open the blade he drew a thin line across his palm, his gaze dropping as the blood began to well up from his sliced flesh. Fisting his hand, he allowed several drops to fall to the parchment over his signature, watching as it sizzled like fat on a hotplate. Cora glanced down at the document, watching in satisfaction as he rolled it up and handed it to her.

'There, all done.' She tucked it into her pocket although given the size of it, there was no way it should have fitted. 'I will of course need something that belonged to each of them.'

She looked across at Charles' expression.

'You do have something of theirs?'

'No,' he replied thoughtfully after a moment, 'but I can get something. It will only take a couple of days.'

'Well I suggest you do,' she told him quietly. 'You have three days Mr Connell, any more than that and the deal is void.'

16.

Danae stared down out of the window, gazing thoughtfully at the now still and silent lake. She hadn't been in Mercy since that night; the three of them had left as soon as Charles had learned of Olivia's fate.

From that moment he had been consumed by one thought and one thought only, find a way to bring Olivia home. She could understand that. If she had a child of her own she imagined she would feel the same way, but they still had other responsibilities.

She sighed silently, a small frown marring her brow. It was different for Charles and Davis. Although they may have some sympathy for the people being attacked, it wasn't personal for them. They hadn't lived and breathed Mercy for the last few years as she had.

She'd agreed to settle in Mercy, at first to keep an eye on Olivia's aunt Evelyn, when Charles knew Evelyn was nearing the end of her life. After all she'd come to visit him at Morley Ridge and she'd known at the time, even if she'd not said the words aloud. They both knew that she was dying, just as they knew the house would pass to Olivia and that she would come to claim it. No matter how painful the memories of Olivia's childhood had been, she would be helpless against the call of blood.

Taking one last look at the lake, Danae turned back into her niece's room. She'd barely reached the airport when she'd received a message from Charles, asking her to go to Olivia's house and retrieve a personal item of both Olivia and Theo and overnight them to Louisiana.

She frowned as she scanned the room, wishing Charles had been a little more specific. Did he mean something with an emotional attachment, or something with trace elements of DNA? She wandered over to Olivia's dresser and lifted the lid of her jewelry box. She stared at it blankly for a moment. She'd never seen Olivia wear much jewelry, with the exception of the moonstone necklace the Goddess Diana had given her, and a small delicate pair of gold earrings in the shape of tiny stars. The other problem of course was, as Olivia had inherited the house and all its contents, she couldn't really be sure what belonged to Olivia, and what had belonged to past generations of Wests. Shutting the lid with a tiny clang and a frustrated breath she turned back into the room. Something with DNA it was then.

She moved over to the chair tucked in the corner of the room next to the fireplace and picked up a discarded sweater. It was soft to the touch and a light grey color. Holding it up in the dying light she realized it was a man's size. She held it closer to her face and inhaled gently. It smelled like Theo. Bingo. She folded it carefully and pulled a clear plastic evidence bag from her pocket. Placing the sweater inside she sealed it and tucked it under her arm. Her gaze swept over the room, but nothing really jumped out at her.

She headed into the adjoining bathroom and flipped on the light, staring at all the cosmetics, bottles and tubes of cream lined up on the counter. No, those wouldn't be any good, not personal enough. Then her gaze landed on a soft bristled hairbrush and she smiled. Judging by the few long hairs tangled up in the bristles and the feminine design she was willing to bet it was Olivia's. Pulling another clear bag from her pocket she sealed the brush up too. Flicking off the light, she headed back to the bedroom and to her backpack, which she'd left sitting on the neatly made bed.

She'd just finished sliding the two items into her bag and zipped it closed when she heard the front door open and close downstairs, followed by the sound of footsteps. Slipping the backpack on quickly, she pulled her gun from the waistband at the back of her jeans and released the safety. Creeping silently down the stairs, she could hear noises coming from the library. Whoever it was in the house they weren't taking the trouble to make themselves quiet.

Veronica bent down scanning one of the lower shelves, looking for a particular book she remembered seeing previously. Skimming along the spines she picked out the one she wanted, plus an extra couple that looked promising. She straightened up and as she did, a movement in the doorway caught her eye.

Her heart jolted and she let out a yelp of shock as she found herself staring down the barrel of a gun. The books tumbled harmlessly from her hands and for a moment she froze in fear, until her eyes began to process the person in front of her. She took in the long icy blonde hair, which tumbled free over one shoulder and rested against a leather jacket. Cool, pale blue eyes regarded her carefully and as recognition dawned, her heart once again began to settle.

'God,' she breathed, 'you just took ten years off my life.'

'Sorry,' Danae shrugged as she relaxed her aim and re-set the safety, tucking her weapon into her jeans at the small of her back.

She didn't seem too sorry Roni noted in irritation.

'Took you guys long enough to get here, we've

been trying to reach you for weeks,' Roni frowned. 'Where's Charles and Davis?'

'Not here.'

'What? Where are they?'

'Someplace else,' Danae replied. 'I'm here to help you.'

'You?' Roni stared. 'Just you?'

'Yeah, just me princess,' she repeated dryly.

'Sorry,' Roni shook her head, 'that came out rude.'

'You think?'

Roni rolled her eyes and bent down to retrieve the books she'd dropped. 'How much do you know?'

'Jake's been leaving me messages,' Danae hooked her thumbs casually in her pockets. 'I know you've got the Soul Collector on the loose and that he's stolen a shit load of souls.'

'I don't suppose you know how to kill him?' her brows rose questioningly.

'I got a few ideas I'm working on, there are some things you can do to protect yourselves from him, but they're all short term.'

'Well its better than what we've got at the moment, which is a big fat zero.'

'You know, I've thought about this a lot on my way back to Mercy. I used to read through old police files, it was kind of a hobby. I liked to read through anything weird or unexplained, and seeing as it's Mercy there was always plenty of weird and unexplained. One of the files I read was on a spate of unexplained deaths back in the thirties. Records weren't quite as good then, but there were police reports. Eyewitnesses reported a tall man in black, with white hair and a strange black hat at the scene of each attack.'

'You think it was him back then?'

Danae nodded. 'From what I remember, it all gels with what's happening now. A few of the younger stronger vics ended up in comas, but they didn't survive for long.

Back then, there weren't the same life support capabilities there are now.'

'So, why did he go quiet for the last eighty years? We just assumed that because the first recorded attacks took place around the same time the gate was opened, that he came through with all the others.'

'He did.'

'I'm sorry I'm lost,' Roni shook her head in confusion.

'There was some evidence to suggest someone banished him from this world around '34 and trapped him on the other side.'

'Who?'

'That I was never able to figure out,' she replied. 'The original attacks took place in the same towns as this time around, again he seemed to stick in and around Eastern Massachusetts. These seem to be his preferred hunting grounds.'

'I wonder why?'

'Probably the same reason so many others are attracted to Mercy and the surrounding areas, because there is magic here, running just under the surface. It calls to those with supernatural origins or abilities.'

'Maybe we can figure out who banished him the first time around and recreate whatever spell or ritual they used?'

'Maybe,' Danae nodded. 'I was going to pull the police files and go back over them.'

'I guess it's a start,' Roni sighed.

'What are you doing?' Danae's eyes narrowed and her head tilted, as she tried to read the titles on the spines of the books Roni had in her hands.

'I'm trying to figure out what he's doing with these souls. I don't suppose you know?'

'I've heard rumors,' she shook her head, 'but nothing concrete. Information on him is sketchy at best.'

'Well what do you know?' Roni perched herself

comfortably on the arm of the sofa.

'Charun, is often mistaken for our boy Charon. He's a demon and used to run with the female demon Vanth. Story goes, they parted ways a couple dozen centuries back. Don't know why, but she continued to guide souls to the afterlife, whereas Charun went serious dark side.'

'Why?'

'I couldn't say exactly,' she replied carefully.

'But you have an idea don't you?' Roni's eyes narrowed on Danae's face suspiciously. 'So if he's not guiding souls to their afterlives, what is he doing with them?'

'I've heard stories…' she answered reluctantly, 'but I don't think you're going to like the answer.'

'I can handle it.'

'From what I understand he keeps them and he feeds off them.'

'What?' Roni's face paled.

'Told you, you wouldn't like it.'

'How long does he keep them for,' she asked quietly, 'I mean before he…' she swallowed convulsively, trying to hold back the bile threatening to choke her.

'I don't know the mechanics of it.'

'But some of them may still be alive?'

'Alive?'

'I don't know…trapped somehow?' Roni bit her lip thoughtfully. 'We have video footage of him and he is putting the souls into glass bottles of some sort.'

'I guess it's possible,' Danae mused. 'If he doesn't consume them straight away and somehow stores them, then yes… maybe some of them are still alive, if that's what you want to call it.'

'Fiona seems to think that if we can find them and free them, the ones who still have their bodies hooked up to life support could, I don't know…'

She mimed two halves joining with her hands.

'The theory is sound I suppose, but we'd need to find them first.'

'I wonder how he's choosing his victims?' Roni murmured absently.

'What?'

'How's he choosing them?' I've looked through the files, the victims are all different ages, genders, ethnic backgrounds. There's no clear pattern.'

'Emotions.'

'Emotions?' she repeated slowly. 'I don't follow.'

'He's a demon,' Danae began, 'he doesn't need to consume human souls to survive. At first he was content to just do as he was supposed to.'

'Guiding the souls, like Vanth,' Roni replied.

'Yeah, but somewhere along the line I'm guessing they became irresistible to him. You hear in all forms of religions, faiths and mythologies about the blinding radiance of the human soul. We as humans, are capable of incredibly intense and complex emotions, and when we feel those intense emotions they show in our auras. After all an aura is nothing but an extension of the soul, kind of like an echo of what we're feeling inside. The stronger the emotion the brighter the aura, and the more appealing the soul.'

'You're saying that it's the intense emotions of the soul he's feeding off, not the souls themselves.'

'Yeah, like a junkie looking for his next fix. He'll continue to drain the soul until its nothing but dust.'

'So he chooses people who are experiencing intense emotion at the time.'

'It's not just that,' she clarified. 'Going on what I read in the original police files, some of the victims' relatives reported that the vics themselves had been complaining of someone following them, stalking them even, some for days, some for weeks before they were finally attacked. It's like if he's desperate, if he's jonesing for a hit, he'll take them quickly, but in other cases he'd taken his time. It's like he enjoys the hunt as much as the feeding.'

Roni's eyes widened and her face suddenly drained of color.

'What is it?'

'In the woods the other night, Jake and I...we were...it was following us, but it didn't attack.'

'What were you were doing at the time?'

'We were kissing,' Roni swallowed uncomfortably.

'I'm guessing by the look on your face there was some intense emotion going on there.'

Roni nodded.

'Damn it,' Danae hissed, 'where is Jake now?'

'He was heading back to my apartment after his shift, to feed Beau.'

Danae grabbed her phone from the pocket of her leather jacket.

'Let's go,' she turned and headed toward the door as she punched in Jake's number.

They both rushed down the porch steps to where Roni's car was parked.

'Shit, he's not picking up, give me the keys.'

Roni grabbed them out of her pocket and tossed them to Danae.

They jumped into the car and tore down the driveway in a loud hiss of churning gravel.

'Keep trying him,' Danae urged as she hit the main road and floored it.

Roni pulled her own phone out and scrolled through to Jake's number and hit connect. Another two tries and he finally picked up, as they headed close to the outskirts of town.

'JAKE!' Roni almost cried in relief when he finally answered.

'Roni?' he seemed to sense her panic, 'what's happened? What's wrong?'

'Give me the phone,' Danae demanded, snatching

it out of Roni's fingers. 'Jake?'

'Helga?'

She let that one go. 'Yeah it's me, where are you exactly?'

'I'm just across the street from Roni's apartment. Why the hell are you with Roni? Is she okay? What's going on?'

'She's fine for the moment but you're not.'

'What the hell are you talking about?'

'Look I need you to listen to me very carefully. The other night in the woods when you and Roni felt the Soul Collector following you....'

'Yeah?'

'...it's got your scent Jake, it's hunting you. It's probably been tracking you for days.'

'Are you shitting me?'

'No, it's not going to stop once it's got you in its sights.'

'What about Roni? Is she a target?'

'I'd probably say that's a big fat yes, but as long as she's with me she's safe. You're vulnerable out there on your own in the dark.'

'What do we do?'

'You need to get to consecrated ground.'

'Seriously?'

'Use your head Jake, no matter how far off the reservation its gone, it's still a demon. It can't cross hallowed ground.'

'Fuck,' Jake swore. 'St Josephine's on Ashmore is the nearest.'

'Head there now, run! don't stop for any reason. We'll meet you there.'

Jake crossed the street and stepped up onto the sidewalk. As he did he suddenly caught the pungent scent of lilies and a shiver ran the length of his spine. He turned slowly, his eyes widened and his heart began to pound like a bass drum. The tall dark figure raised its face and scented the air, almost as if it could smell his fear and adrenalin.

'Jake!' Danae shouted, 'Jake! Can you hear me?'

He took a deep steadying breath. 'Protect Roni,' he whispered.

Dropping his phone he pulled his gun free. He put five bullets into its chest as he backed up, but it didn't even knock it back a pace. The Soul Collector simply paused and looked down at his chest, blinking curiously at the slightly steaming holes in his long dark overcoat. He looked up, fixing his shiny black beetle-like eyes on Jake once again.

Jake took one look at him and turned and ran.

'Jake!' Danae shouted into the phone. She heard the gunshots and then the line went dead. 'Damn it,' she threw the phone into Roni's lap and floored it, tearing around the corner in a squeal of tires and burning rubber.

Jake's lungs were burning as he tore down the street. He ducked down an alley he knew let out onto Ashmore. From there he only had to make it fifty yards to the old church. It was darker down the alley than he realized and he stumbled as he clipped a dumpster, but kept going. He flew out into the street, into the blare of horns and a set of headlights as a car swerved, narrowly avoiding him.

He spun around getting his bearings, his eyes landing on the huge stone building down the street, with wide steps leading up to a large set of old wooden doors. He felt a rush of icy air brush past him and he pushed himself further, faster, his legs burning with the effort as his nose and mouth flooded with the ominous scent of lilies. The church was so close he could almost reach out and touch it.

A sudden rush of black fog swirled in front of him and as he skidded to a halt he found the Soul Collector baring his way. His chest rose and fell with harsh breaths. He tried to drag air into his lungs, and his heart pounded. So, it was going to end this way after all.

He took one last deep breath and raised his weapon in defiance. He let loose a shot, hitting dead center of its forehead. The Soul Collector didn't even flinch, his jaw moved slightly, and then he spat the bullet out, watching as it clattered harmlessly to the ground.

His hand shot out and Jake gasped in pain. He looked down to see its arm sticking out of his chest. He could feel his heart slamming hard and his breath came out in a labored wheeze. His skin turned grey and his lips pale, as he felt a great wrenching tear deep inside him.

Charun withdrew his hand and his eyes widened at the blazing white ball of energy beating and pulsing in his palm. He opened his mouth and sucked in a deep breath, his dark eyes rolling back in pleasure. He removed a bottle from the folds of his heavy coat and tipped Jake's soul into it, before stoppering it tightly and tucking it back into his clothes.

Roni watched through the windshield in horror as Jake's body dropped lifelessly to the ground. Her door was open and she was running toward the tall dark figure before the car had even rolled to a stop.

'Roni NO!' Danae flew out of the car, but she was too late, Roni was far ahead of her and launching herself at Charun in absolute rage.

Roni couldn't even think, couldn't breathe, all she knew was she had to get Jake's soul back before the Soul Collector disappeared again. She launched herself at him, clawing and kicking.

He turned to her and if he was at all surprised by her sudden attack, his expression gave nothing away. He brushed her aside, as if he were swatting away an annoying insect. He grabbed her by the throat, studying her intently for a moment before his mouth opened in a disgusting smile, revealing rotten teeth.

His hand pressed against her chest as she struggled and kicked. Suddenly he paused, pressing against her chest again. Unlike the others he was not able to penetrate her chest cavity to retrieve her soul. He looked down in shock, his beetle like eyes narrowing when he caught the glint of something shiny at her throat.

He ripped open the collar of her jacket and hissed. Pressed against the warmth of her skin and glowing brightly was a small crescent moon. It was the amulet Jake had given her the night they had closed the gateway. The same amulet that had come from the Goddess Diana herself.

Charun's head suddenly snapped back and a thin line of dark blood appeared on his cheek. He threw Roni to the ground in rage and turned to see Danae standing in front of him, a glowing whip made up of pure magic dangling from her hand.

He growled and started toward her, but she flicked it with an expert snap, opening a wound along his chest. He clutched it with his hand as blood spurted through his fingers. He brought them up to his face, almost as if he couldn't believe he was injured. He looked up at her with hate-filled eyes and bared his teeth, growling as he turned in a swirl of his dark coat and disappeared.

Roni had hit the stone steps with a sickening crunch. Her arm and shoulder jolted painfully, and her head rang like a bell. She could hear a high pitched whine in her ears, and as she reached up to touch her temple she felt the wet stickiness of her own blood. She looked over to Jake lying motionless on the floor and crawled over to him. Rolling him over onto his back she pressed her fingers to his throat and leaned close to his mouth to check his breathing.

There was no pulse.

'Oh no you don't Jake,' she muttered as she started chest compressions, 'you're not getting off that easy.'

She leaned over and breathed into his mouth.

'Call 911,' she screamed at Danae breathlessly.

She vaguely heard Danae speaking urgently on her

phone, but she paid no attention. Her head was throbbing, her arm and shoulder screaming like an abscessed tooth, but still she kept going. She had to keep him alive long enough for them to get him on life support.

It seemed like an eternity later when the ambulance finally screeched to a halt beside her, lights flashing as two paramedics rushed out to help her.

'Deputy Hanson,' one of them recognized Danae as he crouched down next to Veronica.

Danae nodded, as her eyes drifted to the ground and the shallow pool of blood that looked so dark it was almost black. Her eyes narrowed thoughtfully.

'Hey Owen,' she called out to the paramedic, 'you got a spare syringe?'

He rustled in the bag he'd set down next to them, pulling out something in a sealed hygiene bag and tossing it to her as he turned back to his patient. Danae ripped open the bag and knelt down, sucking up as much of the blood into the syringe as she could, before wrapping it carefully back in the open packaging and tucking it in her pocket. She watched as they loaded Jake into the back of the ambulance with Roni hovering over him, blood trickling down the side of her face.

'I'll ride with him,' she told them bluntly.

'I'll follow in the car and meet you there,' Danae replied. Roni nodded and climbed up into the back of the ambulance as they were closing the doors.

Danae stood watching in silence as they pulled away, sirens blazing, and headed for the hospital. She retrieved Jake's weapon from the foot of the steps and flicked the safety back on. Reaching into her pocket she pulled out her phone and scrolled through to the number she wanted.

'Hello?' a familiar voice answered on the second ring.

'Louisa.'

'Helga?' she replied in confusion

Damn it, that name was going to haunt her for the rest of her life.

'Louisa, listen to me,' Danae answered patiently. 'Are you at the hospital?'

'Yes why?'

'They're bringing in Jake now.'

'WHAT?' she shouted down the phone. 'What happened?'

'The Soul Collector got to him before we could.'

'Is he…?' she couldn't even bring herself to finish that sentence.

'He had no vitals and he's unresponsive.'

'No…' she breathed painfully.

'Louisa I need you to listen to me. Roni is in the ambulance with him, she pretty much got to him immediately and gave him CPR until the paramedics arrived. There is still a chance to get his soul back and save him, but right now I need you to use whatever authority you've got.'

'What do you mean?'

'They won't let you work on him as he's your brother. Whatever you do, whoever is treating him, do not under any circumstances let them pronounce him. You have to get him onto life support as quickly as you can, do you understand?'

'Yes,' she replied. 'I have to go they're pulling up now.'

The emergency room was a blur to Roni as they rushed him into the trauma room. She was barely aware of anything going on around her, all she could see was Jake through the window as they lifted him off the stretcher and onto the table so they could work on him, attaching tubes and monitors.

Louisa burst through the door and looked down at her little brother on the table. Sachiv looked up from where he was intubating him and glanced momentarily at her.

'You shouldn't be in here.'

'Sachiv,' her eyes were pleading.

'Don't interfere,' he moved around the table confidently and full of authority as they worked to try and save Jake.

'Damn it,' he looked up at the silent monitors, 'how long has he been down?'

'Thirty minutes.'

He sucked in a deep breath.

'Sachiv,' Louisa stepped in close.

He turned his deep brown eyes on her.

'Don't let him die, please.'

'He's been down too long, his brain has been starved of oxygen.'

'Please I need you to trust me, you have to get him onto life support.'

'Even if I do,' he hissed as he continued to work, 'there's no guarantee he'll ever come back off it. Is that what you want for your brother, to live in a permanent vegetative state? Is that what he would want?'

'Look I can't explain it right now, I just need you to trust me…to trust I know what I'm doing.'

'Dr Achari we have a rhythm.'

'Please just give him a chance, that's all I'm asking.'

His eyes suddenly narrowed on Louisa's, as if he'd seen something he'd missed all along.

'Outside now,' he ordered.

'Not until you promise me,' she stood her ground.

He gave the barest nod of his head.

She did as he asked. She knew him, she knew he would do whatever he could for her brother. She stepped out and noticed Roni staring numbly at the window, not moving. Louisa swore softly when she saw the congealed blood at her temple and her pale clammy skin.

She flagged down a passing nurse to bring her a kit to clean and dress the wound.

'Veronica?' Louisa touched her arm gently.

Roni turned as she felt a slight pressure on her arm and found herself staring into blue eyes exactly the same shade as Jakes.

Her heart clenched painfully.

'You should let me take a look at that head wound,' Louisa told her softly as she led her to the chairs.

Roni stared at her with eyes glassy with shock.

'Danae told me you gave Jake CPR until the paramedics got there,' she took the tray from the nurse and opened it.

'He had no pulse,' she whispered.

'You probably saved his life,' she began to clean the wound gently.

'Is he...?'

Louisa grasped Roni's hand tightly. 'He's strong, he's going to make it.'

They both looked up as Sachiv stalked out of the door.

'He's stable for now,' he told them as they both stood, 'they're moving him to a private room. Miss Mason you can go with the nurses while they get him settled if you wish. I'm afraid I need to speak with Dr Linden.

Roni nodded and disappeared through the doors toward Jake, as Sachiv grasped Louisa's arm and pulled her firmly into the doctors' lounge, checking they were alone before shutting the door firmly.

'Okay what the hell is going on Louisa and don't bullshit me.'

'I don't know what you mean.'

'The hell you don't,' he scowled. 'Jake's eyes are drained of color like the other victims and you know what happened to them don't you?'

'Sachiv,' she sighed.

'Don't lie to me,' his voice softened slightly, 'I can't help these people if I don't know what I'm dealing with.'

'I can tell you the truth,' she swallowed nervously, 'but you won't believe me.'

'Try me,' he folded his arms.

She blew out a long tired breath. 'Alright,' she shook her head, 'just try not to have me committed or anything will you.'

'Stop stalling and start talking.'

'They all had their souls stolen by a demon name Charun, who is also known as the Soul Collector.'

'That's not funny.'

'Do you see me laughing?' she sighed. 'Look Sachiv, you've been in Mercy long enough to start noticing that things around here aren't exactly normal.'

He studied her face silently as if to try and gauge if she was lying or just delusional.

'You actually believe that, don't you?' he asked after a moment.

'Do you remember back during the winter storms, when we had patients admitted with all those weird diseases?'

'How could I forget?'

'You said to me, that it was as if there was a Raksasha loose in Mercy.'

'That was a joke, admittedly in bad taste but Raksashas are not real, they are a tale told by housewives to frighten children.'

'No they really are real, and we really did have one loose in town making people sick.'

'Louisa…I think maybe the stress is finally getting to you.'

'Look I don't expect you to understand, or even believe me. You asked for the truth and I gave it to you. What you do with that information is up to you, but right now I'm going to see my brother.'

She stormed out of the room leaving him looking after her in bewilderment. It didn't take her long to find Jake's room, as they had clustered all the coma patients together in adjoining rooms. She stepped quietly into the room and watched as Roni sat staring at Jake's ashen face, his hand held carefully in her own.

'He's going to be okay,' Louisa stopped next to Roni and stroked her shoulder reassuringly.

'You don't know that,' Roni whispered finally.

'No, I don't,' Louisa swallowed hard, 'but it helps to keep telling myself that.'

They both looked up as another familiar shape filled the doorway.

'I've found a way to locate him,' Danae told Roni.

Roni turned back to look at Jake before leaning forward and kissing his forehead.

'Look after him,' she told Louisa. 'I don't care what you have to do, but keep him alive.'

'Where are you going?' she asked as Roni headed toward the door.

Roni paused and when she turned back her expression had not only hardened but was filled with resolve.

'I'm going to get his soul back.'

17.

Olivia perched on the edge of a low cabinet staring at the empty circular table surrounded by four chairs. Her hands were propped under her chin, and her elbows rested comfortably on her drawn up knees. Her fingers tapped out a restless staccato on her cheek and her eyes narrowed thoughtfully.

Sam and Theo had disappeared together in search of the gateway to the Underworld and Bridget was busy trying to find a spell to made the compass work. She'd tried to help Bridget but found herself unable to concentrate, and time and time again her unruly thoughts had been drawn back to Fiona and the Soul Collector.

She supposed it had only been a matter of time before her preoccupation with Fiona would inadvertently draw her back to her eccentric friend's home. She would have thought, if there was anyone she could've communicated with from the other side it would have been Fiona.

Unfortunately, as Bridget had explained to her, Fiona was not able to sense Olivia as she would another spirit, simply because Olivia was not a true spirit. She still wore her mortal body, which put her out of sync with everything else. Even so, there had to be some way to speak with them, and even if she couldn't sense her properly Fiona still had to be her best shot.

A sudden thought occurred to her, maybe there was a way after all. She swung her legs down and reached for the backpack which she always carried with her. Unzipping it she rummaged around until her fingers closed round the warm familiar leather of Hester's Grimoire.

Pulling it out, and laying it on her lap, she brushed her fingers lightly over the cover, smiling softly to herself when she felt the low thrum of power pulse through it. She opened the book carefully and watched, as once again the ink swirled and twisted on the aged pages until it settled into words. She flicked through the first few pages and then paused. There had to be a quicker way of doing this.

She slid her palms underneath the book so she was holding it loosely in her hands.

'I need a spell to allow me to see and hear the real world,' she whispered to the book.

The page twitched slightly and then suddenly, as if it had been caught by the draught from an open door, the pages fanned out, flicking through the book until it reached the page it wanted, and then it stopped abruptly. Olivia looked down and smiled.

'Thank you' she murmured as she read through the incantation. It was pretty straightforward.

Jumping down from her seat on top of Fiona's cabinet, she moved closer to the table. Pulling in a deep breath, she reached deep inside herself for her magic as she spoke the words aloud. For a moment it seemed as if nothing had happened, but then suddenly she caught a flicker at the edge of her vision. She tucked the book carefully back into her backpack. The strange flickering came again, followed by a shifting of the light, and a blurred shape emerged pacing around the room. Olivia blinked a couple of times and focused. Slowly the colorful blur began to sharpen and before she knew it she was staring at Fiona.

Fascinated, she followed the woman around the

room, watching as she laid a huge roll of paper on the table. Olivia leaned over the table and saw Fiona unfurl it and pin it at each corner with a heavy object.

It looked like a map. Her eyes narrowed as she leaned in closer and studied it. It was a map of Mercy. Even more curious now, her gaze turned back to Fiona, who was bustling around the room lighting candles.

Once the room was bathed in a warm golden light, Fiona turned to several bowls she had placed at intervals around the room, each made from a heavy metal and filled with herbs. Those too were lit and left to smolder, filling the air with a sweet smelling smoke.

Fiona suddenly stopped, and looked back toward the door, as if she'd heard something. She bustled out of the room and reappeared minutes later followed by two guests. Olivia peered around her and instantly recognized Roni and Danae. Even better. Although they too didn't seem to be aware of her presence, Olivia found that, unlike last time, she could now hear every world they said perfectly.

'Did you get everything?' Danae asked.

Fiona nodded, 'we're good to go whenever you're ready.'

'I need a bowl and the ink.' She removed her leather jacket and slung it over the chair, retrieving something that was wrapped in a disposable medical bag. 'Is it India ink?'

'Yes' Fiona replied, setting the bowl in front of Danae and alongside it a small glass bottle filled with pure black liquid. 'Are you sure this is going to work?'

'I can't see why not,' Danae shook her head as she unscrewed the lid of the bottle and poured half its contents into the bowl. 'I've used this spell many times.'

'Ever used it on a demon though?' Roni asked.

'No, this will be a first, but there's no reason to think it won't work in exactly the same way.'

'I hope you're right,' Roni breathed.

'Okay, let's get this show on the road,' Fiona clapped her hands and rubbed them together eagerly. 'I've never seen a tracking spell before.'

Danae removed the syringe from the opened packaging, and expelled the blood contained within it, into the bowl of ink. Discarding the empty syringe, she picked up the bowl, cradling it carefully in both her hands and swirling the dark liquid around, murmuring in a low voice. After a few moments, she poured the ink out of the bowl directly onto the map in a giant black ink splotch.

Veronica and Fiona both stared at the black blot.

'Is that it?' Fiona asked suspiciously.

Danae resisted the urge to roll her eyes. 'Give it a minute would you?'

Slowly the ink began to move, sliding across the page leaving no trail or dark smudge behind it. It rolled this way and that, changing direction at random, as if the gradient of the map kept changing.

Suddenly it split into two, gliding across the paper effortlessly then it divided again into four and again into eight. Now, as it slid and undulated across the map it began to leave behind tiny dots of ink, some spaced widely apart, some congregated together in a larger volume. This continued for a few more minutes, until the ink disappeared and the dots were left spread all over the place.

'What does it mean?' Roni asked.

'It's a tracking spell,' Danae replied as she thoughtfully studied the map, 'it tracks every location in Mercy that the Soul Collector has been to.'

'He's been busy,' Fiona mused, looking at just how many dots were spread ominously across the town limits.

'Look at this,' Danae pointed to a section of the map North-West of the lake, deep in the woods.

When they looked closer, they could see a large amount of dots, so many of them, they congealed into a small black splotch of ink and blood.

'He's spent a lot of time at this location,' Danae frowned, 'but there's nothing there. It's just woodland, which leads down to the shore of the lake.'

'There must have been a reason he returned to this location so many times.'

Olivia leaned over the map at the location they were discussing and recognized it immediately. It was the Bachelier place. Located close to the lake, concealed by the woods, stood the small cabin which Thomas Walcott had taken her to when he'd kidnapped her the previous year.

At the time he'd been using her as bait, to lure her father in so that he could kill him, and after that he'd fully intended to kill her too. During the time she'd been there, he'd kept her drugged and tied up in the small cabin.

The cabin had belonged to his maternal grandmother, Clea Bachelier, a hoodoo woman who'd moved to Mercy back in the day, and married the former Chief's Grand-daddy. Being an upstanding pillar of the community, and the Police Chief himself, he'd insisted she change her name to Clare in an attempt to hide her colorful heritage.

Why would the Soul Collector be drawn to that place in particular? Olivia wondered. She cast her mind back to the cabin, swallowing back the memory of the pain and fear. She'd been drugged most of the time, so her recollections were still fairly hazy at best. But it seemed there was something, something she was forgetting. It tickled at the back of her mind dancing just out of reach. She'd been sitting in the chair she remembered, forcing her mind back to a place it didn't want to go. Her hands had been taped tightly to the chair. She unconsciously rubbed the skin of her wrist, as if she could still feel the pinch.

She'd heard a sound outside…a merrily tinkling sound, like glass. She'd tried to look out of the window, and she couldn't, so she'd scooted the chair forward and strained her neck, trying to catch a glimpse and she'd seen…glass, brightly colored glass.

A bottle tree. Olivia stood abruptly and her mouth fell open. Her mind tried furiously to fill in the blanks. She'd seen a bottle tree outside the cabin. Dozens, and dozens of brightly colored glass bottles, suspended from the branches of the old gnarled tree. She remembered thinking, she'd seen something similar on a trip to New Orleans. Bottle trees were old world magic which had come over on the slave ships from Africa. The bottles were used to trap evil spirits, which were then in turn, supposed to be destroyed by the rising sun.

She wasn't exactly sure what was going on, but it had to have something to do with that bottle tree. It was too big a coincidence for it not to be.

'Right,' Roni straightened up, 'we should head out there and take a look.'

'Hold on there, G.I Jane,' Danae frowned. 'I'll admit you tackling a soul stealing demon was pretty damn bad ass, but it was also pretty stupid. You got lucky last time. There is no point us heading out to the woods if we don't know what we're walking into.'

'I know,' Roni replied, 'and if these were normal circumstances I'd be saying exactly the same thing, but these aren't normal circumstances. We need to find the souls before they are destroyed. It's the only hope we have of returning them to their bodies.'

'Look,' Danae breathed patiently. 'I know you want to help Jake, I do too. But he won't thank me if I end up getting you killed or worse.'

Olivia's head snapped up at the mention of Jake.

'What? What's happened to Jake?' she stepped closer to her friend. 'Roni what's happened to Jake?'

It was no use they couldn't hear her, or even sense her presence. Damn it, she should have used a spell that worked both ways. It was all very well being able to see and hear them, but it didn't do any good if she couldn't communicate with them in return.

'Veronica,' Danae replied sympathetically, 'I will do whatever I can to make sure we get Jake's soul back, but we need to be smart here. We can't go in all guns blazing.'

'I'm not suggesting that at all,' she shook her head, 'but think about it. We sneak in, take a look around is all I'm suggesting. If we are unlucky enough to run into him, you have your whip, which seems to be able to harm him.'

'What about you?'

'You saw what happened outside the church, he doesn't seem to be able to harm me while I'm wearing this.' She pulled the small crescent moon suspended on a long silver chain from the collar of her shirt.

'Where'd you get that girl?' Fiona's eyes narrowed in interest as she stepped closer.

'Jake gave it to me, when we were helping to close the gateway. He said it came from the Goddess Diana herself. Olivia, Theo and Jake all had one.'

'And he gave it to you?'

'Yeah,' Roni muttered dejectedly, as she stared down at it. If he hadn't given it to her, he'd have been wearing it at the time he'd been attacked and he would've been safe.

'Don't do that,' Danae told her firmly, as Roni looked up into her eyes. 'He wanted you to have it, and it saved you. I know Jake, and I know he wouldn't have traded your soul to save his.'

Roni's eyes filled with tears and her expression tightened. 'I want him back, I don't care what it takes.'

Danae studied her with a grave expression, finally she nodded slowly.

'Alright' she conceded with a sigh, 'you'd better take this.'

She handed her a gun that looked familiar.

'Jake's gun?' Roni frowned. 'Why? I mean, what's the point? It didn't do Jake much good.'

'I've switched out the magazine for something a

little special I cooked up.'

'I don't understand?' she shook her head.

'The bullets in that magazine have been dipped in holy water and blessed by a priest,' Danae told her. 'Charun is a demon, those bullets won't kill him, but they will hopefully slow him down a bit.'

Roni nodded. Checking the safety she tucked it into the back of her jeans.

'Let's go then.'

'You girls be careful,' Fiona frowned in concern 'and call me as soon as you can.'

Olivia watched worriedly, as her young aunt and her friend headed out of the house, while Fiona anxiously stalked her living room, snuffing out candles and cleaning up.

This wasn't good at all. If she was understanding correctly, the Soul Collector had taken Jake's soul, and they were heading out directly into its path. She couldn't help her friends while she was stuck in the Otherworld, and it was killing her.

She thought of Jake's body lying in a hospital bed, wired up to machines which were keeping him alive, while his soul was God knows where. She had to do something, and where the hell was her father? Why wasn't he helping them? Why were Roni and Danae heading out into the woods on their own?

God, there were just too many questions she didn't have answers to. She needed Bridget, she'd been in the Otherworld waiting for her for the last three hundred years. If anyone knew a way to contact the others in the real world it would be her.

Scooping up her backpack from the floor and sliding it onto her back securely, she focused on Bridget's cabin and watched as her surroundings blurred around her and she re-materialized in the cabin with Bridget staring at her in annoyance.

'Where did you get to?' she asked crossly with her hands propped on her hips. 'You were supposed to be helping me figure out the compass?'

'Sorry,' Olivia replied, 'I guess I got distracted. I was thinking about Fiona and the Soul Collector, and before I knew it I was sitting in her living room.'

Bridget harrumphed as her eyes narrowed.

'Well, I suppose it's easily done. After being here a while you learn to tune out random thoughts, and focus your energies.'

'I am sorry Bridget, but I could really use your help.'

'What in the name of the Goddess do you think I've been doing?'

'No, not with the compass, with something else.'

'What?'

'I saw Fiona and my friends.'

'How?' she asked suspiciously.

'I used a spell from Hester's Grimoire, which allowed me to see what was happening in that room in the real world.'

'You have my sister's Grimoire?' she blinked in surprise.

'Yes,' Olivia nodded.

'With you?'

She nodded again.

'May I see it?' she asked slowly, her tone unreadable.

Not really seeing any reason not to, Olivia slipped her backpack from her shoulders and unzipped the bag, reaching in. Her hands once again grasped onto the warm leather of the book and drew it out, gently setting it on the table in front of them.

Bridget's eyes widened and she took an involuntary step forward. Her eyes lingered on the triple moon etched deeply into the leather, and the tree of life beneath it. She reached out with trembling fingers, hesitating for a moment before she finally grasped the cover and opened the book.

Strangely enough the words weren't swirling on the page like it did when Olivia was holding it, but rather lay static and lifeless on the page.

'You can read this?' Bridget asked after a moment.

'Yes,' she replied, 'although it's strange. Sometimes it shows me just regular spells, ones that would have been commonplace in your time, ones that Hester would have used on a regular basis. Then there are times, when I ask for something in particular, and it shows me exactly what I need, only it's not exactly a spell, more like instructions.'

'What do you mean, you ask for it?'

'Exactly what I said, I ask the book to help me and it shows me exactly what I need. When I was back at home, it showed me how to create a weapon that would kill a Hell Hound, and in Fiona's living room it showed me how to make it so I could see and hear what was going on in her room.'

Bridget stared at her silently.

'Bridget?' Olivia asked after a moment.

She closed the book slowly and handed it back to Olivia, watching as she zipped it back into her backpack.

'Bridget are you all right?' Olivia asked in confusion.

She blinked, and continued to watch her in uncomfortable silence.

'Olivia,' she finally spoke, 'there's something you need to know about the bo…'

'We've found it!' a sudden voice interrupted.

They both turned as Sam and Theo reappeared in the corner of the cabin by the door.

'What?'

'We've found the gateway to the Underworld, I knew we were getting close,' Sam grinned.

'So where is it?' Olivia asked.

'The entrance is a mausoleum in the cemetery,' Theo stepped closer and wrapped his arms around Olivia dropping a light kiss on her upturned lips.

'You're kidding?' she turned back to Sam, 'a mausoleum?'

'Yeah I know,' he laughed, 'not subtle are they.'

'Guess not,' she shook her head.

'Have you made any progress with the compass?' Theo asked her quietly.

'No,' she replied, 'but there is something else.'

'What?'

'Theo,' she breathed heavily as her eyes darkened with worry, 'it's Jake.'

'What about Jake?' he asked in concern.

'The Soul Collector, he's taken Jake's…'

Suddenly there was a huge roar and they were all thrown to the ground as it began to shake violently. It was much worse than the previous times it had happened. Furniture toppled, everything around them smashed to the floor and this time the beam cracked in half and fell, crushing the table. Theo rolled over to Olivia trying to protect her from falling debris, but as she looked up she saw the whole back wall of the cabin disappear into a swirling undulating wall of blackness.

The chairs scraped across the floor and flew into the darkness. Everything that had fallen to the ground began sliding toward it, as if caught in the path of a tornado sucking up everything in sight. Olivia saw her backpack begin to slide toward that yawning black hole and without thinking, she struggled out from beneath Theo, and scrambled forward to grab it. She felt herself caught up in a riptide of air, and she began to slide along the wooden floor toward the darkness. Theo reached out and grabbed her wrist dragging her across the floor toward him.

'It's the Void, its expanding,' Bridget yelled above the ominous grinding and cracking. 'Everybody get out!'

Bridget scrambled toward the doorway, reaching out as Sam grabbed her hands and pulled her through the door out into the open. Theo pulled Olivia closer, grasping a hand to stop her from sliding back, while her other fist wrapped tightly around the strap of her bag to keep it from being pulled into the crushing blackness.

They clawed and pulled themselves across the floor, but it felt as if the cabin had tilted. It now sloped down toward that ominous, gaping maw, which lead straight into the Void, an endless well of nothingness that consumed everything in its path.

They crawled forward trying to reach the door, but they just kept sliding back, caught in the suction, as debris and other items flashed past them, disappearing into the black behind them. There was nothing left for them to grip onto.

Theo felt the molten metal embedded in the flesh of his arm begin to flow down to his palm. He fisted his hand and felt his palm close around the hilt of his knife. He stabbed it viciously into the wooden floor, causing it to crack and spew jagged splinters. For a moment it slowed their momentum, Olivia clung to his other hand desperately, but slowly the blade simply began to gouge out a channel in the floor, and they were once again sucked toward the Void.

Theo felt someone grab his wrist, and he looked up to see Sam materialize in front of him, then everything around them shifted and blurred. The three of them dropped to the dry grass outside Bridget's cabin, in a tangle of bodies and limbs.

'Thanks,' Theo panted heavily.

'Don't mention it,' Sam breathed just as heavily. The three of them looked up in time to see what was left of the cabin collapse in on itself, and disappear into the crushing blackness of the Void.

Olivia glanced across to see that the Void now not only encompassed the majority of the lake and surrounding woods, but her own house was also gone. Taking a deep breath and reminding herself it wasn't real, that her house still existed in the real world, she turned back to the swirling wall of darkness in front of them. It didn't seem to be stopping, she thought with a frown, which suddenly turned to alarm as the grass at her feet began to disappear.

'It's shifting again,' she scrambled back and felt Theo yank her to her feet.

The four of them ran, the ground still trembling under their feet and opening up behind them, snapping at their heels like a vicious animal. They headed into the woods to the North West, stumbling and trying to keep their balance.

Slowly everything began to still and calm, the ground behind them stopped disappearing and stabilized. They finally stopped, breathing heavily with exertion and tentatively they emerged from the tree line to the shore of the lake.

Only a tiny sliver of the once huge lake remained. Everything else had been consumed by the Void which stood immovable, shimmering and undulating in front of them like a giant wall.

'I guess that means Nathaniel and Isabel have taken out another Crossroad,' Sam frowned. 'That's three now.'

'He's right,' Theo breathed heavily, 'we've run out of time. We need to get to the gateway now, and cross over to the Underworld, before this world disappears completely. We'll just have to figure out the compass when we get there.'

Olivia stood, silently staring out over what little remained of the lake, her heart sinking. She knew they were right, but everything inside her screamed out at the thought of leaving now. She knew she'd made a promise to Hades, and it was one she absolutely intended to keep, but there was something she had to do first.

'Olivia?' Theo touched her arm gently, startling her out of her thoughts. 'Olivia, did you hear us? We have to go now, before the cemetery gets pulled into the Void and we lose our only chance to cross over.'

She turned back to him, her eyes dark.

'I can't…' she whispered.

'What?' he frowned in confusion.

'I'm sorry Theo,' she shook her head, 'but we have to go back to Mercy…'

18.

'What do you mean?' Theo frowned in confusion, 'why would you want to go back to Mercy?'

'I was trying to tell you before,' she replied, 'the Soul Collector has taken Jake's soul. Theo…he's dying.'

'No,' he whispered.

'Roni and Danae have tracked the Soul Collector to the Bachelier cabin on the north west of the lake. Do you remember when Thomas Walcott kidnapped me?'

'How could I forget?'

'That was the cabin he took me to.'

'Why would the Soul Collector go there?'

'I don't know,' she shook her head, 'maybe because its isolated? Or maybe it has something to do with the bottle tree outside the cabin?'

'Olivia…' he began.

'Look, Jake's down and I don't know where my father is, but he doesn't seem to be helping them. God knows what else has been going on in Mercy, or how many other people have been hurt, but I do know Roni and Danae are on their way to the cabin, and they have no idea what they are walking into. They are going to get hurt if we don't do something.'

'Olivia, I know you want to help them, I do too,

but we can't,' Theo replied. 'There's just no way to do it. This world is on the verge of collapsing, even if we could find another gateway that leads back into the real world...'

'There is...there has to be. Hades told me when he first sent me here to find you, that there was a way back to the real world, another gateway.'

'And that may be true,' Theo continued, 'but over half of this world has already disappeared into the Void. There is no way of knowing if it was pulled in and destroyed, and even if we go and look for it, there's no guarantee we'll even find it in time.'

'Theo...' she whispered.

'I know,' he replied softly, 'Jake is my best friend. I'd give anything to help him, but I just don't see a way to do it.'

'Theo's right,' Sam spoke up, 'there isn't time and besides you gave Hades your word.'

'You think I don't know that?' she hissed, 'but this is my mess to clean up.'

'Why would you think that?' Theo frowned.

'Because it's my fault,' she closed her eyes against the wave of guilt and nausea. 'That night at Boothe's Hollow, I had my chance to stop my mother from freeing Nathaniel and I failed. I should have killed her when I had the chance, and because I hesitated they escaped. If I had done what I was supposed to, they would have never taken Charon, and the gateway would never have been opened, and the Soul Collector wouldn't have escaped into our world. All those souls he has taken, that's on me.'

'No its not Livy,' Theo stroked her arms comfortingly. 'Please don't do that to yourself. Of course you hesitated, no one should ever be expected to kill their own mother. We both failed to stop her from releasing Nathaniel, but what happened after? Every decision they have made since, every choice, that's on them.'

'Olivia,' Sam interrupted sympathetically, 'you need to stop blaming yourself and just accept there are some things you can't do anything about.'

'I don't accept that,' her eyes blazed angrily. 'I'm not going to abandon the people I care about.'

'You know she's right,' a smooth amused female voice spoke up behind them. 'There is a gateway, and it's still accessible...for the moment.'

They all turned to see a woman sitting demurely on a fallen log. Her gown clung indecently to every curve and dip of her body, and her long dark hair fell over one shoulder in sinuous loops and curls. Her dark fathomless eyes regarded them curiously, even as her lips curved.

'Who are you?' Sam frowned.

'Persephone?' Olivia whispered.

She smiled in amusement, 'at least the little witch recognizes me.'

'Where is the gateway?' Olivia asked as she stepped closer.

'You know the time traveler did make an excellent point, you made a promise to Hades.' Her brow arched as she looked directly at Olivia, 'and my husband is not known for tolerating disobedience, and oath breakers.'

'I have no intention of breaking my promise to Hades,' Olivia replied carefully, 'but I have to help my friends. I'll be back in time to stop Nathaniel from reaching the last crossroad.'

'Some might say, that's cutting it a little fine.'

'So what are you saying?' she shrugged, 'that I have to sacrifice the people in my world for what... the greater good?'

'Sometimes a sacrifice is unavoidable.'

'And sometimes it is avoidable,' Olivia stood her ground, her firm gaze never wavering. 'I'm telling you I can do this, I can stop the Soul Collector, and be back in time to go after Nathaniel and my mother.'

'You don't know how close he is to the fourth crossroad, you can't be sure how long you have.'

'What do you want from me Persephone?' she

frowned. 'To just abandon the people who are important to me?'

'Maybe I just want to see if you have a backbone.'

'What?'

'You've already defied him once,' her gaze flicked to Theo for the barest hint of a second, 'and you lived to tell the tale. Like I said, my husband tolerates no disobedience, and yet, he seems uncharacteristically lenient with you. I do believe he is almost fond of you.'

'Is that a problem?' Olivia asked carefully.

'Not at all,' Persephone's mouth curved. 'Perhaps I just wanted to see what all the fuss is about.'

'What do you mean?'

'I'll tell you the location of the gate…I'll also tell you that Nathaniel is much closer than you think to the fourth gate. You don't have much time, so,' she smiled slowly, 'we'll just see exactly what you're capable of.'

'A test?'

'If you like,' Persephone shrugged elegantly.

'God,' Olivia shook her head, 'you and Hades really were made for each other.'

'Thank you,' she replied in amusement.

'Olivia are you insane?' Sam hissed. 'This is completely crazy. Do you really think you can jump back to the real world, deal with a soul stealing demon and be back here in time to cross over to the Underworld, before this world is sucked into the Void? You don't even have a plan. Just what the hell do you expect to do with this demon when you find him? Theo?' he looked across at him, 'will you talk some sense into her?'

Theo shook his head ruefully. 'If there's one thing I know about Olivia, it's that you can't tell her what to do, but I'm also pretty sure she's already got the beginning of a plan.'

She smiled at him. 'I do as a matter of fact.'

'What are we going to do with a soul stealing demon?' he asked curiously.

'We're going to use that,' she turned and looked at the Void.

'The Void?'

'Exactly. We grab him, pull him back through the gateway, and toss his ass into the Void.' She began to rummage through her backpack, as she looked across to Bridget. 'You said it yourself, anyone who goes into the Void never comes back out.'

'That is true,' she replied thoughtfully.

'Exactly how do you plan to grab him, and get him back here, without him either killing you, or ripping your soul out?' Sam frowned.

'By using this,' she smiled and when she pulled her hands free of the bag, she was holding the two halves of the demon collar.

'Well I'll be damned,' Sam murmured. 'Where the hell did you get one of those?'

'Nathaniel and my mother used it on the Ferryman, when they kidnapped him.'

'And you were able to remove it?' Persephone asked curiously, 'without causing him harm?'

Olivia nodded. 'He told me that it cancels out the supernatural abilities of whoever is wearing it. It also depletes their strength. If we can get this on him, we should be able to easily drag him back through the gateway.'

'It's still risky.'

'There's something else,' she looked up at Theo. 'Roni was wearing the crescent moon I gave to Jake. She told Danae that because she was wearing it, the Soul Collector was unable to harm her. You and I have the other two parts of the pendant, so I'm guessing that will give us some measure of protection too.'

'I suppose that just about covers everything,' Theo replied, 'so where's the gateway?'

Olivia turned toward Persephone, waiting expectantly.

'You already know where it is Olivia.'

'More riddles,' she fought the urge to stamp her foot childishly. Persephone, it seemed, was just as bad as Hades when it came to not giving a straightforward answer.

'Think about it.'

She didn't want to think about it. Just for once, she'd like someone to just answer the fucking question. How the hell was she supposed to know where the gateway was that allowed spirits to sneak into...huh... Her brow folded into a thoughtful frown...the bottle tree.

'It's the bottle tree,' she turned back to Persephone, her mind frantically trying to piece it together. 'There's a gateway by Clea Bachelier's cabin isn't there? She could see them, that's why she put the bottle tree there, to stop any evil spirits from escaping the spirit world into our world.'

'Clever girl,' Persephone murmured. 'Now ask yourself this. What are the bottles for, what were their purpose?'

'To trap evil spirits. When they were caught in the light of the sunrise they would be destroyed.' Olivia chewed her lip, 'but not just evil spirits though.'

'Go on,' Persephone encouraged her.

'Any spirits, the magic she used to trap the spirits in the bottles would work on any spirits, and spirits are just souls without mortal bodies. So, theoretically the bottles could be used to trap a human soul. That's what he's doing isn't it? The Soul Collector is using Clea's bottles to imprison the souls he's stealing. That's why he's spent so much time at the north west wood, because that's where he takes the souls after he's harvested them. Because they aren't evil they wouldn't be destroyed by the sunrise, they would just remain trapped. It's no longer a bottle tree, it's a living, breathing tree of souls.'

Persephone sat back smiling, 'so what are you going to do?'

'We're going to set the souls free. If we break the bottles the souls should be able to return to their bodies.'

'I bet that'll get his attention,' Theo replied. 'We won't have to go looking for the Collector, if we start setting souls free he'll come to us.'

'Let's go then,' Olivia picked up the two halves of the collar and shoved them into her pockets before pulling on her backpack.

'There is one more thing,' Persephone stood slowly.

'There always is,' Olivia breathed, turning back to face the Goddess.

'The gateway is one way only. If you go through the door will snap shut behind you.'

'You mean we can't get back?'

'You need to find something to tether yourself to on this side and wedge the door open.'

'I'll do it,' Sam offered. 'Bridget, can you tether them to me by magic?'

'Yes,' she nodded, 'I believe I can.'

'Then I'll wedge the door open and when you're ready I'll pull you back through the gateway.'

'Okay then let's go,' Olivia agreed.

Bridget and Sam both disappeared in a blur. Theo reached out and took Olivia's hand as they turned back to look at Persephone one last time.

'Thank you.'

'Don't thank me just yet Olivia,' she replied. 'If you fail my husband, I doubt even his fondness of you will be able to save you.'

Olivia blinked and she disappeared.

'We can do this,' Theo squeezed her hand reassuringly.

She nodded, and for a moment their surroundings blurred and then Olivia found herself staring at the small cabin she'd tried very hard to forget. A chill ran down her spine, and her palms grew sweaty.

'It's okay Livy love,' Theo stroked his hand down her spine.

She took a deep breath and turned to look at the bottle tree, which clanged in the wind. It looked quite ordinary and harmless.

'Okay Sam, so where's this gateway?'

'Give me a minute will you?' he murmured as he closed his eyes. He inhaled deeply and stood still, his head slightly cocked as if listening to something they couldn't hear.

'There it is,' he opened his eyes and pointed to a space a few meters from the tree. He held up his hand, his palm outstretched, and suddenly the air began to shimmer and undulate. It was like looking at the ripples on a pond.

'Is that it?' Theo asked.

Sam nodded.

'How did you do that?' Olivia asked curiously.

'A guy's got to have some secrets,' he grinned turning to Bridget. 'Okay Bridge, do what you have to.'

'Don't call me Bridge,' she frowned. 'It's Bridey if you insist on being so familiar.'

His smile softened fondly, 'okay then Bridey, if you wouldn't mind handcuffing me to those two maniacs please.'

'Of course,' she indicated for Theo and Olivia to step forward. 'Hold out your right hands if you please.'

The three of them stood in a rough circle, their right hands joined together at the center. Bridget laid her own hands over the top, and began to mutter softly. Her voice was so low it caught on the wind and was swept away, before they could make out any of the incantation she was using. Olivia stared down at their joined hands and saw bright golden threads appearing. They wound themselves round and around their hands, glowing brightly until it caught and pulled tight, seeping into their skin.

'Okay that should hold you,' she told them. 'Olivia and Theo you take a couple of steps back. You won't be able to see the threads, but you should be able to feel them.'

They did as Bridget suggested, and both felt a curious pulling at their wrists.

'Feel that?' she asked them.

'Yes,' Theo replied. 'So how are we going to signal when we want you to pull us back?'

'Pull on the thread hard, three times,' Bridget told them both. 'Sam will be able to feel it.'

'And if I pull the thread hard, it means get your asses back her because we are being sucked into the Void, okay?' Sam told them bluntly.

'Okay,' Theo took Olivia's hand, and turned toward the shimmering gateway. 'Are you ready?' he looked down at her.'

'As I'll ever be,' she swallowed hard. 'Okay, let's go.'

They both stepped forward and straight into the strange disturbance. It felt like stepping through water, but they didn't get wet although it had a strange fluid like consistency to it. The transfer was instantaneous. As they stepped out of the other side of the gateway, they were still looking at Clea's cabin, however it was now night time. Olivia stumbled and Theo reached out to steady her.

'Are you okay?' he frowned.

'Yeah I'm fine,' she swallowed back the sudden wave of nausea and dizziness. 'I don't like gateways.'

The nausea passed and she steadied on her feet, looking up at the cabin. It was dark and silent, which only seemed to make it even more creepy. She hated the place, she'd love nothing better than to see it burned to the ground.

Looking up to the sky she realized that although it was dark and lit by stars, there was no moon. So why was the cabin highlighted by a bright moonlit glow?

'Olivia,' Theo whispered behind her.

She turned to look and her mouth fell open on a

gasp.

The old gnarled tree in front of them speared up into the sky, lit by dozens and dozens of glowing bottles. It was so bright, and tall, it looked like the Christmas tree at Rockefeller Center. Before she even realized she was moving, Olivia walked toward the tree until she was standing directly under the lowest branches, looking up at the bottles of light. It looked as if every single bottle was filled with a trapped fairy as the lights bobbed and weaved, and butted against the glass.

'Look at them all,' Olivia breathed.

'There are more than one soul in each bottle,' Theo frowned. 'There must be hundreds of souls trapped in here.'

'Then it's time for them to go home, don't you think?' Olivia looked up at Theo.

'Yes I do,' he smiled as he reached up and unhooked one of the bottles. He removed the cork and turned it upside down. The ball of light shot out of the bottle and circled Theo twice in a mad dance, before shooting up high into the sky and disappearing. He dropped the empty bottle to the hard ground, watching in satisfaction as it smashed.

Olivia smiled and reached up for a bottle of her own. As Theo had done she released the cork and upended the bottle, watching as two smaller lights escaped into the dark night. Theo had already reached for another, and before they knew it there was a growing pile of glass at their feet, and the night sky was lit by dancing lights, making it look like it was filled with insanely large fireflies.

'We can't reach the ones higher up,' Theo frowned, throwing another bottle to the ground.

'I have an idea,' she grabbed Theo's hand and pulled him away from the tree. She reached down inside herself for the heat and light of her magic. It unfurled liked a sleepy dragon roaring to life, flooding her body with magic and when she stretched her arms up to the sky several large dragonflies made up of pure flame burst from her hands and shot into the darkness.

They circled the tree climbing higher and higher, leaving a trail of fire in their wake. Their bodies glowed brighter and brighter until they were almost white with heat. Suddenly a bottle exploded raining down glass shards, then another exploded and another. Every bottle the dragonflies touched exploded, and before long glass dust rained down to the ground and the night sky was flooded with hundreds of white glowing balls of light, as the souls escaped.

Olivia looked up smiling, with Theo by her side. For one single moment they stood in awe of the sight before them. It was like the sky was filled with hundreds of Chinese lanterns. The sight was breath taking.

Everything else was forgotten, her mother, her father, Hades, the book, it all faded away and she breathed in the air which pulsed with magic and love and joy. She could feel them, every soul, every emotion, and for a second, it was so overwhelming she wanted to cry.

'You feel it too, don't you?' Theo whispered, looking down at her with a smile.

She nodded, unable to put into words how it felt to stand in the presence of the raw beauty and radiance of the human soul.

Theo was the first to notice something was not right. He felt a shiver run down his spine, as if he'd just been doused in cold water, and his mouth and nostrils suddenly flooded with the pungent scent of lilies.

He turned to Olivia and opened his mouth to speak, when he saw two hands with long white spindly fingers wrap around her torso and jerk her backward.

Sam shifted uneasily from one foot to the other, his hand pressed up against the shimmering patch of light. He glanced nervously up at the sky that previously had been filled with a strange, pale blue, diffused light. Now it began to boil ominously, dark black clouds swept in, butting up close to the wall of nothingness that was the Void. The clouds themselves churned and lit up at random, with little micro bursts of lightning, as if they were charged with some sort of electricity.

The wind picked up and began to howl, pulling and tearing at his clothes, buffeting his body in the strong air current. He grasped onto the gateway with both hands and stared. All he could see was his own distorted image reflected back at him, misshapen and grotesque, like a house of mirrors at a carnival.

He took a deep frustrated breath and his fingers tightened into fists. If only he could see what was going on, on the other side. He hoped it was going to plan he thought, as he cast one more glance at the threatening skies, because he had the uncomfortable feeling they didn't have very long.

Persephone had told them Nathaniel was closer to the fourth Crossroad than they realized, and his adrenalin was now pumping as the ground trembled beneath his feet slightly. A warning...he knew this was a bad idea. They should have just headed straight for the gateway to the Underworld. There was no way they were going to pull this off.

'Stop it Sam,' Bridget told him calmly above the howl and shriek of the wind.

'You know this is a bad idea, you know what's at stake,' he yelled back.

'I do, and believe it or not, so do Olivia and Theo. They have not made this decision lightly. But to expect them to turn their backs on those they hold most dear, is to ask them to fundamentally change who they are.'

'And sometimes you have to sacrifice what you want for the greater good...for your duty.'

'That's your father talking Sam,' she told him bluntly. 'It's time for you to grow up, and start thinking for yourself...it's time for you to decide, what kind of man you are going to be.'

'You don't know anything about me, or my father.'

'I know exactly who your father is, and I know exactly what you both are.'

'Have you told Olivia?'

'No,' she shook her head, her hair whipping across her face as the wind picked up again. 'That's not my place. You'll tell Olivia the truth, when you're ready to tell her, and she's ready to hear it.'

'Not going to happen,' he shouted back, barely able to hear his own voice. 'If there's one rule you don't break, that's the rule you don't break.'

'Rules are meant to be broken.'

'Not this one.'

'Oh no? What about Scarlett then?'

'Don't!' he warned, his eyes flashing dangerously. 'Don't bring her into this.'

'Sam, I don't have much time,' she yelled back 'Believe it or not, I am trying to help you. A war is coming, everything we think we know is about to change. All the lines will be redrawn, and when the dust settles, this world, the mortal world, and every other, will look nothing like it was. It's time to throw away the rule book, and start thinking for yourself. The old rules and loyalties don't work anymore, you have to trust yourself.'

'What the hell would you know?'

'I know plenty. You think I have waited around here for the last three hundred years for my own amusement?' she replied hotly. 'You think my sister was the only one who could see what is yet to come? I stayed behind here, not only to guide Olivia, but to warn you. Walk your father's path, and you will lose yourself, and Olivia and the others will fail. Finding Infernum is only the beginning. The other four books still exist, and one by one they are waking, and when they do they will start calling for their masters. You cannot allow them to fall into the wrong hands. You cannot allow your father, or Azariel, to gain possession of any of the books.'

'What do you know of Azariel?' he hissed.

'It doesn't matter, all I know is neither of them must gain possession of the books.'

'You're wrong,' Sam shook his head. 'Even if the others still exist, Terra was destroyed.'

'No, it wasn't, it was saved and hidden just as the others were. They are all hidden on Earth, and they need to be recovered, and protected at all costs.'

'This is insane,' he shouted angrily. 'You're asking me to go against my own people, to commit treason.'

'I'm asking you to think for yourself, to do what's right. Your father and Azariel, are more interested in fighting each other than saving all of humanity. They will use the books as weapons, and everyone will suffer. Olivia needs you and so does Scarlett. You have yet to even begin to comprehend your role in the coming days.'

'How do you kn…'

He broke off suddenly as the ground lurched beneath his feet. Bridget was thrown to the ground and it began to shake violently. He held onto the gateway with everything he had, knowing that if he lost his grip the gateway would snap shut and Olivia and Theo would be trapped on the other side.

The violent shaking continued, as the ground heaved and cracked beneath them. A loud splintering sound rent the air. Sam looked across in horror as the little Bachelier cabin collapsed and was sucked into the Void, which had once again began to creep inexorably forward, devouring everything in its path. The bottles in the tree began to clank and shake as it moved closer.

Damn it! There was no time left, any moment now the Void was going to swallow the gateway. He gave an almighty tug on the threads, which bound him to Olivia and Theo, screaming their names desperately into the gateway, praying against all odds that they had heard him.

19.

Olivia's breath caught in her throat as she found herself yanked backward. She felt a dry papery cheek brush against hers and her flesh began to crawl. Rank fetid breath gusted across her face as she dug her feet in and tried to stop herself being dragged back. Her dragonflies, which had been circling the tree detonating the glass bottles, now turned as if sensing her danger, and dive bombed the dark figure holding Olivia in its furious grip. His dry white skin sizzled and blackened, like paper, wherever they touched. He opened his mouth to howl in pain, revealing his rotten teeth, but no sound came out. It was as if he didn't have a voice.

He swatted at them, trying to beat them back. He threw Olivia to one side as Theo tackled him to the ground, punching him square in the face. His head snapped to the side, but he gave no indication that it had hurt him at all. He turned back to Theo, his dark beetle like eyes burning with hate. He knew what they had done, Theo realized, as the demon peeled back its lips into a thin dangerous snarl. He now had no intention of trying to harvest their souls, but wouldn't stop until he'd killed them both.

Theo felt the molten metal of his blade flow hotly down his arm, to pool in his palm. He tightened his fist and felt it wrap around the cool, hard hilt of his knife. He raised his arm to strike, but before he could he felt the thread around his wrist pull tight and violently yank him backward, causing him to land on the hard ground on his back. The Soul Collector looked across to Theo noting the thread around his wrist, burning bright gold and leading back towards the gateway. Theo struggled to rise to his feet, but suddenly found himself pinned to the ground, the cruel dark figure of the Soul Collector sitting astride him, wrapping its long tapered fingers around his throat and squeezing tightly.

Olivia gasped as she felt her dragonflies reabsorb back into her body. She fumbled in her pockets for the two halves of the collar. She pushed herself to her feet and rushed toward the demon, but the thread at her wrist pulled tight once again and jerked her right off her feet. The breath was knocked unexpectedly from her lungs as she began to slide back towards the gateway.

'No! No! Not now Sam!' she growled, as she pulled hard on the thread, wincing as it bit painfully into the tender flesh of her wrist.

She could see Theo lying on the floor, pinned by the huge black shape that was slowly choking the life from him. Theo's legs kicked, and his body twisted, as he tried to shake him loose. Olivia crawled agonizingly across the ground, her fists tightly wrapped around the two halves of the collar.

Suddenly the sound of a shot split the night air, and the Soul Collector jerked roughly, as if his body had been impacted by a bullet. His grip on Theo's throat loosened, and he turned to glance into the tree line where two figures were emerging with guns drawn. Taking advantage of his momentary distraction, Olivia surged forward, leaping onto his back and pressing the collar around his neck. It sealed together with a bright flash of green light, and an audible click.

He reared up and fell backward, clawing at his

neck. Olivia tumbled to the ground and watched as his mouth fell open in an attempt to scream, but the only noise that emerged was a strange sound that was somewhere between a disgusting burble, and a mournful moan. Tearing her attention from the disturbing sound, she crawled over to Theo, as he coughed and tried to draw in a desperate breath.

The Soul Collector staggered to his feet, stumbling back, tearing lumps of his own flesh from his throat in an attempt to free himself from the torturous collar. Olivia looked over to the Gateway, which had reappeared and was fluctuating strangely. Another desperate tug came on the threads which bound them to Sam.

'Olivia we have to go now,' Theo yelled as he pulled her to her feet.

Danae and Roni emerged from the woods, their mouths fell open and their eyes widened in shock as they witnessed the Soul Collector stumbling backward, gripping his throat as if he were choking, and Olivia and Theo climbing to their feet.

Olivia glanced across to the tree, which was now almost dark. There were still maybe a dozen bottles left glowing. There was no time to save them. She turned toward the two figures running toward them.

'SMASH THE BOTTLES!' she yelled at them, as both she and Theo turned, and rushed toward the stumbling demon. Grabbing an arm each, they powered him back toward the strange flickering disturbance in the air. There was a sudden flash of light, and they were all gone.

'Did I really just see that?' Roni breathed heavily, 'and... what the hell did I just see?'

'If I have to guess,' Danae sucked in a deep breath of her own, 'I'd say that Olivia and Theo found a way to pull the Soul Collector through to the Otherworld.'

'You mean he's gone, for good?'

'I guess so,' she shrugged as she turned and

glanced at the tree, scuffing some of the glass on the ground with her boot thoughtfully.

'Olivia wanted us to smash the bottles,' Roni frowned.

'I'm guessing that was what they were doing when Charun showed up.'

Roni looked up into the tree at the few bottles left suspended from the branches half way up. Each bottle fluttered with a dancing ball of white light.

'The souls,' Roni breathed, 'he was storing the souls in the bottles.'

'Looks like Olivia and Theo set most of them free,' Danae replied. 'What do you say?' she smiled, 'shall we finish the job for them.'

'I'd love to,' Roni grinned, as they both raised their weapons and aimed.

Dr Achari snapped the latex glove at his wrist and leaned over the young lady laid out on the cool shiny metal slab. He sighed as he looked at the latest victim, so young, barely more than twenty, newly engaged, and so happy by all accounts. She'd collapsed in the restrooms of The Cauldron, one of the most popular restaurants in town and been dead before the paramedics had even gotten to her. He felt sorry for the girl's fiancé. From what he'd heard from the paramedics, he'd only just finished proposing to her before she'd collapsed.

He peeled back her eyelids, and sighed again. Her eyes were completely colorless, exactly the same as Jake, Mr Bailey and the others. This was getting out of hand. He didn't know what Louisa's game was, whether she truly believed all the crap she'd been spouting about a demon stealing souls, or if it was some kind of joke. Of course, he didn't really believe that for one second. Louisa would never joke about a patient's life, especially not when it was her own brother lying on the table.

Which led him to conclude, she truly believed the

story she'd told him. He didn't want to think that. Louisa had been a good friend to him ever since he'd moved to Mercy, but it was clear she was under some sort of delusion. Obviously the stress had finally gotten to her, and caused some sort of minor breakdown. It was really the only explanation. He would have to say something, he had to. It was his responsibility to put the patients first and if Louisa wasn't mentally sound, then she shouldn't be in charge of patient care.

He leaned over to look at his notes, picking up the tape recorder on the metal table next to him and hitting the record button.

'Dr Sachiv Achari,' he spoke clearly and concisely, his voice echoing slightly around the cool sterile room. 'The subject is a female, twenty-three years of age, approximately one hundred and forty pounds in weight, and one point seven meters in height. Slim build, otherwise fit and healthy, no notes in her medical files.'

He smoothed back her pale blonde hair from her pretty, heart shaped face and checked through her hair and scalp.

'There appears to be no evidence of external injury. The iris appears to be drained of color, but otherwise the eye itself seems to have sustained no damage.'

He stepped back and picked up the scalpel.

'I will proceed with the usual 'y' incision.'

He leaned forward to press the tiny sharp blade, but paused millimeters from her skin, as he caught a sudden bright light in his peripheral vision. Straightening up, he turned to look at the strange light. His eyes widened, and his mouth fell open. He took an involuntary step back, still clutching the scalpel tightly in his frozen fist. He could see a glowing ball of bright white light, about the size of a grapefruit. It hovered in the air, before it darted to the left, stopped and then darted back to the right, as if it were looking for something.

Abruptly, it flew toward the table and hovered over the corpse of the young woman. Sachiv was about to step forward and shoo it away, but it suddenly plunged down into her body, through her chest. The body arched off the table, and her rib cage ignited with a bright flash of light under the sheet which was covering her.

Suddenly she inhaled a large noisy breath and her eyes flew open. She sank back to the table her eyes darting around nervously. Sachiv could do nothing but stare in complete disbelief, his mouth hanging open as she sat up slowly, clutching the sheet to her naked body. She looked down at the small tag attached to her toe, and then down to her body in confusion. He could tell the moment she realized where she was. Her eyes flew to Sachiv and then to the scalpel in his hand… and then, she started screaming.

Louisa's eyes flew open and she shrugged the blanket off, uncurling herself from the uncomfortable chair and stretching the kinks out of her back. Yawning slightly, she stood and checked Jake's vitals, before resetting the monitors.

She smoothed his hair back from his forehead and dropped a kiss against his cool skin. Biting back the tears she pulled in a deep breath, glancing down at her watch. She was about to settle back down in the chair, when she turned in surprise. A bright ball of light shot in through the window, straight through the glass, as if it weren't even there. She watched in fascination, her mouth hanging open, as it reared up and plunged into Jake's chest. His body jolted violently and arched upward, his torso glowed momentarily beneath his hospital gown, and the monitors went nuts. His arms flailed wildly as he tried to drag in a deep breath, but couldn't because of the breathing tube. He began to choke, and frantically reached up to pull the tube from his throat.

'Jake stop!' Louisa pinned his arms to his waist,

putting all her weight behind it. God damn it, he was strong.

She wrestled with him, as he tried to pull himself up.

'Can I get some help in here?' she yelled as several nurses and student doctors rushed past the room. It was a pretty safe bet that if Jake had woken up, the other coma patients probably had as well.

A young brown haired nurse ran into the room, and helped her to restrain Jake.

'Jake…' Louisa grabbed his face, and forced his wild blue eyes to meet hers. 'Jake, calm down its me…' gradually he slowed his frantic movements and turned to look at her. 'There, that's it,' she crooned softly as she stroked his face soothingly, 'you need to calm down.'

He watched her with wide eyes, as she relaxed her grip on his hands. He raised one hand and touched the tube taped to his mouth.

'Okay,' she nodded, glancing across at the monitors. 'I'm going to take the tube out, but you need to remain calm, okay?'

He nodded slowly.

'Josie,' she turned to the nurse, 'can you help me?'

They both tucked a hand under each of his arms and helped him to sit up. Raising the bed and tucking some more pillows behind him, the nurse switched the oxygen off and unhooked the tube. Switching off another machine and moving it out of the way, Louisa removed the pieces of tape holding the tube in place, and grasped the end firmly.

'Right, on the count of three, I want you to exhale as hard as you can okay?'

Jake nodded.

'Okay…one…two…three.'

Jake blew out as hard as he could, and as she pulled the tube out firmly and handed it to the nurse, he began to cough.

'I'll get him some water,' Josie picked up the discarded tubing.

'Thanks,' Louisa turned back to her brother who had fallen back against the cushions.

'Where's Roni?' he croaked in a whisper.

'Jake,' Louisa frowned, 'I don't think you should be worrying about that right now.'

'Where…is…she?' he grabbed her wrist tightly.

'She's…,' Louisa sighed, 'she went after the Soul Collector with Helga,' she frowned and shook her head, 'I mean…Danae.'

'Damn it,' he croaked, grasping the sheets to push them back.

'What the hell are you doing?' she shoved him back against the bed, and ripped the sheets from his fingers. 'You're not going anywhere yet.'

'I have to find Roni,' he pushed himself up again, 'she's in danger.'

'I'm here…I'm here…'

Louisa looked up in relief, as Roni rushed through the door, breathing heavily as if she'd been running.

'Thank God,' Louisa sucked in a breath.

Roni crossed the room to Jake's bed and took his hand.

'I'm here and I'm fine,' she looked down at him smiling, 'and you're okay.'

Jake grabbed her hand firmly and yanked her toward him. Caught off balance she fell onto the bed and he wrapped his arms around her tightly.

'You're okay,' Roni whispered more to reassure herself than him, her eyes filling with tears.

She pulled back just far enough so she could look into Jake's eyes.

'I had the strangest dream,' he croaked, running her silky hair through his fingers. 'I dreamed you were shooting bottles with my gun.'

She chuckled lightly and reached back to the

waistband of her jeans, pulling out his gun.

'What, you mean this one?'

'Why have you got my gun?' he frowned. 'What the hell happened?'

'Your girl is pretty bad ass.'

He looked up to see Danae leaning against the door jamb with a cocky smile.

'What?'

'We arrived just in time to see you getting your soul ripped out of your chest, when Roni here sprints after the soul stealing demon and flat out tackles him, like a linebacker.'

'What?' Jake's face drained of color and he turned to Roni angrily. 'Are you insane, putting yourself in danger like that? What the hell were you thinking?'

'To be honest I stopped thinking at that point,' Roni replied ruefully. 'I just knew I couldn't let him escape with your soul.'

'Jesus Roni,' he raked his hand shakily through his hair.

'Look she's making it sound worse than it was,' Roni told him. 'He couldn't hurt me, because I was wearing your amulet.'

'To be fair,' Danae interrupted, 'you didn't actually know that at the time. It was just sheer dumb luck that thing worked.'

'Not helping,' she hissed.

'We'll discuss this later,' Jake threw Roni a look. 'Why don't you tell me what happened after.'

'He got away,' Roni continued, 'but not before Danae managed to get some of his blood. She used a tracking spell and we managed to track him to the north west woods.'

'Where the Bachelier place is,' Danae supplied.

'Why was he there?' Jake frowned.

'It seems he was using the old Hoodoo bottle tree Clea Bachelier put up, to trap the souls he'd stolen, so he could feed off them at his leisure.'

Jake suppressed a shudder at the thought of the demon feeding off his soul. 'So how did you stop him?'

'We didn't,' Roni told him softly. 'It was Olivia and Theo.'

'What?' Louisa piped up, 'they're back? Where are they? Are they hurt?'

'No, they're not here, and I don't think so,' Danae answered each of her questions in turn.

'Where are they then?' Jake asked.

Danae shrugged.

'I don't know,' she replied. 'There was some sort of disturbance in the air, close to the tree. I'm not a hundred percent certain, but I think it may have been a smaller gateway than the one we saw on the lake. Olivia and Theo grabbed the Soul Collector, and dragged him through. Then they disappeared too.'

'And the souls?'

'Released,' Roni told him, 'all of them. Those who are able to, should return to their bodies, like you did. The others should be able to move on, to whichever afterlife they are destined for.'

'Jesus,' Jake rubbed his eyes in exhaustion, 'so we still don't know where Olivia and Theo are?'

'No,' Danae shook her head. 'I just hope wherever they are that they're okay.'

Olivia and Theo hit the ground hard and rolled out the reach of the Soul Collector. The wind howled like a hurricane, tearing at their hair and clothes, raking their skin with its severity. They scrambled back out of the way as the gateway crumbled, and disappeared into the encroaching vortex of blackness. The Soul Collector began to slide across the ground, caught up in the suction of that great black gaping maw. He stopped struggling with the collar glowing at his shredded bloodied throat, and rolled over onto his stomach clawing frantically at the earth, trying to stop his inexorable slide back toward oblivion. His eyes were wide with madness, and his mouth was agape, rimmed with frothing spittle.

The wind picked up pace, until it was like being caught in the path of an approaching tornado. Bridget's feet were pulled out from under her, and she slid across the ground toward the Void and the demon desperately trying to claw his way out of its path of destruction.

'BRIDGET!' Olivia screamed, as she reached out and caught Bridget's hand.

Theo's hand snatched out and grabbed the back of Olivia's backpack to stop her from being dragged forward, and he reached back with his other hand, so Sam could grab him and anchor him to something.

Bridget cried out in pain, as the demon grabbed her ankle and sunk his sharp claw like nails deeply into her flesh. He speared her calf with the claws of his other hand, and began to painfully claw his way up her body, tearing her flesh as he went.

'Olivia let me go,' Bridget cried in pain as he embedded his claws into her lower back.

'NO!' she shook her head.

'You have to,' she whispered through the pain. 'Just remember…it was always meant to be you…'

'NO!' Olivia screamed and reached out desperately, but Bridget ripped her hand from Olivia's grasp. Rolling over she wrapped her arms and legs around the demon, rolling them both to the edge, and over into the darkness.

'Olivia we have to go,' Theo dragged her back and hauled her to her feet, as the wall of nothingness inched closer to them. 'WE HAVE TO GO NOW!'

He grabbed her hand and dragged her away from the edge. She felt Sam grasp her other hand, and the chaos around her blurred and shifted. She found herself running, being dragged along by Sam and Theo. In the distance she could see the giant wrought iron archway, and the words

'MERCY CEMETERY' in elegant, spidery letters.

She risked a look behind them, and her stomach leapt in fear. Despite them running flat out, the world they knew was disappearing behind them fast, consumed by the roaring black inferno churning up everything in its path. She pushed herself to move faster, her breath was coming in big labored gasps, and her heart hammered in her chest. The muscles in her legs screamed in protest, and her backpack banged painfully against her spine with every step, but she didn't dare stop, or even slow down.

Her palms were sweaty with exertion, and she kept losing her grip on Sam, and then Theo. Sam allowed her to release his grip, and kept pace next to her, but Theo wouldn't let her go. His death like grip on her hand would have been amusing under any other circumstances, but at this particular point, she couldn't be anything other than profoundly grateful. They ran under the huge archway and down the small winding path, which ran between rows and rows of gravestones.

Behind them came a loud ominous grinding, the heart stopping sound of metal twisting and bending under great strain, but they didn't dare turn back to look. If they had they would have seen the great iron archway folding in on itself, and disappearing into the wall of blackness.

They cut across graves, leaping over decorative borders and urns, trying desperately not to trip and fall. They skirted around smaller mausoleums, and towering statues of Angels, but nothing survived. All fell before the destructive might of the Void, they all crumbled into the deep well of forever, never to be seen again.

'Is it much further?' Olivia panted, as she stumbled from sheer exhaustion.

'It's not far,' Sam turned back in time to see Olivia trip over the decorative edging of an old grave, which had been partially concealed by overgrown weeds.

Olivia felt her foot tangle and she went down, unable to stop herself. She rolled over, helpless to do anything, but watch the endless Void rushing toward her. She felt strong familiar arms lifting her, Theo pulled her roughly into his arms and began to run once again.

'Sam, get to the entrance!' Theo breathed heavily.

Olivia looked up, and saw a large rectangular building with pale walls, which may have been white once but had faded to light grey. It was surrounded by majestic Greek style columns, small archways lined the walls, where windows would have been. There was a pitched roof and on the smooth front gable was the name West deeply etched into the stonework.

It was weird, she'd been to the West section of Mercy cemetery, back in the real world. She'd explored it thoroughly with Theo when they were searching for Charlotte West's grave, and she'd never come across a family mausoleum like this one. They skidded to a halt outside the entrance, which was a heavy oak door overlaid with an iron gate.

'Hurry up and open it,' Theo dropped Olivia to the ground holding onto her tightly.

'I'm working on it,' Sam breathed heavily as he laid his hands against the rusted metal.

Olivia and Theo turned, pressing their backs closer to Sam, and shoving him forward, as the Void churned up the grounds in front of them. Gravestones were ripped loose and swallowed, trees were yanked roughly out at the roots and devoured. Grass, paths, urns and flowers all toppled helplessly into the Void.

'SAM!' Olivia yelled above the noise, 'ANYTIME NOW WOULD BE GOOD!'

'YOU'RE NOT HELPING!' he hissed in frustration.

'SAM!' Theo shouted in desperation.

'Got you,' Sam breathed as the door swung inward and all three of them leapt into the dark entrance, to find themselves tumbling into a deep well of blackness, like Alice falling down the rabbit hole.

Part 2.
The Underworld

20.

Like Alice, it felt as if they had been falling through the dark silence forever, with no concept of time or distance. Olivia began to wonder idly if the Underworld was so far below the surface, it was indeed located at the very center of the Earth. Or maybe it wasn't under the Earth at all, but somewhere else entirely. She was so lost in her wandering thoughts, it came as a surprise when they finally hit the ground with a collective humph, in a vicious tangle of arms, elbows and bodies.

'Get off,' Olivia wheezed. She wasn't sure who it was, but someone was crushing her.

'Sorry,' Sam whispered and the pressure on her chest eased.

'Olivia?' she heard Theo's voice in the darkness, and she felt a hand groping her breast.

'That'd better be you copping a feel Theo,' she whispered.

His quiet chuckle made her smile, despite her aching limbs. 'Sorry,' he replied, running his hand down her arm to touch her hand.

'Hang on a minute, this is no good, I can't see a damn thing.' Olivia snapped her fingers and two of her dragonflies burst into flames, but rather than the warm gold and red of her Earth fire, they blazed the fiery black and sapphire blue of Hell fire.

The dragonflies hovered close, casting an eerie

blue glow over them, but it was enough to see by. The guys were already standing and Theo leaned down and grasped a hand, pulling her gently to her feet.

'Are you okay?' he cupped her neck gently as he checked her for injuries.

'I'm fine,' she smiled, 'just bumps and bruises.'

'You went down pretty hard in the cemetery.'

'I'm good,' she nodded. 'I banged up my elbow a bit, but like I said it's just bruises. What about you?'

'I am uninjured,' Theo reassured her.

'Sam?'

'I'm good,' he turned to them both. 'So this is the Underworld?'

'I take it you've never been before?' Olivia asked curiously.

'Nope, first timer,' he replied. 'So I hope you weren't hoping for a guide, because I've got no clue.'

'I guess we will just have to figure it out together.' Theo took Olivia's hand, and turned to look around, unable to see anything outside of the circle of blue light. 'I can't see anything,' he frowned. 'Why don't you try the compass?'

Reaching into her shirt, she pulled out the small golden compass, flicked the lid open and stared down at it. Nothing happened. She shook it a few times and waited. Definitely nothing. She was beginning to wonder if Hades realized he'd given her a dud. Either that, or he was having a joke at her expense.

'Zip,' she snapped it shut irritably.

'So now what?' Sam frowned, 'there's nothing here. We could end up wandering aimlessly for eternity.'

'Well I don't have that long,' Olivia sighed. 'I just want to go home, so let's find my mom, and get this done.'

'Any ideas?'

'I guess we just start walking,' she shrugged, and squeezing Theo's hand reassuringly, they set off at a brisk pace.

'You know we could be walking in completely the wrong direction,' Sam grumbled.

'Not helping,' Olivia blew out a frustrated breath.

'Sorry,' he muttered.

They walked in silence for the most part. There was something about the darkness that seemed to set a quiet reflective mood. Olivia's mind wandered, and she found herself relaxing. She could now feel the low hum of power beneath her feet, and that feeling of eternal vastness. She cocked her head unconsciously as they moved, trying to listen. It almost felt like the darkness was whispering to her. To the left, at the edge of her peripheral vision, she thought she caught something. She turned her head quickly, but it vanished.

'What is it?' Theo asked in concern.

'Nothing,' she murmured, 'I just thought I saw...' she shook her head. 'Nothing...never mind.'

They pressed on into the darkness, their way lit by the glow of her dragonflies, but after a while the strange apparition came again, ghosting along at the edge of her vision, dancing just out of sight. She turned her head again, and caught a wisp of fine smoke-like vapor.

'I don't think we're alone,' Olivia whispered to Theo, as he wrapped his arm around her and pulled her in closer.

The ground under their feet gradually began to change, and the smooth surface changed to a more uneven gravel-like consistency. Even the ground itself seemed more uneven, rising and falling in mounds and dips. They began to pass by boulders and outcroppings of dark grey rock. The strange silvery blue smoke once again brushed past them, this time remaining visible. Theo sucked in a sharp breath, as a pale ghostly figure swept past them, followed by another. All three of them stopped and looked around, realizing they were surrounded by them. Like a bloom of jellyfish, they drifted along silently, completely unaware of the three mortals standing in their midst.

'Are they ghosts?' Theo asked.

'Shades,' Sam murmured, as an old man sailed past him, blissfully ignorant.

They were, for the most part, in human form. They were made up of a thin wraith like mist and seemed to be hollowed out shells of their former selves, content to drift along, not knowing or caring about anything around them. Although they still had heads, arms and torsos, their legs had disappeared to be replaced with filmy, tentacle-like tendrils, which floated and billowed, as if they were underwater.

'I think I know where we are,' Olivia whispered.

'What?' Sam frowned, 'where?'

She suddenly grabbed both Sam and Theo, and dragged them behind a large outcropping of rock.

'What the hell Olivia?' Sam grumbled.

'We can't follow them,' she shook her head.

'What's going on Livy?' Theo asked, his voice low and soft. 'Where are we?'

'Erebus,' she whispered, 'a place of darkness between Earth and Hades.'

'Hades?' he asked in confusion.

'Hades the place, not Hades the person,' she clarified. 'The first level of the Underworld was named for the God that rules it.'

'Okay,' Theo guessed, 'so this is what? A place where the dead pass after dying?'

'That's exactly what it is,' she nodded.

'So this is an in-between place', Sam spoke up, 'not the actual Underworld?'

'No,' she looked over and pointed. 'That's the Underworld.'

As they turned to look, Theo gasped and Sam's mouth fell open in disbelief.

'Holy mother of God,' Sam breathed, his eyes wide. 'That thing must be nearly five hundred meters tall.'

Olivia gazed up at the colossal stone gateway. She

realized Sam was probably right, and at around five hundred meters, it was probably higher than the Empire State Building. The word, 'Hades' was etched deeply into the crest of the arch, and the rest of the stonework was engraved with lettering that she couldn't make out at this distance. Inside the great stone archway were two gigantic thick oak doors, each adorned with a huge black metal ring, serving as a handle that no mortal could ever possibly open.

'We need to get closer,' Olivia whispered. She glanced up at her dragonflies, which were now hovering close to her shoulder, and had dulled to a muted throbbing blue, as if they knew to make themselves as unobtrusive as possible. 'Stay low, and use the rocks as cover.'

'Olivia,' Theo frowned, 'I don't think the shades can see us, and even if they can, I don't think they care.'

'It's not them I'm worried about,' she replied.

'What then?'

'That,' she pointed.

'Jesus Christ,' he gasped. 'What the fuck is that?'

Olivia's mouth curved in fleeting amusement. Theo never swore, but he'd obviously been around Jake and Tommy too much, as the word had fallen easily from his startled lips.

She turned back to the creature he was staring at, which prowled back and forth across the gateway. It was enormous, and padded slowly on thick paws. Its body sleek, shiny, and black, glimmered in the pale light of the huge torches, which burned either side of the vast doors, in gigantic braziers. Three heads sprouted from its powerful shoulders, as it growled at the shades approaching the gates.

'Cerberus,' Olivia breathed. 'He's Hades' pet.'

'That's a pet?'

'He guards the gateway. From what I understand, he's there to prevent anyone trying to escape the Underworld, rather than to stop anyone trying to enter,'

Olivia told him.

'That's probably because no one has ever been stupid enough to try and break into the Underworld before.'

'Well you're wrong about that,' Olivia muttered, 'but we don't have time for a history lesson right now. I don't think he would try to stop us from entering, but I sure as hell don't want to put it to the test. Besides, we don't know what we're walking into on the other side.'

'Then how are we supposed to get in?'

'I don't know yet,' she shook her head. 'Let's try to get closer, I can't see much from here.'

'Maybe we should just go up and knock?' Sam suggested. 'That thing is Hades' pet, and Hades did tell you to come to the Underworld. I don't get all the creeping around.'

'Because, Hades himself told me that there has been an uprising. We don't know who is loyal to Hades and who would just hand us straight over to Nathaniel. We can't take the risk; we can't be seen.'

Nodding in agreement, they did as she suggested, creeping forward slowly, using the rocks as cover until they were only about ten meters from the gate itself.

Set out at intervals in front of the gate, were nine tall thick columns, and each bore one word. Below that word, was a mortal suspended by chains. The first one was a fairly young looking male, and although he seemed more or less unharmed, his face was filled with indescribable grief. The next one, was a middle-aged female whose expression bore the marks of great anxiety. Next to her was another a male, by the looks of it, but she couldn't tell for sure, as it was ravaged by disease. Flies buzzed around it and its skin was red, raised and angry, covered by boils.

She ran her gaze along each column, taking in the object lesson, an old woman, and then a man, so emaciated he was barely more than stretched flesh over a skeleton, with dark sunken eyes. The next appeared to be dead, and next to her, one whose face was filled with absolute agony. The last one seemed to be sleeping.

'What are they there for?' Theo whispered.

'I'm not sure,' Olivia murmured. 'Maybe they're warnings, or object lessons or fears. I don't know.'

'I wonder what the words say?'

'You can't read it?' she asked in surprise.

He shook his head and she turned to Sam. 'Can you read it?'

He shook his head too.

'You can?' Sam asked her in surprise. 'That's one of the ancient languages. There are very few who can read it.'

'What does it say?'

She went along the row reading each one in turn.

'Grief, Anxiety, Disease, Old Age, Fear, Hunger, Death, Agony and Sleep.'

'Jesus,' Theo raked his hand through his hair. 'I don't know what they're for, but I'd just as soon not end up as one of them.'

'I hear you,' Sam agreed, 'but there's no other way through.'

'Yes there is,' Olivia spoke up suddenly. She didn't know where the words had come from, or why she knew they were true, but as she turned to face them she could feel it deep inside her, a knowledge that had been sitting there all along, just waiting for her to need it.

'Not far from here, there's another way in, a secret way.'

They followed behind her curiously, as she ducked down behind the rocks, and began to head away from the gigantic gateway. The further away they got, the more they realized, it wasn't just a single gateway in the middle of nowhere, like the one on the lake outside her house had been. This gateway split a huge rock wall, which speared up into the blackness, as high as the gate itself or possibly even higher. They turned quietly, and followed the perimeter, creeping along the edge of the huge black wall like thieves, until Olivia stopped abruptly.

'This is it,' she smiled.

'Err…Olivia,' Sam paused, 'it's just a wall.'

Theo frowned, Sam was right. He couldn't see anything but the wall, stretching into the darkness.

'Livy, are you sure?'

She took a step closer to the wall, and then a step to the left, and disappeared.

'Olivia!' Theo rushed forward.

'What?' she reappeared.

'How did you do that? Sam asked suspiciously.

'It's just an optical illusion,' she beckoned them closer. 'Look…'

They stepped closer and realized there was an alcove cut into the wall, which they couldn't see until they stepped forward. Once inside there were stairs cut into the rock, which led upward.

'How did you know this was here?' Sam asked carefully.

'I don't know,' Olivia shook her head, as she began to climb. 'It's like the knowledge was there, stored inside my mind, but I didn't think of it until Theo said there was no way through the gateway. It kinda feels like Déjà vu.'

Theo and Sam shot each other a concerned look, before climbing up after her. It seemed to take forever to reach the top of the steps. Their calf muscles were burning in protest, and they were breathless, as they finally emerged onto what appeared to be a walkway or parapet, which had been carved straight into the rock face.

'God, that was…'

Olivia clamped her hand over Sam's mouth, and dragged both him, and Theo down to the hard ground, so they were concealed behind the low wall. She placed her finger over her lips, and then pointed.

Sam turned his head to look. They had emerged

on the other side of the wall, and now had a good look at the gateway from the inside. It looked much as it had from the front, with an exception. Instead of a monstrous, gigantic, three headed dog prowling back and forth, there was a row of strange, vicious looking birds perched on the arch of the gateway, looking down and watching the emerging shades, like vultures trying to decide which corpses to pick over.

Sam's eyes narrowed as he looked closer, and he shuddered in revulsion. Each of the birds had the body and wingspan of a bird, but the head and face of a woman with a cruel pointed beak instead of a mouth. Harpies, he thought in disgust. They hunted for the Erinyes, and were never far from them.

His gaze swept down to the gateway, which opened onto the shore of a river. Beside it lounged three incredibly beautiful, identical, black haired women. They wore diaphanous gowns of blue black, which were draped with jewels, and protruding from their shoulders were leathery looking, bat-like wings.

'Damn it,' Sam whispered. 'The Erinyes.'

Olivia looked over to the three, exotic looking, female creatures. She knew exactly what they were, the Furies, as they were more commonly known.

Alecto, Megaera and Tisiphone, the three Goddesses associated with the souls of the dead. They avenged crimes against the natural order of the world, particularly crimes by children against their parents, such as Matricide and Patricide, and their punishment was to inflict madness upon the murderer.

Now, although Olivia hadn't committed matricide as yet, she had set fire to her parents' house with her mother in it, and she did intend to cause her mother some serious harm if she got her hands on her. It was a bit of a grey area, and one she preferred not to flash up on the Furies' radar. Probably best to just avoid them at all costs.

She looked over to Sam, who was pointing and

indicating for them to start moving away from the gateway and further into the dark Underworld. Nodding in agreement, she turned and nudged Theo to get him moving. They crept silently along the wall, until it began to descend.

Once they reached the bottom, they hid amongst the bushes and shrubbery, which lined each bank of the river. A light suddenly appeared in the darkness, hovering over the mist covered water. It glided slowly closer, bypassing them and heading for the shore.

'Come on,' Sam mouthed, but Olivia was still, watching that strangely familiar light.

'Wait,' she mouthed back.

As the light drew closer to the shore the mist parted, and a small boat appeared. It was a wooden skiff, and from one end hung an old fashioned lantern. It bumped gently against the shore, and a familiar figure stepped out of the boat, onto the sand.

'Charon,' Olivia whispered.

Charon stepped out onto the sand, and glanced up as one of the Furies broke away from her sisters and headed straight for him.

'Charon!' she hissed acidly, 'you have some nerve showing your face here.'

'Megaera,' he sighed in resignation, 'what's the problem this time?'

'You have been plotting against us, whispering in Hades' ear, poisoning him against us to gain his favor.'

'I don't need to gain his favor,' he replied blandly. 'I already have it, it's called loyalty. If you and your sisters weren't so volatile and self-serving, then maybe he might be more inclined to listen to you.'

'Carrion,' she hissed, 'you think you're better than us? You think to trap us here, while the rest of the Underworld is on the verge of war.'

'That was Hades' decision not mine.' His eyes narrowed, as he noticed the blood red apple in her sister

Alecto's claw like hand. It had three bite marks in it, revealing the white flesh of the fruit, and the poisonous black seeds at its core.

Shaking his head in frustration, Charon leaned to one side to look around the three of them, and saw the smirking woman reclined on a rock beside the gate.

'Eris,' Charon grated from between clenched teeth, 'I should've known.' He shook his head in disgust his eyes narrowing. 'Now is really not the time to be causing mischief. And as for you three,' he turned back to the Furies, 'you should know better than to take anything from Eris, especially one of her apples of discord.'

'Please,' Eris rose gracefully from her perch, shaking out her long soft blonde her, her startlingly blue eyes twinkling with mirth. She smoothed the fine gossamer of her scarlet colored gown against her seductive form, and bit into a shiny crimson apple. 'You know what those morons are like for snatching food.'

'I really don't have time for your games Eris,' he glared angrily at the stunningly beautiful Goddess of Chaos.

'Forget those idiots,' she dismissed the fuming sisters with a casual flip of her hand. 'I was simply amusing myself to pass the time, while I waited for you.'

'And why would you do that?'

'I know how highly Hades thinks of you,' she trailed a long red nail along the bare flesh of his arm. 'I thought you could put in a good word for me.'

'And why would I do that?'

'Because I would be very, very grateful,' she purred, looking up at him from beneath devastating lashes. 'I can be a valuable asset for Hades. Just let me loose amongst Nathaniel, and the other traitors, and allow me to do what I do best. A few apples, a few seeds of discontent, and the insurrection will fold before it even gets off the ground. I could be a great ally Charon,' her expression hardened, 'or I can be a formidable enemy.'

'Is that a threat?' he arched a brow in amusement.

'It's a friendly warning,' she replied coolly. 'I've served my time for that unfortunate incident in Palestine.'

'Unfortunate incident?' he snorted. 'Eris, you started a war.'

She shrugged elegantly, 'I want off the gate.'

'Not likely.'

'Why?'

'Because you can't be trusted, just like the Furies.'

'The triplets? Please...' she rolled her eyes, 'they aren't even in the same league as me.'

'I will of course relay your offer to Hades. What he chooses to do about it will be up to him.'

Eris watched with icy blue eyes, as Charon headed toward the two shades waiting by the shore. He held out his hand, watching dispassionately, as the shades reached into their own mouths, one by one, and removed a coin from under their tongues, and handed them to him. Nodding he stepped aside, allowing them to glide effortlessly onto the skiff, and settle against the small wooden bench at the bow.

Charon stepped into the skiff, and pushed away from the shore with his pole. He turned back to Eris, as the boat slid silently into the mist.

'If you want to win Hades' favor Eris,' he told her bluntly, 'no more apples for the triplets.'

Eris rolled her eyes, as the boat was swallowed up by a heavy curtain of mist.

He poled along the waterway in silence, the water of the Acheron lapping soothingly at the sides of the boat. His two guests sat at the fore, staring blankly into the mist. Suddenly, he caught a muted, blue glow, throbbing in the curtain of mist. His eyes narrowed and he slowed his movements, trying to make out the foreign shape in the distance. It hovered in the mist and then danced to the left weaving across the air, making its way closer until it broke through the fog and hung before him, sparkling with delicate blue black flames.

His eyes widened in shock, as he recognized the burning dragonfly. His head whipped around to make sure he could no longer be seen by the occupants on the riverbank. Satisfied that they were well disguised by the mist, he turned back to the dragonfly.

'Take me to her,' he whispered to it.

Shivering in delight, it danced in the air and then shot back into the mist. Charon dug his pole back into the bed of the river, and pushed off again, picking up speed, and chasing the strange glowing creature of flame.

After a moment, it shot across to the bank at the right hand side of the river. Adjusting his course, the small skiff suddenly bumped gently against the bank, and Charon stepped out onto the soft springy turf amidst the bushes and shrubs.

'Olivia?' he whispered into the darkness.

She stepped out from where she had been concealed, and his face broke into a smile. He threw his arms around her, and pulled her in close, hugging her tightly.

'What the hell are you doing here?' he breathed quietly.

'We're here to find the last Crossroad,' she replied.

'We?' He looked up and saw Theo. 'I see you found him then,' he grinned and hugged Theo too.

'Charon,' Theo greeted him.

Charon pulled back, stiffening as he caught sight of Sam.

'What is he doing here?' he asked coolly.

'He's our friend,' Olivia gave a puzzled frown, 'he's here to help us.'

'Are you sure about that?'

'What do you mean?' she asked gazing back and forth, between the two men staring warily at each other.

'Like Olivia said,' Sam answered. 'I'm here to help them.'

'When has one of your kind ever done something to help someone else. Your first loyalty will always be to Heaven.'

'So you know what I am then.'

'And I know who you are. When your father realizes where you are, he will bring the others, and they will tear this place apart looking for you, and that's something we cannot afford right now. It'd be like pouring gasoline on an already raging inferno,' Charon replied angrily.

'That won't happen,' Sam shook his head. 'The world my father trapped me in no longer exists. As far as he is concerned, I was lost to the Void. Trust me, no one is looking for me.'

Charon's voice lost some of the heat, and his expression now bore more confusion than anger. 'You don't intend to tell him you're still alive? You don't intend to return to your people?'

'No,' Sam breathed quietly, voicing aloud for the first time the decision that had been inside him all along, even if he hadn't wanted to acknowledge it. 'I'm not going back.'

'Why?' Charon asked, genuinely puzzled.

'Because I'm not like them,' Sam spoke quietly. 'It's time to start thinking for myself.'

'Interesting,' Charon's eyes narrowed, studying Sam as if he was some kind of obscure specimen under a microscope.

'Charon,' Olivia tugged on his arm pulling his attention from Sam. 'We need to get to the Crossroad before Nathaniel does. How much do you know about what's going on?'

'A lot more than you,' he shook his head and glanced around nervously. 'We can't talk here. All of you, get in the boat and get down; you mustn't let anyone see you.'

Detecting his sense of urgency, they all clambered

into the boat and lay down on the bottom boards, so they couldn't be seen.

'What about them?' Theo asked looking over at the two shades still hovering at the stern.

'They won't even notice you.' Charon climbed back into the boat and pushed away from the bank. 'You said you're here to find the last Crossroad?'

'Yes,' Olivia whispered.

'You haven't got long, Nathaniel has already destroyed four of them. The whole Underworld is up in arms, not just this one but all of them.'

'I don't understand?'

'All of the Hell dimensions are connected to each other, pieces of a whole, but ruled by separate entities. Hades all the way down to Tartarus is ruled by Hades, Sheol is ruled by the Hebrew God, Hell is controlled by Lucifer.

'Okay I get it, so it's like a huge theme park divided into different sections.'

'What's a theme park?' Charon frowned.

'Forget it,' she shook her head.

'Anyway, all the other demons originated in Hell. They serve Lucifer, but they have broken some of the oldest, most ancient laws governing the Hell dimensions by coming into Hades' Underworld and destroying the Crossroads. It's a declaration of war.'

'Lucifer allowed this?'

'Lucifer is still locked away in a cage in the deepest pits of Hell where he was cast down.'

'So, it's a coup?' Olivia frowned. 'Nathaniel is looking to overthrow Lucifer, and he needs the book to do it.'

'And his brother Seth.'

'Fuck,' she muttered.

'Mortals,' Charon murmured rolling his eyes.

'We still need to get to the Crossroad before him. Do you know how to find it?'

'No, I haven't got a clue, none of us do. We still don't even know how he managed to find them. They aren't static; they fluctuate in and out of synch with the rest of the Underworld. That's how they stay hidden. They are never in the same place for long.'

'So how is he finding them?' Olivia frowned.

'I just don't know.'

'How am I supposed to find them?'

'I don't know that either…but I know someone who does.'

'Who?'

'I can take you to Hecate. If anyone knows how to find the Crossroad, she will.'

'Hecate?' Olivia replied, 'the Goddess of the moon?'

'Pagans,' he shook his head in exasperation, 'only half right as usual. Hecate is the Goddess of Crossroads, and Entranceways.'

'Oh.'

'I just have to take these shades to the Judges, and then I'll take you to Hecate.'

'Thank you Charon.'

'Don't thank me yet, she's notoriously difficult to deal with.'

Settling back onto the uncomfortable bottom of the boat, she reached for Theo's hand and felt his fingers entwine with hers. Looking up, she watched as they passed beneath a huge Elm tree, so vast its branches spanned the entire width of the river. She watched idly as pictures and images flitted across the leaves.

'What's that?' she murmured.

'Don't touch it,' Charon warned, looking up at the beautiful ancient tree in disgust. 'False dreams cling to every leaf. Trust me, it wouldn't be good for you if you were to touch it.'

'But it's so beautiful,' she whispered.

'You witches,' he shook his head, 'so drawn to

nature. It may be beautiful, but that is what makes it so dangerous.'

Olivia settled down again and after a while the gentle rocking of the boat and the soothing lap of the water began to lull her toward sleep. Suddenly, she felt a gentle bump as the boat slid against the shore.

'Stay here,' Charon whispered, and for pity's sake don't let anyone see you.'

He climbed out of the boat, and the two shades followed him obediently. Too curious for her own good, Olivia risked a small peek over the edge of the boat.

The shore sloped upward to three gigantic stone seats, which resembled thrones, and braziers which burned between them. Three old men sat in the seats, towering over Charon who appeared dwarfed in comparison.

'Minos, Rhadamanthus, Aeacus,' Charon bowed respectfully.

The shades drifted forward to be judged and he began to back away quietly.

'WAIT!' Minos suddenly roared, standing up to his full immense height. 'What is the meaning of this treachery Charon!'

'My lord?' Charon swallowed nervously.

'You have brought mortals into our presence!' his voice boomed all the way down to the banks of the shore.

'My lord,' Charon began slowly.

'Bring them forth and let them be judged!'

21.

'WHAT HAVE YOU DONE?' Aeacus thundered, as he too rose from his chair. 'This is heresy, you flaunt our laws by bringing mortals into our realm!'

'My lords,' Charon took a step back trying to placate them.

Rhadamanthus sat watching, quietly curious.

'You know mortals are forbidden here,' Minos hissed. 'You will be punished for this.'

'Enough!' Aeacus roared. 'Bring them before us!'

'My Lord,' Charon tried to intervene, 'if I could but explain.'

'Olivia,' Sam hissed as she began to move.

'Sam, we don't really have a choice, they already know we're here. We might as well face them. The quicker we do, the quicker we can be on our way.'

'She's right Sam,' Theo replied. 'I don't think we have any other choice. We're in their realm now, and at their mercy.'

'Not if I can help it,' Olivia muttered sourly, as she sighed in frustration. She really didn't have time for this.

She sat up, as Theo climbed over the side and leaned in to helped her out. Sam trailed behind them and they started up the embankment toward the three giant men. There really was no other way around it, they were going to have to confront them.

She stared up at the imposing sight of the three colossal old men towering above them. Two of them were glaring murderously, the other seemed content to remain in his seat watching with interest as events unfolded.

Olivia tried to focus, but her mind seemed to keep wandering. Everything around her seemed to hum with a strange vibration. She could feel the undercurrents of power running through the ground beneath her feet, the vast ancient power in the very air, as she drew it into her lungs.

A strange kind of dreamy lassitude fell over her and oddly, she found herself feeling at ease. She could sense the tension in Theo's body, in the rigid set of his jaw and shoulders. Sam, who was now on her other side, flanking her protectively, was radiating nervous energy. She should have been afraid, and her logical mind was telling her to be careful. The ancient men before her looked upon them as nothing more than mortal insects, and yet she found she did not fear them. If anything they were really annoying her.

'Alright Minos' she sighed, 'you have my attention. You can stop shrieking like a fishwife.'

His eyes widened and his nostrils flared in anger, almost as if he couldn't quite believe what he was hearing.

'INSOLENT MORTAL!' he thundered. 'HOW DARE YOU!'

'Olivia!' Sam hissed, 'what are you doing?'

'Be quiet Sam,' she told him quietly.

'I WILL HAVE YOUR SOUL FOR THIS!'

'No,' Olivia replied coolly, 'you won't.'

'You are a very, very foolish mortal,' Aeacus leaned closer to her, his eyes narrowing dangerously.

'You think so Aeacus?' she replied calmly.

'I will have the flesh stripped from your bones and fed to Eurynomos, then I will personally condemn your soul to the fields of punishment for all eternity,' Minos growled dangerously.

Olivia yawned insultingly and glanced down at her watch.

'Are you quite done with your empty threats old man? We do have somewhere we have to be and you're interfering.'

Minos sputtered furiously, almost as if he was so angry he couldn't even form the words.

A small chuckle had Olivia glancing across to the third seated man who was watching her in amusement, his eyes twinkling with mirth.

'Something amusing you Rhadamanthus?' she asked casually.

'Perhaps I am just enjoying the very rare sight of Minos rendered speechless. As someone who very much enjoys the sound of his own voice, it is a rare occurrence indeed.'

'Glad I stopped by to entertain you,' she replied dryly.

'Tell me girl,' Rhadamanthus leaned forward, 'how is it you know who each of us are?'

Olivia stared back at him thoughtfully, that was an extremely good question. She'd seen their names in the history books of course, but the moment she'd approached, she'd instinctively known which was which.

'Lucky guess,' she answered cagily.

'Very lucky,' he smiled in amusement.

'Rhadamanthus!' Aeacus growled, 'stop conversing with it and let us pronounce its punishment.'

'Aeacus,' he sighed in resignation, 'you really are getting to be as bad as Minos. Use your head, can you not tell this one is different?'

'Olivia,' Sam growled under his breath, 'will you stop provoking them. These are the Judges of the Underworld.'

'Judges?' she scoffed, 'more like crotchety old

men, who just like the sound of their own voices too much.'

'Crotchety?' Aeacus sputtered indignantly, 'how dare you speak to us like this!'

Rhadamanthus seemed content to sit back with a small smile playing on his lips.

'Theo,' Sam hissed, 'do something before she gets us all killed.'

'What do you expect me to do?' he asked. 'If she's not going to listen to the Judges of the Underworld, what makes you think she'll listen to me?'

'We really don't have time for this,' Olivia sighed. 'I'm here because Hades asked me to come. If you have a problem with it, then I suggest you take it up with him.'

'Hades?' Both Aeacus and Minos echoed, while Rhadamanthus leaned forward in interest.

'Yes, Hades,' she repeated.

'You lie!' Minos roared reaching out to pluck her from the ground.

She felt her power burst out of her, like a dam bursting its banks, sudden and violent. The vast ancient power she'd felt in her own world, when she'd called forth Hell fire, paled in comparison to the power she summoned now that she was surrounded by the source of it. A great wall of Hell fire exploded in front of her, knocking Minos back several paces, and throwing him toward his stone throne.

Aeacus took an involuntary step back in shock, and Rhadamanthus chuckled lightly.

'It seems the child has power,' he looked across at Olivia meeting her eyes. 'Tell me child, why are you here?'

'That is my business,' she replied quietly. 'If you want to know, you are welcome to ask Hades, but for now I suggest you let us go on our way. From what I understand, Hades doesn't like to be crossed.'

'What is your name child?'

'Olivia West.'

'Olivia West,' his mouth curved, as he spread his hands. 'Then by all means, you are free to depart.'

'Rhadamanthus!' Aeacus hissed.

His held up his hand silencing his companion.

'Thank you Rhadamanthus,' she replied quietly as they turned and headed back toward Charon's boat.

'Olivia?' he called softly, causing her to pause and turn back toward him. 'You be sure to come back and visit me sometime.'

She smiled in amusement, 'I may just do that.'

They headed back to the boat in silence and climbed in. Olivia settled herself down on the small bench. There didn't really seem much point in hiding now, and she didn't feel like lying back down on the floor of the boat. She pulled off her backpack, and planted it between her feet, rolling her shoulders to ease the ache, and as she looked up she found Theo, Charon, and Sam all staring at her.

'What?' she asked innocently.

'No one has ever spoken to the judges that way,' Charon frowned.

'Well then, I'm sure it's a refreshing change of pace for them,' she replied.

'Holy Hell Olivia,' Sam shook his head incredulously, 'you have balls of steel.'

'No, I'm just sick of them all thinking it's okay to throw their weight around, because they think they're a big deal.'

'Olivia, they kind of are a big deal,' Theo answered.

'It just gets my back up,' she frowned, 'the way they refer to us. The way they say 'mortals' like we're some kind of sub species. Yet we're the ones they call, when the world needs saving,' she pouted moodily.

Theo started chuckling, leaning forward and kissing her.

'Is it any wonder I fell in love with you,' he shook

his head in amusement.

She kissed him back, and entwined her fingers with his.

'Charon, can we go to see Hecate now?' she asked. 'I have to get to the Crossroad before Nathaniel, and I really don't want Hades pissed at me anymore than he already is.'

Charon nodded in understanding and used the pole to push the small boat away from the shore.

'So where are we going?' Theo asked.

'We are on the River Acheron at the moment. Not too far upstream, the river forks and splits off into the River Styx. The Styx circles the Underworld seven times, that is how we'll reach Hecate's temple.'

Theo nodded, and settled more comfortably onto the bench next to Olivia.

They set off along the river, and before long they did indeed branch off onto the River Styx. The rhythm of the boat, and the gentle lap of the water was lulling, and time began to slip past unnoticed.

Sam stared down absently into the murky water of the river, and his thoughts began to drift. He'd done it, he'd finally done the one thing he'd dreamed of for longer than he cared to admit. He'd defied his father. Not only that, he'd betrayed his people. He'd become a traitor…because, he'd chosen Scarlett over his own people. He had put his own desire to protect her ahead of those of his own kind, his own father.

He frowned unconsciously, Olivia was right. He needed to talk to Scarlett, he needed to explain to her…to tell her…what? What exactly was he going to tell her? That his father had convinced him to use her? She'd never forgive him, and it was all his father's fault. Everything was his father's fault. If he hadn't convinced him to betray the one person he cared about most in the universe, he wouldn't have to pretend he was dead, that he'd been lost to the Void.

A painful thought suddenly occurred to him, he could never go home. How could he explain the truth to Scarlett, when he couldn't go home? He was in an impossible situation. If he stayed away and let them believe he was lost, he would never see her again, but if he returned home, he would be forced to betray her and he would lose her anyway.

He suddenly felt a wave of hate flood his body, hot and vicious. He found himself clenching his fists, maybe he should return home and kill his father. After all he deserved to die. He felt the anger spike even more as the back of his neck began to burn. He could do it, he could kill him.

'Sam,' Charon spoke softly, 'don't do that.'

'What?' he snapped angrily.

'Don't stare at the water.'

'What?' he looked up at Charon, and as he met his eyes, he could feel the anger begin to drain. Shame flooded his cheeks. Had he really just been thinking moments earlier of murdering his own father?'

'The Styx, is not called the river of hatred without reason,' he told him quietly. 'It will feed and amplify, any feelings of hate you have. Do not to look at the water for too long. Try closing your eyes, and focusing on something else.'

Taking a deep breath, he looked up to see Olivia's blue black dragonflies dancing just ahead of them. Focusing on them, he tried not to think about his father, nor the fact he was now alone, adrift in the world with no plan, and no one to count on but himself.

Olivia tucked her hand further into Theo's, and rested her head on his shoulder. Everything felt different down in the Underworld. It was like every atom and molecule pulsed with that strange ancient well of power she drew her Hellfire from. She could feel it all around her, throbbing like a heartbeat, calling to her, drawing her in. Like it was trying to tell her something, but its voice was too faint for her to understand.

'Hecate's temple,' Charon startled her out of her thoughts.

Olivia looked across to the furthest bank. On either side, the river was flanked with thick dark bushes, and undergrowth, obscuring much of her view, but somewhere above she could just about make out a flat rectangular white building, glowing eerily in the darkness.

The boat bumped the bank gently. Charon jumped smoothly ashore and moored the boat securely. Olivia pulled her backpack on, as Charon reached out to help her step across. He stepped back, as Theo and Sam followed curiously.

'This way,' he told them and disappeared into the brush.

There was no daylight in the Underworld. It was a world of perpetual night, but it was not dark, far from it. As they stepped through the brush to follow Charon Olivia drew in a startled gasp. It was like stepping into a strange alien world.

The path ahead of them was filled with trees and plants she couldn't name, and had never seen before, and probably never would again. The leaves, buds, and petals, glowed with a strange phosphorescent light, dozens of vibrant electric shades of blue, green, red, yellow, orange, pink, and purple. It was like a whole jungle of plants and flowers, lit with an ethereal glow, and it was beautiful.

Bright eyes glowed in the shadows, and the air was filled with a strange buzzing sound, like insects were flitting around, just out of sight. The peculiar glowing forest was teeming with life, with creatures she couldn't even begin to put a name to. She walked along slowly behind Charon, her dragonflies hovering over her shoulder.

'There is beauty in darkness, is there not?' Charon smiled.

'It's incredible,' Olivia breathed in wonder.

The undergrowth suddenly parted in front of her, and Olivia paused in awe. She'd seen pictures of Greek temples, ruins of temples, partially reconstructed temples, but they had always been rather sad, and tired looking, ravaged by the passage of time in the mortal world.

The building in front of her was nothing short of breath taking. It was small by comparison to other temples and structures, but rather than detract from it, it made it lovelier somehow, more intimate.

It looked rectangular in shape, with steps leading up to several tapered columns, slimmer at the top than the base. A frieze ran across the front of the pitched roof, but from this angle Olivia couldn't make out the designs depicted on it.

She realized as they mounted the steps, that the columns and the pitched roof, were only part of the entrance way. Once past the grand columns, it opened out into a lovely courtyard with a pool.

It wasn't a rectangular building as she'd first thought, but rather a collection of interconnecting buildings, more like a villa than a temple.

Suddenly Olivia understood, that although Charon referred to this place as Hecate's temple, it was in fact, her home, not a temple that would have been a place of worship for the mortals, to honor their Goddess.

A tiled walkway surrounded the pool, and was edged with more columns, which led inside. They followed behind Charon, who strode ahead confidently, as if he knew exactly where he was going.

They entered an open room which overlooked the pool, and where a huge bed sat before them, framed by a canopy of fine, diaphanous material, and covered with thick cushions in jewel colored tones.

Amidst the cushions lay a body, elegantly draped in a gossamer light material, which covered pale smooth skin. Hair as black as midnight, spilled over the pillows in thick coils and curls.

Several wine jugs, were piled up on the floor at the side of the bed, one tipped over on its side, allowing a rich crimson liquid to spill across the tiled floor.

'Hecate?' Charon approached slowly. 'Hecate?'

The figure murmured and stretched slightly, but otherwise did not acknowledge him.

'Hecate?' he sat down on the bed next to her and placed his hand gently on her back, shaking her lightly.

'Go...way...' the slurred response came from the cushions.

'I can't Hecate,' he apologized. 'We need your help, and we don't have much time.'

'Isay...goway...' she slurred again. 'I don... talk anyone.'

Charon sighed, as he scooped up one of the jugs, and sniffed.

'Dionysus' wine,' he shook his head.

'Is she drunk?' Theo asked.

'Unfortunately,' he replied. 'I don't think we're going to get her to talk when she's like this.'

'Is this usual for her?'

'No, it's not actually,' Charon frowned.

'Well shit,' Olivia swore. 'I'm sorry Charon, but we don't have time to be delicate.'

She walked briskly over to the bed, and taking a deep breath, she rolled the drunken Goddess onto her back and helped her to sit up.

Hecate raised her face to peer blearily into Olivia's eyes. Even drunk, she was a stunningly beautiful woman, with pale porcelain skin, jet black hair, and startlingly green eyes, even if they were a bit bloodshot.

'Mortal?' she frowned.

'Hecate, I need your help to find the Crossroad.'

Hecate's eyes filled with tears. 'Gone...all gone...'

She reached shakily for the wine jug in Charon's hand, and threw her head back draining what was left.

'I think we've just found the reason why she's

drunk,' Charon murmured.

'Stop that,' Olivia told her irritably, as she took the jug away from her and handed it back to Charon. 'Hecate, I need you to focus.'

'They're gone,' she whispered. 'I felt them die…it was like being ripped apart…they have stood since before all of us…and I felt its faltering heartbeat. I felt the magic die.'

She tipped her head back, and began to wail.

'What is she talking about?' Theo whispered to Charon.

'She is the Goddess of Crossroads and Entranceways. She must be tied to them in some way. There must have been some sort of deep connection for her to feel their destruction so intimately.' He looked her, his expression filled with sympathy. 'She is in so much pain.'

'Maybe we should leave her Olivia,' Theo told her gently, 'leave her to her grief. We'll find another way.'

'There isn't enough time to find another way,' she shook her head. 'I wish there was, but we've already lost too much time going back to Mercy to stop the Soul Collector. We have to get to the last Crossroad before my mother and Nathaniel. We have to stop them.'

'I know that, but look at her.'

'Hecate?' Olivia turned back to the grieving Goddess. 'Hecate, please listen to me.'

Hecate's head dropped forward heavily, her wails quieting to deep shuddering sobs, as she fell against Olivia. She felt her heart wrench for this woman crumbling in her arms. She could sense the amount of pain she was in, and it simply floored her. She wasn't in the least bit surprised the Goddess had tried to drown the pain with booze, especially booze that was made by the God Dionysus, the God of the Grape and wine-making himself. She was willing to bet his label packed quite a punch, judging by the state of Hecate.

She found herself unconsciously rocking the tiny Goddess, smoothing her hair back, and murmuring soothingly in her ear. There had to be some way to reach her, all she needed was the location of the last Crossroad.

'Hecate?' she tried again, 'I really need your help.'

'What good would it do now? It's all lost…'

'Okay,' Olivia sucked in a breath, 'unfortunately we're going to have to get drastic.'

She struggled to remove her backpack, while juggling the intoxicated woman, until Theo stepped forward and took a firm hold of it, while she slipped her arms out.

'Hold onto that for me,' she told him, as she stood and dragged the Goddess to her feet, wrapping Hecate's arm around her neck and across her shoulders.

'What are you going to do?' Charon asked suspiciously.

'I'm going to sober her up.' She edged toward the pool, half carrying half dragging Hecate with her, 'or possibly drown her,' she added.

'Are you insane?' Charon hissed, 'she is going to be spitting mad.'

'I don't care if she's mad, as long as she's sober enough to understand me,' Olivia replied, standing at the edge of the pool.

'You might want to stand back,' she warned them, grasping hold of Hecate firmly. 'Please don't be mad at me,' she murmured, and then she plunged them both into the cold water of the pool.

Hecate breached the surface of the pool, sucking in a great big shocked gasp of breath, her eyes wide. Olivia grabbed her head, and shoved her under the water again, while she flailed and kicked. After a couple of seconds, she allowed her to breach the surface and suck in another lungful of breath, before dunking her again. When she finally came up for the third time, Olivia could see, not only that her eyes were clear, but they were blazing with absolute fury. She released her grip on her, and stepped back.

Hecate stood waist deep in the pool, her gown now completely transparent, and molded to her naked breasts and torso. Her black hair streamed down her back, like glossy black tar. The whole building began to shake and tremble in response to the blinding fury in her green eyes.

'Stop it Hecate,' Olivia told her firmly, raising her hands, as they burst into flame, the glowing sapphire of her Hell fire banked low in warning. She didn't want to fight the Goddess, she just wanted her attention.

Hecate's eyes focused on the Hellfire churning in Olivia's outstretched palms, and her eyes lost a little of the murderous fury. The trembling of the building ceased, but she still fixed her gaze on Olivia, angry and demanding answers.

'I'm truly sorry,' Olivia told her, 'but I needed to talk to you.'

'You are a mortal?' she asked flatly.

'Yes I am.'

'How is it you can summon the ancient fire?' she demanded.

'I don't know,' Olivia told her honestly, 'I just can.'

'What is your purpose here? Why did you come to the Underworld and how?'

'Hades sent me.'

'To what purpose?'

'To find the last Crossroad, to stop the demon Nathaniel.'

'You seek Epsilon?'

'Epsilon?' Olivia replied in confusion.

'Epsilon is the fifth, the most ancient, and the most powerful of all the Crossroads.' Her eyes closed painfully, 'and it is now the last of its kind.'

'I can save it,' Olivia whispered.

'What?' Hecate frowned.

'I can stop Nathaniel from destroying the last Crossroad. I don't know what he is planning on using it for, but I can guarantee that once he has what he wants, he will destroy it, so no one else can use it.'

'If the last Crossroad falls, the balance will shift, everything we have ever known will be thrown into the hand of Chaos,' her voice was low, and her eyes fathomless. 'Everything will end.'

'Then help me.' Olivia let her fire peter out, and reached out toward the Goddess imploringly. 'I will stop them, I swear. Help me save the last Crossroad…help me save Epsilon.'

'How?'

'Tell me how to find it,' she replied.

'You can't,' her eyes burned, as she shook her head helplessly. 'It is buried in the farthest, deepest pit of Tartarus. It is as far below Hades, as the Earth is below the Heavens. A deep, dark abyss of eternal torment, a dungeon for the suffering of the wicked. It is the prison of the Titans, of Prometheus, and of Kronos himself.'

'Kronos?' Olivia breathed, 'the father of Hades and Zeus?'

'Yes' she replied. 'Your friend Charon there will tell you. The Phlegethon is the river of fire, and it leads to the depths of Tartarus, but even if you reach it, you will never survive long enough to find Epsilon. If Kronos, or Prometheus don't find you first, there are thousands of other damned creatures that will, and Hell fire or not, you are still but a mortal.'

'I still have to try,' Olivia shook her head. 'I made a promise to Hades, and now to you, I will do everything in my power to stop Nathaniel, and to save the Crossroad.'

'Even if it costs you your life?'

'Yes,' Olivia whispered.

'Nobility,' Hecate shook her head, 'a quality, we immortals sometimes underestimate.'

She waded slowly through the water, until she was standing toe to toe with Olivia. She raised her hand and traced her cheek gently.

'Daughter,' she spoke softly, 'life is precious. Do not throw yours away on a hopeless promise.'

'I gave my word,' Olivia stared straight in her eyes. 'I keep my word.'

Hecate's gaze dropped on a helpless sigh, to Olivia's throat, where a small glint of gold caught her attention. With a puzzled frown she reached out and hooked her slender finger under the chain, pulling the compass free from Olivia's drenched shirt.

Hecate's mouth fell open on a startled gasp. 'Where did you get this?' she breathed.

'Hades gave it to me.'

Hecate's hand fisted tightly around the compass and she squeezed her eyes shut, sucking in a deep shaky breath.

'Are you truly set on this path daughter?'

'I am.'

When she opened her eyes, they glittered with hope, and fear, in equal measure.

'Then go with my blessing,' she answered softly, 'and when you reach Tartarus use this.'

'I don't know how?' Olivia shook her head. 'It doesn't work.'

'It will,' she replied.

Olivia nodded.

'There is one more thing,' Hecate warned. 'Do not let Kronos find you, and no matter happens, under NO circumstances let him get his hands on the compass. Do you understand?'

'I understand,' Olivia breathed.

Nodding at the agreement between them, Olivia stepped back feeling a chill run down her spine, and seep into her bones, she wondered if she would ever feel warm again.

22.

'What is it Theo?' Olivia asked softly, looking up at him, as they drifted lazily along the river.

He'd been quiet ever since they'd left Hecate's place, not that Theo was overly chatty at the best of times. He'd always been quiet and reflective, preferring to sit back and just take everything in until he felt the need to give his opinion, but this was a whole new level of silence and it was painfully obvious something was bothering him.

'Nothing,' he murmured, staring at the gentle lull of the water.

She tugged on his hand, until he turned to look at her. 'No lies, remember?'

He sighed and glanced down at their entwined fingers.

'Did you mean what you said to Hecate?'

'Which part?' she asked in confusion.

'The part where you said you were willing to risk your life.'

She let out a deep breath. 'Yes, I did mean it,' she shook her head in resignation. 'Do I want to? The answer is no. What I want is to go home with you, and live an incredibly boring, safe life together.'

He looked up and met her whiskey colored eyes.

'But that's not the cards that were dealt us Theo,' she continued. 'It took me a long time to accept that. If things hadn't turned out the way they did, if I hadn't been different in the first place, you would never have been pulled through time, and we would never have met.'

'Do you really think this is the price you have to pay, for having me?' he frowned. 'This isn't some debt you feel you have to pay?'

'No,' she replied, 'it's just the way things are. That's what everyone has been trying to tell me, only I've been too stubborn to listen. We're different Theo. For whatever reason, we've been thrown right into the middle of this mess, and it's up to us to fix it. We can't do that unless we commit to it one hundred percent, and maybe, just maybe, if we're lucky, we'll come out the other side and get the chance to grow old together.'

'I hope so,' he kissed the back of her hand as she pressed her forehead to his and sighed.

'Me too.'

'I won't let anyone hurt you, you know,' Theo promised. 'I may be secure enough to stand back and let you mouth off at Immortals, but if anyone tries to hurt you, they'll have to come through me first.'

'I know,' she brushed her lips against his. 'I love you,' she told him softly.

He smiled against her mouth, 'I'll never get tired of hearing you say that.'

'Then I'll say it often,' she replied. 'You know, I won't let anyone hurt you either. It's you and me Theo.'

'Right until the bitter end?' he asked in amusement.

'Something like that,' she smiled, 'but I prefer to think of it as, right until the happy end.'

'You don't believe in happy endings.'

'Maybe this time I'll make an exception.'

'If you two get any more cloying, I may vomit,' Charon sighed.

'Then stop listening to a private conversation,' Olivia turned to look at him in amusement.

'It's not as if I'm doing it on purpose,' he replied.

'What about you?' Olivia asked curiously.

'What about me?' he continued to plunge the pole steadily into the water, and push them forward.

'What happened to you and Charlotte?'

'My wife is at our home, which is located along the West bank of the Acheron,' he smiled.

'You married Charlotte?'

'Hades was gracious enough to allow Charlotte to remain here with me, and she was gracious enough to consent to be my wife.'

'Awww,' Olivia smiled sentimentally, 'I'm so happy for you. I really wish I could visit her, after all, she is my great, great aunt, and she did save my life.'

'I'm sure you'll get the chance to, sooner or later. Something tells me this won't be your only visit to the Underworld.'

'Why do you say that?' she frowned in confusion.

'I don't know,' he shrugged, 'just a feeling.'

'Hey! You know what?' Olivia suddenly laughed in realization.

'What?' Charon replied.

'If you married Charlotte, that technically makes you my uncle.'

'What?' he repeated dryly.

'Yeah,' she laughed again, 'you're like, my great great uncle.'

'Gods have mercy,' he sighed, rolling his eyes.

'I doubt they will,' she replied, her eyes glittering with suppressed mirth.

'Tell me something Olivia.'

'What?'

'How did you know who the judges were?'

'I don't know,' she answered honestly. 'I guess it was the same as the passageway past the Gateway. The knowledge was there, deep inside me, only I wasn't aware of it until I needed it.'

'You are a very strange mortal.'

'So I keep being told,' Olivia muttered. 'So… can I call you uncle Charon?' she asked in amusement.

'Not if you expect me to answer,' he murmured.

Olivia chuckled lightly. 'Charlotte is well then?'

'Yes' he nodded, 'she is very happy.'

'Won't she worry where you are?' Olivia asked. 'I mean, you did kind of drop everything to help us.'

'You have read Charlotte's journals?' he asked.

She nodded.

'Do you remember her mentioning that she could see into the spirit realms?'

'Yes I do,' Olivia recalled.

'Well, that was really only the beginning. Once she cast off her mortal body and all its restrictions, her gift flourished. She is able to see across many of the realms, including the Underworld.'

'So you can't hide from her?' Olivia laughed in delight.

'No,' his mouth curved, 'she knows where we are, and she knows what we are doing.'

'Sam?' Theo spoke up suddenly, as he eyed their friend. 'Sam?'

Olivia looked over and found Sam sitting numbly, with a glazed lethargic expression.

'Sam?' Theo leaned forward and shook him lightly.

Sam looked up slowly and frowned. 'Who are you?' he murmured absently, before turning back to the water and gazing at, with a kind of dreamy lassitude.

'What's wrong with him?' Theo asked Charon in concern. 'Why doesn't he know who we are?'

Charon sighed, 'I was afraid of this,' he shook his head. 'Don't worry the effect will only be temporary.'

'I don't understand,' Theo frowned. 'What's going on?'

'We have now left the River Styx, and we are travelling the River Lethe,' Charon told them. 'It is the river of forgetfulness.'

'Are you sure he's going to be okay?' Olivia asked worriedly.

'I'm sure,' Charon assured them. 'Once we leave this river he should be fine.'

'Why is it affecting him and not us?' Theo asked.

'I suspect that has something to do with Olivia.'

'What do you mean?' she asked suspiciously.

'Like I said Olivia,' Charon shook his head, 'there is something very strange about you. I'm not sure what it is. I knew it the moment I saw you back in the mortal world, but since you have been down here my suspicions have only been confirmed.'

'What? Because I knew a short cut across the wall, and because I took a lucky guess at which judge was which?'

'It wasn't a lucky guess Olivia and you know it, besides there have been other things.'

'Such as?'

'Your ability to summon Hell fire, your ability to read the ancient language as if born to it. There are creatures who have existed here in the Underworld for thousands of years, and they can't read our language, but you can. I think, that whatever makes you so unique is also protecting you against the effects of the river.'

'But what about Theo?'

'You two are more or less permanently attached to each other. You don't even realize you are doing it. You naturally gravitate to each other, holding hands, touching. I would imagine the connection between you, is passing your protection to him.'

'Huh,' she replied thoughtfully, 'poor Sam. So do mortals usually freak out on the rivers?'

'I don't know what you mean by freak out,' Charon frowned.

'Do they usually act out of character, or display strange behavior?' she clarified.

'I don't know really,' he shrugged. 'We don't usually get mortals down here, but then Sam here is different anyway. You must have figured out by now that he's not human.'

'I did know that actually,' Olivia nodded.

'Sam's not human?' Theo replied in surprise.

'Oh,' Olivia murmured, 'I forgot you didn't know that.'

'I just thought he was like us, and that his ability to travel through time was a gift, like Olivia's fire or my visions.'

'No,' Charon shook his head, 'he's definitely not human, and what he truly is, that makes him susceptible to the effects of, not just the rivers, but the Underworld itself.'

'What do you mean?'

'I mean, that your friend there is making a huge personal sacrifice to help you here. His kind don't belong down here, especially not for prolonged periods of time. The longer he remains here, the sicker he will become.'

'Damn it,' Theo swore, 'why didn't he tell us?'

'It is possible that he doesn't know,' Charon told them. 'This is the first time he has been here and as I said, his kind don't come down here.'

'You keep saying his kind,' Theo frowned, 'what exactly do you mean? If Sam isn't human, then what is he?'

'I'm sorry Theo, but it's not my place to say. If Sam wants you to know, he'll tell you himself,' Charon shook his head. 'All I can say is, that he's from higher places than you can imagine.'

'Oh my God,' Olivia breathed. 'When you first saw him, you said his first loyalty will always be to heaven…he's from heaven, isn't he?'

'I can't say,' Charon shrugged, 'so stop asking. If you want to know, ask him, once he stops drooling.'

'You're an ass,' Olivia replied dryly.

Charon's mouth curved in amusement as he looked downstream. Suddenly the river forked to the right.

'What's that?' Olivia asked.

'That is the River Cocytus and it's pretty potent; even you should feel its effects.'

'What do you mean?'

'The closer we get to Tartarus, the stronger the effects of the river.' The boat began to turn and split off into the new waterway. 'You might want to cover your ears.'

'What? Why would…' Olivia suddenly clapped her hands over her ears as an insanely high pitched shrieking filled the air around them. Theo did likewise.

Sam woke violently from his dreamlike state and covered his ears.

'What the hell is that?' he shouted.

'The Cocytus,' Charon yelled calmly above the noise, seemingly unperturbed by the disturbing sound. 'It's the river of wailing.'

'What's making all that noise?' Olivia yelled.

'They are,' he replied, nodding toward the water.

Olivia looked down and shuddered in revulsion. The River Styx had been much the same as a regular river, murky and mud-like. The Acheron's waters had been clear, and the Lethe had a strange pale cloudy quality to it, but this river, the Cocytus, was an eerie, unpleasant, glowing kind of green, and within the churning waters hundreds of bodies floated beneath the surface, arms outstretched imploringly, and mouths hung open in a never-ending scream.

'Who are they?' Theo asked.

'The damned,' came the reply. 'They are tormented souls, being punished eternally for their mortal sins.'

'Is there no hope for them?' Olivia asked quietly, her voice barely carrying over the mournful wails.

'No,' Charon answered in sympathy, 'not for them. They lock themselves in that torment, because they are the ones who can't see past their own sins and failures. It is a punishment of their own making. They are the ones who can't change, because they don't want to.'

'It's so sad,' Olivia breathed.

'Don't waste your pity on them Olivia,' he told her. 'There is nothing you can do.'

'Perhaps, it is not that they don't want to, but they don't know how to,' she answered.

'Maybe, but there is still nothing that can be done,' he replied looking up and pointing. 'Look ahead…'

They turned and saw the river once again forked to the right. Suddenly the air turned smoky, and was filled with a nasty sulfur-like smell.

'The Phlegethon,' Charon murmured, 'the river of fire.'

The screams and wails of torment faded away to be replaced by a strange sound. It was like a mixture of the crackle of an open fire, and the roar of an opening furnace. They turned down the channel, and the green glowing water was slowly replaced by a thick, slow, churning movement.

Olivia looked down and gasped at the sight of the river, which could now barely be called a river at all. Instead of water, it was hot molten lava, which glowed a bright, white hot mixture of red and orange, with a cracked, perpetually moving crust of black char.

'Charon,' Olivia swallowed thickly, 'you do know your boat's made of wood, right?'

'Relax Olivia,' he replied, 'the boat cannot be damaged.'

'Are you sure?'

'Yes,' he chuckled, 'stop worrying about the river, and start worrying about what's at the end of it.'

'Tartarus.'

'Exactly,' he replied soberly. 'I've never heard of

any mortal surviving Tartarus.'

'Thanks for the pep talk,' she replied dryly.

'Olivia,' he sighed, 'I can't go with you.'

'It's okay Charon,' she frowned, 'I didn't expect you to.'

'It's not that I won't, it's that I can't…' he tried to explain.

'What do you mean?'

'Tartarus is at the very end of the river; I can't move beyond its borders. My powers don't extend beyond the rivers.'

'It's okay,' she assured him.

'It's not okay,' he frowned. 'I'm worried about you, about all of you.'

'Stop worrying,' she told him bluntly. 'Like you just told me, some things you can't change and this is one of them. Besides,' she added with a smirk, 'I'm different, remember? The usual effects of the Underworld don't apply to me.'

'That's not what I said, and you know it,' he replied blandly.

'Well,' she winked, 'close enough.'

Charon sighed and rolled his eyes. 'I now understand why Hades finds you so frustrating.'

She laughed in amusement. 'Oh lighten up Charon, we're the ones facing impending death.'

'I will never understand mortals,' he shook his head.

'You don't need to understand us, you just need to have a sense of humor.'

'Isn't that the truth,' Sam muttered.

'Er Charon?' Theo spoke suddenly, his gaze fixed on something ahead of them. 'When you said Tartarus was at the end of the river, please tell me you meant that the river ends on the banks of Tartarus?'

'Not exactly,' Charon admitted as Olivia turned to look.

The roaring was getting louder, almost like a waterfall. Steam rose up obscuring her view.

'What do you mean, not exactly?' she yelled above the noise.

'Tartarus is technically separate from Hades.'

'As in… a separate world?' Theo asked.

'Yes, technically.'

'What does he mean yes, technically?' Olivia looked back to Theo.

'He means that the end of the river, and Tartarus, are separated by the Void.'

'WHAT?' she shouted, turning back to Charon. 'AND YOU'RE JUST TELLING US THIS NOW?'

'You'd better get ready,' he warned.

'Ready to what?' she asked suspiciously.

'To jump.'

'TO WHAT?' her voice went up another octave.

'Still got that sense of humor?' Charon asked dryly.

Theo pulled her to her feet and helped her into the backpack, making sure the straps were tight.

'Oh no' she shook her head, 'I did not agree to this,' she sat back down and crossed her arms. 'Killing a demon…fine, finding a lost crossroad…check, facing off a God…no problem, JUMPING THE VOID? Not a chance in Hell.'

'It's, not a chance in Hades, actually and you don't have a choice Olivia.' Charon glanced over the side as they neared the end. 'There's only one way into Tartarus, and you only get one chance.'

'It's okay Livy,' Theo pulled her to her feet.

'Are you mad,' she glanced over the edge. 'It's not okay. What about this can you possibly think is okay?'

She started to tremble in his grip and her voice rose in panic.

Suddenly Charon raised the pole above his head and plunged it hard down into the river. There was a loud grinding as it anchored on the bottom, slowing their approach until the boat finally ground to a halt, hanging over the edge, the bow still in the lava and the stern suspended out into the blackness of the Void. Two waterfalls of lava cascaded thunderously down either side of them, split by Charon's boat, tumbling down into the Void far below until they disappeared from view. Olivia glared over the edge into the blackness and stumbled, a wave of dizziness washing over her.

'Are you okay Olivia?' Sam frowned.

'I may have a slight problem with heights,' she swallowed.

'Livy you can do this.' Theo cupped her chin, 'don't look down, look across…'

She glanced across the Void and saw what he was talking about. There was a rocky outcropping not far away, slightly below them. It looked utterly terrifying, but it was do-able. They could make it.

'What about you?' she turned back to Charon.

'Don't worry about me,' he smiled, 'it's the end of the river. I'll simply return to the beginning.'

The pole scrapped alarmingly along the molten riverbed, and the boat suddenly slipped a bit further, starting to tilt into the Void.

'You need to go now!' Charon shouted, as he tried to hold his grip on the pole.

'I'll go first,' Theo told them. 'Sam?'

Sam looked at him, 'don't worry I'll make sure she gets to you.'

He nodded, 'Olivia, do you want me to take the backpack?'

'No,' she shook her head trying to suck in a deep calming breath to ease her racing heart, 'I've got it, it's my responsibility.'

'Okay,' he kissed her roughly, 'you can do this alright?'

She nodded, watching as he turned and leapt

across the Void. Her heart stopped for a moment, as he hung suspended in the air, falling through the blackness. Then he hit the rock, and rolled to absorb the impact.

'Olivia!' he climbed to his feet and held out his arms to her. 'You next.'

'You'd better catch me or I'll never speak to you again,' she shouted over, as she stepped up onto the edge. With a quick prayer to every God, Goddess and Deity she could think of in the space of two seconds, she braced herself and leapt.

For those dizzying seconds, while she felt herself flying through the air, time seemed to stop, and all she could hear was her heart thundering in her ear, and then suddenly Theo's arms wrapped around her, and they both tumbled to the ground in a tangle of bodies.

'You two should get a room,' a calm voice spoke next to them, and when they both looked up Sam was smiling at them in amusement.

'Did you just translocate across the Void?' she asked accusingly.

'Yes.'

'So, you just let me jump, when you could have translocated us over here?'

'It's always good to face your fears Olivia.'

'You should start running now Sam,' she warned dangerously, 'because I'm going to kill you.'

He stepped back laughing lightly. 'I'm joking,' he sighed, his face becoming more serious. 'The truth is I don't know if I could have taken all three of us. I don't feel right...' he shook his head. 'I didn't want to risk it.'

'Fine' she sulked, slightly mollified, 'I forgive you then.' She held out her hand, so he could help her up off the floor.

She stood up and brushed the pieces of rock and dust off her jeans, as Sam leaned in to help Theo up. She looked up at the boat overhanging the edge, for a second she saw Charon, and then the boat shimmered and disappeared completely.

'Do you think he got back okay?' she murmured.

'I hope so,' Theo stepped close, and looked up at the waterfall of lava.

'We should get moving,' Sam told them, looking over his shoulder nervously. 'Cronus rules here, we will have to be very careful.'

Theo nodded, taking Olivia's hand as they picked their way over the uneven rocky ground, toward the dark horizon. There was no vegetation, no trees, just darkness and what looked like volcanic rock. The air was tinged with heat and the scent of brimstone. Olivia's dragonflies pulsed gently with blue fire, hovering close to her shoulder nervously, as if to not draw too much attention to themselves.

'Why don't you try the Compass again?' Theo suggested.

Nodding in agreement they paused, as she pulled the golden chain from her collar and flipped it open, looking down at it expectantly.

Nothing.

'Are you shitting me?' Olivia hissed angrily. 'After all this, and the damn thing still won't work.'

'I guess we'll just have to keep moving.' Theo took her hand again, and they set off across the rough terrain.

'So Cronus is Hades' father then?' Theo asked quietly as they moved.

'Yes he is,' Olivia replied softly. 'Cronus was born from Uranus, the Sky, and Gaia, the Earth. He overthrew his father's rule, and took his sister Rhea as his wife.'

'His sister?' Theo's eyes widened in shock.

'You'll find it's very common amongst the ancients,' Sam told him, shrugging casually. 'Believe me, the Egyptians, and the Romans were just as bad.'

'So anyway,' Olivia continued in a quiet voice, 'Cronus and Rhea took the throne and ruled as king and queen, but Cronus learned that he was destined to be deposed by his own sons, just as he had in turn usurped his father's throne. He sired the Gods Demeter, Hestia, Hera, Hades and Poseidon by his sister Rhea, and as soon as they were born he devoured them in an attempt to prevent the prophecy from coming true.'

'Devoured?' Theo frowned skeptically, 'you mean he actually ate his own children?'

'That's the myth,' Olivia nodded, 'and he devoured them, not ate.'

'Is there a difference?'

'He swallowed them whole, so they remained intact, and anyway they're Gods, so they can't die. Then when the sixth child, Zeus, was born, Rhea and Gaia hid him from his father, and instead gave Cronus a stone wrapped in baby blankets to swallow.'

'This is so disturbing,' Theo shook his head.

'Anyway, there are many different accounts, a lot of variations, but the general consensus is that once he was grown, Zeus either cut open his father's stomach to free his siblings, or gave him some sort of emetic to force him to expel them, by disgorging the contents of his stomach.'

'That's disgusting.'

'So…after that, Zeus and his brothers and sisters overthrew Cronus and the other Titans, and cast them down into Tartarus.'

'Shush,' Sam stopped and listened, 'there's something going on up ahead.'

Olivia pulled her dragonflies in close, their flames banking down so they were barely visible as they crept forward in the darkness. In the distance a dim glow appeared, which grew brighter as they approached.

They sneaked up to the edge, hidden behind a wall of rocks, and peered over into the sooty red and orange glow. A great pit yawned open in front of them, spanning miles, and dropping down deep into the heart of Tartarus.

Filled with stairs and ladders that were carved painstakingly out of the rocks, it was a hive of labor and industry. Ragged, heavily chained slaves pushed metal carts filled with rocks. Great pulleys heaved up more carts, full of rock, forges burned, releasing greasy smoke and filling the air with sparks and firebrands. The sound of hammers, and anvils rang out through the air.

'God, it's like the mines of Moria. Are you sure we haven't dropped into Middle Earth?' Olivia whispered, but when she turned both Sam and Theo were staring at her blankly. 'Seriously? Lord of the Rings? The Hobbit? None of this ringing a bell?' she shook her head in disgust. 'You two should be ashamed of yourselves. I'm guessing a Frodo reference would be wasted on you both right now.'

Sam shook his head slowly, 'I don't know where we're heading, but I'm pretty sure we want to avoid that place.'

'Agreed,' Theo nodded, casting a look around. 'I can't see much, but the ground seems to be sloping down, and away from here.'

'Okay, let's head that way then,' Olivia nudged Theo and they started moving once again.

Slowly the sounds of the fire pit seemed to fade away, and the air cooled, marginally. The darkness returned, and once again her dragonflies brightened and took the lead.

Suddenly, the ground ahead of them changed color, and from where they were approaching, it seemed to transform from a dark sooty black, to white stone. They moved cautiously, not knowing whether the surface was solid, or not. Stopping at the edge, Olivia reached down and ran her fingers over the surface. It was white stone, and it was cool and smooth to the touch.

'It seems stable enough,' she turned back to the others, but as she straightened up the ground suddenly began to tremble.

They all stumbled back a few paces, watching dumbfounded as the white stone surface began to rise up from the gravel and rock. It unfolded itself, and began to stretch up, higher, and higher, as it rose into the dark sky.

Olivia's head tilted back, and her mouth fell open as she watched it grow. When it finally stopped, she found herself staring at a huge figure of a man, easily as tall as the statue of Liberty. He was half naked, and completely colorless, as if he were a statue carved in exquisite detail, except the sculptor had not bothered to paint him.

But he wasn't a statue, he moved with the same lithe grace and economy of movement, as a regular man. He looked down at them, and as his milky white eyes locked on hers, she sucked in a deep breath.

She wasn't sure how, but she knew exactly who he was. Her heart began to hammer in her chest, and her blood ran cold.

'Oh my God,' she whispered, 'Prometheus…'

23.

Olivia stared open mouthed, mesmerized by the gargantuan Titan in front of her, barely registering Theo pulling her protectively behind him.

As Theo raised his arm, the metal embedded within his skin didn't just melt and flow down to his hand, to coalesce into his knife, but instead burst into bright blue and silver flames, which ignited the whole of his arm in glowing blue vines. The knife itself throbbed and glowed with power.

Prometheus's eyes flicked over to Theo and narrowed in interest. He leaned over and effortlessly scooped him up from the ground. He grabbed one of his legs between his cool stone fingertips and dangled him upside down, as if he were a fascinating insect he was about to pick the wings off.

'Put him down Prometheus,' Olivia told him calmly.

Prometheus looked down, and his eyes widened in surprise. Olivia stood with her bow of fire drawn and aimed directly at him. Her gaze narrowed on him with total focus, as she regarded him as nothing more than a target. A black and blue bolt of pure Hell fire vibrated against her knuckles, just waiting for her to let it fly.

Sensing his moment while the Titan's focus was on Olivia, Sam drew in his strength and flashed into Prometheus's hand, grasping hold of Theo and translocating them both to the ground. Prometheus started in surprise, glancing at his empty hand and then back at the two men now on the ground, as if he couldn't quite understand what had happened. Finally, he turned his gaze back to Olivia, studying her intently.

'It's you...'

Olivia wasn't sure what she had expected him to sound like, maybe some kind of thunderous sonic boom, but nothing prepared her for the soft lulling timbre of his voice. It coiled around her like a blanket, and held her softly.

Her gaze lost some of the sharp focus and she lowered her bow just a fraction, her eyes puzzled. She could feel him, she realized with a frown of confusion. Being in his presence was slightly overwhelming, as she could sense the vastness of his consciousness. This was a being who had stood from almost the beginning of time, watching worlds spin from chaos.

He brought with him a feeling of timelessness, as old and immovable as the Universe itself. It was comforting. This was not the being she had been warned of, she felt no hostility from him, only curiosity and...relief? He was pleased to see her, that much she could understand. She lowered her bow, and let the flames peter out, taking an involuntary step toward him.

'Olivia,' Theo started forward in concern, catching her arm gently to still her movement.

'It's okay Theo,' she laid her hand on his in reassurance, her gaze moving back to Prometheus as he watched her silently. 'He won't hurt me...,' she whispered.

'You don't know that,' he frowned, 'Hecate said...'

'Hecate does not know everything,' Prometheus spoke softly, causing them both to stare up at him. 'She certainly should not presume to know my mind, nor predict my intentions. I was here long before she came into being.'

'And we're just supposed to believe you?' Theo asked bluntly.

'That would be your choice,' the amusement was reflected in his voice. 'Believe, or do not, it does not concern me, but the female is right I intend her no harm.'

He kneeled down beside them and extended his hand for Olivia to step forward.

'Olivia,' Theo warned.

'It's okay Theo,' she smiled softly as she brushed his hand from her arm, 'I know what I'm doing…trust me.'

Theo pulled in a deep breath, his mouth fixed with resolution as he allowed her to pass. She stepped onto Prometheus's outstretched palm, holding onto his thumb for balance as he lifted her high into the dark sky, until she was level with his face.

'What is your name mortal?'

'Olivia.'

'Olivia,' he replied softly his mouth curving into a smile. 'I have waited a long time for you.'

'I don't understand.'

'You know who I am?'

'Prometheus,' Olivia replied, 'the son of the Titan Lapetus and the Oceanid Clymene.'

'And do you know why I was cast down deep into Tartarus?'

'You stole fire from Mount Olympus and gave it to the mortals, which angered Zeus.'

He smiled slowly, his voice low and soothing.

'I was once known as the greatest benefactor of humanity. I, who tricked Zeus into accepting the bones and fat of the bulls, brought for sacrifices, leaving the true meat to sustain mankind. I, who stole away to Mount Olympus, and took back fire, so that the mortals could flourish. I was worshipped for my beneficence. Even when Zeus cursed me to die in agony every day, only to be reborn every night just so that I could perish again the next day, I never regretted anything I had done for the mortals. Even when Zeus tired of watching me being mutilated every day, and cast me down into the deepest pit of Tartarus, I still did not regret my actions, and do you want to know why?'

'Why?'

'Everything I have done was for one reason, and one alone.'

'What was it?' she asked in confusion.

'To bring you into being.'

'What?'

'The world has waited for you to be born for so long,' he told her. 'I tricked Zeus into allowing the mortals meat so they would flourish, because I knew one day you would come from them.'

'No,' she shook her head.

'The fire I stole from Zeus was not for the mortals. They already knew the secret of Earth fire, they knew how to prepare their food and warm themselves. What use would they have, for something they already held the secret of?'

'The fire you stole from Mount Olympus…' Olivia breathed in understanding, 'it was not just any fire.'

'No, it wasn't. It was the fire of the Gods, ancient, and full of magic.'

'Hell fire.'

'I stole into Zeus and Hera's palace to the great fireplace in their bed chamber. In the hearth burned the fire of the Gods, in all its many colors. I took one single flame of each color, one of the deepest ocean blue, one as silver as the most precious metal, one as red as the finest wine, one as purple as the heavens as the sun begins its descent, and one as green as the endless fields of Elysium. I took these flames and twisted them together, fashioning a single flame of the five ancient fires.'

'What happened?' she whispered entranced.

'I crept away under the cover of night and fled to the mortal world. There I found a young girl, sleeping in her bed. So young, so sweet, with pale skin and dark tresses, barely more than a child. I came to her in a dream. I gave her the flame, and told her to keep it safe, knowing that when she woke with the dawn she would have no memory of our conversation, nor any memory of the flame that lived inside her, lying dormant…waiting.'

'Why her?' Olivia was almost afraid to ask…afraid that she already knew the answer.

'Because I knew one day a child would come from her bloodline, a woman by the name of Althethea.' His white eyes locked on Olivia's, 'you know of whom I speak.'

She did know. As Bridget had explained, Althethea was the mother of Carrigan, the first of the West women, and she was her direct descendant.

'The little girl you gave the flame to…'

'You are of her blood. The fire has awoken, and you are the one destined to wield it.'

'But why?' her eyes widened in disbelief, 'why me?'

'Because it was always you granddaughter,' he looked at her, his expression tender and filled with affection. 'You will shake the very worlds to their foundations.'

'No,' she shook her head in denial.

'You know it is true,' he told her softly, 'it all begins with you.'

'What begins?'

'The dawn of a new era. You will rise, a living banner, and the whole universe will tremble.'

Olivia stared at him, not trusting herself to speak. Not even knowing what to say. The fear and pressure was almost overwhelming. She had never dealt well with being told what to do, and now she was being told… what exactly? That she was supposed to start some sort of revolution?

It was insane. All she wanted to do was go home, crawl under the covers, and maybe sleep for the next month, or possibly three. She didn't want to be given this kind of responsibility, it was too much.

She didn't trust herself, she'd felt the edges of the power she'd summoned. She knew how easy it would be to allow herself to become lost to it. She was pretty sure there was a good reason the ancient fires were the domain of Gods, and not mortals.

'Why do you fear the darkness granddaughter?' Prometheus asked curiously, as if he could sense her thoughts.

'Because it is too easy to lose yourself to it.'

'Child, do you not yet understand?' he asked with a puzzled expression. 'There is no such thing as darkness. What you perceive as darkness, is only an absence of light, and you…you are a living flame.'

'I can't,' she whispered. 'I just want to go home…'

Prometheus's eyes suddenly widened and he hissed violently, twisting to look out across the barren wasteland behind him. A bright red flash lit the darkness, and the ground began to tremble, accompanied by an earsplitting roar of anger.

'Cronus!' Prometheus growled.

Despite the anger and hate twisting his features, he lowered Olivia carefully to the ground and deposited her next to Sam and Theo.

'Protect her with your last breath,' he commanded them before straightening to his full gigantic height.

'ATLAS! OCEANUS!' He bellowed with an almighty roar.

The face of the stark black cliff next to them began to crack and shake, before sheering away. Olivia and the others stumbled back to stop themselves from being showered with falling rocks and debris, watching wide eyed as the colossal chunk of detached rock unfolded, and straightened until he stood as tall as Prometheus.

'Atlas!' Prometheus turned to his brother, 'Cronus approaches. We must stop him.'

'CRONUS!' Atlas growled in disgust, his voice rough and gravelly, as he turned to face the approaching sooty glow.

Olivia turned in puzzlement as she heard the unmistakable boom and hiss of a giant wave. She clutched on tighter to Theo, and took an involuntary step back at the sound of violent rushing water. She drew in a startled gasp, as a huge wave rounded the edge of the cliff face and crested over the rocks.

Like water released from a broken dam it rushed, and churned toward them ominously. The three of them stumbled back, knowing there was nowhere for them to hide, no way they could outrun that violent wall of water. But as it reached them it faltered and tumbled into a ball, before unfolding like a huge transformer, Olivia thought randomly, watching as it stood as tall as the other Titans.

Before them stood an awe-inspiring Titan, who held the shape of a giant man. But rather than flesh and blood he was composed entirely of rushing, churning sea water, which seemed to be in perpetual motion, giving the appearance of rippling transparent skin.

A huge boom shook the rocky ground beneath their feet, causing them to stumble and hold on to each other for balance. Looking up to the dark skies, now lit with a deep sooty red glow, Olivia drew in a sharp breath.

A gigantic man stood, taller than Prometheus and his brothers, his flesh a blackened charred crust, and beneath the splits and tears, burning hot lava churned and rippled. When he opened his mouth wide and bellowed it was like being caught in front of a giant furnace. Even from a distance Olivia could feel the blast of heat, which scorched her cheeks and made her skin feel dry and tight.

'CRONUS!' Prometheus roared.

Cronus paid him no heed, his mouth opened again, letting loose a bellowing screech. His wild red eyes fixed on Olivia and suddenly she felt the compass burn hot against her skin. She took an involuntary step back. He knew, somehow he knew she had the compass.

Cronus stalked toward them, the ground trembling and heaving with each titanic step, completely unconcerned with the Titans gathered in front of him, shielding them.

'OCEANUS! TAKE THEM TO SAFETY!' Prometheus growled, as he headed for Cronus, breaking into a run.

Cronus, seeing the giant stone man heading toward him, halted his advance and braced himself. His hands outstretched into claws, and his lips peeled back into a snarl.

For just a second time seemed to slow and then the whole world shook, as the two Titans collided. The shock wave knocked Olivia, Theo and Sam to the ground, and when they looked up in stunned awe, they could see the two Giants locked together.

Prometheus grasped Cronus by the arms and spun him into the cliff face, and the whole rocky side collapsed inward leaving a gigantic indentation. Rocks and dust rained down and the ground heaved. Cronus straightened himself and charged Prometheus, tossing him to the ground as he brought his fist down dead center of his chest. A huge depression appeared in Prometheus's torso, with deep cracks spreading outward like a spider's web. Atlas roared in fury and tackled Cronus, driving him to the debris strewn floor before he could bring his fist back down to Prometheus again.

Having seen enough Oceanus turned back to the mortals, scooping all three of them up in one hand and placing them on his shoulder. He took three long strides, his enormous legs eating up the distance, before he collapsed to his knees. His legs below the knees turned to rushing water and he rolled forward fluidly, his shape disintegrating into a huge wave that flooded across the terrain like a Tsunami.

The God-like shape disappeared entirely and Theo, Olivia and Sam suddenly found themselves being swept along, immersed in a frothing, violent torrent of water. They could do nothing but hold onto each other desperately, trying not to get separated, and riding the flood, as if it were white water rapids. They swept along, too fast to even focus on their surroundings, or note the direction they took.

The water broke violently over their heads time and time again, as they clutched onto each other for dear life, taking huge gasps of air whenever the massive churning rolls of water would allow their heads to break the surface. Then suddenly, without warning, they found themselves washed up on a rough, gravelly surface of black sand. They sprawled out, soaked to the skin, chests heaving as they tried to fill their lungs with much needed air.

Olivia pushed herself shakily to her knees and looked up. The vast wash of churning waves had reared up into a writhing wall of water directly in front of them. The water rippled and frothed and a face appeared in the churning water.

'Daughter of Fire,' his voice burbled wetly, 'remember this day.' His aqua eyes held hers and hers alone. 'Remember who your allies are…NOW RUN!'

He turned in a huge rush of water, and washed away in the same direction he had come.

'Come on,' she pulled herself to her feet, turning toward Sam and Theo. 'We have to go, I don't know how long they can hold Cronus.'

Theo rolled to his feet and stumbled toward Sam, who was still lying on the harsh black sand breathing heavily, his face pale.

'Sam!' Olivia dropped to his side, 'what is it?'

'I don't know. When I translocated myself and Theo, it took more out of me than it should have.'

'It's the Underworld,' Olivia told him, 'it's poisoning you. You shouldn't be here.'

'I know.'

'You know?' she frowned, 'then why? We could have found a way to get you out of here, another gateway, or you could've used the gateway into our world. Why come down here with us if you knew you were going to get sick or worse.'

'Because you're my friends, and friends don't let each other down,' he breathed heavily. 'Sometimes you just have to do what you feel is right, and damn the consequences.'

'I wonder who he learned that from,' Theo replied dryly, casting a glance at Olivia.

'It's fine,' Sam tried to lift himself up weakly. 'I'm fine, go…I'll catch up.'

'No way,' Theo leaned down and heaved him to his feet, wrapping his arm around his neck for support. 'It's all of us, or none of us.'

'Theo's right,' Olivia took Sam's other arm and wrapped it around her neck. 'There's no way we're leaving you.'

He nodded weakly as they set off, moving as quickly as they could with Sam leaning heavily against them.

'Do you even know where we're heading,' Theo asked after a moment.

'I don't have a clue,' Olivia shook her head, 'just as far away from the Titans as we can get.'

They set off again, but Sam was beginning to tire and gradually their pace slowed.

'We can't keep running,' Theo stopped after they'd travelled a little further, 'we're not going to get far.'

'Shit,' Olivia swore, looking around. 'There's nothing here but barren wasteland. There's nowhere to even hide,' she replied desperately.

Pulling the compass from her collar she flicked it open.

'If you are ever going to work, now would be the time,' she breathed, as she stared down at the dials and hands.

Nothing.

She growled angrily, shaking the compass as if that would make it work. Glaring down at it in disgust she hissed at it, 'God damn it, would you just work…'

The needle twitched.

'Son of a bitch…' she frowned, wondering if she'd just lost it, and imagined that small hopeful movement.

'Move,' she breathed quietly and the needle twitched again, this time spinning in a small circle.

There was no way she'd imagined that. She closed her eyes and shook her head in exasperation.

'It cannot be that simple…' she muttered, opening her eyes again and looking down at the innocent looking object. 'I'm such an idiot.'

'What is it?' Theo asked taking Sam's full weight from her.

Olivia looked up as the ground shook, and a great angry bellow split the still air, which was suddenly filled with an acrid burning stench, and a sooty red glow.

'No time to explain,' she turned to Theo and took his hand. 'Sam hold onto Theo, and no matter what happens do not let go!'

They looked across to see a huge figure behind them, glowing ominously in the darkness.

Clutching Theo's hand desperately, she raised the compass to her lips.

'Take me to the Crossroad…'

Her soft whisper caught on the air like a sigh. Suddenly the compass began to warm in her hand, the golden metal glowed brightly, and all the dials and hands began spinning. There was a strange kind of ticking sound, and the darkness around them began to shift and swirl.

It was the same strange dizzying feeling she'd had as a child, when she'd held her arms out and spun around and around, really fast, until dizzy with delight she'd collapsed to the ground in helpless laughter.

She didn't collapse to the ground this time, but the world did spin, and spin around them, while her stomach swooped and lurched, filled with sick and terrifying excitement.

Abruptly it began to slow, and she swayed on her feet, slightly unbalanced as she tried to regain her equilibrium.

The first thing she noticed was that it was no longer dark. She glanced up into the sky, which was ablaze with great swirls of purple and pink, as if she were witnessing a sunset. Heavy storm clouds drifted across the skies, punctuated every so often by a micro spike of lightning. The air felt heavy with expectation, but also dry and charged with static electricity.

Her gaze dropped from the sky, to where the three of them were standing. They were in some sort of passageway only there was no roof, and she could still glance up to the sky. They seemed trapped between two walls made up of large heavy sandstone blocks, which stretched up several meters in height. There were no doors or exits, but the passageway stretched in either direction for miles. Frowning in confusion, a few meters from them she noticed heavy vines climbing the wall to the top. She wandered toward them, with Theo helping Sam along behind her.

'Is this the Crossroad?' Theo asked dubiously.

'I don't know,' she frowned, stopping in front of the thick toughened vines. 'We need a better vantage point.' She tugged the vines a couple of times experimentally, before starting to climb.

'Stay here,' Theo told Sam, as he dropped him down to the dusty stone ground and propped him against the wall. 'We'll be right back.'

Sam nodded slowly; he still looked weak, but some of the color was starting to return to his face and his breathing wasn't quite so harsh and labored.

Theo climbed quietly up behind her. By the time he had reached the top, she was already standing on the top edge of the wall. He pulled himself up beside her.

'I thought you had a problem with heights?'

'It isn't that high,' she looked down to where Sam sat tiredly, 'besides, before you wanted me to jump the Void. That's completely different.'

She turned back to the view in front of her, her gut churning in a mixture of awe and frustration. Laid out below them, stretching out endlessly, was a giant circular maze of sandy colored walls.

'It's a labyrinth,' she breathed, turning to Theo who was looking out in confusion. 'I'm guessing a David Bowie reference would be equally lost on you.'

'Who?'

She shook her head and sighed. 'You know if we ever get home, we are going to snuggle in bed for a month and have a movie marathon.'

He took her hand comfortingly and squeezed, smiling down at her. 'Sounds good to me.'

She turned back to the labyrinth laid out in front of them, her eyes narrowing, as she studied something in the distance. 'There...' she pointed to the center of the labyrinth.

Theo squinted slightly as he looked in the direction she indicated.

'What is that?'

'It's the Crossroad,' she murmured, 'that's Epsilon.'

'You mean we have to find our way through this giant puzzle to get to the Crossroad?'

'Maybe...'

'What is it?'

'I don't know,' she mumbled absently, her attention fixed somewhere on the twisting stone passageways.

The sky churned and lit above them with the oppressive heaviness of an approaching storm. She had a strange sort of feeling, a kind of prickling of the skin, not enough to make her feel cold, but more like an awareness.

Something pulled at her, tugging deep inside, something familiar. Everything in her yearned toward it, filling her with helpless love, and bone deep sorrow. The kind of deeply scored pain, that only one person had ever made her feel.

A lump began to form at the back of her throat, burning painfully as she tried to swallow past it. She could feel her heart pounding in her chest, and her hands gripped tightly into fists, forgetting she was holding Theo's hand as her nails dug into his skin.

'Olivia?' he called to her softly, 'what is it?'

She blinked back the sudden sheen of tears blurring her vision.

'I can feel her,' she whispered. 'She's down there…in the Labyrinth.'

'Who?' he asked in confusion.

'My mother…'

24.

Isabel looked at the giant blocks of sandstone, her gaze absently drifting up to the top and to the sky, which swirled and rumbled, crackling with energy. It was as if it knew they stood right at the precipice of an event so huge, it was going to shift the balance of everything. It hung poised, holding its breath, waiting for the right moment to unleash all of its fury.

Nathaniel watched Isabel carefully, a small smile curving his lips. It was almost too easy to manipulate the witch, he'd been doing it ever since she was sixteen years old. Ever since she'd been old enough to understand her own power, or lack of it rather, and the legacy of her family. Of course she wasn't as powerful as some of the West women that had come before her, but that lack had only made it easier to plant the ideas in her mind.

It was pathetic really, she'd actually believed she held the upper hand, that he would allow her to get her hands on Infernum. His eyes narrowed as she stood, staring blankly, waiting for him. He'd feel sorry for her, but she was a human, and his lip curled in disgust. They were maggots, crawling across the face of their world, infesting and devouring everything in their path.

'Nathaniel?' Zachary appeared behind him, 'they approach.'

Nathaniel turned away from the witch, and focused on the two men as they stopped a few meters from them. Both tall, and with a slim elegant build, they looked like they were more suited to Wall Street than a labyrinth in the deepest, darkest pit of the Underworld. Although some might argue there wasn't much difference between the two.

The taller of the two had dark hair, just slightly too long so that it brushed the arch of his dark winged eyebrows. He had startling eyes, so pale they looked like blue ice. He wore a dark grey suit with a black shirt, open at the collar, revealing the line of his throat, his skin a pleasing golden color. His companion was dressed much the same, in an expensive looking tailored, dark colored suit, but his hair was lighter, more of a golden brown, as were his eyes.

'Ash,' Nathaniel greeted him, his lip curling in barely concealed disgust.

Ash turned his pale blue eyes on the demon, his black hair gleaming in the dying light. His gaze swept over Nathaniel, noting his ragged and torn clothes, the tattered and rotten flesh hanging from his frame, until he reached the ruins of his face.

Part of his jaw had been eaten away by the magic contained in the blade Theo had stabbed into his throat, and the damage had now spread. The decay had crawled up the side of his face, and eaten away, until he had no ear left on that side of his head. The hair was also gone, his scalp now covered in sparse tattered chunks. The damage had also spread downward, eating away the skin of his neck and shoulder, revealing nothing but gaping wounds and raw sinew.

'Nathaniel,' Ash replied coolly, his lip curling slightly in revulsion.

A sudden growl had Ash looking across to Zachary, who was glaring at the man at his side, his black eyes blazed, and his lips peeled back in an angry animal-like snarl. Ash looked down to his associate, who in turn was glaring daggers at the younger demon, with barely concealed hatred.

'Oh,' Ash mused mildly, 'I'd forgotten about that unpleasantness between you two.'

Zachary took a step toward them, and Ash's gaze hardened.

'You might want to call off your dog,' he warned coldly, 'or the consequences will be severe.'

'I could say the same to you,' Nathaniel rasped in a strange grating voice, almost as if his vocal chords were rotting away.

Ash gave a cool smirk, before addressing his associate. 'Cyrus,' he spoke smoothly, 'that's enough.'

Cyrus looked up to Ash and straightened, unfurling his clenched fists, but his eyes still blazed with contempt, as he continued to watch Zachary warily.

'Now, shall we conclude our business?' Ash looked to Nathaniel. 'I have upheld my end of our bargain. I gave you the locations of the five Crossroads. Is everything in place for me?'

'It is,' Nathaniel replied grudgingly, 'they are ready to move on your orders.'

'Good,' he inclined his head in acknowledgment.

'There is just one more thing,' Nathaniel answered.

Ash raised a perfectly winged brow questioningly, 'there always is with you demons.'

'I need to get to the center of the labyrinth.'

'That was not part of the deal.'

'I'm making it part of the deal, or the deal is off. Hades draws near, I can feel him. If he interferes now, neither of us get what we want.'

'Not afraid of a God, are you?' Ash asked in amusement.

Nathaniel glared hatefully at him, through one empty socket and one filmy white eye.

'Very well,' he shrugged after a moment, 'but as it was not part of our original agreement, you now owe me a debt.'

'Agreed,' he grated from between clenched, blackening teeth.

'Nathaniel!' Zachary hissed, not at all happy with the thought of a debt being owed to them.

'Silence!' he snapped, as he turned back to Ash and nodded.

Ash slipped his hand into his pocket, and when he withdrew it he was holding a strange glowing blue sphere.

'Isabel,' Nathaniel commanded, watching in satisfaction as she wandered over to him unquestioningly and stood beside him.

Ash held the bright stone up and unfurled his long elegant fingers, so that it sat in the palm of his hand. It was round and smooth, about the size of an orange. It seemed to be constructed of some sort of transparent glass, allowing an unhindered view of the magnificence at its center, as it pulsed and throbbed like a beating heart. Deep inside the sphere was a churning, primordial mass of energy, glowing blue, and punctuated every so often with micro bursts of electricity.

'Incredible,' Nathaniel murmured, his gaze hungrily fixed on the jewel.

'Focus demon,' Ash replied in amusement, 'the sphere was not part of the agreement.'

He held up the round glowing object, and as he turned it, a deep crack, gouged into the surface of the glass, could be seen. It seemed to be missing a small shard. Nathaniel didn't have time to dwell on that little detail, as the giant stone wall began to shimmer. It disappeared and in its place stood an archway, which led into a seemingly endless tunnel, dimly lit by occasional torches.

'This will lead you straight to the center of the labyrinth, and to the eastern entrance of Epsilon,' Ash told him.

Nathaniel nodded begrudgingly. He entered the archway, followed obediently by Isabel. Zachary cast one more disdainful look at Cyrus, and followed the others.

Cyrus watched silently, until they disappeared into the gloomy tunnel, before turning to his companion.

'I hope you know what you are doing Ash,' his voice was laced with disgust, 'consorting with demons. You know their kind cannot be trusted.'

'Of course I do,' Ash smiled coolly. 'Why do you think I brought the Sphere? It was no easy task to smuggle it out without its absence being noted.'

'You knew he would alter the details of your agreement?'

Ash shrugged, 'now he owes me a debt, which could prove useful.'

'I still think it's a mistake, especially having anything to do with that carrion Zachary,' he spat in disgust.

'You need to let that go Cyrus,' Ash replied, his eyes narrowing. 'Jerusalem was a long time ago.'

'Not nearly long enough,' he hissed.

'And when this is all over you can do whatever you want to Zachary, but not until then. Do I make myself clear?'

Cyrus nodded grudgingly.

'I still don't understand why you had to give him the locations of all five Crossroads. He's already destroyed four of them...you do know he's going to start a war, and that the war will spill over onto Earth? Azariel will be furious.'

'Azariel and Thomas are too busy trying to destroy each other to even notice what is happening on Earth, and that's exactly what I am counting on.'

'We need to be careful,' Cyrus warned. 'If Nathaniel gets his hands on Infernum...'

'He won't,' Ash shrugged. 'Do you really think he has what it takes to go up against Hades? To go against the will of a God?' he rolled his eyes. 'Hades will exterminate him, like the insect he is.'

'But Infernum is no safer in the hands of a God than it is in the hands of a grasping, conniving demon.'

'Hades has no interest in the book,' Ash replied coolly, 'and neither do I. What would I want with that poisonous filth? All I care about is Caelum.'

'It's a dangerous game Ash.'

He tucked the throbbing blue sphere back into his pocket, and rolled his shoulders.

'It was never a game,' he smiled slowly. His pale blue eyes glittered and as he straightened, his huge wings unfurled, stretching and spanning several feet in length. Smooth and incredibly soft to the touch, they were covered in jet black feathers.

'I think it's time the Angels once again walked the Earth,' he smiled.

Olivia and Theo walked slowly, with Sam between them. Although he no longer needed their assistance, and could move unaided now they were not running, it was still difficult for him to keep up with them, and the strain was showing clearly on his face.

'We should probably let you rest again,' Theo frowned, looking at Sam in concern.

'No,' he shook his head, 'we don't have the time. We'll never make it to the center of the labyrinth if we keep stopping.'

'Theo's right Sam,' she told him absently, 'take a minute.'

'What is it?' Theo asked her, sensing the change in her mood.

'I'm not sure,' she murmured, her attention someplace else entirely. She could feel a strange hum of power. Something had shifted inside the labyrinth, something was different. She couldn't explain how or why she knew, it was as if she was somehow connected to it.

For a moment the compass had burned hot against her skin, hot enough for it to sting. She lifted it from her collar and turned it over in her hands, flicking the lid open. It was now pulsing with a strange blue glow, like it had woken from a long slumber.

'Show me the way to the center of the labyrinth,' she whispered impulsively.

She wasn't sure what she'd been expecting, but the wall in front of her suddenly shimmered and changed. When she looked up, her mouth fell open in surprise. A huge archway had opened up in the sandstone before them.

'How did you do that?'

'I didn't,' she replied, 'the compass did.'

She looked down at the compass in her hand. It felt strange, alive somehow, throbbing in her hand like a heartbeat, and pulsing with light.

'Did it glow blue last time?' Theo frowned.

'No it didn't,' she answered, slightly puzzled.

She studied the face of it, which still looked the same. The dials and hands were all motionless, but somewhere underneath was where the strange pulsing light was coming from.

She laid her fingertips lightly against the face of the compass and twisted. It turned and released a tiny secret mechanism, flipping open the whole face, which held the dials and hands. Beneath it was a tiny secret compartment, and set at its center was a very strange looking precious stone of some sort.

It looked like a deep blue sapphire, but it seemed to hum as if it were somehow alive. It didn't look like any jewel or precious stone she'd ever seen. It wasn't cut or smoothed into a pleasing shape, but rather was a jagged shard, as if it had split away from a larger piece.

'Olivia?'

She looked up from her curious inspection of the shard and compass, to see what he was staring at. The strange long corridor which had opened up, was now lit by torches and seemed to run deep into the labyrinth.

'Looks like it leads directly to the Crossroad.'

'Yeah,' Olivia muttered thoughtfully. 'I guess it's time to call some back-up.'

'Hades?' Theo asked.

She nodded. 'He's going to be pissed if he doesn't get first shot at Nathaniel. Besides, if he can keep the demon busy, I'll deal with my mother.'

'And you're okay with that?' he asked softly.

'I'll have to be,' she answered quietly, looking up at Theo. 'I didn't ask for any of this, but she has to be stopped. If it's not me, it'll just be someone else.'

'Then let it be someone else,' he stroked her arm comfortably. 'No matter how okay you think you are with this Olivia, she's still your mother.'

'I'm not okay with this,' she shook her head in frustration, 'I'm not okay at all, but she's my responsibility.'

'We'll see,' Theo murmured. 'Go ahead, you may as well call Hades.'

She gave a small nod of agreement and closed her eyes, lifting her face to the sky and sending out the thought.

'Hades,' his name echoed in her mind, loud and resounding, like a bell.

'You don't need to shout Olivia,' the smooth voice came from behind her. 'I can hear perfectly well.'

'Hades,' she greeted him dryly, noting that he still wore battle armor, which was even more dented and stained than the last time she'd seen him.

'Olivia,' he replied, his tone just as acerbic. 'I hear you have been stalking through the Underworld like a natural disaster.'

'I don't know what you mean,' she shrugged innocently.

'Is it true you shouted at the Judges?'

'I didn't shout.'

'But you did treat them disrespectfully.'

'Where I come from respect has to be earned.'

'Not here it doesn't. They are thousands of years older than you, and when I left them Minos was a rather unhealthy shade of purple, and Aeacus was almost having an apoplectic fit.'

'I'm sure they'll get over it.'

Hades mouth twitched slightly.

'And what about Hecate?'

'What about her?'

'You threw her into her pool of contemplation.'

'Is that what it was called?'

'So you don't deny it?'

'It wasn't so much throwing her in, as dunking her a few times.'

'Dunking her a few times...' he repeated slowly.

'I am a little sorry about that,' she conceded ruefully. 'I genuinely liked her, but unfortunately I needed to speak with her, and I couldn't do that while she was drooling into a wine jug.'

He pinched the bridge of his nose in exasperation, shaking his head slowly. 'Do I even need to start... on you disobeying me and returning to the mortal world?'

'I didn't exactly disobey you. I never said I wouldn't go back there, I just said I'd find the Crossroad, and TA-DAH!' she spread her hands and innocently indicated the tunnel behind her which led to the last crossroad.'

'You seriously have the audacity to stand there and argue semantics with me?' he ignored the tunnel for the moment.

'We can sit if it's more comfortable for you,' she shrugged.

'I told you to forget the others in the mortal world, let them deal with it, and concentrate on finding your mother.'

'And I told you, I was not going to abandon the

people I care about,' she replied. 'Look we solved a problem, the Soul Collector is gone, everyone in Mercy is fine, and we found the last Crossroad before Nathaniel.'

'Overachiever,' Sam muttered as she threw him an impish smile.

'Everything worked out okay,' she replied, 'what more do you want from me Hades?'

'A little bit of deference would be nice,' he murmured.

'My mother is here,' she told him quietly, 'and if she is here, then Nathaniel is here. I kept my word to you Hades. I'm sorry if I'm not the kind of fawning mortal or subordinate you're used to, but that's not going to change. If I say I'm going to do something I do it, I'm not going to apologize about how I go about it.'

'Of all the obstinate, frustrating, headstrong females…' he growled, 'you're enough to drive a God to drink. I'm not surprised Hecate was halfway through a jug of Dionysus' wine if she saw you coming.' He glanced across at Theo, 'you have my deepest sympathy.'

Theo's mouth curved in amusement, but he wisely chose to keep his comments to himself.

Olivia smiled impishly, 'admit it Hades, you're having fun for the first time in centuries.'

He shook his head, with a deep long suffering sigh of resignation. 'Well I'm certainly not bored.'

'So, is all forgiven?'

He chuckled lightly, 'I have no idea why I'm so fond of you Olivia.'

She rose up on her toes and kissed his cheek affectionately. 'I'm fond of you too, even though you are grouchy and demanding.'

'Grouchy?' he frowned.

'And demanding,' she clarified.

'Do you ever get the last word with her?' he asked the others.

'No,' Theo and Sam replied together.

Hades' gaze fell on Sam for the first time. He was propped up against the edge of the wall near the archway, his skin pale, and with the kind of clammy appearance of a sick person. His eyes were strained and his breathing was shallow.

'You are a young one aren't you?' his eyes narrowed, as he studied Sam carefully. 'You should not be here.'

'So everyone keeps telling me' Sam replied, from between clenched teeth.

'I don't remember giving you permission to cross into the Underworld.'

Sam glared up at the God towering above him. 'I am Olivia and Theo's friend, I came to help them.'

'Not helping them much at the moment are you?'

'I'm fine,' he replied angrily.

'No, you are not Sam.'

'You know who I am?'

'Who yes, and what,' he frowned. 'Some of your elders are powerful enough to withstand the darkness, and power of the Underworld, but you are not. You are too young, too unskilled, you have yet to come fully into your gifts. You should not be here, you must leave at once, or you will die.'

Sam gritted his teeth, pulling himself up by sheer force of will, and holding himself upright.

'I will stay as long as they are in danger.'

Hades stroked his chin thoughtfully, his dark eyes glittering with interest as he studied Sam.

'You are not at all like the others of your kind, are you?' he muttered turning toward the other two. 'You do keep some interesting company Olivia.'

'Hades,' Olivia replied softly, 'stop poking at him. He stays with us. We will care for him.'

'A noble sentiment,' he turned to Olivia, 'but one that will not serve you, or him well. He is in no condition to go into battle.'

'Battle?' she frowned, 'who said anything about a battle?'

'What did you think was going to happen?' he shook his head, 'that Nathaniel and I would meet, and exchange harsh words?'

'Well no, but…'

'Olivia, he has been using a small army of demons to break the Crossroads. He and your mother are not alone…and neither am I.'

Olivia turned and looked over his shoulder, and behind him stood a tall Greek warrior, grim and formidable, wearing a short kilt and closely fitted armor. He had a large round shield strapped to his left arm, and a long spear in his right. He also carried a short sword, which she recognized as a Xiphos, which was sheathed at his hip.

He looked every inch an imposing Greek warrior, with one exception, she could see the wall behind him straight through his body. He was as thin and insubstantial as mist.

'He's a shade?'

'Don't let that concern you,' Hades smiled as another warrior materialized next to him, and then another, and another. 'They are lethal, as many of my enemies have already discovered. Although,' he mused thoughtfully, 'I'd have liked to have had a few dozen Spartans.'

'Why can't you?' she asked curiously.

'Politics,' he replied cryptically.

She wisely chose not to question him any further.

When she looked behind him once more, there was a small army of ghostly warriors staring back at her.

'Well Sam?' Hades' gaze locked on him, 'what is it going to be? I can send you back to the mortal world, it will take you a while to recover your strength, but you will, eventually. If you remain here much longer, I cannot guarantee you will survive.'

'I stand with my friends,' he replied coolly. 'I may not be at my full strength, but I can still fight.'

Hades stared at him thoughtfully. 'Loyalty…' he mused, 'is something I value very highly.'

Seeming to come to a decision, he pressed his hand to Sam's chest, causing him to gasp in shock. Sam felt fire roar through his veins, burning him alive. His face broke out in a sweat and his heart beat uncontrollably against the vicious wave of pain building inside him.

He let out a roar of pain as the wave crested, and then Hades released him. Leaning forward and resting his hands on his knees, he sucked in a deep shaky breath, but when he straightened he instantly felt different. The weakness, which had been spreading through his body like a plague, was gone. He felt strong, and charged with a strange kind of energy.

'It will not last,' Hades answered his puzzled expression.

'What did you do to me?'

'I gave you what you needed,' he replied calmly. 'As I said it will not last, but it will at least keep you alive long enough to get out of the Underworld, that is…' he smiled in amusement, 'unless the demons kill you first.'

'I'd like to see them try,' he replied coolly.

'You might need this.' He held out his hand and balanced across his palm was a black bladed sword.

Sam reached out slowly, taking the blade from Hades' hand. His fist wrapped around the hilt, and he sliced and cut through the air experimentally a few times. It was so light, perfectly weighted and counterbalanced. It was an incredible weapon.

'Thank you,' he replied quietly, puzzled at the enigmatic God standing before him. Everything he knew about Hades, everything he'd ever been taught about the God of the Underworld, didn't match up to all he'd witnessed since being in the Underworld, and it was…unsettling to say the least.

'Theo,' Hades turned toward him, 'I understand you have a very unusual weapon. May I see it?'

Theo narrowed his eyes thoughtfully, regarding the God in front of him. Nodding his head in consent after a moment, he pulled back his sleeve. Hades leaned forward and grasped Theo's arm in his long elegant fingers, turning it over so he could examine the vines of blue, black and silver etched deeply into his flesh.

'Fascinating' he murmured, his eyes widening slightly, as the tentacles of metal began to soften and slide down his arm to pool in the palm of his hand. Theo flexed his fingers, and they wrapped around the hilt of his blade.

Hades studied the large hunting knife with its silver vines and tiny leaves around the hilt, and its blue black blade, which glowed with an ancient language, which Theo was certain Hades was able to read.

'The blade itself is imbued with two of the ancient fires,' he looked over to Olivia. 'You were responsible for this?'

'I didn't exactly do it on purpose,' she muttered.

'You never do Olivia,' he rolled his eyes, and returned to his thorough scrutiny of the extraordinary blade.

'Well,' Hades spoke after a moment, 'as impressive as that is Theodore, it just won't do. These are demons, and you certainly won't do much damage with that tiny little blade.'

His fist gripped Theo's so they were both holding the weapon tightly. Theo watched in interest, as the blade rippled and began to grow, elongating into a slightly curved and elegant sword.

When Hades finally released his hand and stepped back Theo turned the blade over in his hand, studying it closely. It still looked exactly as it had before, retaining all the same characteristics and markings, only now it was a sword instead of a knife.

Satisfied Hades stepped to the entrance of the

long tunnel. 'Well,' he smiled coldly, 'I do believe it's time to kill some demons.'

25.

Danae blinked in surprise as her phone started ringing. Grabbing it up before it had a chance to ring off, she hit connect.

'Charles! Finally,' she breathed in frustration. 'Would it kill you to return a fucking phone call?'

'What do you think I'm doing?' he returned dryly.

'Really? After two days of trying to reach you and my idiot brother, you finally feel like returning my calls?'

'Danae,' he replied irritably, 'I really don't have time for this.'

'Everyone in Mercy is fine by the way,' she told him sarcastically, 'and the Soul Collector is gone.'

'Good...' Charles murmured, 'that's good...'

'Are you even listening to me?'

'Danae, now is not a good time. I have someplace I have to be.'

'Then why did you bother calling me at all?'

'To tell you to stop calling. I'll speak to you when I'm done.'

'Charles, don't you dare hang up on me,' she warned.

The line went silent for a moment.

'What do you want Danae?'

'I saw Olivia.'

'WHAT?' Charles asked in confusion, 'what the hell are you talking about?'

'Olivia came back.'

'What? How? Why didn't you tell me before?' he demanded.

'What, like two fucking days ago maybe?' she deadpanned.

'Stop swearing at me,' he snapped irritably.

'I can't help it,' she snapped right back. 'I'm royally pissed off right now.'

'Just tell me what happened, where is Olivia now?'

'She's not here, she went back to the Otherworld.'

'Why?'

'Just shut up and listen,' she sighed, reaching deep down inside for her patience. 'The Soul Collector was at the old Bachelier place out in the north west woods by the lake. He was using Clea's spirit bottles to trap the souls he was harvesting. Roni and I showed up just as Theo and Olivia were taking care of business. They grabbed the Collector and pulled him back through the gateway they'd come through and all of them disappeared.'

'She's still alive?' he breathed in relief. 'If she reappeared in our world her mortal body must be undamaged.'

'She looked just fine to me.'

'So there's still a chance to pull her back to this side permanently.'

'That's just it Charles,' Danae shook her head. 'Whatever it is you're planning, I don't think you should go through with it.'

'What are you talking about?'

'I don't think Olivia and Theo were dragged back through the gateway. I think they chose to go back through, which means they're dealing with something we know nothing about. We should hold off until we've at least found a way to communicate with them.'

'No.'

'Charles,' she breathed heavily, 'I know you're worried about her, and I know you want her back, but just take a step back and think about this for a moment. If you go barging in there using Hoodoo, which is some pretty heavyweight old world magic, you could end up doing more harm than good.'

'You don't know what you're talking about,' he replied stiffly, 'you're just guessing. How do we know that they aren't desperate to get back, but they had to return to the Otherworld to deal with the Collector? How do you know he didn't pull them back through?'

'Charles please, I have a really bad feeling, just hold off a few days that's all I'm asking. Let's just see if there's another way we can contact them.'

'I can't,' he replied quietly, 'I'm sorry...'

'Charles...Charles...'

The line went dead.

'Damn it,' she swore as she redialed his number. No service. He'd obviously switched his phone off. Growling in frustration she rang her brother's phone again and got his answering service.

'Davis listen to me, you have to stop Charles. No matter what you do, don't let him try to pull them back from the Otherworld. It's really important he doesn't interfere. Please call me as soon as you get this message...'

'Charles, are you ready to leave?' Davis poked his head around the door. 'Julien has the car waiting for us.'

'I'm coming,' Charles nodded, taking one last look at his cell, before he turned to follow his brother.

The warm night air was filled with music and laughter as they stepped out into it, heading toward the dark shiny sedan parked in front of the building. A drunken party of Midwesterners rolled past them, stumbling and laughing loudly. Davis took a step back to avoid them, and accidentally collided with Charles.

'Sorry,' he frowned, waiting for them to pass,

before climbing into the car.

'No problem,' Charles replied. As Davis disappeared from sight he pulled out Davis' phone, which he'd snagged from his pocket, pulled up his messages and listened.

'Davis, listen to me, you have to stop Charles. No matter…' having heard enough Charles hit delete and then pulled out his own cell phone from his pocket, depositing them both in the nearby trash before climbing into the car.

Nodding to the driver, they pulled away from the building, and headed out of the city. Much as it had the last time, as the sounds of the city began to fade away they were replaced with the soothing sounds of Katydids, and bush crickets.

The air hung hot and heavy, and laden with expectation. Charles tensed, as he sat gazing out of the window. He was doing the right thing, he couldn't let doubt creep in now. Olivia needed him, he had no doubt of her capability to take care of herself, but damn it, she was his child. He couldn't leave her stranded on the other side, he was going to bring her back no matter what.

In what seemed like no time at all the car slowed, and drew to a halt down by the murky water of the Bayou. Once again, the small wooden boat awaited, with the same tall, thin, dark skinned man who never uttered a word. He seemed perfectly content to carry them across the sluggish water, which was heavy with vegetation and algae.

The boat rocked and waded through the water as he removed a neatly pressed handkerchief from his pocket and dabbed the light sheen of perspiration from his face and neck.

The same rickety, ramshackle building floated into view, held up on spindly stilts, and rising up out of the swamp in mismatched levels. The boat bumped gently along the long, thin, wooden walkway and Charles looked up at the lonely cry which echoed through the air. It was a night heron, swooping in to settle on a low branch and watch him with indecipherable eyes. They reached the door and knocked, standing back and waiting patiently until it swung open.

'I'll wait here,' Davis decided, as he pulled out a small can of mosquito spray, and applied it liberally to every inch of his exposed, fair skin.

Nodding in agreement, Charles stepped into the cabin and stopped short, glancing around in confusion, wondering if he was in the right place. Gone was the mad, pink, shag pile carpet and neat white furniture. There were no longer any china plates, bearing scenes of the English countryside, hanging from the walls, in fact there was not one frilly curtain, plump cushion, or pink bow anywhere.

Instead there was little furniture, just a plain unadorned wooden table and chairs tucked into the corner of the room, a low brown cracked leather couch was pushed against the other wall, and crammed into every other spare inch of room were old glass fronted display cabinets, and bookcases of varying shapes and sizes.

Laid out carefully on each shelf was a hoard of strange treasures, and Charles found himself wandering the room, slowly studying each shelf curiously, his nervousness all but forgotten.

It was like an Aladdin's cave. Tiny little bottles with glass stoppers lined the shelves, along with old faded leather bound books, some in languages he had never even seen before. There were several crystal balls, and bell jars containing dried herbs, or preserved rodents and amphibians. A large snake skin filled another jar. Other shelves held candles of varying colors, jars filled with a strange black colored dust, Tarot cards, and cards with strange unknown illustrations. On a small table were runes, bones and large bottles.

There was a scientific porcelain model head and shoulders, with sections of the brain mapped out on its shiny white scalp. Beside a brass telescope, was a large lidded container, which looked, quite disturbingly, as if it contained endless looping coils of intestines.

Charles stopped up short, when he came across a cabinet containing, what looked like, a desiccated and blackened human hand. Fascinated, he stepped closer, reaching out towards it.

'I wouldn't do that if were you Cher.'

He turned back to see who had spoken, and his eyes widened slightly.

'Cora?' he asked uncertainly.

'Who else were you expecting Cher?'

'You look different.'

'When I am working there are no masks, no pretenses, just truth.'

'So this is the real you?'

'As you see,' she shrugged.

She stepped bare footed into the room. Gone was the cute little Englishwoman with her perfectly sculpted curls, and neatly buttoned up cardigan.

Before him stood a slightly older woman with a kind of timelessness about her. If he had to peg her age, he'd have put her close to his own, although he imagined she was probably far older than she actually looked.

Her long jet black hair was pulled back from her face in a mass of complicated braids, falling down her back in thick ropes, which were almost dreadlocks, interwoven every now and then with gold rings.

Her skin was a pleasing deep golden honey, her eyes dark and edged with black Kohl. She wore a dark dress, which clung to her abundant curves like a second skin. There was a kind of overripe lushness about her, and an appealing sensuality.

Dark beads hung around her neck, entwined with several strange pendants, which hung down past her breasts almost to her waist. Her nails were painted black and her hands were unadorned, with the exception of a single signet ring of gold, inlaid with a large black stone of polished onyx.

He turned back to the cabinet, and to the strange blackened hand.

'It's a hand of glory, isn't it?'

'Did you come for the tour?' she asked in amusement, 'or did you bring the items I requested?'

He handed her the bag he was holding.

'Good,' she took it from him slowly, her gaze holding his. 'I was beginning to wonder if you were coming back, your time was almost up.'

'We have a deal.'

'Yes we do Cher,' she muttered studying him thoughtfully. 'Shall we begin then?'

As she moved aside his gaze fell to where a large sigil was drawn out on the wooden floor. Spaced at intervals were strategically placed thick, stumpy black and white candles, more symbols were scrawled in a circular pattern around them, and herbs were scattered everywhere. He watched as she laid the sweater and hairbrush in the center of the circle, and retrieved a jar of black dust from one of the shelves.

'What's that?' he asked curiously.

'It's Goofer dust,' she replied, as she knelt on the ground, unscrewed the lid, and pulled out a great handful scattering it across the symbols.

'Goofer dust?' he frowned, 'isn't that usually used for hexing?'

'Usually,' she agreed, 'but it can also be used for coaxing and coercion. It has many uses, depending on the blend.'

'What's in that one?'

'A little of this, a little of that,' she shrugged, 'graveyard dirt, snake skin, ash, salt, powdered bones. Do you really want a lesson on magic?'

'Sorry,' he smiled, 'I'm a teacher by nature. I always was too curious for my own good.'

'A teacher?' she raised one slender brow.

'High school history.'

'I do like a man who respects roots,' she stood and placed the jar back on the shelf, dusting her hands on her skirt. 'Okay, shoes and socks off, and come and stand over here.'

'Sorry?'

'You heard,' she replied, 'bare feet, and hurry up we don't have all night.'

Bending down to do as she asked, he untied his shoes and removed them. Tucking his socks neatly inside, he wandered over and stood opposite Cora, feeling the dust and herbs beneath the soles of his feet.

'Okay then Cher,' she grinned, 'let's get this show on the road.'

Nathaniel glanced down the gloomy corridor and saw a faint light in the distance. They groped along in the darkness, for what seemed like forever, and when they finally reached the end and stepped out they found themselves facing a tall curved wall.

No longer the warm pale yellow sandstone of the labyrinth, these walls were bleak and imposing, made of solid, tightly packed grey stone. Slightly to the left was a huge arched doorway, from which, hung a heavy wooden door, with large metal hinges. A curved letter 'E' was burned deeply into the door, scarring the wood.

'Epsilon,' Nathaniel muttered, the ruin of his mouth trying to curve into a smile, but merely succeeded in achieving a terrifying grimace. 'Zachary,' he turned as the younger demon appeared next to him, 'summon the others.'

Zachary nodded and closed his eyes, reaching out to his brethren. Slowly, they started appearing around the circumference of the huge wall. Men, women, children, all of varying shapes and sizes and all with blood red eyes.

A middle aged woman with red hair approached.

'Saffire,' Nathaniel turned to look at her.

'My lord,' she nodded in greeting, 'an archway has

opened up, in front of the west entrance to Epsilon.'

'Hades?' he growled.

'Not just Hades my lord, he has the witch with him.' She spat in contempt, casting an accusing look at Isabel, who was completely unperturbed by her presence.

'Take the others and head to the tunnel, make sure no one reaches the Crossroad.'

She nodded and moved toward the new, brightly lit archway, beckoning the other demons to follow.

'You too Zachary,' he told his second in command. 'No matter what happens, Hades and the girl must not reach the Crossroad.'

'Of course,' he replied.

'How about you Isabel?' Nathaniel asked slowly. 'Would you like to watch, while we kill your daughter?'

Isabel stared at him blankly, as if she couldn't quite comprehend what he was saying. Either that or she just wasn't concerned enough to show any reaction. Nathaniel chuckled, a disgusting wet burbling kind of sound.

'Go,' he commanded.

Zachary bowed and disappeared toward the west entrance.

Nathaniel turned and looked at Isabel, who was staring at the wooden door.

'Open it,' he whispered to her. It had to be her of course. As a demon, he would not be able to touch the door, but that didn't mean he couldn't step through it if someone opened it for him. Once inside, all he had to do was get Isabel to make a deal with the keeper. Annoyingly, this was also something he couldn't do, because it had to be a human. Still, he had her now. Isabel was his to control, and all he had to do was get her to ask for the location of the book.

He watched in interest, as Isabel reached out, slowly grasped the cool metal handle and twisted. Despite no one probably having used it for centuries, possibly even longer, the door swung open easily, with no hint of rust, or creaking hinges. A breeze rushed through the open doorway, tugging at Isabel's hair, brushing it back over her shoulder, and revealing the silvery burn mark which marred the skin on the side of her face.

Slowly she stepped across the threshold into the darkness beyond, with Nathaniel silently gloating, as he following behind.

Olivia walked in silence alongside Hades, with Theo and Sam just slightly behind her to her right, and behind them the ghostly forms of the army of shades glided silently along the sandy ground.

'Are you feeling okay?' Theo whispered to Sam.

'I feel a bit strange,' he admitted quietly, 'but I'll be okay. What about you?'

'What about me?'

Sam nodded toward the impressive blue black sword in his hand. 'Do you actually know how to use that thing?'

Theo shrugged, 'what's to know? The pointy end goes into the other man.'

'Seriously?'

'What about you then?' he indicated the sword Hades had given to Sam. 'You don't even look old enough to shave yet, are you sure you know how to use that?'

'Don't let the face fool you Theo, I'm a lot older than you think, and I have been training since I was old enough to pick up a sword. It's the way of my people, we are first and foremost warriors.'

'If you say so,' Theo replied.

'Look, stay close to me, and try not to get yourself killed. Olivia went to a lot of trouble to pull you out of the Otherworld. I doubt she wants to go back and start looking for you all over again.'

'I thought the Otherworld was destroyed when it was pulled into the Void?' Theo frowned in confusion.

'No,' Sam snorted, 'there's no way you can destroy the whole of the Otherworld, it's too vast. It's probably one of the largest of all the different realms, because it more or less caters to each soul personally. What you saw fall into the Void, was simply the manifestation of the afterlife you subconsciously created.'

Theo stared at him blankly.

'Think of the Otherworld as a fruit, a raspberry for example. If you look closely it's not one fruit, but rather lots of tiny little segments, which bind together to form the whole. It's the same with the Otherworld. There are millions of tiny little pockets of it, and each one belongs to a different soul.'

'Oh I see,' Theo replied.

'What was that?' Olivia stopped suddenly in front of them, listening intently. 'Can you hear that?'

'Yes I can,' Hades growled, drawing his own sword. 'DEMONS!' he hissed in disgust.

Olivia's expression hardened, as she raised her hands, and when she drew them apart her bow burst into sapphire flames. Two of her dragonflies, double their usual size, blazed brightly with Hell fire, and hovered over her shoulder protectively.

'We'll take care of the demons,' he told her quietly. 'Whatever happens, you have to get to the Crossroad and stop your mother from making a deal.'

Olivia nodded, her eyes widening as she saw the first wave of demons scrambling down the tunnel toward them.

The demons were like a swarm of insects. Defying all the laws of nature they flooded every surface of the tunnel, clinging to the walls and ceiling, as they headed toward them. As if that was not bad enough, she suddenly heard a cold baying sound, followed by a familiar growl, and when she looked, dozens of Hell hounds ran with them in a pack.

'Shit,' she swore, and let loose a bolt of pure black

flame, aiming for the alpha of the pack. She gave a smirk of satisfaction, as it hit true, and the drooling skeletal creature exploded in a shower of ash and dust.

Hades watched her carefully, his expression indecipherable, as she aimed and took out another three in quick secession.

'Hell fire won't work on demons,' Hades warned her, his eyes locked on the demons rushing forward.

'I know,' she muttered, taking out another hound. 'You take out the demons, I'll deal with the dogs.'

Grunting in agreement the shades surged forward down the tunnel. 'PROTECT THE GIRL!' Hades roared at them, as he rushed forward.

Sam and Theo suddenly appeared, flanking her. It was carnage, fighting in such close quarters. The shades were unstoppable, claws and weapons simply passed straight through them. None of the demons could get a grip on them long enough to do any damage, yet the shades' weapons plunged into bodies, and hacked off appendages with sickening accuracy.

Theo and Sam seemed to be doing fine on their own, and soon the bodies were piling up either side of them. Olivia continued to rain down blazing arrows on the Hell hounds, watching as they detonated, one by one. The air was filling with a disgusting choking ash, which rather disturbingly, smelled like barbecue.

'GET TO THE CROSSROAD!' she heard Hades shout from somewhere deep in the melee.

'Theo!' she called out to him, but she'd lost him in the press of falling bodies.

Theo and a smaller demon were circling each other. Theo held his blade loosely in his fingers ready to strike, and yet he couldn't bring himself to do it. The demon in front of him looked no more than a ten-year-old child. His mind was telling him it was a demon, but he still couldn't bring himself to deliver the killing blow.

'Theo!' Sam yelled, as he plunged his blade easily

through a female's throat, and spun around, running another through with one clean thrust. 'Stop playing with it, and just kill it!'

'It's a child!'

'It's not a child,' he growled, 'kill it now!'

He could hear Olivia calling out to him from somewhere further down the tunnel, and he knew he had to find her. Giving a roar of disgust and frustration he raised his sword, but before he could strike, a shade appeared behind the boy and ran the demon through. Theo watched the innocent looking form slide lifelessly to the floor that was now stained black with blood.

'Come on,' Sam grabbed his arm and shook him.

They climbed over body parts and corpses, until they reached Olivia.

'We have to get to the Crossroad now!' she shouted, as they approached.

Nodding in agreement Sam went first, cutting and hacking his way through to clear a path for them, as Theo hung back to protect Olivia, killing anything that got too close to her.

'There's so many of them,' she breathed heavily as they climbed over more dead.

'They're not called the hordes of Hell without reason,' Sam panted. 'I can see the end of the tunnel, keep moving.'

They finally burst out of the end of the tunnel, but something grabbed Olivia's ankle and she hit the ground hard. She rolled over to see a hand grasping onto her leg. The hand was attached to an arm, and part of a torso, but that was it. She screamed and kicked at it, but it held firm.

It yanked her hard, scraping her back against the hard ground, as it dragged her back toward the tunnel. Theo grabbed her and pulled her back toward him, as Sam seized a spear from a nearby corpse and thrust it through the wrist of Olivia's captor, pinning it to the ground and forcing it to release her ankle. She scrambled back out of the way and Theo hauled her to her feet, pushing her behind him protectively.

'STOP THE GIRL!' Zachary shrieked, and suddenly several more demons spewed out of the tunnel heading toward them.

Isabel stepped calmly through the doorway, followed closely by Nathaniel, and the door slowly swung closed behind them. The pathway, which led to the center of the Crossroad, was much as the others had been, grey flagstones inscribed with an ancient language too worn to decipher correctly.

The Crossroad was similar to all the others, with four pathways intersecting at the center and ending at the four compass points, and a large doorway. The whole Crossroad itself was enclosed within a tall circular wall, which was covered with ancient scrubby looking vines. It was dimly lit, and although there seemed to be no direct light source there was a low glow, which just seemed to emanate from everywhere, and yet nowhere, at the same time.

Isabel drifted down the path, absently gravitating to the center, while Nathaniel glanced around warily, looking for the keeper. This Crossroad may have been similar in design, if not in size, but he knew Epsilon was the oldest, and the most powerful of all the Crossroads.

Isabel stopped in the dead center and glanced around.

'What do we have here?' a strange voice crackled from beside them.

Isabel peered into the darkness on either side of the path, and as her gaze became accustomed to the gloom, she made out an old lady sitting in a rocking chair, knitting something of no clear shape, from a rather unsavory and unattractive looking ball of rough, brownish grey, yarn. The woman rocked back in her chair, her needles clicking furiously, as she watched them.

'Come into the light,' Nathaniel commanded.

She cackled in the darkness. 'I don't take orders from demons.' She leaned forward far enough for the light of the Crossroad to highlight her old and misshapen face, 'especially you Nathaniel...'

'YOU...' his eyes widened, and he exhaled slowly...

'I've waited a long time to cross paths with you again,' she hissed, revealing rows of blackened teeth.

'I wondered what happened to you,' he smirked. 'The last time we met you looked a lot prettier.'

'The last time we met I ended up sentenced to the Crossroad,' she glared at him hatefully.

'Water under the bridge,' he shrugged, 'we're here to do business. Isabel...' he called to her, his gaze still fixed smugly on the stooped old woman, 'come here and ask her for the location of the book.'

'Still flogging that dead horse are you?' the old woman asked insultingly.

'Isabel...' Nathaniel turned toward her, 'ask her for the location of the book.'

Isabel turned her dark whiskey colored eyes on him, and the blank look drained from her eyes, to be replaced with a sharp defiance.

'No,' she whispered quietly, her mouth curving into a slow smile.

'What?' he hissed. 'I said, ask her for the location of the book.'

'Did you really think it was that easy?' she answered smoothly. 'Did you really think I would be so easily manipulated?'

He took an involuntary step back in shock. Gone was the unstable, demanding woman he'd first encountered when she raised him from the devil's trap. Gone was the lethargic, dreamlike state she had dwelt in for the last several weeks. Gone, was the mask of a broken mind and impending madness, and in front of him stood an icy cool, dangerous woman, very much in control of her own mind.

'Stupid…stupid little demon…' she tutted slowly, as the old woman began cackling in delight behind her.

Ignoring Nathaniel, she turned to the woman and smiled coolly. 'I'm here to make a deal.'

She shot a smug look at Nathaniel, and turned back to Isabel, rubbing her dirty hands together in delight. 'And what exactly is your heart's desire?'

Her voice, when she finally spoke, was dripping with ice, and her smile was so sharp it could have sliced with the precision of a scalpel.

'I want… to be the most powerful witch who ever lived…'

26.

'NO!' Nathaniel growled and stepped forward, only to be pushed back by an invisible barrier.

'Ah, ah, ah,' the old woman shook her head gleefully, 'no interfering while terms are being discussed. This does not involve you, demon.'

He hissed and stalked the edge of the barrier, baring his rotten teeth, his face livid with rage.

'He looks very angry,' she smiled delightedly.

'Yes he does,' Isabel replied mildly, 'but his mood doesn't concern me. I have told you what I want, can you give it to me, or not?'

'Of course I can,' she spread her hands widely. 'There's very little I can't do, but that kind of power won't come cheap. The question is, what are you willing to pay?'

'Name your price.'

Isabel watched, as the old woman studied her carefully. She tugged at the long lone hair protruding from her chin, and sucked her teeth loudly in consideration.

'Well,' she murmured, 'your request is not uncommon, and it is really upsetting Nathaniel, which is very pleasing to me, and so I am willing to deal.' She beckoned Isabel closer with one craggy finger.

Isabel leaned in, as the old woman whispered in her ear. Her eyes widened a fraction, and she turned sharply toward her, almost as if to ascertain if she was serious. She took an unconscious step back, her face troubled.

'Not so easy, when it actually has a price on it, is it?'

Isabel stared at her, her mind churning. Everything she had ever wanted was right there within her grasp, all she had to do was reach out and take it. There was a small voice at the back of her mind, telling her that it was too much, the price was too steep, that she would lose something she would never get back. But that voice was pushed ruthlessly aside, and when she straightened her spine and stared straight into the old woman's eyes, she nodded slowly.

'Agreed.'

She clapped her hands together in delight, cackling loudly.

'Very well, let us shake on it and be aware that it is binding, there is no changing your mind, or going back now.'

'I understand.'

She held her hand out. Isabel reached out and clasped it firmly, gasping loudly as she felt a strange kind of wrenching deep inside her.

Suddenly, her body flooded with energy. She could feel the heady whip of power, as it surged through her veins like adrenalin, while her mind was filled with centuries upon centuries of knowledge.

As her hand was released, she stumbled back gasping heavily. Her heart rate gradually began to settle, and she straightened, her eyes no longer the warm aged whiskey color of the West women, but now a bright vivid lavender. She ran her fingertips gently across the raised skin of her burn scar, and felt as it smoothed out and disappeared. Her hair darkened and the white streak at her temple disappeared. She stared down at her hands, turning them over, as her skin tingled with a power, so vast it made her want to rip the top off a mountain, just to see if she could.

'Intoxicating isn't it?' the old woman's eyes glimmered in amusement.

'It's incredible,' Isabel whispered. 'All my life I've felt the lack, known every woman in my family was strong with the magical gift, but not me. I had to strain for it, to beg, borrow, or steal the power, but not anymore, now there is nothing I can't do, and once I have the book in my possession there will be no one to rival me.'

'Be very careful Isabel,' she replied, 'it does not come without a warning. Absolute power, corrupts absolutely. Be very careful you are not consumed by it.'

Isabel cast a cold smile in her direction, before turning back to the seething mad demon, growling on the other side of the barrier.

'You can release him now,' Isabel told her. 'I will deal with him.'

The old woman smiled cagily.

'The deal is done,' she shrugged, and the barrier disappeared.

'ISABEL!' he roared, flying towards her, his rage palpable.

'Stop,' she held her hand up lazily, and he froze, struggling as if he were held captive by invisible bindings. 'Stupid demon,' she spoke coolly her voice laced with disdain. 'You're even more arrogant than I am. Did you really think I didn't know you were manipulating me? I've known it, ever since you first started whispering to me from the devil's trap.' She shook her head, 'and you thought I didn't have any patience. I knew that sooner or later you would have to bring me to the Crossroads, because you needed a human to make a deal.' She leaned in close to him, as he bared his teeth. 'You were so busy gloating at a West woman, who didn't have the strong magical gifts of her predecessors, that you didn't stop to fully understand the gifts I did possess. I've been able to read your intentions since that first day, every plan, every machination all there, wide open like a book. It was so easy to play you, to allow you to believe you had control of me.'

'Why?' he growled, 'why keep up the pretense?'

'Because it amused me to play you at your own game,' she scoffed. 'Did you think I didn't know why you were really destroying the Crossroads? That I didn't know what you took from the keepers?' she sneered. 'Such a shame it was all in vain. You see you will never be free, you will stay locked up in that meat suit I put you in, until I decide to let you out.'

'It's too late Isabel,' he hissed, 'it is already weakened. It is only a matter of time until it breaks down, and then I am going to rip your throat out…'

'You think so?' she laughed.

She raised her hands and slowly she mimed tying two laces together and knotting them tightly. Nathaniel hissed in pain, as the rotting flesh of his body, which had split open and begun to decay, suddenly wrenched itself back together, and sealed itself shut.

Large, angry looking stitches began to appear all over his face and body, closing all the gaps, and pulling the suit of flesh back together tightly. When she had finished he stared at her hatefully, looking even more like Frankenstein's monster than he had before.

'There,' she smiled sweetly, 'all tucked in, safe and sound.'

'You bitch,' he spat.

'You're welcome. Now for the finishing touch, just in case you have any more doubts as to who is in charge.'

She snapped her fingers and two large shiny metal cuffs appeared at each wrist, the kind that wouldn't have looked out of place on a genie in a magic lamp.

'What have you done?' he growled, struggling against the invisible bonds holding him.

'That…' she smiled cruelly, 'is a Witch binding,

and trust me Nathaniel, those cuffs make your demon collar look like a Tiffany necklace.'

He growled and struggled even more. 'I'm going to strip the flesh from your corpse, you fucking bitch.'

'Temper, temper,' she tutted. 'You're not going to do anything of the sort,' she smiled gloatingly. 'Those cuffs not only suppress any supernatural abilities, but they also bind you to my will. You are my slave now. You no longer have any free will. Welcome to a life of servitude.'

'NO!' he growled.

Isabel yawned, 'that's enough Nathaniel, you really are becoming quite annoying now.'

She flicked her wrist, and several vicious looking stitches appeared across his mouth, firmly sealing it shut.

The old woman howled with laughter, while Nathaniel glared at her murderously.

'There, that's better,' Isabel told him. 'Did you ever wonder why you were never able to take the book from my family Nathaniel?' She waited pleasantly for him to answer, knowing full well he couldn't. 'No? It's because you were never meant to have it. You continually underestimated the West women, especially me, and now you are going to stand by my side and bear witness, as I gain possession of the book, because it was always meant to be mine.'

He stared at her in hate filled silence.

'You know, she wouldn't have been able to tell you the location of the book, even if I had asked for it.'

His eyes cut across to the keeper, who was now rocking in her chair comfortably, smoking a long, strange, thin looking pipe.

'She's right,' the keeper nodded.

'See, there you go,' Isabel continued, as his eyes swiveled back to her. 'Underestimating the Wests again. If Hester was powerful enough to seal you in a devil's trap for three hundred years, do you really think she wasn't able to hide the book somewhere you'd never find it? She was an incredibly gifted seer, she knew you'd find a way to the Crossroad, and so she devised a way to conceal it from every supernatural creature, including a Crossroad keeper.'

She released the invisible bonds holding him, and he didn't move, just stood there staring at her.

'It was hidden by a West, and it has to be found by a West,' she smiled coldly. 'Have you figured it out yet? To find the book, you must first find Hester, before she comes into her gifts fully, before she can see ahead to the Crossroads, back to when the book first passed into her possession.'

His eyes widened in understanding, but he was unable to say anything.

'That's right,' she smiled, as she gestured absently, and the air behind her began to ripple, throbbing with a strange purple light. 'We're going back to the night you murdered her mother.'

Cora stepped back frowning.

'What's wrong?' Charles asked in concern.

'I can't pull them back from the Otherworld,' she replied, 'because they are not there.'

'What? Where the hell are they then?'

'Shush,' she gestured at him absently, as she closed her eyes and concentrated.

He dropped down on his haunches, watching her as she sat cross legged on the floor amidst all the scattered herbs and candles, waiting patiently.

Minutes passed, and he grew anxious. When she finally opened her eyes and looked directly at him, the feeling only intensified.

'They are in the Underworld.'

'No,' he shook his head in denial, 'it's not possible, there's no way.'

She frowned again, as she focused on them. 'It's difficult to tell what's happening, but they are in Tartarus, the lowest most dangerous pit of the Underworld.'

'Tartarus?' he breathed heavily, as full blown panic began to set in. It was the feeling only a parent could know, the feeling of utter helplessness when your child is in danger. 'That's where Zeus cast down the Titans.'

'I know,' she mused. 'It's strange, I can't focus on them. It's like, they keep phasing in and out of sync with everything else, like they're someplace separate and yet not. I can't really describe it.'

'You have to pull them out.'

'I can't,' she stood abruptly, and dusted the herbs from her dress.

'What do you mean you can't?' he scowled. 'We had a deal.'

'We had a deal for a ride out of the Otherworld,' she told him bluntly. 'Tartarus is Hades' domain and no offense, but you've paid nowhere near enough. One measly favor, is not enough for me to go up against a God.'

'Then how much is enough.'

'Cher, can you hear yourself? Some things should not be messed with. If they are in Tartarus, then there's probably a good reason why they're there.'

'There is no good reason to be in Tartarus,' he disagreed. 'I want her back, I don't care if I have to sell my soul to Lucifer himself.'

'Lucifer has no authority in Tartarus,' she replied dryly.

'Stop being deliberately obtuse,' he growled. 'Can you bring them back or not?'

'It's a lot more difficult,' she scowled back at him. 'At best, I could only bring one of them back, not two.'

Charles closed his eyes, and sucked in a deep breath. If he only brought Olivia back and left Theo in the Underworld, there was a good chance his daughter would never speak to him again. She'd certainly never forgive him. But really, what choice did he have? He had to get her back. Okay, so she probably wouldn't speak to him ever again, but at least she would be alive and back in the real world where she belonged. His heart ached at such an impossible choice. If he brought her back, he'd still lose her anyway. He slowly opened his eyes and fixed them on Cora.

'Name the terms.'

'Cher, I urge you to reconsider.'

'Name the terms,' he repeated slowly.

'Fine,' she replied coolly. 'I want your ability to plant suggestions in people's minds.'

'What?'

'You think this is a walk in the park for me? You're asking me to spring someone from the Underworld, to go up against a God? The price has to be worth the risk, and mind control is a very rare gift indeed.'

He didn't even want to think about why she wanted his ability to plant thoughts in people's minds, his conscience could only take so much in one day.

'Fine,' he whispered, 'just bring her back.'

'Damn Cher,' she shook her head as she retrieved a small glass ampoule from a nearby shelf, 'she must really mean a lot to you.'

'You have no idea,' he muttered.

She removed the glass stopper, and stood in front of him. 'Are you absolutely certain about this Cher? There are no refunds.'

He nodded silently.

Sighing in resignation, she began to speak in a low tongue he couldn't understand, something ancient with a strange guttural quality to it. A tickle began at the back of his throat, and he coughed. She continued to mutter, and the tickle got worse, and suddenly he was coughing uncontrollably, trying to suck air into his oxygen starved lungs, but something felt as if it were trying to force its way up and out of his throat. He gave a final cough and heaved, as a pale amber colored mist smoked out from between his lips.

Cora scooped it up in the ampoule, and replaced the stopper. Charles dragged a deep lungful of air into his chest, blinking rapidly to clear his watery eyes, his gaze fixed on the swirling amber smoke in the ampoule.

'Okay then,' Cora shook her head, slipping the ampoule into her pocket. She began to remove various other containers from the shelves, emptying them out and arranging things on the ground, adding to the symbols and sigils. She stood slightly off center and raised her arms, her voice once again beginning to murmur in the strange guttural language.

'I truly hope she forgives you for this Cher,' she murmured, as the candles suddenly flared up, the flames burning with a bright green fire.

Sam leapt forward as the demons began spilling out of the tunnel, desperately trying to reach Olivia. Theo rushed forward running one of them through, as Sam swung his sword and decapitated another.

'OLIVIA OPEN THE DOOR!' Theo yelled.

She scrambled toward the entrance to the Crossroad and grasped onto the metal handle, turning it and swinging the door open.

Both of them began edging back toward the open gateway.

'Theo go!' Sam swung in front of him, blocking another demon.

'Not without you,' Theo ducked under Sam's arm, and slid his blade easily through the demon in front of him.

They looked at each other and then both dived through the gateway as Olivia tried to slam the door shut. Several demons rushed forward to stop them, but the second their skin touched the closed door, it began to blacken and smoke, causing them to howl in pain and release their grip. The door swung shut with a resounding crack.

Breathing heavily Olivia turned. The center of the Crossroad stood just ahead of her and she could see a strange purple glow. In front of it was her mother and Nathaniel.

'NO!' she shouted and took off. Pulling out her bow while on the run, she took aim and let loose a black bolt.

Isabel turned at the sound of her daughter's voice. She saw her rushing toward them with a blazing bow made of pure blue flame, and letting loose a bolt. She smiled as the bolt hit her shield and exploded in a shower of black sparks, and when they had cleared, both she and Nathaniel were gone.

'NO!' Olivia screamed in frustration.

'I could help you, you know,' a crackly voice spoke from the shadows.

Olivia jumped, and turned her bow in the direction of the voice. 'Step into the light,' she replied, her eyes narrowing dangerously.

An old woman hobbled out onto the Crossroad. Olivia could see she had been sitting in an old fashioned wooden rocking chair, her bleak shapeless knitting tucked into a basket next to it.

The woman herself had iron grey hair underneath a strange looking knitted hat. Her face was old and lined, with a wicked long hair poking out of her chin. She wore an old fashioned dress and around her hunched shoulders she wore a shabby moth-eaten shawl, which crossed over her chest and was tied up at the small of her back.

In fact, the woman wouldn't have looked out of place during the French Revolution, sitting at the bottom of the steps of Madame la Guillotine watching the Aristocrats being led to their deaths. She looked like the kind who would sit there, cackling in delight as heads rolled.

'You're the keeper?' Olivia asked suspiciously.

'Yes,' she nodded, eying Olivia's bow with

interest, before her gaze flickered to the two large dragonflies hovering over her shoulder.

'What's your name?' Olivia lowered her bow slowly.

The old woman blinked and stared at Olivia, slightly puzzled, as if no one had ever bothered to ask before.

'Marguerite,' she replied after a moment, ambling slightly closer to Olivia, and looking over in curiosity as Sam and Theo appeared by her side.

'The woman who was just here...'

'Yes,' Marguerite replied, 'you're her daughter aren't you?'

'Unfortunately.'

'You look like her,' her eyes narrowed as she studied Olivia intently.

'So I'm told,' she answered coolly. 'Did she make a deal?'

'She did.'

'And what was it? What did she ask for?'

'Sorry,' Marguerite grinned, revealing dirty rotting teeth. 'Don't ask, can't tell.'

'Where did you send her then?'

'I didn't send her nowhere,' she shook her head.

'You must have,' she murmured thoughtfully, 'she doesn't have the magical ability to open a portal herself. That takes a lot of power.'

Suddenly understanding, she turned back to the old woman. 'That's what she asked for, wasn't it? She asked for power?'

'I have to admit you West women are a lot smarter than people give you credit for,' Marguerite replied.

'Damn it,' Olivia turned to Theo, 'they could be anywhere.'

'I can tell you where they've gone.'

Olivia turned back to her suspiciously, 'in return for...?'

She clapped her hands together in delight at the prospect of another deal.

'I have to admit,' she pursed her wrinkled old lips, 'you're not my usual class of customer.'

'What's your usual class?'

'Desperate and very selfish,' she replied, 'but you,' she shook a finger at her thoughtfully, 'you're something different. You are human, there's no doubting that, but there's something else.' She leaned in close and inhaled deeply, sniffing at her. 'God fire,' she smiled widely, 'you hold the secret of God fire.'

'What?' Olivia frowned in confusion.

Marguerite stroked her chin thoughtfully, tugging at that stray nasty hair, and studying Olivia as if she were really seeing her for the first time.

'I have a deal for you,' she told Olivia after a moment. 'I'll tell you where they went and in return…'

'In return…' she prompted her to finish.

'You must return to the Crossroad and free me.'

'I'm sorry, what?' she replied, frowning as if she'd misheard her. 'I think you're a bit confused, I don't have that kind of power.'

'Not yet,' she answered vaguely as if she knew something Olivia had not yet figured out. 'When you come into your gift fully, you must return and free me from the Crossroad.'

She looked up at Olivia, giving her best sad eyes, and stooping a little lower.

'I'm so old now,' she told her weakly. 'I'm so tired, all I want is to be at peace.'

Olivia rolled her eyes, 'you do know you're not fooling anyone with that little old lady act. You could probably throw us off the Crossroad and halfway across the Universe without even breaking a sweat, so let's cut the shit here. No deal.'

She straightened up pouting, and sighing.

'No deal?' she repeated. 'Now who's fooling who?

There's no way you're leaving here without your mother's location.'

'I didn't say I was,' Olivia shrugged, 'but let's be realistic here. A location, in return for freeing you from an eternity of servitude on the only remaining Crossroad? Hardly seems like an even trade. You need to sweeten the pot.'

Her eyes glittered with interest and she blew out a breath. 'Fine, what do you want, more power?'

'No thanks,' Olivia replied casually. 'I'm quite happy the way I am.'

'What about your friend over there?' she nodded in Sam's direction. 'That patch job Hades gave him isn't going to last long. I could send him out of the Underworld, where he'd be safe.'

'No thanks,' Sam answered. 'Wherever these two go, I go.'

She turned to Theo and her eyes narrowed, as she studied him.

'What about you?' she asked.

'What about me?'

'I could give you back your sister.'

'What?' he whispered.

'Sweet little Temperance. Wouldn't you give anything to have the little one back again, to have a second chance, to give her the life she deserved?'

For a second Theo's heart thudded painfully, before finally shaking his head.

'No.'

'Theo,' Olivia whispered, 'this is your one chance. You could have her back.'

'It's not right Olivia,' he told her quietly, 'everything has a natural order. She died a long time ago, even if it feels like only yesterday to me. It wouldn't be a kindness to pull her back from wherever she has moved on to. If being here with you has taught me anything, it's that anything is possible. I can only hope she's in a good place, that she's with our mother, and that she is happy and free from pain.'

Olivia smiled softly, stepping close to him as she grazed his cheek with her fingers and brushed his lips tenderly with hers. 'You're a good man Theo.'

He looked up at Marguerite. 'No deal.'

She growled softly in frustration. 'There must be something you want?'

'Sorry Marguerite, if you want out of the Crossroad, you're going to have to up your game.'

'Alright,' she answered after a moment, 'not only will I tell you where your mother and Nathaniel are, I'll send you after them.'

'Now you're talking,' Olivia replied. 'All three of us?'

'All three of you,' Marguerite nodded.

'Then we have a deal.'

Marguerite held out her hand. Olivia looked at her dirty cracked nails and filthy skin as she took her hand, reluctantly shaking it and trying not to cringe.

'The deal is done,' she let go of Olivia. 'Your mother and Nathaniel have gone after your ancestor, Hester West.'

'Well she's nothing, if not consistent,' Olivia muttered.

'When have they gone back to?'

'They are going back to when she is still a child, still vulnerable. She said something about the night the demon killed the child's mother.'

'Damn it,' Theo swore. 'He's going back to the night the girls were brought to my family's farm, the night Sam pulled me out of the fire and brought me to Mercy.'

'If they interfere in that event,' Olivia shook her head in fear, 'not only will you have never been brought forward to Mercy, but the girls won't escape. And if Hester doesn't survive, I'll never be born.'

'Shit,' Sam swore, 'we have to go back to 1695

then.'

Theo nodded.

Olivia looked up at Marguerite, 'send us back then.'

'Remember our agreement,' she warned.

'I will come back for you, I promise.'

Marguerite nodded, and suddenly the air shimmered next to them, the same strange purple color as before.

'Well, I guess we're going back to the 17th century then,' Sam frowned, sighing in disgust. 'I didn't even like it the first time around.'

Olivia and Theo looked up at him in surprise.

'What?' he frowned, 'I told you I was older than I looked.'

Theo took Olivia's hand, and they turned toward the strange rippling portal.

'And this will take us back to that night?'

'Yes,' she replied.

Suddenly the floor began to shake, causing Olivia to take a step back in surprise.

'What was that?'

At the very center of the Crossroad a bright green light exploded, rippling outward. Ropey vines of green flame crackled and wrapped around Olivia's waist and torso, grabbing her tightly and tugging hard.

'Theo!' she yelled in panic.

'What are you doing?' Sam yelled at Marguerite.

'It's not me,' she shouted. 'Someone is trying to pull her from the Underworld.'

'Stop them!' Theo growled, as he grabbed onto Olivia's arms to stop her from sliding backward.

'I can't,' she stepped back shaking her head, 'it's not part of the deal. My powers are bound by the Crossroad. Unless it's part of a deal, I can't do anything.'

'Sam!' Theo shouted, as the green flames licked up his arm, burning as they went, but leaving no marks.

He gritted his teeth against the pain, as she began to slide back once again.

'You have to go now!' Marguerite shouted, 'I cannot hold the portal open much longer.'

Sam took a deep breath and braced himself. With a war like cry of defiance, he charged into Olivia, knocking her into Theo and throwing all three of them through the portal.

They disappeared, and a gigantic explosion of green fire burst outward violently. When the dust finally settled the Crossroad was gone, and so was Marguerite.

Hades stepped over the bodies littering the ground and waded through the smoke, glancing around. The Crossroad was nowhere to be seen, nor was Olivia, her mother and Nathaniel. He knew once the Crossroad had disappeared, they would not be able to find it again. His lips peeled back in an angry snarl as one of the shades approached, and dropped a broken bloodied body at his feet.

Zachary looked up at Hades, one of his eyes swollen shut, and his face covered in blood.

'Where were they going?' he asked.

'I'll not tell you anything,' he spat blood at Hades' feet.

'You'll feel differently soon,' Hades replied coldly. 'You'll find I can be very persuasive.'

The shade grabbed him by his collar and dragged him face first across the hard sand covered stone, taking layers of skin off.

Hades looked up at the strange green glow hovering in the smoky air, and let out a deep frustrated breath.

'Wherever you are Olivia' he muttered, 'I hope you make it out alive...'

Keep Reading…

The Guardians Series 1
Book 4

Witchfinder

If there is one rule you don't break, it's 'Don't mess with Time'.

All of a sudden Olivia and Theo find themselves thrown back in time to 17th century Salem. Isabel and Nathaniel are hell bent on finding Olivia's ancestor, Hester West, who was the last of the West women known to have had possession of Infernum. It is the most powerful book ever to have existed and Hester is the one person who knows its current location.

The problem is, if Isabel and Nathaniel find Hester they will change the events of the past. Theo will never have been pulled through time to present day Mercy and will never meet Olivia. Even worse, if Hester is harmed in any way, Olivia will never be born in the first place.

The stakes have never been higher. Trapped in the past at the height of Witch Fever, Theo must not only try and keep Olivia safe from the religious fanatics, who have never seen a real witch in their lives, but he must face his brother Logan and the past he left behind. And this time, if he fails, Olivia will be the one hanging from the tree on Gallows Hill.

1.

Olivia groaned and rolled over, pressing her face into the grass and inhaling deeply. Her fingers instinctively flexed, and dug into the earth. Lifting her head suddenly she inhaled again. She could actually smell the grass.

Looking up into the sky she could see endless blue, and fluffy white clouds. Gone was the strange bruised light of the Otherworld, or the oppressive darkness of the Underworld. This was pure sunlight. She lifted her hand slightly and her skin glowed, and she could feel warmth tingling on her skin.

Pushing herself up, she tilted her head and listened. She could hear the birds in the nearby trees. She closed her eyes and pulled in a deep breath; she was back in the real world.

Her eyes narrowed as a new sound began to intrude upon her awareness, something unfamiliar, a strange kind of pounding noise.

Hands suddenly grasped her and hauled her to her feet, dragging her across the grass. She kicked back and spun around, her brow creasing in confusion when she realized it was Theo.

'Theo,' she breathed.

'Shush,' he warned, his gaze anxiously darting between the forest of trees which surrounded them. He suddenly pulled her behind a thick tree trunk and pushed her down, so they were both out of sight.

The pounding sound got louder, and louder. The curiosity gnawed at her, but she resisted the urge to poke her head around the tree to see what was going on.

'Theo,' she whispered.

Suddenly, he clamped his hand over her mouth and pulled her in as close as he could. Her eyes widened as two horses thundered by. She caught a brief glimpse of their retreating forms as they passed by. Each horse bore a rider, dressed in some sort of dark clothing, although she couldn't quite make it out from this distance.

Theo finally let out a breath and some of the tension drained out of his body. He looked down at Olivia, cupping her face gently in his hands.

'Are you okay?' he asked softly in concern.

'I'm fine,' she placed her hand over his.

'I thought we'd lost you there for a moment,' he frowned. 'What the hell happened back at the Crossroad? What was that green fire?'

'I have no idea,' Olivia shook her head. 'It came out of nowhere, and wrapped around me. I could feel it pulling at me.'

'Did it harm you?'

She shook her head. 'Did it hurt you?'

'I felt it,' he replied, 'when I grabbed you. It felt like it was burning, but it left no mark.'

'Well, we're here now,' she stood slowly. 'Where's Sam?'

'I don't know,' Theo answered worriedly, 'but he can't be far. We have to find him before anyone does.'

'Who were those riders?'

'I have no idea.'

'Then why did we hide?'

'Olivia, this is the 17th Century and you're wearing jeans and a backpack.'

'Oh,' she looked around, but all she could see

were trees and grasslands. 'Are you sure we're in the right place? The right time even?'

Theo looked around quietly, his eyes shadowed.

'Theo?' she looked at him in concern, noting his strained expression.

'We're not far from Salem Village, my family's farm is a couple of miles west of here. We need to get someplace safe and out of sight, until I can steal us some clothes. Once we blend in we can look around, but we need to be careful until we can establish the date. People around here know me, the other me,' he shook his head in irritation. 'The past me, must be around here somewhere. I can't risk anyone seeing me in two places at once.'

Olivia nodded, 'we'd better find Sam.'

Theo took Olivia's hand and led her through the trees, all the while glancing around warily.

'I know where we are,' he replied suddenly. 'It's the apple orchard belonging to my neighbor, James Wilkins.'

'Is that water I can hear?' Olivia asked as she tilted her head and listened.

'There's a small stream that runs along the border of his land.'

It didn't take long to locate Sam. They seemed to have been thrown down roughly in the same area, although unfortunately for Sam he must have taken the brunt of whatever the strange green fire had been back at the Crossroad. He was barely conscious when they reached him.

Olivia dropped down to her knees beside to him and rolled him over. He was pale and his body wracked with violent tremors.

'What do you think is wrong with him?' Olivia looked up at Theo in worry.

'I don't know,' he frowned, 'but if it hadn't been for Sam, we'd never have gotten you through the portal. Whatever that strange green fire was, it must have undone whatever it was Hades did for him. He's probably suffering from the after effects of being in the Underworld for so long.'

Olivia stroked his face gently in concern. 'Do you think he'll be okay?'

'I don't know,' he shook his head, 'we don't even know what he is.'

'I wish Louisa was here.'

'Me too,' Theo glanced around, 'but for now, we're on our own. Not too far from here, James has a barn he uses to store the apples in. We should be able to hide in there for the moment.'

'Are you sure?'

He nodded, 'Logan and I used to hide in there when we were children.'

She climbed to her feet, watching as Theo heaved Sam off the ground and slung him easily over his shoulder.

Luck appeared to be favoring them for the time being, and they managed to cut back through the orchard toward the barn without anyone seeing them. The barn itself was pretty far from the farmhouse, so they snuck in, dropping Sam down on the hay strewn ground and tucking him into the corner near a huge barrel of apples.

'Now what?' Olivia asked.

'Now we wait for it to get dark. I'll slip out and see if I can sneak up to the main house and steal some clothes for us. Once we can roam around a little more freely we can make a plan.'

'God,' she frowned, 'this is a nightmare. Sam's pretty much out for the count, we've got to try and avoid not only the past you, but anyone who knows you, and as if that weren't bad enough, there are now two Nathaniels.'

'I know,' he replied in frustration. 'If the one with your mother wasn't bad enough, the Nathaniel from my time is in his true form, and much more powerful. He'll know we're out of time, the second he sees us.'

'We'll just have to make sure he doesn't see us

then.'

'That's easier said than done,' he shook his head. 'He's looking for Hester too remember?'

Olivia sighed and closed her eyes, rubbing her temples tiredly.

'Are you alright?'

'It's just a lot to take in,' she breathed, 'and I'm tired.' Her stomach growled loudly, 'and hungry apparently.'

'Here,' he reached into one of the barrels, and grabbed a couple of apples, 'eat these. I'll see if I can find some clean water.'

There was a sudden scuffling noise, and the sound of the barn door opening.

Olivia pulled her legs in and slid behind one of the large barrels of apples, holding onto Sam carefully, while Theo hid behind another.

'Hello?' a small timid voice called out. 'Hello?'

Olivia frowned, it sounded like a child's voice.

'Theo?' the child's voice called out.

Olivia glanced across at Theo and saw his eyes widen, as he instinctively turned in the direction of the voice.

'Theo, I know you're here, so you might as well come out.'

Unable to help it, Theo unfolded himself from his hiding place, stepping out into the light that streaked in from an opening higher up in the building. His heart stopped, as his gaze landed on the small dark haired child.

'I've been waiting for you,' she smiled.

'Tempy?' he whispered.

She smiled widely, and held her arms out for him.

He dropped down slowly in front of her and she wrapped her arms tightly around his neck. He folded his arms around her tiny body and crushed her to him, not wanting to let go, afraid that it wasn't real. His eyes burned with tears, and he found he couldn't swallow past the hard knot of emotion burning at the back of his throat.

Temperance pulled back and grinned.

'I brought you some clothes.' She looked down at him, in his jeans and boots. 'Your clothes are very strange. Where are your friends? I brought some for them too.'

'What?' he replied in confusion.

'The lady with the gold eyes, she's here too isn't she? And the boy with black hair?' she turned and retrieved the sack she'd dropped by the door. 'You'd better hurry up and change. Mr Wilkins is at market today but he'll be back soon.'

'Tempy,' he whispered, 'how do you know about the others? How did you know to find me here?'

'I saw you silly,' she shook her head.

'You saw me?'

'In a dream,' she smiled. 'There was another lady there that time. She wore a green dress, and had a bow and arrow. She told me you needed me to help you.'

She pulled out some clothes, and handed them to him as he sat staring at her in disbelief.

'I got one of Mary's dresses for your lady friend,' Temperance frowned. 'I hope Mary doesn't notice, she gets awful mad lately.'

'Mary?' his eyes widened as the pieces began to fall into place. 'Tempy, is Mary back at the house?'

'Of course she is,' she replied as if it was the most obvious answer in the world. 'She's back at the farm with the other you.'

'Tempy, is Mary sick?' he asked carefully.

'You know she is,' she answered seriously, 'the sickness is in her mind, and she's getting real bad.'

Theo closed his eyes and drew in a shaky breath.

If Temperance was still alive, and Mary was at the height of her madness, it could only mean one thing. The year was 1685. He wasn't sure what that strange green fire was, which had interfered back at the Crossroad, but something had obviously gone terribly wrong. They'd been thrown back ten years too early.

Glossary of Terms in Greek Mythology

Hades: - used to denote both the God of the Underworld and the Underworld itself.

Hades the God: He drew lots with his brothers Zeus and Poseidon, when they were dividing up the World after they had overthrown the Titans. Zeus gained the earth, Poseidon the sea, and Hades the Underworld

Persephone: daughter of Demeter, the Goddess of the harvest. Seduced by Hades and taken as his wife.

Hades the Underworld: In front of the entrance to the Underworld, live Grief, Anxiety, Diseases and Old Age. Fear, Hunger, Death, Agony, and Sleep also live in front of the entrance, together with Guilty Joys.

On the opposite threshold is War, the Erinyes, and Eris. Close to the doors, are many beasts, including Centaurs, Gorgons, the Lernaean Hydra, the Chimera, and Harpies. In the midst of all this, an Elm can be seen where false dreams cling under every leaf.

Erebus: Meaning deep, darkness. A place of darkness between Earth and Hades. This was the region of the Underworld, where the dead pass immediately after dying

Cerberus: The three headed dog who guards Hades the Underworld to keep the souls in. He was generally viewed as a pet of Hades the God.

The Erinyes (also known as the Furies): These were the three Goddesses associated with the souls of the dead, they avenged crimes against the natural order of the world. They consist of Alecto, Megaera, and Tisiphone. They were particularly concerned with crimes committed by children against their parents such as matricide, patricide, and un-filial conduct. They would inflict madness upon the living murderer, or if a nation was harboring such a criminal, the Erinyes would cause starvation and disease to afflict the nation.

Eris: She was the Goddess of Chaos, Strife and discord.

Charon: He is the ferryman who carried the souls of the dead down the River Styx, to the gates of Hades, where they were to be judged. It was customary for the souls to pay a coin to the ferryman for his trouble. To this end, the relatives of the deceased would place a coin in the mouth of the dead.

Minos, Rhadamanthus and Aeacus: These are the three judges of the Underworld. Aeacus held the keys to Hades, Rhadamanthus and Aeacus judged the souls between them, but Minos had the final decision.

Eurynomos: a daimon (or spirit) of the Underworld, who eats all the flesh of the corpses, and leaves only the bones.

The Fields of Punishment: the place in the Underworld

where people are punished for evil deeds, using a variety of methods of torture.

Hecate: A goddess, whom Zeus honored highly. She is most often shown holding two torches, or a key. She was variously associated with crossroads, entrance-ways, dogs, light, the moon, magic, witchcraft, knowledge of herbs and poisonous plants, ghosts, necromancy, and sorcery. Through the honors bestowed upon her by Zeus, she had influence in all parts of the universe, but preferred to reside in the Underworld, where she became a handmaiden to Persephone.

Dionysus: The God of the grape harvest, winemaking and wine, ritual madness, ecstasy and fertility.

Prometheus: He was one of the Titans. He stole fire from Zeus to give to the humans. As a punishment he was chained to a rock by Zeus, and sentenced to have his liver eaten each day by an eagle. At night, it would re-grow so that he would suffer the same torment again. Finally, he was cast down into Tartarus.

Cronus: He was the youngest leader of the Titans, and the father of Zeus, Hades and Poseidon. He ruled during the so called Golden Age, until he was overthrown by Zeus, and imprisoned in Tartarus.

Tartarus: The deep abyss that was used as a dungeon of torment and suffering for the wicked, and as the prison for the Titans.

The Five Rivers of the Underworld:

- **The Styx** – the river of hatred, which circles the Underworld seven times.
- **The Acheron** – the river of pain.

- **The Lethe** – the river of forgetfulness.
- **The Phlegethon** – the river of fire, which leads to Tartarus.
- **The Cocytus** – the river of wailing.

Other Titans:

Lapetus: – Father of Prometheus

Clymene: Daughter of Oceanus, therefore an Oceanid. She was also the mother of Prometheus.

Atlas: The God of astronomy and navigation. He was brother to Prometheus, and son of Lapetus and Clymene.

Oceanus: The God of the sea, and father to Clymene.

Author Bio.

Wendy Saunders lives in Hampshire, England with her husband and three children. She spent twelve years caring for her grandmother but when her grandmother passed away she decided the time was right to pursue her own dream of writing. Mercy is her debut novel and the first of a five book series.

Also in this series
Book 2 The Ferryman
Book 3 Crossroads
Book 4 Witchfinder
Book 5 Infernum

Come find me!
On my official website
www.wendysaundersauthor.com
Don't forget to subscribe to my mailing list via my website to receive a free copy of my e-book Boothe's Hollow, a companion/prequel short story to Mercy.

On Facebook
www.facebook.com/wendysaundersauthor

On Twitter
www.twitter.com/wsaundersauthor

On Instagram
www.instagram.com/wendysaundersauthor

If you would like to rate this book and leave a review at Amazon or Goodreads.com I would be very grateful. Thank You.

Printed in Great Britain
by Amazon